At First Glance

by
Susan L. Tuttle

Bling!
Romance
Lighthouse Publishing of the Carolinas

AT FIRST GLANCE BY SUSAN L. TUTTLE
Published by Bling!
an imprint of Lighthouse Publishing of the Carolinas
2333 Barton Oaks Dr., Raleigh, NC 27614

ISBN: 978-1-946016-64-5
Copyright © 2018 by Susan L. Tuttle
Cover design by Elaina Lee
Interior design by Karthick Srinivasan

Available in print from your local bookstore, online, or from the publisher at:
ShopLPC.com.

For more information on this book and the author, visit: www.susanltuttle.com.

Brought to you by the creative team at Lighthouse Publishing of the Carolinas (LPCBooks.com):
Eddie Jones, Shonda Savage, Jessica Nelson.

Library of Congress Cataloging-in-Publication Data
Tuttle, Susan L.
At First Glance / Susan L. Tuttle 1st ed.

Printed in the United States of America

PRAISE FOR *AT FIRST GLANCE*

"It was a treat to read a romance novel featuring two characters who don't fit our unrealistic standards for beauty! I cheered for Penny and Jonah as they dealt with old scars, grappled with the meaning of worth, and fell in love with each other for all the right reasons. Heartwarming!"

~Becky Wade
Christy and Carol Award-winning author of *My Stubborn Heart*

Susan Tuttle's debut novel, At First Glance, is a fun romance with deep undercurrents of truth. Tuttle gets to the heart of what we all really want at our cores - to be truly seen and loved the way we are. Through the story of two families with an inordinate amount of heartache, and a heroine with massive insecurities, Tuttle shows the ultimate healing of perfect love through her pretty-perfect hero, Jonah Black. Fans who enjoy a sweet combination of humor, heart, and the beauty of unconditional love, will find this story a wonderful addition to their reading list.

~Pepper Basham
Author of the *Mitchell's Crossroads* series

Susan Tuttle's *At First Glance* is such a refreshing read! Her unique characters tugged on my heart from the opening scenes and the plot moves along at a great pace. The underlying theme is one that will engage women of all ages: What is true beauty? And what happens when you find it in the most unexpected place... or person? Readers, get ready to make room on your bookshelf for Susan Tuttle!

~ Melissa Tagg
Author of *Made To Last.*

In *At First Glance*, Susan Tuttle creates true-to-life, flawed characters who sometimes look for love and redemption in all the wrong places — and the wrong people. Her debut novel is woven through with romance, honesty and hope — and not an ounce of sappiness. I'm looking forward to more from this new author!

~Beth K. Vogt
Christy and Carol Award-winning author of *Somebody Like You*

Where do you search for your value? Woven with a powerful theme, laced with splashes of humor, and filled with fresh, witty dialog, Susan Tuttle's debut novel, *At First Glance*, will enchant romance readers of all ages and leave you with a sigh of pure delight! I can't wait to dive into more sweet romances by Susan Tuttle!

~Dora Hiers
Author of Heart Racing, God-Gracing Romance

Susan Tuttle's debut novel sings with wit and humor, but also an unconfined tenderness as it explores true beauty and self-worth. Tuttle's mastery to blend a palpable romance, characters layered with complexity and heart, and meticulous attention to details, results in a stellar love story, proving she's one to watch in the contemporary romance genre.

~Jessica R. Patch
Author of the *Seasons of Hope* series and *Unleashing Love*.

ACKNOWLEDGMENTS

As is often said, no author completes a book by themselves. There are so many people to thank along the way who've helped either through prayer, encouragement, or their time. But let me begin by first thanking Jesus Christ. Quite simply, any success or good thing that comes out of me belongs to him.

I also have to give a huge thank-you to the friends I've made along this journey. To the ones who read this story in its roughest state and helped me polish it. Jessica Patch, Dawn Crandall, and Joanna Politano, you ladies have pushed me as a writer, and I love you for it. Thanks to my agent, Linda S. Glaz, for believing in me and this story and being its biggest champion; you fight for authors and their voice, and I'm blessed to have you in my corner. Lastly in this writing arena, I have to thank my editor, Jessica Nelson, for taking on this new author. I so appreciate you answering all my questions and for making my debut a wonderful experience. Your comments helped tighten my writing, made me grow, and yet maintained the heart of this story. Thank you.

Finally, I want to thank my friends and family. Mary Jo Kleyn, you were the very first person to read any story by me (one that is now stashed safely in a drawer) and urged me to pursue publishing. Your faithful encouragement through the ensuing years means more than I can ever say. Thank you, my dear friend. Kelli Tipton, you have taught me what friendship means. You never waiver in your support and love for me, and always, always, always find a way to make me laugh. Thank you for helping me learn that being myself is more than enough. To my siblings, thank you for making sure that as the youngest I could never stop talking if I wanted to be heard—in your own crazy way, you helped me fall in love with words. And a special thank you to my only sister, Beth, who helped me learn all about perfumes for this story. The only portion of the sisters inside this book that resembles us is the use of the word "Princess!" To my parents who have loved me, always believed in me, and ensured I had a bedrock of faith; you've made sure I pursued who God wanted me to be—even when it was hard—and cheered me on along the way. For that I will always be thankful. Lastly, to my children, Corydon, Ella, and Raleigh, I am blessed daily by you and couldn't be prouder of who you're becoming. Be open to travel wherever God calls you, even when that road is difficult. Remember he will never leave you or forsake you. And to my husband, Doug; I am forever grateful that I gave you more than one glance. My friend first, you will be My Love always.

DEDICATION

For Jesus; may my firstfruits always be yours.

Chapter One

For once, she should have listened to Mom's advice. If she had, maybe then she wouldn't currently resemble a grape about to burst.

Penny Thornton sucked in her stomach and tugged on the zipper of her dress. There. Now if she didn't breathe, or move, she'd be all set.

"Penny! Are you in that dress yet?" Mom's voice drilled into the dressing room.

Penny looked in the mirror. "I am not coming out there."

Voices murmured on the other side of the door before it bounced open. She'd been so focused on the ... absolutely stunning, super-mini, purple dress her sister had picked out she'd forgotten to lock herself inside.

Not that she'd be able to escape Mom and Belle anyway.

Mom's voice thinned. "Penny Rose, you are coming out here. You will not ruin this day for your sister."

No. Wouldn't want that. "This dress doesn't fit me." And she wasn't simply talking about the size ten marked on the tag.

"It's not Belle's fault you didn't go on that diet or that you refuse to take my advice and wear Spanx." Mom walked in, shut the door, then spun Penny to face the silver-gilded mirror. She yanked on the zipper. It didn't budge. "Honestly, Penny, would it hurt you to finally try and lose a few pounds?"

A few pounds, a few inches, dye her hair blonde, and hide the scar. Then she'd be all set for Mom.

"I'll see what I can do." Penny stepped away from Mom's jarring tugs. "But no matter how hard you pull, I'm still a size fourteen." She sidestepped Mom and backed up to the wall, one hand clutching the front of the dress to her chest. But her long-held grip on the hope that Mom and Belle might one day accept her for who she was slipped.

Maybe if she finally gave into their demands. Lost some weight ...

Penny closed her eyes and inhaled the scent of sugar and roses. Being with them messed with her head. It's why she'd moved to Chicago. With her free hand, she squeezed the bridge of her nose. Today required an extra dose of patience.

When she opened her eyes, Mom stood with her arms crossed, glaring.

Penny sighed. "Even if I lose weight, this dress isn't me."

"It's couture." Two words that sounded awfully like *of course it isn't*. Mom opened the door and beckoned in a bridal consultant. "Can you please clip my daughter into this dress so she can join the rest of the wedding party?"

The woman scurried in, white clips in hand. Inserting a small piece of fabric into the opening, she quickly secured the last inches of Penny's dress. "All set."

"Good." Mom pointed to the hall. "Now get out there. Belle is in her dress, and she wants to see how everything looks together."

A drum roll beat through her mind. Here came the firing squad.

"Fine." Maybe once Belle saw this monstrosity on her, she wouldn't choose it for the wedding. Strapless and made of royal purple chiffon, it fell fitted to above the knee. Tight creases gathered in criss-cross patterns covering the entire length. As if that wasn't enough, Belle had added a diamond brooch above the right hip where those creases met in one large swirl. There was no way this dress could flatter anyone. Unless the rest of Belle's bridesmaids were all five-two and weighed ninety pounds.

Penny rounded the corner and stopped.

Oh. They were.

Belle turned from the mirror. "You took longer than the bride."

The four tiny girls standing around Belle giggled with their professionally manicured fingertips covering their mouths.

Penny met her gaze. "Sorry. The dress doesn't exactly fit."

Belle shushed her friends, stepped down from her pedestal, and sashayed over. A princess cut ball gown hugged her top half tightly then flared into a big poof at the waist. Cinderella at her finest. Crystals covered the bodice and ran along the hem, and their sparkle matched the gleam in Belle's blue eyes. "I can see that." She walked around Penny then stopped in front of her. "It definitely shows off your killer long legs. And if you lose those pounds before the big day, you should be all set."

"It's not like I'm grossly overweight, Belle. Most women have hips, you know." And apparently, hers were the only trait Mom and Belle saw. After her last disastrous date, she wondered if it was all anyone saw.

"I know. I only want you to look your best. That's all." Belle turned back around and fluffed her hair. "Trust me. You'll thank me come my wedding day."

Not if she still insisted on picking this dress.

"Seriously, Belle—" Penny began.

Men's laughter drifted in from the hall.

"Oh! Cover me!" Belle shoved Penny in front of her.

Mom ran toward the voices, hands waving circles through the air. "Not yet, boys! Not yet!"

Penny craned her neck to find her little sister cowering behind her. "What's going on?"

"Micah had the guys downstairs trying on tuxes so we could see the whole wedding party together. I was supposed to be out of my dress by now, but we waited so long for you—" She narrowed her eyes.

A black-clad saleslady floated into the room, a warm smile on her face. She crossed to Belle. "Coast is clear. Let me help you out of your dress and then we'll let them in." She eyed the grape dresses. "Oh, wait until you see the men in their tuxes. You have a beautiful wedding party."

Belle straightened. "I hope to." She cast one last look at Penny before following the saleswoman. "I'll be right back."

The four other bridesmaids perched nearby on a soft gray couch lined with fuchsia piping. Rather than joining them, Penny walked to the large window overlooking the tulip-lined street. In another month, the masses would descend upon Holland, Michigan, to see those tulips.

She ran a hand softly across the light gray velvet curtains. Parting them to tip her forehead against the cool glass, Penny shut out the voices in the room. Being here pulled all her old anxieties to the surface. It would have been smarter to stay home. Except she'd determined that this wedding would somehow draw them closer—at least her and Belle.

Right. It was only driving a larger wedge.

Releasing the curtain, she refocused on the room. Belle glided back in on three-inch heels which pointed out under her black wide-leg trousers. Her blush blouse had a deep v-neck, creating the perfect spot for her rhinestone-encrusted 'B' pendant hanging on a silver chain. Or maybe those were actual diamonds. There was nothing Mother wouldn't buy her princess.

"Send them in," Belle directed.

Micah entered and swept Belle into his arms. "Hey, beautiful."

Penny's heart pricked at that term of endearment. She ached for it to be used on her, but it had long ago been made clear that Belle was the only one in this family fit for that name.

Watching her now, it was hard to disagree. Micah and Belle were a life-size Barbie and Ken. His chiseled arms, her toned middle. His golden blond hair only a shade darker than hers—and neither of them had a strand out of place. Mom could rest easy knowing her grandchildren would all be blue-eyed beauties.

Four other men followed Micah into the room. Not one of them glanced her way. The Royal Court on the couch with their golden legs and silky hair snagged their immediate attention.

"Where's Jonah?" Belle asked.

"His train arrived late. He's downstairs still putting on his tux. He'll be right up."

Penny took advantage of the fact that the groomsmen were occupied flirting with the bridesmaids to study them. They were all in perfect shape, GQ hair, and not one appeared to be over six foot tall. Exactly the type of guys who'd always followed her sister around. The only time they'd paid Penny attention was in an attempt to get Belle's number. She'd hoped Chicago would be different.

It was—only not in the way she'd thought.

Plenty of men had found her a great ear for advice about their girlfriends. Her momentary foray into online dating had quickly proven not to be a fit for her, and the few dates she'd snagged from real-life connections somehow turned into episodes of Antique Road Show with her as the appraiser. Last month was the worst. Her client had flirted his way through his deceased parents' estate sale, selling her on his hard financial state as expertly as she sold his items. And she'd fallen for it. Given him a large discount. The final night he'd asked her to dinner, shown up with a thank you, her check—and his girlfriend.

No more dating for her. Seemed all she attracted were men who were more interested in what she could give them than they were in a relationship.

Belle began the introductions. "Most of you guys all know each other, but for those who don't; Chad, Tim, Blake, and Justin, this is Kelsey, Taylor, Ava, and, Brittany."

Penny cleared her throat.

"Oh, and my big sister, Penny." The men flicked their glances her way and then back to the Royal Court. Belle stepped forward. "I want to take a few pictures, and we're running low on time. Micah and I have dinner plans with our parents, so let's pair you up." She tugged on one of the guy's arms. "Chad, you're the best man, and you'll pair perfectly with Kelsey."

"Belle, doesn't the maid of honor typically walk with the best man?" Last she checked, she held that role.

Belle pulled her aside. "Mom mentioned the height difference and how it may play out in pictures, so we swapped you and Kelsey." She wrung her hands. "Honestly, I didn't think you'd be comfortable walking with him. Especially in heels."

"I wouldn't be comfortable, or your wedding party wouldn't look perfect?"

Belle had the good grace to grow a deeper shade of red. "You're my sister. I knew you'd understand it didn't matter where you stood. Micah didn't want to hurt Chad's feelings."

Because men cared about those things.

"Fine." Penny sighed. Arguing wouldn't close any of their distance. "Who am I walking with then?"

"Micah's cousin, Jonah Black. I told Micah he had to pick someone tall enough for you to walk down the aisle with, and Jonah's the perfect fit. Wait until you meet him." Belle grinned, and her eyes sparkled. "He's from Chicago too."

Her look and tone said she was up to something, but Penny was too exhausted to try and figure it out. She nodded over to the Royal Court who had their heads together whispering. "Go pair up the rest of your group."

"You're not mad then?"

"No, Bella Rose, I'm not mad." Try hurt. Focusing on that wouldn't grow them closer, though, so Penny squeezed her in a hug. "Whatever you want me to do to make your day special, I will. I promise."

A deep voice rumbled into the room. "Sorry I'm late."

Penny turned. A towering hulk of a man strode their way. Soft around the middle, he resembled a linebacker who'd spent more of the season pounding back cheeseburgers than players. And he was bald, no less.

"Jonah's here," someone called out.

Of course he was Belle's idea of her perfect pairing.

Except that wicked glint filled her little sister's eyes again. She *was* up to something. And the pit in Penny's stomach said she wasn't going to like it.

"Remember that promise." Belle waved at Jonah and smiled back at Penny. "I plan on holding you to it."

Chapter Two

Jonah Black rushed into the room and nearly bit his tongue. The purple of his tie wasn't only an accent, it was apparently the wedding color, and he was currently engulfed in a sea of it. Like being drowned in a vat of grape juice.

Seriously. Who picked this ... wonderful color? He swallowed the comment pushing against his lips. Bad enough he was late, best he keep his words in check, or Mom would definitely roll over in her grave. He squelched the urge to apologize to her.

Micah came over to greet him. "You didn't miss anything. Belle's ironing out an issue with her sister, so we're still waiting for our directions."

Jonah's gaze traveled across the room to the two ladies in the corner, and his brows rose. Belle's sister was not what he expected.

He'd met Micah's petite, blonde fiancée before, so when Micah had informed him he'd be escorting her sister down the aisle the mental picture he'd conjured up was a far cry from the stunning black-haired woman who currently towered over Belle—in her bare feet nonetheless.

Micah's shoulder nudged his. "I know, right?"

"Huh?"

"Hard to believe they're from the same family, isn't it?"

Jonah laughed. "Same could be said of us."

"We're cousins. They're sisters. Though Belle's—"

He was cut short by the sisters' arrival. "Jonah." Belle wrapped him in a hug. "Good to see you again." She made introductions then pulled Micah away. "You two get to know each other. I need to pick the handkerchiefs you boys will wear, and then we'll line you up."

Penny extended her hand. "Nice to meet you, Jonah."

Her tone was even, her handshake firm, and her eyes held his. She was taller than he'd first thought but still shorter than him by a good three inches. Her hair brushed past her shoulders in soft waves, and deep green eyes shone behind the longest lashes he'd ever seen. She had a classic beauty that didn't match the purple dress she'd squeezed herself into.

What one wouldn't do for family. "Nice dress." He smirked.

Her jaw tightened. "Only slightly lovelier than your vest and tie. Pull that thing much tighter, and your face will match the ensemble."

"Touché." His finger went between his collar and topknot. "I hate being late. I took my frustration out on the tie." He dropped his hand. "And it certainly didn't help when I saw what color I had to put on."

Perfect teeth flashed up at him. Her smile was great. "I can handle the color; it's the style. But I have no say. They've been waiting their whole life to dress me up."

"They?"

Penny nodded to an older, perfectly coiffed blonde woman in the corner. Petite and wearing a bone-colored suit with matching heels, Penny didn't get her height from this woman.

"My mom and Belle."

"They don't like how you typically dress?"

She giggled. No, the word giggle didn't suit her—the sound was too hearty.

"No. They don't." Her fingers toyed with the broach at her hip. "I don't share their affinity for glitter. We stopped shopping together about the time I decided my clothes shouldn't sparkle more than my personality."

"So you're loving that pin at your waist."

"I'm planning on stringing it up and breaking out my disco moves at their reception."

Laughter poured from him. "Nice. I'll brush up on my Electric Slide."

Her fingertips smoothed over her lips as her shoulders shook. Her mom turned and glared, and immediately Penny stilled. "She's going to ban me from this wedding just like she did their pageant world."

He leaned in, unsure he heard her correctly. "Come again?"

Surprised eyes found his. Didn't she realize she'd spoken out loud?

Curiosity snagged him. Unfortunately, so did the bride.

"Over here, everybody," Belle called.

Once Belle had everyone placed, the two he thought were named Chad and Kelsey stood beside the happy couple. The remaining group fanned out from there, ending with him and Penny. Strange that Penny wasn't maid of honor.

Beside him, she fidgeted with the part of her dress stretched across her hips.

Belle and Penny's mother stood beside her youngest as they faced the group. She clasped her hands together. "Nearly perfect." Her gaze landed on Penny. "We're ordering the suits and dresses today, so no one gain one ounce. The seamstress can take away material, but she can't add any."

Warmth worked its way up Jonah's neck. What kind of person said something like that? He leaned down. "You look great, by the way."

Penny tugged the top of her dress up. "And you need glasses." She spied her sister. "Belle, are we finished?"

"Once the seamstress takes your measurements."

A woman in a black suit approached wielding a long white tape, and Penny followed her to a dressing room.

Micah clapped Jonah on the back and took a key from his keychain. "Belle's asking Penny if she'll drop you at my place. Sorry you had to get a taxi earlier, but if I'd been even a minute late, Belle wouldn't be speaking to me right now."

"No problem. And I can take another taxi to your place. No sense inconveniencing Penny."

"No way. This is Belle's doing, not mine. Trust me, let Penny take you home. It will save us all a bunch of grief."

Jonah caught Belle grinning at him. She gave a little wave and swept into Penny's dressing room. He had the feeling she was up to a little matchmaking.

Hmm … couldn't say he minded.

"You what?" Penny tied the belt that cinched her shirtdress and slipped into her floral ballet flats. She'd been right. She didn't like what Belle was up to at all.

"Well, he needs someone to drive him to Micah's house. Everyone else has plans for the night." Belle reclined against the pink chenille couch in the dressing room.

"And you assumed I didn't?"

"Do you?" Belle raised her brows.

"As it happens, yes, I do."

"Plans that involve another person? Not simply going home, putting on sweats, and scanning deals on the computer?"

"I'm in the middle of pricing an estate. I have work to do."

Belle picked a loose string off her sweater. "Dropping Jonah off is on your way. And if you two happened to stop for dinner …"

"I'm not interested in a set-up, Belle." Private romantic failures were embarrassing enough; she didn't need to fall on her face in front of Belle. Especially not with Micah's cousin. There'd be no hiding from that humiliation— ever. "The only thing I want right now is to open my store. And I'm close." So close. Just a few more sales and her bank account would finally look healthy enough for that loan. That meant she could actually start visiting possible spaces to house her little antique shop. Excitement flooded her then quickly dried with Belle's next words.

"But Jonah is perfect for you."

Because as far as Mom and Belle were concerned, tall, heavy, and bald equated to her match. She swallowed back the bubbling frustration. Those two so easily climbed inside her head. She shook away their thoughts. It didn't matter what Jonah looked like. Didn't matter that he had a two-minute conversation with her that had pulled out laughter. She was through sticking herself out there only to be let down. "Whether he is or not, I already told you. I'm not looking."

Her sister tipped her head and stood. "Come on. One night. You can even talk work with him." Her sing-song words plucked dread through Penny's middle.

"Why is that?"

"For starters, he and Micah's grandmother isn't doing well, and Jonah is in charge of her estate. He seemed really interested when I told him what you do."

No wonder he'd been so friendly outside. Like others, he probably thought charm could land him a deal. She didn't need to hear any more.

"Not. Interested."

They stared each other down.

Finally, Belle retreated. "Can you at least drive him home?"

If it would end this conversation. "That I can do." Penny walked to the door. "He is on my way, so there's no sense in him paying an Uber driver."

Belle squealed. "You know, that's how it all started for Micah and me."

Penny shook her head. Let Belle think what she wanted. Nothing was starting up between her and Jonah Black.

Jonah met Belle and Penny as they exited the dressing room. The green shirtdress she wore hugged her curves and fell just below her knees. It reminded him of something Grace Kelly or Audrey Hepburn would wear—not that he'd ever admit to knowing that fact. It definitely fit her better than the purple number from earlier. Not to mention how it made her eyes stand out.

"I hear you're my ride?"

Her smile didn't reach those eyes. "I am. You wearing that tux home?"

His lip twitched. "Tempting as that sounds, I was just waiting to make sure I had a ride before heading downstairs for measurements. I know they volunteered you, so if you had other plans ..."

Penny waved him off. "You're on my way."

"Give me a few minutes, and I'll be ready." He found alterations, and the seamstress approached him with her measuring tape. He stopped her. "I'm not at my normal weight right now."

She tipped her head.

"But I will be by the wedding."

A patronizing nod. "I'm sure you will, but I need to take your measurements as is."

Jonah sighed. He knew a chunk of the weight would be off by the wedding in late June, but there was no use convincing her. She probably heard this song at most fittings.

"Can I order a tux in a lower size, too?"

The seamstress covered her laugh with a cough. "It's your money."

"If you don't mind, that's what I'd like to do."

She nodded as she wrapped her tape around his waist. After she finished, he gave her a size larger than he'd have ordered a year ago and then got dressed. While he wouldn't change this weight gain for anything, he itched to shed the pounds. Now that Gavin was stronger, they could work on taking them off together.

Jonah grabbed his suitcase and climbed the stairs two at a time. Penny hadn't seemed thrilled to be his chauffeur, so he didn't want to keep her waiting. There was something about her that clicked with him, and he wouldn't mind getting to know her better.

She sat on the sofa tapping her iPhone. Her gaze met his.

"You ready?" she asked.

"Sure, unless you need to finish what you were working on. Belle mentioned you work estate sales." A business owner himself, he knew things couldn't always wait. "I'd love to hear more about it."

Her eyes narrowed, and she slid her phone into her purse. "Not much to tell." She stood. "I'm parked out front."

He followed her to a silver Mercedes E-Class. "Nice car."

"It's my mom's."

He stowed his suitcase in the backseat then slid into the black interior. "I appreciate you taking the time to drive me home."

"Like I said, you're on the way."

"Sure I can't interest you in dinner?"

She started the car. "I'm sorry. I have a lot to get done tonight."

He understood. What he didn't understand was where the coolness was suddenly stemming from. "Maybe another time?"

"My schedule's pretty full."

They rode in silence for a few minutes. Penny turned on the radio and flipped stations until she hit one with Adele singing.

"I hear she's coming to Chicago early this summer." Jonah watched her.

"Micah says you're from there, too?"

"Yep."

Not exactly a fountain of information. And he didn't get the feeling it was due to shyness. Not after how open she'd been inside. Something was obviously bugging her. Didn't know her well enough to ask, but he had seen her sarcastic side. Maybe he could reach it again. Distract her from whatever ate away the smile she'd worn earlier.

"You know, just because you talk to me doesn't mean I'll assume you're confessing your undying love."

Her crimson face swung to his. "What?"

"Just saying I won't mistake friendliness for an invitation to propose marriage."

A low chuckle accompanied her head shake. "Good to know." She slid her gaze back to the road. After a few moments, she broke the silence. "Sorry I've been a brat. My Mom and sister tend to put me on edge."

Ah. Family, not business, was bugging her. Not too surprised there.

"Can't imagine why. They seemed lovely."

Based on her shoulders relaxing and the way she grinned, she'd picked up on his sarcasm. Nice to see her smile return too.

She flicked on her blinker and switched lanes. "That concert's sold out by the way. I tried to get tickets."

"Sorry. I heard they sold fast." He leaned back in the deep leather seat. "So how long have you lived in the city?"

"Ten years." She toggled the heat down. "You?"

"I grew up around the Lincoln Park area."

"Is that where you live now?"

"I do."

"Your family still in the area?"

A twinge of sadness pricked his heart. He still wasn't used to Mom being gone. "Not everyone. Only my sister, nephew, and Gran are still close-by."

"I guess that's nice if you get along."

"I'm sensing you and your sister aren't the best of friends?"

Penny glanced his way. "We aren't enemies."

Interesting answer.

She exited the highway and turned right onto 16th Street. "Baker Lofts, right?"

"Yep."

And it was coming up all too quickly. He liked Penny. The dry sense of humor. How she refused to speak badly about a sister who obviously didn't always treat her the best. Her wavy black hair, green eyes, and smile that stood out. Not to mention her style. Not flashy, but classic.

"You taking the train home tomorrow?" he asked as she pulled up to Micah's building.

"Sunday morning, actually."

The car idled. Jonah stepped out, grabbed his suitcase, and leaned in the open door. He wanted to ask her out but already knew her answer. "I'll say good-bye here then. Thanks for the ride."

"No problem." She smiled.

Yep. He could get used to that smile.

He barely had the door closed before she pulled from the curb. As he walked to the front door of the lobby, he pulled out his phone and called Micah.

"Mind if I stay till Sunday?"

Chapter Three

She'd survived the weekend. Barely.

Thankfully, only Dad wanted to bring her to the train station. She couldn't handle one more of Mom or Belle's digs—not that she'd spent much time with them. Avoidance was not beneath her.

Dad pulled into the parking lot and circled. It was busy for a Sunday morning.

"You can just drop me at the door," Penny offered.

"I'll walk you in." He pulled into a spot and cut the engine.

"Okay. If you're offering, I'm accepting." Penny hopped out and rounded to the trunk, hauling out her suitcase. Dad immediately grabbed it from her. "Thanks."

He draped his free arm around her shoulder and kissed her temple. "No thanks necessary. I needed some more time with my Lucky Penny. I miss you when you're not home."

Penny leaned into him, inhaling his Old Spice cologne as they walked toward the train station. "I miss you too."

His long, thin legs moved at a leisurely pace. "Sure you don't want to stay for the week? You hardly got to see your mom and sister."

As if that was a bad thing. But Dad never seemed to acknowledge the tension between them.

He reached out and held open the door for her. Penny ducked under his arm and into the train station. "I've got an estate sale scheduled for next weekend, and I don't even have everything catalogued or priced." They walked through the small building, past several benches full of people, and outside to the platform. "You could come to Chicago and help me, though."

He shook his head. "I wish I could, sweetheart, but Grandma and Grandpa need me at the barn sale. Donations flooded in, and they can't keep up with it all. I'm not sure how we'll get it all priced and organized."

Their annual charity sale. It's where her love for antiquing began. She'd hoped to help but was beyond busy herself—especially since she was so close to her goal.

"Sorry I can't make it this year." Penny sidestepped a stroller.

"They know you're busy."

"Sounds like it's going to be a big one."

His weathered cheeks crinkled into a smile. "Hope so. They want to fund our youth group's mission trip. Least that's what they told the church."

Penny checked her watch. "Speaking of church, you should get going. Mom won't be happy if you're late." She leaned over and kissed his cheek. "Tell Belle and Mom I said good-bye."

His face darkened. "I hope your sister's at church for me to tell her. She stayed out again all night." He swallowed and stared off into the distance for a moment. "I worry about her."

"I know." Penny squeezed his arm.

A moment passed. Slowly, Dad shook his head. "How'd my girls grow up so fast? You're in Chicago, and now Belle's getting married? Where'd the time go?" He wrapped her in a hug, and his wet cheek pressed against hers.

She pulled back and wiped his tears. Dad's heart was so tender, so full of love; it almost made up for the lack of love from Mom.

Almost.

Taking her bag, she gave him a light push. "That time is still ticking, and it'll make you late if you don't get out of here."

"All right." He kissed her forehead. "I'm going. Don't be a stranger."

With a wave, Dad disappeared through the door. Penny rolled her suitcase over to a concrete bench and sat. Within minutes, her train rolled to a stop. She hauled her suitcase into the entryway and through the tight aisle before stuffing it above the first open seat she came to and sitting. Digging out her laptop and headphones from her backpack, she settled in.

"This seat taken?"

Her focus remained on her computer. "Yes." By the work she needed to spread out. And this morning there were plenty of other seats free on the train.

"Looks open."

She pushed her headphones into her ear. "I'm saving it."

"Huh. Thought you came home by yourself."

Her gaze flew up and collided with Jonah's eyes scrunched around the edges in that impossible smirk he possessed.

"And I thought you were going home yesterday."

His smirk deepened. "I was, but Micah and I had some catching up to do."

"Funny, I thought he spent the weekend with Belle."

The train jolted forward, and Jonah grabbed the luggage compartment above. "Mind if I sit to talk?"

Resigned to the fact he wasn't going away, Penny pulled her backpack off the seat beside her. "Be my guest." So much for spreading out.

"Thanks."

He stowed his rolling carrier above their seats and plopped down. His leg and broad shoulders encroached on her seat, and she pushed herself against the window.

"They sure don't give you much room, do they?" He scooched closer to the aisle.

"That's why I typically drive."

"You have a car in the city?"

"You don't?"

Stubble graced his chin. So. He could grow hair. By the looks of it, it would be dark. Was he really bald, or did he shave? If it was his choice, someone needed to tell him to make a different one.

She shook the rude thought from her head. One weekend with Mom, and she was back in her brain again.

Jonah leaned back. "You disagree?"

"Uh"—she tipped her head—"disagree about what?"

"That we can cut down on pollution by carpooling or using public transportation." Scenery sped by outside. "I get that most people live in towns without great public transit, but in Chicago, you're all set; you don't really need a car. I use mine as little as possible."

He was an eco-nut.

Penny turned back to her laptop. "I still prefer my car."

"Fair enough." Jonah reached into his bag and pulled out a copy of Forbes magazine.

How long did she need to wait before putting her headphones on again and attempting to work? Ten minutes? That seemed fair.

Jonah propped a foot over his knee, and his thigh pressed into hers. He scooted back the other way. "Sorry. Like I said, not much room."

Her knees pressed into the seat in front of her. "I understand."

"How tall are you, anyway?"

"Six foot."

"I thought so. You certainly don't get your height from your mom."

"Ha! You think? She would have loved that though. If she could have strapped a brick to my head growing up, she would have tried it. Much to her dismay, I surpassed her height by the time I was twelve."

His magazine lay in his lap. "I'm guessing your father is tall?"

"Six-five."

"And she didn't mind that?"

Penny wound the cord to her earbuds around her fingers. "Not until she realized I had his genes." Though that had only been the icing on the cake. Mom had found Penny lacking years before. "Sorry, but I've got a lot of work I need to get done."

"Right. Estate sales and antiques. I'd still love to hear about them. I may have need of your expertise soon."

For his grandmother's estate. Thank you, Belle. "Maybe at the next wedding function we're summoned to, we can chat, but I really need to finish a few things for this weekend's sale."

He watched her for a moment. "No problem. I've been waiting to read this."

Somehow he didn't seem like a guy that read Forbes.

She planted her headphones back in her ears and flipped her music on, but not before she thought she heard, "For the record, I like tall women."

Warmth flooded her, and she twisted to look at him. Jonah's gaze was on his magazine. He turned. "Need something?"

She narrowed her gaze. Watched him. Had he said that or was she hearing things? Because she'd fallen into this trap before. Interpreted interest in her expertise for actual interest in *her*.

His brow rose.

Not chancing it. "Nothing." She turned back to her computer.

A moment passed before she snuck a peek from the corner of her eye. He still focused on his magazine, but his lips twitched.

He was playing with her. But it was a game she didn't want to join.

Jonah didn't say anything for another hour, pretty sure he'd already said enough. He hadn't meant for that last comment to slip out.

He flipped another page to make it appear he was reading. The magazine in his hands might as well have been *Glamour* for all the interest he had in it right now. His focus rested solely on the woman to his right, and he couldn't break it. Didn't want to anyway.

Even if she'd become a bit prickly.

He ran a hand over his bald head. Beside him, Penny stared at her computer and twirled a long piece of hair between her fingers. Her work had her full attention.

His eyes trailed over her smooth skin and stopped to watch her teeth nibble at her silky red lips. She tipped her head, and the light caught her face at a different angle, revealing a faint scar from the edge of her lip halfway up her cheek. Faint, but there. Both times he'd spoken with her, he'd missed it. Not that it mattered, just made him curious.

She turned. Caught him staring. She tugged out one of her headphones. "Yes?"

He nodded to her computer. "About ready for a coffee break?"

"I don't drink coffee."

Okay. Maybe she wasn't perfect.

She laughed. "I know, shocking in this day and age, right?"

"I'm wondering how you manage to function."

Penny dug into the largest purse he'd ever seen, a brighter blue version of her navy dress. And she had yellow shoes on.

Her voice drifted to him. "Oh, I do caffeine, but as tea." She grabbed her wallet full of even more color—the woman was a walking box of crayons. Beautiful.

Penny flipped the wallet over, but not before he saw the name "Penelope" on it. "Shall we find some snacks?" she asked.

Jonah stood and held his hand out for her to walk in front of him. If he'd known it'd be this easy to distract her, he'd have tried earlier. "I'll follow you."

They walked the narrow aisle to the end of the car, his hips bumping into the edges of every seat. "Penelope, huh?" When she didn't answer, he continued, "It suits you."

"You'd be the only one to think so." The words drifted over her shoulder.

"Apparently not, or you wouldn't have it on your wallet." And he happened to like the name too.

She half turned, brows scrunched as if she was trying to figure him out, then kept walking toward the concession stand at the far end. Midway down the aisle, the train lurched. Penelope stumbled backward into him, and Jonah grabbed her waist. A light scent—flowers maybe—floated past his nose. She smelled great. She felt even better nestled against him. "Gotcha, Penelope."

She glanced up, her cheeks a soft pink. His fingers tightened around her waist as the train rolled around another corner. Soft pink turned to red, and she pushed away.

"Thanks for catching me." Penelope tossed the words over her shoulder and barreled down the aisle.

When they reached the snack cart, she selected a bag of nuts and another of Peanut M&M's. Jonah opted for a bottle of water, a pack of cinnamon gum, and a large coffee. Luckily he could drink it black because they were out of creamer.

He nudged Penelope out of the way when she tried to pay for her snacks.

"I got it."

"Thanks, but I can buy my own." She pulled out a ten.

Jonah laid his twenty on top of her bill. "Take mine," he said to the man and then looked at Penelope. "I owe you for the ride home on Friday."

She stuffed her money back in her wallet. "Thanks." Then scooped up her treats. "But you didn't need to do that."

"Didn't think you expected me to." Jonah pocketed his change and motioned for her to walk in front of him again.

She brushed past, tossing out her words as she did. "You'd be right. Zero expectations."

He had a feeling she wasn't simply talking about their snack purchase.

Penny's hands skimmed the tops of seats as she made her way back to their car. No way she was tripping again. How embarrassing for Jonah to grab her thick waist. Ugh. At least she had a dress on—no muffin top there.

And he called her Penelope. No one did that anymore. She'd long ago given up on asking.

Yet with Jonah, she hadn't needed to ask. He hardly knew her, but with one look at her wallet, he decided he knew what suited her.

What bothered her wasn't only the fact he was right, but that the name sounded so right on his lips. A thought she refused to entertain.

She slid into her seat and grabbed the thermos of tea from her purse.

"You like nuts?"

Penny turned to Jonah. "Referring to yourself?"

Jonah's mouth opened. Closed. He shook his head. "You crack yourself up, don't you?"

She shrugged. "I share my father's dry sense of humor. More often than not it gets me in trouble."

"I like it." Jonah took a swig from his water bottle and then pointed toward her snacks. "But I was referring to your choice of food."

She ripped open the tops of both bags and dumped a little of each into her hand. "What I like is chocolate. I figure if I add enough nuts to it, I'll get my protein too. Make it healthier."

"Uh-huh."

"It's my dream world. Let me live in it." She popped the handful into her mouth and poured another.

Jonah chuckled. "Same world my mom lived in." He unwrapped a stick of

20

his gum. "She always carried a pack of Dentyne, but chocolate had her heart. Maintained that anything brown was calorie-free, fat-free."

"Sounds like a woman I'd love to meet."

The words were out before they registered in her brain. Jonah turned away. Embarrassed? So much for him not taking her friendliness as a come-on. Fine by her, silence gave her room to work, which was exactly where her focus should have remained.

With his gaze still caught out the window, she rolled up her snacks, slipped them into her purse, and grabbed her headphones. Pushing them back in her ears, she caught Jonah's glance. His eyes watered.

And then it clicked.

He'd said lived, not lives.

She tugged her headphones off. "I'm so sorry."

"Don't be." He shrugged. "You didn't know. And I'm the one who brought her up."

"No. I'm sorry you lost someone you obviously loved. A lot."

He had a great smile—made his eyes crinkle around the edges and sparkle like polished silver. How come this was the first time she noticed it? Or his striking eyes. "Thanks."

Silence inflated its awkward bubble around them. Talking about loss did that. Especially when she couldn't relate to his. And wouldn't. At least not with her mom.

Penny shook her head.

"You okay?" Jonah's brow furrowed almost like he could read her mind and didn't like her thoughts. Not because they were awful, but because he could see the root of them. Could see her pain.

Now she was making things up. Jonah wasn't a mind reader.

"I'm fine." She flipped open her laptop. "Just have a lot of work to do, and time is ticking away."

He held her gaze for a moment longer. "Okay." He held up his Forbes. "I'll stick my nose back in this thing and let you get to it."

His attention returned to his magazine, and loneliness slipped in to replace its warmth. What was wrong with her? She refused to be interested in him. Had more than enough work to do. And yet ...

"You play Scrabble?" she blurted.

He smiled. "You like losing?"

Penny brought the game up on her phone. "No. And that's why I never lose."

His laughter rumbled over her, and the cloud of loneliness lifted. Okay. So maybe not romance material, but Jonah Black was shaping up to be fantastic friend material.

"There's a first time for everything."

Sure was. But she wasn't losing a thing to him. Not this game. And definitely not her heart.

Chapter Four

"Hey, roomie." Lacey Conson smiled from her perch at the counter, the Sun-Times spread across the surface, her orange juice and oatmeal beside the paper.

Penny dropped her suitcase onto the floor. "Sunday off?"

"Thankfully."

"That why you're enjoying a late start to your day?"

Lacey smiled. "More like late finish to last night. I met someone."

Penny retreated to the door. "He's not here, is he?"

"Relax. We stayed at his house. I followed the rules, even if you weren't home." Her hazel eyes lit up. "I think he may be 'the one.' Wait until you meet him."

Penny shuffled into the kitchen. "If he was 'the one' he'd treat you like the lady you are, not sleep with you after one night."

A snort came from the counter. "I swear you are an eighty-year-old woman trapped in a thirty-one-year-old body."

"I'm not old, just old-fashioned. Least that's what I've been told." She flipped the burner on under her kettle and opened a cupboard to choose just the right teacup for this morning. She needed it after Jonah beat her at Scrabble. No one ever bested her at that game. The man was a walking dictionary.

Her eyes landed on the light pink roses blooming along one of her cups and saucers. Aynsley china, signed by Bailey himself. Perfect. She pulled it out. "Is it really so incomprehensible to believe you should take things slowly? Be with only one man who really loves you?"

"No. What's crazy is not sampling all the others first." Lacey flipped her caramel colored hair over her shoulder. "How are you going to learn about chemistry without experience? And trust me, men want experience."

Penny dropped a tea bag into her pink teacup. "Not the kind of man I eventually want to date."

"Honey, they all want it. Some just might not admit it."

She pushed her saucer along the counter and plopped into the seat next to Lacey. "So what are you up to today?"

"Thought maybe I'd go for a run along Lake Shore. You want to come?"

"Because I run."

Lacey pushed her dishes over to the sink. "Fine. But at least get outside. A little pink in your cheeks would do you good."

"I will. Promise. But I've got to get a few more things priced. The Wilton's estate sale is next week. The supposed money from their parents' collections is burning a hole in those kids' pockets."

"They've got good stuff?"

"Decent. Problem is the collections were worth far more to Allen and Frances in sentimental value than in actual value. I don't think their kids recognize the difference."

"Good luck with that."

"Thanks."

Lacey yanked her hair into a ponytail. "Just keep picturing that cute little antique store you want."

"I know. I'm so close."

"And this sale will bring you one step closer." With a wave, she was gone.

Penny grabbed her laptop but didn't make it more than twenty minutes. Lacey was right. It was far too nice a day to stay inside. After a quick change of clothes, she snuck out for a walk.

Stepping into the sunshine, Penny peeked down the street. Wicker Park bustled with activity. She headed up to Damen. Her taste buds begged her to turn right; she opted for left. If she wanted to visit Leitzia's Bakery, she better walk the block first.

Everything about this area suited her. The fun shops, little brownstones, walkways and Wicker Park itself all within walking distance reminded her of home without all the inconveniences of living there. Here she could be herself without hearing it wasn't enough.

One day, she'd prove it was. Maybe that would finally soothe the ache inside.

She turned right on Schiller, and the park stood on her left. Children's voices mingled in with traffic. The air had warmed since morning and held the promise of spring. She could actually smell the grass that carpeted the park. Of course, it was only the beginning of April, and that meant the weather could plummet back down to winter coat status. She hoped not. It would be awfully cruel after a day like today.

"Clooney! No!"

The voice came from her behind, and before she could turn, the largest mutt she'd ever seen charged through the dog park's gate and straight past her. Penny leapt for the leash and ended up eating dirt. She sat up and brushed gravel from her hands as the dog continued down the street, a young boy chasing after him.

"Gavin, stop!"

The boy eked out a few more paces before bending over and dragging in deep breaths. His mother flew by and threw her arm around her son.

"Gavin. You're in no shape to chase Clooney."

Worry pinched the mother's face as she led her son to a nearby bench where he struggled to catch his breath.

Penny walked over. "Everything okay?"

Two sets of concerned eyes looked up.

"My dog."

"Hush, Gavin. I'm more worried about you than I am about that stupid dog."

Penny stared at the boy. When he ran by, she'd guessed him to be around ten, but his face was that of a young teen. His head was shaved bald, his skin pale, and he carried a few extra pounds, to say the least. He didn't look too good.

Down the street, Clooney barked. Gavin tried to stand, but his mother restrained him.

"Stay. You're not strong enough."

Penny eyed his protruding stomach and chubby cheeks. *That's what you get for too many video games and potato chips.* The bitter comment died on her tongue, and she snapped her head back.

Gavin's mother watched her. "Are you all right?"

Penny shook her head. "Yes. Just attempting to dislodge my mother from my brain."

The woman's eyes widened. "Oh. Okay."

And now she thinks I'm crazy.

"I can go get him," Penny offered. It was the least she could do after her awful thoughts.

Gavin pulled some dog treats out of his pocket before his mom could disagree. "Here."

Penny took them with a cautious glance toward Gavin's mom.

She studied her and then Gavin's hopeful face before resting her gaze on Penny. "Thank you."

"No problem." Down the sidewalk, Clooney danced in circles, happy to be free. His leash dragged along the concrete behind him.

"Here, Clooney," Penny called out. "You want a treat boy?"

Clooney stopped dancing and sat.

"That's a good boy." Penny approached, treat held out. She reached for the leash, and Clooney bolted.

"You have got to be kidding me."

Ten feet away, Clooney stopped and danced some more. Penny edged closer and repeated the offer.

Clooney sat and smiled. A dog who smiled. She was in trouble.

"What kind of mutt are you, anyway?"

Whatever he was, he was huge. Either that or it was his mass of caramel colored fur poofing out.

Penny held out the treat again, taking slow, measured steps. Clooney's eyes widened as the treat inched closer. She had him this time. No reaching down for the leash, this time she was stomping on it. Two feet away, Penny leapt. Clooney was faster. With a bark, he bounded away and twirled in another circle.

"Oh, you think this is funny, do you?"

Another smile. Darn dog.

"Fine." Penny pocketed the treat. "You don't want a nice, warm home with all the food you could eat and a boy who loves you, then you go right ahead and keep running. I'm not chasing you. I'm sure Gavin can find another dog who wants to live with him."

Penny spun on her heel and strode back toward Gavin. She made it halfway before something nudged her leg. She pivoted and stared at Clooney's wet nose and big, brown eyes.

"You decided you want to come home?"

Clooney sat.

"All right, but this is your last chance. You run again, and you're on your own."

The dog nudged her pocket.

"I'll give you a treat *after* you let me pick up that leash."

One ear picked up as Clooney tilted his head. Penny stepped on the leash, then closed her fingers around it. Once she had a firm grip, she gave him a treat and then headed back to Gavin and his mom.

"Here you go." She handed the leash off to Gavin's mother.

"Thanks so much." Gavin smiled up at her. Some color had returned to his cheeks, but he still appeared out of breath.

"Yes, thank you. I'm Rachael, and this is my son, Gavin." She extended her hand, and Penny shook it.

"I'm Penny. Glad I could help."

Rachael nodded to Gavin. "We are too. Gavin's had some health issues lately that have taken a toll on him. He's getting better now, but not quite as fast as he'd like. My brother gave us Clooney to help get Gavin outside and walking."

Health issues. She wanted to knock herself over the head for thinking the worst of the poor boy.

"Are you a George Clooney fan?" Penny asked.

Gavin smiled. "Nope. Clooney's a girl. She's named after Rosemary Clooney."

Penny patted the dog. "No wonder you ran from me. I kept calling you 'boy.'" Then she peered over at Gavin. "I'm surprised you even know who Rosemary Clooney is."

"My nana, uncle, and I watched a lot of old movies together when Nana and I were both sick. *White Christmas* was one of my favorites, and Rosemary Clooney was one of Nana's favorite singers."

"How's your nana doing now?"

"She passed away a few months ago," Rachael spoke softly.

What was it with her and bringing up dead people today? First Jonah, now these two. "I am so sorry." Penny rubbed her hands together as silence settled around them. She cleared her throat. "Well, I should get going. Keep a tight hold on that leash."

Rachael smiled. "I think Gavin will stick with going to the gym alongside his uncle for a while rather than walking Clooney."

"Yeah. I finally got cleared by my doctor to work out. My uncle hired me a personal trainer at Emerge Fitness. I'm gonna start this week. Ever been there?"

"Nope." Though it was close.

"Maybe you should check them out sometime."

She was almost offended by his possible implication. Almost. But could she blame him for judging her by the same yardstick she'd used on him?

"Maybe." Clooney started to tug on her leash. "Good luck getting Clooney home."

"Thanks again." Rachael helped Gavin to his feet, and they started in the opposite direction. Penny watched them for a bit before continuing her walk. Except she'd just chased a dog and hadn't planned on that extra exercise. So ... she turned around and headed for Leitzia's.

A few feet from the bakery, her phone rang. She slid a finger across the screen. "Hey, Belle. What's up?"

"You left without saying good-bye."

"You weren't home."

Belle's theatrical sigh blew through the phone. "You could have waited for me."

"And miss my train? You weren't home all weekend."

"Well, if you'd fixed your car earlier, you'd have had it this weekend and wouldn't have to catch a train."

"They needed an extra part—"

"Anyway. I wanted to let you know that Mom and I told them to order the dresses."

That wasn't news. "I assumed that's why they took my measurements, and I put down a deposit."

"We had them order yours in a size ten."

Now that was news. "What?"

"I know it's a tad smaller than what your measurements indicated—"

"A tad? It's two sizes smaller!"

"Mom and I wanted to help you reach your goal."

"My goal?"

Belle's voice lowered. "You said you'd lose weight before my wedding."

"Yeah. Like a couple of pounds. Belle, I'm not overweight." Not too much, anyway.

"Do you know the body you could have with that height? Honestly, Penny, I only want you to realize your full potential."

Penny gripped her phone tighter. "My potential has nothing to do with my waistline." Maybe one day they'd all believe that. At least Belle hadn't mentioned the scar for once.

"How would you know when you've never actually tried to lose the weight? You'd be so beautiful with only a little work. You have no clue what you're missing out on."

Oh, she knew. She'd missed out on it her whole life. Love. Acceptance. A place to belong. All because she couldn't attain their version of that one word: beautiful.

"Look, Penny," Belle spoke into her hesitation. "They placed the order when I spoke with them on Friday evening. Do you really want to miss my wedding because you can't fit into it?"

And there it was. The ultimatum they'd always lived but never stated quite so clearly: fit in or stay out.

Silence stretched across the line. Penny's reflection stared at her from a storefront window, a battle waging inside. She couldn't compete with Belle. Had never been able to. Still, it hadn't prevented her from hoping one day to fit in based on who she was. That finally they'd believe she was enough. Accept her. But maybe a little change was the compromise to finally see it happen. Maybe effort on her part would bring effort on theirs. Exhaustion weighed her down. How badly did she want their approval?

"Fine, Belle. I'll see what I can do."

Apparently a lot. Like twenty pounds worth.

Belle's squeal nearly caused her to drop her phone. "Oh, Penny! You won't regret it!"

They hung up, and Penny stared at Leitzia's. With a sigh, she turned and headed for home. No coffee and pastry now. She pulled up the internet on her phone and typed in Emerge Fitness. Looked like Gavin's uncle wasn't the only one hiring a personal trainer.

Chapter Five

Jonah watched Gavin finish his last rep at the bench. The boy could barely lift the bar even without weights attached. Yet the smile on his face was priceless. Cheating death tended to do that.

East Fisher, the personal trainer, stood above Gavin and helped him stow the bar. Jonah gave Gavin a thumbs-up. It was Monday, which meant he had three more minutes on the treadmill, and then it was his turn at the bench—minus East. Still wasn't sure what he thought of the cocky trainer, or his name, but East seemed to be handling Gavin well. Pushing him in the right spots, giving encouragement when needed, yet holding him back when he charged ahead. The man had a lot more patience for Gavin's weight than Jonah's.

Not that Jonah was excited about carrying the extra pounds either, but there was no way he'd have let Gavin go through things alone. While he couldn't take on the radiation or chemo, he could shave his head and put on weight right along with Gavin. And now they were going to take it off together.

Gavin sat up on the end of the weight bench and wiped his face. He'd done enough for the day. The treadmill whirled to a stop, and Jonah hopped off and walked over to his nephew. "Good job today."

Gavin smiled. "It's a start."

"Why don't you get a drink and cool down? Then we can shower and grab a burger."

East tossed Jonah a towel. "You're going to undo everything we've done tonight. Get him a protein shake instead."

Gavin's shoulders drooped. Poor boy had consumed his share of shakes. He needed a burger.

"Go on, Gavin. I'll catch up in a bit, and we can figure out what to do for dinner."

East wiped down the barbell. "You need a spotter?"

"I'll be fine."

East's brows whipped up. "My next appointment is late anyway." He pushed a few weights on the bar. "Hundred okay for you?"

"Hundred on the bar."

East chuckled. "Sure."

Jonah's gut tightened. He'd love to tell him to add more but wasn't in the mood to hurt. He'd get back to where he was a year ago, just not in one day. Let East think what he wanted.

It took him five minutes to rip through his three reps, and by the last one, his arms shook.

East grabbed the bar and placed it back on the hooks. "You'll get there, man."

Right about now, if he really cared what others thought, he would knock that smirk off the obnoxious man's face. But he'd learned long ago that what others thought didn't matter. So he stayed on the bench and calmed his breath.

"East Fisher?" A woman asked.

Jonah sat up. Yep. He'd recognized that voice anywhere. "Hey, Penelope." He stood to greet her. He'd thought about her too many times to count in the week since he'd seen her.

Her eyes widened. "Jonah, what are you doing here?" Her ponytail, navy sweats, and orange Hope College tee were a stark contrast to the dresses she'd worn in Holland. Still, she was gorgeous.

"Same as you, I suspect. Working out."

Not that she needed to.

East stepped forward, smarmy smile firmly in place. "I'm East. You must be my seven o'clock?"

She shook his hand. "Yep. They said you'd show me around and help me set up a routine?"

Jonah wished she was aiming that smile at him.

"Definitely." East stepped in close to Penelope. "What happened there?"

Her fingertips covered the small scar, and her face flamed. Jonah clenched his fist. He'd been itching to knock the guy earlier. Now he was ready to scratch that itch.

Penelope spoke quietly. "Um, it's from a birthmark I had as a child."

"Oh." East tipped his head. "I thought maybe you got into a fight or something. It's mysterious. And guys love a little mystery."

Penelope's flaming face turned into a blush, and her grin reappeared. No way she was swallowing this guy's lines.

East nodded to Jonah. "You good?"

"Yep."

Turning, East motioned to an open spot on the floor. "Let's start with stretching, and you can tell me your goals. Penny Thornton, right?"

She nodded.

Interesting that she didn't ask him to call her Penelope.

The two sat on the floor, East's hand on her back guiding her into a stretch. Jonah's jaw clenched. Maybe he should stretch after his workout—wouldn't want an injury from not cooling down properly.

He walked over to them.

Penelope mimicked a position East was demonstrating. He'd asked her something, and Jonah caught the tail end of her response. "—my little sister's wedding."

East watched her as she bent. Jonah didn't like the look in his eye. Or his words. "By the time I'm through with you, no one will notice the bride."

"Ha! I highly doubt that's possible. I'll settle for fitting into the tiny dress she ordered me to wear." Penelope switched to another stretch.

Jonah sat beside her. "And it's such a beautiful dress too."

Her nose scrunched up, and she laughed. The sound almost covered East's response. "With Penny in it, I've no doubt."

What was up with this guy?

Penelope rolled her eyes and grinned at Jonah before zeroing in on East. "You can stop the flattery. I've already paid for the next three months of training."

Jonah coughed to cover his laugh. Penelope was just fine. He stood. "I've got to head to the showers. See you around?"

"With all Belle's wedding plans, I'm sure of it."

That was the best news he'd heard all day.

"So, you should be loose enough to start." East's teeth gleamed white in his deeply tanned face. Dark blond hair and the biggest blue eyes she'd ever seen. And his muscles? She'd checked them out as she watched him with Jonah—not that she'd recognized Jonah until she'd walked over. East's six-pack and chiseled chest, clearly visible under the fitted black Under Armor shirt he wore, had held her attention.

He was her personal trainer? And then he'd started to flirt with her? She enjoyed it for a moment but put a stop to it. This was the real world. Men like him never noticed women like her. Now if Belle were here …

Penny shook her head.

"Everything all right?"

She needed to stop daydreaming. The annoying habit was going to make people think she was crazy. And she was if she thought East was remotely interested in her.

"Yes. Just anxious to start. I haven't been in a gym in years. We're talking gym class in high school."

"You don't look old enough for that to have been too many years ago."

"Again. I've already paid."

He laughed. "Not angling for your money. Just being honest."

His smile put her at ease. "Where do you want me to start?"

East led her to a treadmill. "How about here. Let's see what you're made of."

Jelly. Her knees shook as she stepped on. Yep. Definitely made of jelly. "You're not going to make me run, are you?"

Those blue eyes of his sparkled like sunlight hitting Lake Michigan on a hot summer's day. And she felt the heat. He reached across her and punched the 'on' button, then knocked the speed up to a four. "What do you think?"

Happy her legs were long enough to handle this speed at a walk.

After two minutes, East upped the incline. Her legs burned. How had she gotten so out of shape? At the five-minute mark, East appeared at her side again. He smiled. And pushed the speed up to a six. It was run or fall off.

"Not sure I can do this," Penny called out.

"You are doing it." East leaned against the front of the treadmill. "In fact, you move like a natural born runner."

She groaned. Sweat dripped down her brow, and her lungs screamed. She hadn't even been running a minute. East pushed it up to a seven.

"What are you doing?"

A few heads turned in her direction. She didn't care. This man was crazy.

"I told you. I want to see what you're made of."

Not what he thought. She reached out to punch the speed back down, and East covered it. "Not yet."

Then he punched it up one more time.

She glared at him between panting breaths. He smiled.

"I know you want to stop," he taunted. "Go ahead. There's no need to look perfect. It's not even your wedding. Just your little sister's."

Fire burned through her. Penny punched the speed up one more time. East crossed his arms in front of him. "Trying to take my job from me?"

She couldn't answer if she wanted to. There was no breath left in her body. The treads beneath her feet spun faster than she thought possible. What in the world was she thinking to push the speed this high? She was going to die.

Out of the corner of her eye, she spied someone watching her. She cut a glance his way and noticed it was Gavin from the park. She dared a wave at him, and his eyes lit up. So his uncle had made it here with him. Must be a great guy to take care of his nephew that way.

"You want to slow down?" East stood in front of her.

She shook her head.

"Want to go faster? We could punch it to a ten."

She'd laugh, but that would require air.

East's finger inched toward the speed button, and she shook her head violently.

"Yeah, that would be too fast." He started to walk away and then stopped. "So, about this dress your little sister wants you to wear."

Penny nailed the speed button.

"Miss Penny! I want you to meet my uncle."

Gavin's voice nearby startled her. She lost her footing and wiped out. With a thunk that rattled her teeth, the treadmill propelled her against the back wall. Amazing. Leave it to her to silence a gym.

Nike tennis shoes appeared in her line of sight. "You all right?"

Other than her pride, not much hurt. "Yeah, I'm fine." Penny's gaze drifted up to find Jonah and Gavin peering down at her. Well, of course Gavin's uncle was Jonah. And why not?

He squatted beside her. Thick black lashes lined his steel gray eyes. Mom would pay to have lashes like that.

She shook her head, and Jonah's forehead wrinkled. He leaned in. "Did you knock your head?"

Sweat dripped down her back. "No. Just the rest of me."

He chuckled. "Let me help you up." He grasped her arms and steadied her as she stood.

Penny accepted the towel East held out to her. "Thanks. Both of you."

People made their way back to their workouts, and Jonah turned on East. "Why'd you have her treadmill set so fast?" A deep 'v' sat between his brows, and he towered over East by a good three inches.

East shrugged. "I didn't. She did."

Only because he'd pushed her.

"You're the trainer. You should have kept it at a slower speed," Jonah ground out.

"You're right. I'm the trainer. And she was handling the speed fine until your nephew distracted her."

Red crept up Gavin's neck.

Penny placed her hand on the boy's arm. "It had nothing to do with you. I'm clumsy all on my own." She hopped up and down, shaking her arms. "And I'm fine. See?"

Gavin straightened with a nod. "Good."

"Penelope's the woman who helped you and your mom at the park?" Jonah asked his nephew.

"Yeah. You know her?"

"She's in Micah's wedding. Penelope is his fiancée's sister."

"Cool." He nudged Jonah but remained focused on Penny. "You sure you're all right? That was a great fall. If I had my phone out, you could have gone viral."

Thank the Lord for small miracles.

"Yeah, I'm good."

East's warm voice broke in. "We still have more work to do, Penny."

She pointed at the treadmill. "I am not getting back on that thing."

"Not today at least." He nodded toward the weight machines. "Let's work on your strength training. I'll walk you through the circuit then we'll do some floor exercises for your core."

Jonah and Gavin followed them on their way toward the exit.

"You need dinner when you're done here?" Jonah asked.

"Don't you have to get Gavin home?"

"That's a question, not an answer."

That's right. He wanted to pry information about her job. "Then no. I don't need dinner." She'd already worked a full day and had a pile of pricing sitting at home to tackle. One that involved actual customers.

Gavin folded his hands together and stuck them near his chin. "Please? As a thanks for the other day?" Dang, he was good. The boy's eyes perfectly matched his uncle's, right down to the flecks of silver that lit up with their smiles. And where Gavin went, so did Jonah.

Beside them, East adjusted the first machine to fifty pounds. Five. Zero. "Are you here to work on your body or your social life?"

Could she vote for neither?

But Gavin proved harder to say no to than Belle.

Guess she was a glutton for punishment.

"Fine. I'll meet you for dinner."

Chapter Six

Penny towel dried her hair, leaving it in damp waves that hung down her back. She dressed quickly, then stowed her workout gear. The reflection in the mirror stopped her. What stared back dimmed the brightness her colorful clothes brought out. Her hair was a hot mess. Her pasty skin held no hint of tan. And her hips seemed to have grown since yesterday. Yep. She'd definitely been dreaming to think even for a second that East had been flirting with her. If she had even one of Belle's assets, then maybe.

With a sigh, she picked up her bag and headed out of the locker room. She spied Gavin and Jonah waiting outside. Jonah met her as she came through the entrance.

"Where to?" Penny asked, still unsure how she'd been roped into dinner with these two.

Then Gavin smiled, and she remembered.

"Choppers."

Of course the kid would pick Choppers.

"Up for the walk?" Jonah asked.

"I think I can handle a half-mile."

"After seeing you on that treadmill, I wondered."

She shot him a look.

"Kidding." His deep laughter rumbled over her, sounding as if it came from his toes. Against odds, it relaxed her. Even if she was its target.

The sun warmed her face, and she hitched her gear bag higher on her shoulder. "You're a funny man, Jonah Black."

He slipped the bag from her shoulder and onto his own. "I think I'll choose to take that as a compliment." He set his hands deep in his pockets. "Life's too short to be serious all the time."

Gavin's laughter matched his uncle's. "You're never serious, Uncle Jonah."

"Hey!"

She reached for her bag. "I barely know you, yet I agree with Gavin."

"Tag teamed. Thanks a lot." He sidestepped her reach. "And I'm carrying your bag for you."

Penny opened her mouth, but Gavin spoke first. "Nana's rules."

"Your mom?" she asked Jonah.

He nodded, his mouth pulled to the side as if hiding a grin.

"Guess I can't argue with that."

"Guess not." If he'd been hiding a grin, he wasn't anymore.

She rolled her eyes. Fine. He could win this time. Though his win felt more like hers.

They started down the sidewalk, a comfortable silence filling the air. Penny glanced over at Jonah. His stride was slow considering how he towered over her.

He sneaked a glance at Gavin, and she followed his gaze. The boy's face was pinched, his cheeks red. No wonder they walked so slowly.

Jonah's attention returned to her. "I hope I didn't offend you with my comment about the treadmill. I really was only kidding."

"No offense taken. Don't know what I was thinking, pushing myself so hard." Except it hadn't been her pushing.

"You're really worried about fitting into that dress?"

"No." Yes. And about disappointing her sister. And Mom. She shook her head.

"You do that a lot." Gavin noticed.

"Gavin—" Jonah's ringing cell phone interrupted him. He reached for his back pocket as a rock anthem blared from it. "Sorry. It's my sister." He walked a few feet away.

Gavin shifted beside her. "Sorry 'bout the head shake comment."

She waved a hand at him. "Don't be. I do shake my head a lot. Guess it's my way of getting rid of thoughts I don't want."

"You have that many thoughts you don't want?"

Unfortunately, yes.

Before she could formulate an appropriate answer, Jonah deflated against a wall and rubbed a hand down his face, speaking into his phone. "It's what we prayed for." He uttered a few more words before hanging up and rejoining them. "We need to head back."

They hadn't even made it a block past the gym. Penny gazed up at Jonah. "Everything okay?"

"Yes. But I need to take a rain check on dinner."

"What?" Disappointment edged Gavin's voice.

Jonah put a hand on his nephew's shoulder. "Gigi just passed away."

"She did?" Gavin's eyes widened, and tears filled them. "How's mom?"

"She's okay, but I need to head over and help her with a few things." He wrapped Gavin in a hug and let him cry. Jonah's dry eyes found hers. "Gigi is our grandmother—well, mine and Rachael's."

"Belle had mentioned she wasn't doing well. Still, I'm so sorry." Though it appeared by Jonah's dry eyes and nearly palpable relief, she and Gavin might be the only ones who shared that sentiment. "Go on to your sister's. I can walk home from here."

Jonah released Gavin. "My car's just up the street. I feel bad enough about canceling dinner, let me at least drive you home."

"I'm fine."

"Please?" This from Gavin.

What was it about the boy that always hooked her? "All right." She followed them down the street and back to the gym.

They stopped at a silver Ford Focus. The plug-in kind.

Gavin slid into the back seat of the car, and Jonah held his hand on the passenger door but didn't open it. "I really am sorry about dinner. Can I call you next week?"

Penny bit down hard on her lip. His grandmother just passed, and not only wasn't he upset—the man had apparently prayed for it—he was still asking her about dinner. One he'd hinted last week was to figure out how to sell said grandmother's estate.

"I'm pretty busy next week."

"Then perhaps this weekend?"

His last push shoved her over the edge. "Shouldn't you be more concerned with your family than dinner plans with me?"

He sucked in a breath. "I'm only trying to—"

Gavin popped his head out of the car. "Are you coming?"

Two pairs of blue eyes focused on her. She chose Gavin's and squatted by his window. "You're very sweet to want to see me home, but your mom needs you right now. Go on, and be with her. I'll walk home."

She gently shut the door on Gavin. Jonah stood near her, and as she straightened, he scrubbed a hand over his bald head. "I can't convince you to let us give you a ride?"

"No." She shouldn't have changed her mind in the first place, but Gavin's pleas had cut through her indecision. She couldn't let them again because these past few minutes with Jonah had her more confused than ever. He was a dichotomy. One second caring for her or others, the next, he seemed emotionless. She couldn't figure him or his intentions out. Honestly, she didn't need the headache of trying.

She reached for her bag.

Jonah hesitated but then handed it to her. "All right." He walked around the car and stopped by the driver's side. "If I seem—" His ringing phone silenced him, and he reached for it, though his focus still captured hers. "Hey, Rach. She what?" His jaw clenched. "No, don't do anything. I'll be right there."

He pocketed his phone. "Sorry. I've really got to go. Can I call you later?"

The wind picked up and scattered a few spring buds along the sidewalk. "Go be with your sister."

His piercing gaze held hers for one more moment. He was trying to read her mind again, just like on the train. She shifted her focus over his shoulder.

He sighed, dropped into his car, and drove away.

She squashed the feeling that she'd been unfair to him. Everyone handled death differently, but he showed no sorrow at all. And the topper was him pushing for that dinner. The more she thought about his actions, the angrier she became.

Yes. She'd seen enough of Jonah Black.

Jonah snagged a glance in his rearview mirror of Penelope.

"You should watch the road," Gavin said.

His thoughts were split, but his focus couldn't be. "How're you doing, bud?"

Gavin shrugged. There'd been too many good-byes in his short life. The subject of death didn't need to be studied again. He'd talk when he was ready.

"I still can't believe Penelope was the one who caught Clooney for you the other day."

This earned a small smile. "Told you you'd like her."

"I'm not so sure *she* likes *me*, though."

"Why's that?" Gavin's innocence made a rare appearance.

Jonah cringed. Penelope had only heard half the conversation, and it wasn't the time or place to explain everything. "A misunderstanding." Hopefully.

Gigi's peaceful death had brought the healing they'd prayed for minus all the pain of watching her suffer with Alzheimer's. He'd rejoiced she was free.

To Penelope, he had to have come across as callous.

He parked at Rachael's and stowed his thoughts for later. Gavin jumped from the car before Jonah even cut the engine, racing up the steps. Inside, Gavin already had his arms wrapped around his mom.

Jonah engulfed them both. "How are you doing, sis?"

Clooney bounced around their feet.

Gavin ducked out of the hug and tugged Clooney away.

Rachael lay her head against Jonah's chest. "She's in a better place; I know that, but right now I just want to cry."

Jonah let her soak his shirt. With his free hand, he swiped his own tears. "Think of that reunion in heaven right now."

"I know." Rachael pushed out of his arms and tucked a curl of chestnut hair behind her ear. "But can I be honest and say I'm so over funerals?" Jonah followed her to the kitchen, passing Gavin and Clooney on the couch. As if sensing their somber moods, for once, Clooney was quiet and still.

"Uncle Jonah?"

"Yeah, bud?"

"Is Mom okay?"

He circled back to Gavin and knelt. "She will be." He squeezed his nephew's shoulder. "We all will."

With a trusting nod, Gavin stood. "I'm gonna go upstairs. I've got homework."

Not normal for a thirteen-year-old boy, but nothing about Gavin's life had been normal recently. Jonah hoped that would all change soon.

"Need help with anything, I'll be down here."

"Staying for dinner?"

"How about I call Piece and order a pizza?"

Gavin's smile returned. "Sounds great."

Jonah returned to the kitchen, Clooney on his heels. Rachael sat at the granite island, mug of coffee in hand. She pointed to the coffee pot. "Help yourself."

He opened a cabinet and grabbed a large white mug. After pouring a cup, he added a healthy dose of creamer. Stirring it, he took in the meticulous white subway tile backsplash, the black and white speckled granite countertops, and the stainless-steel appliances. His brother-in-law, Chris, had worked hard to make this Rachael's dream home. Now, with him gone, a huge chunk of her dream was missing.

Jonah swallowed against the lump in his throat. Rachael had experienced too much loss. He thanked God those losses hadn't included Gavin.

He slid onto the stool next to her and patted Clooney's head. "I told Gavin I'd order pizza."

She nodded. "Dad's not coming."

Jonah sighed. Couldn't say he was surprised. "You called him?"

"Yeah, between my calls to you."

"That wasn't a very long conversation."

"He said he was pretty busy. That's the excuse he gave for not being able to make it. Starting a new company out there, he needs to stick around."

While there was truth to that statement, Jonah knew it was still an excuse. "It's still too fresh after Mom. This city, the funeral. It would be too much for him."

"I know. I just wish he was coming."

"Me too." He sipped his coffee, still coming to grips with the fact Gigi was gone. "I'll handle all the details, Rach. Don't worry about a thing."

"Aunt Sharon instructed me to." Her thumb drew circles on her mug. "Said she's too busy with Micah's wedding plans and that you have the house to take care of."

"I can handle both. I'll go to the funeral home tomorrow. Tell me what you and Gavin want, and I'll take care of it."

The sadness in her eyes melted him. "I'll go with you."

"Rach. Let me handle this." She'd arranged enough funerals.

She hesitated, then sighed. "Okay. We can talk to Gavin over dinner, see what's important to him, and then you can make the arrangements." She placed a hand on his shoulder and kissed his cheek. "Thanks, Jonah."

He covered her hand. "Anything for you. You know that."

"I do. And I also know you're going to make some woman very lucky one of these days."

Penelope's full smile, large green eyes, and rich laughter filled his thoughts.

Hopefully, he could shed light on today's misunderstanding because he'd love to get to know her better.

That would make him the lucky one.

Chapter Seven

Tuesday morning dawned bright and much too early. Penny groaned. She needed room-darkening shades and a soundproof window. Shoving off her blankets, she sat up and ran her fingers through her hair.

Tea.

She padded to the door and opened it. A strange man strode down the hall. She screamed and slammed her door.

A few seconds later, someone knocked. "You can come out now," Lacey called. "He's safely tucked in my room."

"What is he even doing here this early?"

"We're going on a run then out for breakfast. Probably end up at the lake."

Penny cracked her door an inch and peered out at her roommate. "You're off today?"

"We both are. He's a radiologist at my hospital."

Penny narrowed one eye. "Wait. Is that Shawn? The guy you told me about last week?" Lacey's relationships never lasted past date three.

Her eyes lit. "It is." She back-walked toward her door. "Catch up with you tonight?"

"Definitely."

Penny closed the door, but Lacey's giggles floated straight through it. Flopping onto her bed, she found the mirror across the room, tugged her hair back, and sucked in her cheeks. With a slight twist of her neck, she focused on her scar, a scowl darkening her features. Just once she wanted someone to find her beautiful. Was that too much to ask?

Footsteps and muffled voices drifted away as the front door opened and closed. House empty, Penny carried her laptop to the kitchen. She'd do better focusing on work than her non-existent love life. She turned on the burner under the water kettle and reached up to choose her cup and saucer. Golden scrolls and a bright yellow background caught her eye. Perfect.

Within an hour, she'd consumed two cups of licorice tea, finalized the pricing on her spreadsheet, and her mood had lifted. She might not have a love life, but she did have a job she loved, and nearly enough in her bank account to call a realtor about opening her own storefront.

Now a shower before heading over to the Wilton house. Today, she could start tagging everything and snap a few pictures for her website. With a click of her mouse, she sent her file to the wireless printer and headed to clean up.

As she stepped out of the shower, her cell phone sang. Belle. She'd return the call once she was in her car. Snagging her hair dryer, she pressed it on, but it didn't drown out the sound of Belle calling again. By round three, Penny set aside her hair dryer and reached for the phone. "Hey, Belle."

"Finally." Sniffles punctuated the word.

"What's wrong?"

"Oh, nothing huge, only Micah's grandmother died. And my sister won't pick up the phone when I need her."

That's right. Micah and Jonah were cousins.

She let the verbal jab go. "Oh, Belle. Tell Micah I'm sorry."

"You can tell him yourself. I called because the funeral is by you on Friday, but there's some convention in Chicago, and the hotels are booked. Micah said Jonah's place isn't an option, so do you mind if we stay with you?"

Another weekend in close proximity with her sister wasn't in her current plans, but considering the circumstances … "Sure. What time Friday should I expect you?"

"We're actually coming in tomorrow around dinnertime." This week suddenly doubled in drama and shortened in time. "Can you make lasagna? It's Micah's favorite."

She fought her gut-level response to Belle's demand disguised as a question. Couldn't fault Micah for wanting comfort food during a time like this. "Sure." Though she'd need to rearrange her Wednesday appointment with East.

After grabbing a few more details, they hung up, and Penny hustled to make it out the door. She drove up to Lincoln Park and high-fived the air when she found an open spot right in front of Frances and Allen Wilton's old brownstone. Inside, she couldn't suppress her smile. This home still held all their love in it. They'd raised a family of six, had holidays with all their sixteen grandchildren, and even spent their last hours together here. Allen passed away only days after Frances. Their children already had removed their precious mementos out of the house and now were anxious to see how much the remainder of the estate was worth.

Penny started with the furniture. Allen had been a furniture maker in his spare time, so while most of the pieces were of no noteworthy name, they were of the highest quality. She'd researched similar pieces online and was comfortable with the tags she placed on them.

When she finished the furniture, Penny switched to smaller items. She headed upstairs, stopping in Allan and Frances's bedroom doorway. Her gaze sought out Frances's collection of old perfume bottles and landed on one in particular.

It was still there.

She crossed the room to where it sat on top of Frances's old dresser. Guerlain's Après L'ondée. Her fingertips brushed the honeycomb stopper, and she pulled back. It was a find. The question was what to do with it.

Other bottles filled the spaces beside the Guerlain perfume. Chanel. Ma Griffe. All vintage and pre-reformulation. Even a collection of small chess-shaped bottles immediately recognizable as Mary Chess's perfumes. Frances collected so many.

But the Après L'ondée.

Penny's hand strayed back to touch its ridged glass. She picked the bottle up but didn't open it, understanding its worth. Typically, gardenias and their light, sweet fragrance were her weakness, but one whiff of the earthy violets wrapped in rain had hooked her on Après L'ondée. She'd only had the pleasure of smelling it once, at an auction she'd attended years ago, but the scent had made its impression. To purchase a full bottle today not only took more money than Penny would spend on herself, but also the luck of finding a vintage one. Even a trip to France wouldn't nab what sat on the dresser.

The wistful desire to purchase this bottle nearly overcame the rational side of her.

With a sigh, she set it down and brought out her camera. While a few of the perfumes she could sell here, most would fare better on the Internet. She snapped those pictures, then carefully boxed up Frances's collection and brought them downstairs. If the sale went well, maybe she'd let herself purchase the Chanel.

Penny set out the scents she'd keep here on a table in the expansive living room, along with other collections of items she'd found in the home. Lladro figurines, antique cherry glass, and even a large thimble collection filled the room. She stepped outside to her car and grabbed a card table to display the thimbles on in groups easy for collectors to sort through.

"I thought this was your car." Robert Wilton, Allen and Frances's oldest, stood on the sidewalk. "I wanted to stop by and see the progress you're making."

More like check the price tags she'd placed on items. Out of all the kids, Robert was the most concerned with the bottom line.

Penny slammed her trunk and returned to the house. "It's going well. I'm nearly finished pricing, and then I'll take the rest of the pictures needed for my site. I want to highlight the furniture and your mother's thimble and perfume bottle collections. It's the unique things that will draw people here."

Robert followed, his short legs striving to catch up to her. "Are you confident everything will sell Saturday?"

"Most of it will." She set down the table. "Whatever doesn't will go home with me, and I'll put it on eBay."

"Right. Barb spoke with me about that." His hand ran over the smooth edges of a Lladro figurine. It was a small boy in a boat with his father, fishing. "I'm going to do one final walk-through and let you know if I have any concerns."

No doubt he would. He seemed to always find something objectionable.

With a nod, Penny started organizing the thimbles stored in dusty boxes on the floor. About halfway through the task, Robert rejoined her in the family room. "Prices seem fair as long as you remain firm. However, I still think the dining room table should be marked higher than twelve hundred."

She stood to take the height advantage. He wasn't the first client to question her abilities, but Robert took it to an entirely new level. "As we've discussed, I research items extensively to ensure my clients receive the best price. And while everything is negotiable at an estate sale, I will not sell anything below its value. That wouldn't serve you well or help my reputation." A truck rumbled past outside. "You need to trust that I want the best for us both."

"I don't suppose I have a choice this late in the game." He strolled to the door. "I'll be back on Saturday during the sale."

"And I'll look forward to seeing you." Not really. But she had to say it.

Now if she could play just as nicely when Belle showed up tomorrow, maybe she'd survive the rest of the week.

Penny shut the oven door, closing in the steam that wanted to escape. Ten minutes uncovered, and the cheese she'd just added to the top of her lasagna would be bubbly brown. The table was set, the salad made, and the garlic bread now baked on the rack over the lasagna, filling the kitchen with wonderful smells.

It was enough to make her smile—if only she expected someone else for dinner.

The door shuddered underneath a knock.

"Want me to get that?" Lacey asked from the couch.

Penny popped a handful of peanut M&M's into her mouth, took a deep breath, and emerged from the kitchen. "No. I got it."

She opened the door to Belle's perfect smile. "Hey, Belle."

Her sister glided in, and Micah followed, carrying all of their bags. He sniffed the air. "Something smells good in here."

Belle continued toward the hall. "Micah, you can bring our stuff down here. I want to freshen up before dinner."

Um, no. They weren't sharing a room together.

"Belle." Penny followed her sister. "Micah's on the couch, and you're in my room with me."

Belle spun on her heel, and Micah caught her before she toppled over. She righted herself, smile firmly in place. "Micah, go ahead and put our things in Penny's room for now." He obeyed, and Belle walked over to Penny, voice low. "Micah is huge. Do you honestly think he'll fit on your fold-out? It's going to be a long week. He needs good rest and his privacy."

All true.

"Fine. He can have my room, but you sleep on the couch. I'll bunk in Lacey's room." She crossed her arms as Belle opened her mouth. "Not married. Not sharing a room."

Belle's eyes nearly touched the back of her head they rolled so far. "You sound just like Dad. And Jonah for that matter." That nearly had Penny changing her opinion of him. "But Micah and I are engaged." She wiggled her ring finger in the air, her diamond sparkling in the hall light as she turned toward Penny's room. "And I'm staying with him."

Penny exhaled. Loudly. Had she really expected any different?

"Belle—"

Micah stepped out and handed Belle a small bag. She clasped it. "Thanks." Then she turned to Penny. "I really need to use the bathroom. We brought our own sheets, so if you don't mind taking yours off, Micah can make our bed while I freshen up."

Yeah. Because that three-hour drive had to be a killer.

She clenched her teeth around the snark.

Lacey appeared at the end of the short hallway. "The buzzer just went off on your lasagna, and I know you don't want me touching it. I can help get their things settled."

"Oh, hey, Lacey. Thanks." Belle disappeared into the bathroom.

Penny shook her head and scooted past Lacey. "Just throw my sheets out here. I'll use them on the couch." She paused at the kitchen. "And, Belle, we're not done talking about the sleeping arrangements!"

The bathroom door slammed shut.

Penny stomped into the room and pulled the lasagna out of the oven. It needed to cool a few minutes. So did she.

Or she'd do something she'd regret.

Inhaling the bubbling aroma of cheese, she prayed for an extra dose of patience along with the right words to use with Belle because her sister was too much to handle alone. And as much as she'd like to ignore everything, talking to Belle could not be avoided. There was no way she'd let Micah and Belle share a room. It went against everything she believed.

She groaned. The whole point in moving to Chicago had been to avoid all this drama.

And yet here it was, smack dab in the middle of her home. Better deal with it or dinner would grow cold.

She crept to the bathroom and knocked gingerly. "Can I come in?"

"It's your apartment." Ice coated her sister's words.

Penny nudged open the door and slipped inside. Belle sat on the edge of the tub, with red-rimmed eyes and a Kleenex in her hand.

Great. She'd made her little sister cry.

"I don't want to fight with you, Belle." Penny sank onto the tub edge beside her.

"And I don't want to feel like a heathen in my own sister's home."

Ouch.

"You're not a heathen. I'm sorry if I made you feel that way, but you know how I feel."

Belle twisted her tissue. "Come on, Penny. You're telling me Lacey's never had one of her boyfriends here?"

"Not overnight. It was part of our agreement when she signed the lease." She caught a glimpse of her little sister, the one who used to follow her around. "Belle, what are you doing? We were both raised the same. I know you know sleeping with Micah isn't right."

Belle's back straightened. "How about you talk to me once you have a boyfriend?"

Double ouch.

"I'm just trying to watch out for you."

"No. What you're trying to do is give me advice about something you've never experienced." Belle jumped up and paced over to the sink. "It's easy to hold to your convictions when you've never had to actually live them. So until you have a clue what you're talking about, don't preach to me."

Tears pricked Penny's eyes. She pushed to her feet. "Fine, but in my home, you don't sleep with Micah until after the wedding. Clear?"

"Perfectly." She strode to the door and opened it. "Can we eat now? I'm sure Micah's hungry."

"It's on the table."

Penny followed Belle down the hall. Lacey and Micah stood around the table.

"Everything okay?" Lacey asked.

"Fine." Belle took Micah's hand. "I'll be bunking on the couch while we're here."

Micah widened his eyes. "Come again?"

"Penny's apartment. Penny's rules." She held her diamond up. "Apparently, this ring isn't commitment enough."

"How about we eat?" Lacey interjected.

Penny mouthed a silent thank you to her friend while they all squeezed around the small table. Micah scooped a huge portion of lasagna onto his plate. "Smells amazing." He bit into the cheesy dish. "Mmm ... it tastes great too. Belle, you gotta have her teach you how to make this."

Belle iced Micah with a glare. "I don't cook. You knew that before you put the ring on my finger." She heaped a portion of salad onto the center of her plate. "Besides, if I made stuff like that"—she pointed to the lasagna and bread—"I wouldn't look like this. Which do you prefer?"

He cleared his throat. "No contest. I'll take you over lasagna any day."

"Good answer."

Penny placed her fork down, and across from her, Lacey bit into her garlic bread with a glare. At least someone had her back. Dinner progressed in silence for a few minutes which was perfectly fine. She wasn't hungry anymore, and the sooner they all were done, the better.

"So have you spoken with Jonah since the fitting?" Belle sweetly asked.

"Not much."

"Surprising. I thought you two were meant for each other. Same values. Same morals." She stabbed a piece of lettuce. "I know how important those things are to you."

Penny matched the narrow gaze Belle leveled at her but said nothing. A thick cord of tension flowed over the table, and she refused to cut it. Instead, she focused on Micah. "I'm sorry about your grandmother, Micah."

"Thank you." He set down his garlic bread and wiped his hands. "She'd been struggling a long time. Alzheimer's. It tore us all up, especially Jonah and Rachael. They've had a hard couple of years."

Ever so slowly, understanding crept in. She'd worked plenty of estates where children had lost a parent to that disease. Seen their relief over that long, tough battle finishing. Why hadn't she connected those dots earlier?

"Your Gigi had Alzheimer's?"

Micah nodded. "We'd hired a live-in nurse for the past two years, but my mom was visiting to talk about finally moving her into a retirement home. Gigi went and had a heart attack, instead. Jonah thinks it was an answer to their prayers." He leaned back in his chair. "No more suffering, and she was better off."

Oh. She'd been harsh. Too harsh. "He was thankful she was whole again and didn't have to suffer." Made perfect sense now.

"Yeah. Something like that."

Awkward silence fell over the table as everyone became lost in their own thoughts. Belle excused herself to the bathroom, and Micah stood. "Thanks for dinner." He picked up his plate. "Want me to just put this in the sink?"

"Leave it. I'll take care of this."

He nodded then drifted to the living room to watch TV.

Penny cleared the dishes and ran hot soapy water. She'd been wrong to judge him so quickly. Being wrong and losing were two things she didn't handle well, and yet she seemed quite accomplished at both around Jonah.

She needed a rematch in Scrabble.

And she owed him an apology.

"So," Penny called to Micah and Belle, "what time is the visitation tomorrow?"

Chapter Eight

Penny hustled down the steps of the Wiltons' brownstone late Thursday afternoon. She tugged out her cell phone and dialed Belle.

Belle's clipped voice answered. "You missed the visitation."

And already felt awful about it. "Sorry, Belle—"

"I'm not the one who needs the apology. Micah and Jonah are."

And she already owed him one. "I know. But something came up." For once she'd been thankful for the issues with Robert. Dealing with him provided a legitimate reason to give into her budding procrastination on that apology to Jonah. Besides, he wasn't expecting it or her, so there was no way her absence was noted.

Belle was silent.

"Belle?"

"Just a sec." A door clicked shut. "Micah is going to be your brother; you should have been there. And I told Jonah to expect you."

"You told Jonah I was coming?" Her voice squeaked. So much for her absence going unnoticed.

"Of course I did."

Penny unlocked her car and climbed in. "I'll apologize to Micah when I see him tonight."

"And Jonah?"

She checked her rearview and pulled out. "Text me his number."

"I'll tell him to expect your call."

"I didn't say—" the phone went dead. Great. She'd planned on texting him. "Thanks, Belle," she muttered. Penny plugged her phone into her car and hit iTunes. Ella Fitzgerald's smooth voice filled the air, and Penny flicked to another song; she needed something stronger right now.

Crow was her least favorite dish to eat.

Her phone dinged, and she pulled into a parking lot. Jonah's contact info. Mouth suddenly dry, Penny picked up her phone and hit send before talking herself out of it.

"Jonah." His deep voice rumbled next to her ear.

"Hey, it's Penny."

"Penelope. What's up?"

Her full name. She couldn't help the smile. "Sorry I missed the visitation."

His voice warmed. "Not a problem. I know you're busy, and you didn't even know my grandmother. You barely even know me."

"But I know Micah and Belle. And I do know you." She hesitated. "Well, sorta anyway."

Someone called his name in the background. "One sec," he said.

"I can call back later."

"No, I was talking to Gavin. He's hungry. Again."

Penny laughed. "Well, go feed him then."

"Care to join us? Maybe get to know me better than 'sorta.'"

His warm voice lured her. Eating out with Jonah would push her for time, but she could probably make it work—if she wanted to.

He argued with her hesitation. "Come on. It's only dinner. Besides, I'll just keep asking until we finally get to have a meal together."

And apologies were best served in person.

"Please, Miss Thornton?" Gavin's voice filtered over the line.

"Oh, that's just low," she said, "using the kid."

"Whatever it takes."

"All right. Where do you want to meet?" A whoop filled the background, and she laughed. "Tell Gavin I'll be glad to see him again too."

"Only Gavin?"

She snorted.

But yeah, only Gavin. He posed no complications.

"Guess I know where I stand," Jonah mumbled, but she could hear the smirk. "Gavin says he's still hungry for that burger. Sounds like Choppers."

Thankfully, that restaurant also served salads. If she ate a burger before one of East's workouts, it'd end up on the floor. "I'll meet you there in ten."

"We're on our way."

Penny slipped into traffic and worked her way over to Choppers. She waited in her car until the guys arrived. The two could be father and son. Tall, bald, slightly overweight, with matching smiles.

She climbed from her car into a wall of heat. Definitely the warmest spring they'd had in years, though that wasn't why she was sweating.

Oh, how she hated being wrong and having to admit it.

Jonah and Gavin walked over.

"Thanks for coming." Gavin stood with his hands in his pockets. Even his stance mimicked Jonah's.

"Thanks for inviting me."

Jonah nodded toward the restaurant. "Shall we?"

Penny started walking. She might as well get the painful apology out of the way before lunch so she could enjoy her meal.

"I really am sorry about Gigi." As much as she wanted to focus on the cracks in the pavement, she met Jonah's eyes. "And I'm sorry if I seemed a little cold when you received the call. I thought—"

His gaze fixed on her, and she stopped. Once again, he seemed to spy every nook and cranny inside of her. She'd never met anyone who gave her such full attention, and it unnerved her.

"Thought what?" he prodded.

Some things were better left unsaid, especially around Gavin. "It doesn't matter what I thought because I know better now. I really am sorry, not only for your loss but for how I acted."

"I wondered if my reaction the other day is what earned me the cold shoulder." Jonah held the restaurant door open for her, but Penny didn't go through.

So, even with an apology, he was still calling her out on her bad behavior. She straightened. "It was an unusual response. You could have told me she had Alzheimer's."

He leaned on the door. "You could have given me the benefit of the doubt."

"I don't know you well enough."

His hand swept in front of her. "Then let's go inside and rectify that."

Behind her, Gavin cleared his throat. "Hungry teen here. Waiting to eat."

Jonah's brow lifted.

"Sorry." Gavin quieted.

Penny turned to him. "No, Gavin. I'm sorry. Let's go on in and eat." She stepped past Jonah. "Am I forgiven?"

His smile wrapped around her heart. She worked to untangle it.

"Like it never happened." Jonah let the door close.

That easily? She waited for the hoop to jump through, for the guilt trip.

Jonah swept a hand out. "Pick a booth, and we'll follow."

She hesitated.

"Or grab a stool along the window, I'm fine with that too."

But that trip never arrived. "Um, a booth is fine." And she took the nearest one.

Gavin slid in beside her.

"Do you know what you want?" Jonah asked.

She peered toward the counter. Grease, French fries, and salt filled the air.

Her mouth watered. Maybe she could order a burger with everything, minus the burger, bun, mayo … flavor.

And the treadmill waited.

"I'll take a salad and a glass of water."

Jonah nodded. "Gavin?"

"Choppak. Everything on it. And bacon." The kid was hungry. "Can I get an extra side?"

"Sure."

"And moz sticks, please."

Penny held in her surprise. Apparently, teenage boys truly were bottomless pits.

Within minutes, Jonah had their food at the table. He'd ordered a salad, too, and joined them, handing out everyone's orders.

Penny opened her Styrofoam container. "So how are you both doing, really?"

Jonah slid a straw over to Gavin. "We miss her, but we know she's in a better place."

Gavin nodded. "Still, it's been really hard on Mom."

"I'm sorry to hear that. It's difficult to lose someone you love."

"Yeah. The last few years have really stunk. Which is why Uncle Jonah—"

"Really should properly thank you for helping with Clooney the other day. Gavin couldn't stop talking about the lady at the park who went after her. Some days I regret buying that dog."

Penny waved him off. "Clooney only needs some training. She'll be a great dog, once she knows who's in charge."

"You volunteering to train her?"

She stilled. "Not on your life!"

With a chuckle, Jonah added dressing to his salad. "Are you going back to Holland this weekend?"

"No. I'm not needed there again for a while. Besides, I've got a busy weekend ahead."

"Date with the boyfriend?"

She laughed. "Uh, no. Work."

Gavin leaned forward. "Do you have a boyfriend?"

"Gavin." Jonah's tone warned.

The boy reddened. "Sorry."

Poor kid. "No problem."

His red cheeks lightened. "So where do you work?

She'd expected Jonah to bring up her work, not Gavin. "I own my own business. I do estate sales."

"You sell houses?" Gavin's arms stretched across the table.

"Not houses, the stuff that filled them while their owners were alive."

Jonah took over the questions. "Do you hold auctions?"

"Depends on what I find when I go through the houses. Some people have everyday items that sell well with a standard estate sale. Other people have incredibly valuable collections. Those I tend to put up online. I rarely do auctions." She sipped her water. Waited to see if he'd maneuver for her help. But the question didn't come, so she continued, "My goal is to keep doing estate sales, only less of them and eventually have my own antique store. A place where I can refurbish pieces and sell them, among other things."

Gavin swirled his soda into a vortex with his straw. "You like old stuff then?"

"I like finding value in things where others don't see it."

Jonah tipped his head. "People often overlook priceless objects."

The steel in his eyes cut at the protective layer around her heart. If she let him, he'd find a way in. That wasn't going to happen.

Penny stabbed at a tomato, desperately trying to ignore Jonah's delving stare and the delicious aroma of Gavin's food. Completely unaware of her war, the boy pushed his container of mozzarella sticks close to her. "Have one. I've got more than enough."

Sure. Because the cheese wouldn't go straight to her hips. Visions of a grape bursting at the seams taunted her. She pushed them back. "No, thanks."

Jonah grabbed one. "Come on. Live a little."

He would say that. Her gaze dropped to his stomach. Obviously he'd 'lived a little' a lot.

And there was her mother again.

Jonah caught her glance and popped the moz stick into his mouth. "Value where others don't see it, huh?" He shook his head and dug into his salad.

Embarrassment curled its way up her body, and she deserved every ounce of the heat.

Jonah cleared their trash from the table, more than ready to leave. An awkward silence filled the space after his loose lips, but when he'd caught her glance at his physique, insecurity mixed with anger, and the words slipped between his teeth.

Penelope held a ten dollar bill out to him. "Here. For mine."

He shoved it back. "I invited you, remember?"

"Um. Not a date, so I think it's okay."

"Doesn't matter." Though it did bug him that she felt the need to clarify.

Gavin stood to let her out of the booth and headed for the door.

She didn't move. "Take my money."

Man, she was stubborn. "No."

Penelope glared at him.

Jonah leaned down, her hair tickling his cheek as he whispered in her ear. "Trying to teach my nephew how to treat a lady, here. Could you help out?"

Penelope sighed, grabbed her purse, and headed for the exit, her light flowery scent lingering behind. They walked out into the blue sky and warm air.

"You really didn't have to pay for my dinner, but thank you."

"We invited you. And when you invite a lady somewhere, you pay. Right, Gavin?"

Gavin shrugged. "So you've told me—not that I'm going to date a girl anytime soon."

Jonah clapped him on the back. "You've got all the time in the world."

"I do." He beamed.

Penelope's hair lifted on the light breeze, and she tucked a strand behind her ear. Her skirt swirled around her legs.

"Want to take a walk with Gavin and me?"

She hitched her huge blue bag up farther on her shoulder. "Sorry, but I've got a date with East."

"Date?" He choked out the word.

She stilled. Her cheeks grew pink. "As in a workout. Don't worry. I'm not delusional enough to think someone like him would look twice at me, but thanks for the inspiring vote of confidence." She spun on her floral heel and stalked off, his mind spinning along with her.

"Smooth, Uncle Jonah."

Because he wasn't already thinking that himself.

"Stay here. I'll be right back."

In a few long strides, he'd caught up with Penelope. He grasped her shoulder and gently twirled her around. "Penelope, stop. That's not what I meant."

She raised a brow at him.

"To be fair, I only said one word."

"Your tone and facial expression spoke the rest for you."

How could he explain? It wasn't disbelief she'd seen. It had been worry. "Well, you heard them wrong."

"Really." She crossed her arms but then softened. "You know what? It's okay. You hit on a sore spot, and I overreacted. Not your fault."

Not intentionally, but he'd still poked at it. He held his words until a loud group passed them by. "I'm a good listener if you want to talk about it."

Her hesitation flared his hope that she'd let him in, but then she gripped the strap of her purse and nodded over her shoulder. "I appreciate the offer, I really do, but I should get going. Don't want to be late for my date with that treadmill." Her small smile fell horribly flat, and she walked away, the imaginary wall between them still fully intact. If he could manage to keep his foot out of his mouth when around her, maybe he'd have a chance at breaking through it.

Chapter Nine

Penny slammed the door behind her, still frustrated by Jonah's words. Or lack thereof. Sure, she'd probably misinterpreted his response, but his face when he thought East had asked her out rubbed salt into a wound that had never healed. Why did no one think she could attract a guy like East?

Maybe because she never had.

"Hey, Penny." Micah grinned at her from the couch. "Your lasagna is even better the next day."

Plates littered the sofa table in her living room where Micah and Belle sat together.

"Thanks. And sorry I didn't make it to the visitation. I got held up at work."

Belle lifted her head off of Micah's shoulder. "You don't exactly work in an office. You could have made it."

Penny sucked in a deep breath. A rerun of *Say Yes to the Dress: Bridesmaids Edition* was on. Was it too much to hope they'd feature the Grape Monstrosity as a bride's fatal mistake? Maybe then Belle would say no to the dress.

"Hello? Penny? You're zoning out."

Penny snapped her attention to Belle's perfectly shaped blonde brows pushed tightly together. "I may not work in an office, but I do have a sale scheduled for this weekend, and the people who hired me showed up for a walk-thru." And it had taken two hours to straighten out the misinformation Robert had relayed to his siblings.

"I think they would have understood that you had a funeral visitation." She scooped up their plates and handed them to Penny. "But I get that your work is important to you. Before Micah"—she kissed him on the cheek—"I only focused on work too."

"Yes. The pageant world will dearly miss you, sis."

Belle's eyes narrowed. Penny retreated to the kitchen before one of those daggers pierced her. She dumped the dishes into the sink. Those nasty words shouldn't have escaped her mouth, but there was only so much a girl could take in one afternoon.

She blamed Jonah.

With a groan, Penny dropped her head to the kitchen counter and tapped it against the hard surface, asking once again for patience—which could be supplied, but it was up to her to choose to extend it. And coupling a wedding and funeral this close together provided ample opportunities. Her sister was having a stressful week. Time to cut Belle some extra slack.

Rolling tension from her shoulders, she glanced at the clock, never more ready for a workout in her life. Now if she could get herself out the door without bumping into Belle again, she'd be set. Sneaking out of the kitchen, she tiptoed down the hall, threw on her sweats, grabbed her bag, and ran for the door. If she were late, East would add another fifty sit-ups to the hundred he already asked of her.

The floor squeaked, Belle sat up, but Penny kept moving.

"Going to work out again tonight, Penny?"

"Yep."

Before her hand touched the door handle, Belle was up and running down the hall. "Wait for me. I'm coming too. You can get me in for free on a guest pass."

Micah pulled his long form up from his seat. "Guess that means I'm working out tonight."

Great. Capping off her evening working out beside Belle's skinny frame. Could this night get any better?

"Fine, but hurry up. If I'm late, East makes me pay for it. And I don't mean with money."

Micah's speed didn't increase. "You hired him. If you don't like how he works, fire him."

And have to deal with their comments when she didn't fit into the bridesmaid dress?

"I'm leaving in five minutes," she called down the hallway at Micah's retreating back.

"I'm a guy. I need about half that time."

True to his word, Micah appeared at the door within two minutes, where they waited another five for Belle. Penny struggled not to strangle her but instead, pushed open the door and hustled them both down the street. "Come on, you two. Pick up the speed."

East knew how close she lived and expected her to walk—he called it her warm-up, even though he put her through another one when she arrived. The man was insane.

"This has got to be one amazing trainer if he is able to get you to move at speeds like this." Belle's laughter followed Penny down the sidewalk. Lucky for her sister, her gym socks were out of reach, or she'd lob one at her—preferably at her mouth.

They made it in record time. East stood at the counter, tapping his fingers. "Hey, gorgeous, thought you were going to stand me up tonight."

Belle plowed into the back of her, and Penny turned around. Belle's eyes were glued on East, and her mouth hung open. Not bothering to hold in her smirk, Penny introduced the two.

"Belle, this is my personal trainer, East." She turned to him. "And East, this is my sister, Belle."

East held out a hand, the muscles in his deeply tanned arms flexing. Belle took it, her mouth now closed and trademark smile in place. "East, it's a pleasure to meet you. I hoped we could work out with Penny tonight? I need to fit into my wedding dress and would love some tips on toning exercises."

His eyes started to slide down her form before a throat cleared behind them. East met Micah's gaze. "Oh, hey, you must be the fiancé."

Micah's lean frame towered over him—it was like Ken meeting G.I. Joe. "That's me."

East motioned them toward the treadmills. "Do you guys like to run? Penny's getting really good at it, and it's typically where I start her for her warm-up."

"Because the mile walk here wasn't enough," Penny joked.

East placed his hand on the small of her back as they walked. Belle's brows shot into her hairline, and Penny slowed down, leaning into his touch. She should ignore it. Should remind herself that he was this way with all of his clients. But with Belle's face mimicking Jonah's earlier, it was too easy to act—and pretend—otherwise.

"Your walk was your pre-warm-up." East's attention shifted to Belle. "She seems to be worried about fitting into her bridesmaid dress. At the rate she's going, though, she's got nothing to worry about. Down a pound in just under a week with me."

"Hopefully, she'll keep it up. It's going to take more than that to fit into her dress."

Penny opened her mouth, but East spoke first. "She will. I'm a great teacher, and she's a great student." He led them through a few minutes of stretches then found three open machines. "Show them what you got, Penny. I'll grab you guys a couple of towels."

Penny stepped up on her treadmill. Fueled by East's belief in her, it was hard to keep her eyes off of him. He bent to pick up a mound of soiled towels from the floor, and his muscles rippled. Literally. She was going to Google the phrase, and there'd be his picture.

East stood, caught her staring, and those blue eyes of his crinkled at the edges. She'd happily drown in them.

He headed for the laundry room. "I'll be right back."

Penny punched her speed up to four. "Start at a four; we'll increase after two minutes."

"No wonder you're here every night." Belle cast a glance at East's retreating form.

Micah waved his hand in front of her. "Right here. The hunk of a man you're marrying."

Belle shoved his hand out of her face. "Whatever. I saw you checking out the aerobics room when we walked by."

His laughter reminded Penny of Jonah's. He leaned over and pressed a kiss against Belle's cheek. "Only realizing how lucky I am that my future wife is one hundred times hotter than all the women put together in that room."

Penny punched her number up to a six.

Belle huffed. "I thought you said we had two minutes."

"That's my Penny—always pushing herself." East stood beside her machine, hands full of towels. His gaze traveled over Belle but didn't remain there. It moved to Penny, and his Adonis smile landed on her.

She melted under the strength of it. The man was lethal.

An hour later, Penny glistened with sweat and had never had a better workout. For all her talk about working out every day, Belle had struggled to keep up. In fact, she seemed a little green.

"I knew I shouldn't have eaten your lasagna." She turned accusing eyes on Penny before focusing them on Micah. "Always pressuring me into something, aren't you?"

He took a step back, his eyes narrowing before he put on a smile. "Let me take you home."

Belle slid into a seat. "I'm not walking there. You need to grab our car from Penny's house."

"Of course. I'll be back shortly."

Penny sat next to her while East went for water. "Everything okay, Belle?"

"Why wouldn't it be?" For once her voice held no emotion.

Let it go ... the thought was there, but even with as awfully as they treated each other, Belle was her little sister. Penny hated to see her upset. "It's just, you mentioned Micah pressuring—"

"I'm not talking about this with you, remember?"

And ... so much for trying.

East returned with a bottle of water. "Here." He offered it to Belle and then took the open seat by Penny. "I shouldn't have pushed you so hard, but Penny led me to believe you worked out regularly."

Belle sipped her water. "I do, just not typically on such a full stomach. I'm not used to such heavy food, but Micah kept raving over what a great cook Penny was and how I had to try her lasagna."

East smiled at Penny. "Good cook, huh?"

"So I'm told."

"Invite me over, and I'll give you the truth—that is if you dare."

The breath left Penny's lungs. Good thing she wasn't delusional, or she'd actually think East was asking her on a date. His charm was all about keeping her business, though. She'd seen him flirt with his other clients. He was exceptionally good at what he did.

But Belle didn't know that.

She turned her smile on East and hoped he followed through.

"How about tomorrow night?"

Belle nudged her. "The funeral is tomorrow. Micah and Jonah need you there."

"Jonah?" East chuckled. "That guy who comes with his nephew? Guess I didn't know you were seeing him."

"Because I'm not seeing him."

Belle grunted. "Not because he isn't interested."

"He's not interested in me." Belle knew it too. But *East's* apparent interest was driving her sister crazy. "He's Micah's cousin, and we're both in the wedding."

"So he wouldn't mind me taking you to dinner?"

"I thought the offer was for me to cook for you."

"I'll take what I can get."

If only she had her phone to capture Belle's face right now. "How about dinner on Saturday at Wicker Park? I'll pack the food; you just show up."

His brows rose. "Taking charge. I like that about you."

Belle's sweet laughter flowed into her dream. "You like that Penny's a stubborn mule?"

This was quickly turning into a nightmare, because only in her nightmares did her sister still embarrass her in front of a cute guy.

East stood. "Her tenacity is what kept her going today when the rest of you quit."

Score one for East! And they were back in dream territory.

Red exploded over Belle's face, and she jumped up. Penny stepped in front of East before Belle could elicit the matching color from his nose.

"Belle, you seem to be feeling better now. Why don't you go check if Micah is here."

With a glare, Belle stalked outdoors. Penny put a hand over her smirk and turned back to him. "That wasn't very nice."

He shrugged. "The truth hurts sometimes. Your sister is nice to look at, but not so much to listen to." His gaze slowly traveled over her. "You, on the other hand, are shaping up to be the entire package."

Man, he was good. Even knowing his motivation, his words heated her. She'd turned into molten lava and may as well have been a puddle on the floor.

The glass door to the gym opened, and Belle leaned her head inside, calling up the short stairway. "Micah's here. Either come on, or you can walk home."

"I'll see you Saturday, then?"

Penny nodded, ignoring Belle's threat. Let them drive off without her. She planned to savor this moment. It was probably the only time she'd be thankful for that stupid purple dress.

Chapter Ten

Something way too loud buzzed by her head. Penny swiped at it, but it only grew louder. Stupid alarm. Next time she was buying one that would wake her up with the sound of rain, or the ocean, or anything she could sleep through.

She swatted at it again, and it quieted. Hopefully, the blaring noise hadn't woken the entire house. That would defeat the purpose of having swapped sleeping spots with Belle last night.

Luckily, the house remained silent. With a groan, she pulled herself off the fold-out and checked the clock.

Friday. Five a.m.

Crazy early. But that's what happened when you overscheduled your weekend.

It was worth it, though, because tomorrow night she'd be on her pseudo-date with East. One Belle was very aware of. She simply needed to get all the cooking done for their picnic, attend Gigi's funeral, and make it through the Wilton sale first.

Cracking her back, Penny padded to the kitchen to warm some water. While the kettle heated, she began pulling recipes, pans, and ingredients out from her cupboards, trying hard to be silent. Three long hours and two cups of tea later, a pile of food in Tupperware covered her counter. Probably fancier than she needed, but just because it wasn't a real date didn't mean she couldn't try to impress him.

"Good morning." Micah shuffled in scrubbing a hand through his messy hair, his eyes still half-closed.

"Oh, hey. I hope I didn't wake you up."

"Nah. I typically get up earlier than this. Belle's the one who likes to sleep in." Micah pointed to her cup. "Coffee?"

"Tea." She nodded to Lacey's pot. "Coffee's in the cupboard above the stove." He started making some as she gathered her things. "Mind if I sneak into my room?"

"Nope. I'll probably turn on the TV. You get ESPN?"

"I have cable, so probably." Sports weren't her thing. "Remote's sitting beside the TV."

Penny closed her door, thankful for this little haven. Her eyes landed on her Bible. She picked it up and settled into the antique chair in the corner, hoping to fill up on peace before her little sister awoke and started draining it.

As if that mere thought woke The Princess up, Belle's voice rang through the hall. "If anyone needs the bathroom, say something now because I'm going to take a shower." Seconds later, the water turned on.

Penny shook her head, her eyes landing on the bookshelf across her room and the one framed picture she still kept of Belle and her. Belle was two, her mouth open in laughter as Penny covered her little sister's eyes in a game of peek-a-boo. How easy it had been to make Belle see her then. Now, more than hands blocked Belle's sight. Years of Mom's rhetoric cast a pall over their relationship. Would they ever find their way through it all to rediscover a relationship? Because beyond all the hurt, she still desired to love and be loved by her little sister.

Her computer dinged an incoming email. Unraveling her past with Belle would require more time than she could offer this morning, but her heart tucked that hope away to pursue later. She dove into her morning devotions followed by finishing all the final details for tomorrow's sale. Nearly an hour, later she stood. Now to find something to wear on that date with East. She'd be too rushed tomorrow to do more than swap outfits after work.

She flipped through the sundresses in her closet, searching for something that made her look good without appearing she'd tried too hard. Wasn't crazy enough to think she'd turn his head, but she could surprise him. Remind him she was a girl. Which shouldn't be hard considering he'd only seen her in sweats. Those baggy things didn't exactly scream feminine. Or grab a guy's attention.

Penny reached in the back for a navy sundress. She held it against her body and faced her full-length mirror.

Her bedroom door opened. "Getting ready?"

Penny spun around and faced a perfectly-made-up Belle. "I know you were taught to knock because we grew up in the same house."

Belle pointed a fuchsia-tipped nail at her. "Tell me you're not wearing that."

Penny held up her dress. "What's wrong with it?"

"Seriously. How did I end up with all of Mom's style genes when I'm the adopted one?"

Handpicked to fit into the place Penny should have filled, Mom passed everything on to Belle. Including her love.

Belle joined her at the closet. Her black taffeta skirt swirled around her knees, showing off her tanned legs. The cashmere sweater she wore had capped sleeves with her rhinestone "B" pendant hanging at her collarbone. Her three-inch black heels must have taken a bath in glitter, and that didn't even touch the sparkle coming from her jewelry. Or the smell of whatever sugary scent Belle was wearing.

"Style is a very subjective word." Penny held out her dress. "This is style to me."

"Well, you're not wearing that. These people are going to be my family. Please don't embarrass me."

Because blinged out was a better way to go.

Penny shook her head. And stuffed her temper. "I'm not wearing this. I have a black skirt and a cardigan."

"Heels?"

Silence.

Belle turned on her. "This is really important to me, Pen. Please."

"Fine." Penny re-hung her dress and then stooped to the floor of her closet. She reached all the way to the back and grabbed a pair of shoes. Two-inch high peep-toes with a small bow. "Will these work?"

"You'll have to paint your toes."

"I am a girl. I have been known to do that." Even if she only maintained it for sandal wearing weather. Otherwise, what was the point?

Belle reached for the black skirt. "I guess this will have to do." She handed it to her. "You're braver than me. I never wear pencil skirts. I always feel they make me look hippy."

Belle didn't have hips, and she knew it.

But she never could resist reminding Penny of hers.

"By the way," Belle said as she double checked herself in Penny's mirror, "Mom called earlier. She wants you to save her and Dad a seat at the church because I'll be up front with the family."

"Fine." Penny grabbed her sweater. "Now if you want me to get ready, you need to get out of here."

"Start with your hair. And you can't get dressed 'til you do those nails." Belle sashayed to the door. "I'll go grab my pink polish and meet you in the bathroom."

"I can paint my own nails," Penny called to her retreating form. "And not pink!"

"Yes, pink." Belle returned.

It was going to be a long day.

Four hours later, Penny reclined in a plastic chair doing her best to tune out her sister's chatter. After the funeral, she'd driven Micah and Belle to the funeral home's reception hall and then discreetly left them to find the farthest table at the back, hoping for some quiet. That hope was short-lived. Belle had yet to elicit a comment from her on the line-up of green garbage trucks outside, and she wasn't about to let it go.

Belle slipped into the chair across from her. "I can't believe you didn't know Jonah's family owned All Waste."

Penny continued shredding the paper napkin in front of her. "And this surprises you because?"

"You've spent enough time with him to have asked what he does."

She dropped the shreds. "I barely know Jonah. Definitely not well enough to ask him for his resume."

Micah pulled out the chair beside Belle and dropped into it. "Belle practically asked for mine on our first date." He kissed her cheek. "Luckily, I could say med student, not garbage truck driver."

Spoken like someone who'd never tried running their own business. It took a lot of mettle and was every bit as impressive a feat as med school—no matter the company. And All Waste was a large one. Their trucks were all over the city.

Belle slid her arm around his waist and patted his chest. "There's a big difference between truck driver and owner. Owner would definitely have still snagged you a date."

Penny mounded up the shreds of napkin. "Not looking to snag a date with Jonah, so this conversation is pointless."

"Penny, darling." Of course, Mom chose that moment to walk past. She stopped and joined them. "You can't afford to be so choosy. I'd think knowing how well Jonah can provide for you would make up for his ... shortcomings."

Penny shook her head and shoved away from the table. "I'm going to get some water."

"Just make sure there's not a piece of cake attached." Mom patted Penny's side. "You have a dress to fit into."

"Which is why I hired a personal trainer. Who, by the way, asked me on a date. Belle can tell you all about him." She brushed Mom's hand off her side. "So I guess I can afford to be a little choosy."

Storming across the room, Penny wove between the tables of people eating their lunch, talking and laughing as if they hadn't just attended a funeral. She grabbed a bottle of water from the refreshment table and stormed out the front door, wishing the spring breeze was cool enough to calm her down.

Jonah leaned against one of the trucks, arms crossed. "Needed some fresh air?"

Seriously? She chuckled. He was standing next to a garbage truck. A sparkly clean garbage truck, but still. "Nice one." Tension melting away, she joined him and mimicked his stance, her shoulder brushing against his.

"I've been known to be funny every now and then." Jonah offered her a stick of cinnamon gum.

"No thanks."

They stood silent for another moment except for the occasional pop of his gum. She peered up at him. "So."

"So."

"You're a garbage collector."

"Yep."

She wrapped her knuckles against the truck. "How long did it take to clean this thing?"

"It's one of our new ones. Hasn't even been on the streets yet."

"I can honestly say, I've never seen a funeral procession of garbage trucks."

Jonah chuckled. "The guys loved Gigi. She hadn't worked in the office for over two years, but they remembered her even when she couldn't remember them. It was their way of saying good-bye and paying their respect."

"It was quite a sight."

"She was quite a lady." His eyes dimmed, and he squinted up at the sky. "Spring was her favorite time of year."

The breeze carried the scent of cherry blossoms on it. "Why'd you call her Gigi?"

Laughter popped from him. "When Rach was pregnant with Gavin, Gigi said she was too young to be called great-grandma, so she had him call her Gigi, and it just stuck for all of us. Secretly, I think it was because *Gigi* was her favorite movie."

It was one of hers, too. "I think I would have liked her."

He turned, close enough that Penny felt his breath brush her face. "She would have liked you."

His eyes were amazing; steel gray mixed with blue. And kind. She'd never looked into them to find anything other than kindness reflected back at her, but she barely had time to acknowledge that revelation before he pushed off the truck. "I should get back inside."

"Yeah, me too. I need to round everyone up." Though she'd rather stay right here. Something about Jonah calmed her.

They walked back to the entrance, Jonah's hands tucked into his pockets.

"Everything ready for your sale tomorrow?"

Surprise lit through her. "How'd you know about that?"

"Micah. He mentioned he and Belle are helping you before they cut out of town tomorrow."

He opened the door, and she slipped past. "Yeah. I typically have a group of college girls who help, but they have finals next week, so most of them are taking the weekend to study. Two of them need the pay badly enough they'll be there, but that's not enough with a house this large."

"I can help."

Penny rubbed her polished nails. Just this morning, she'd practically begged Belle for help. In the end, she'd only agreed because Penny had given in to the pink manicure. Yet Jonah barely knew her, and here he was freely offering up his Saturday.

Penny shook her head. "Thanks, but you've had a crazy week. I should be okay with Micah and Belle."

"You're sure?"

"Yep."

Across the room, Rachael waved them over to where she, Belle, and Micah stood. "There you are. I was looking for you."

"Sorry. I needed some air." Jonah gave Rachael a hug. "Did you need something?"

She addressed the group. "I thought it would be nice for us all to have dinner together before Belle and Micah have to leave tomorrow."

"I appreciate the offer, but I invited my parents over tonight," Penny said.

Belle brushed a blonde lock off her cheek. "Oh, I forgot to tell you. They're not coming."

"What?"

"They're not coming."

"Why?"

Belle shrugged. "I didn't ask, but I guess that means you're free." She turned to Rachael. "I'm not sure if I can make it, though. Unlike my sister, I require a lot of sleep, and Penny corralled me into helping her early tomorrow."

Not how she remembered it.

Penny smiled at Rachael. "Guess I'm free for dinner, but I do have a few things I need to finish tonight, so it can't be too late."

Her face lit up. "Does five work?"

"That's perfect."

Belle stepped out of the circle. "Are you about ready?" she asked Penny.

"Just about."

"Then I'm going to snag Micah." She left to find him.

"Need me to bring anything tonight?" Penny asked Rachael.

"Nope."

"Are you sure?"

Jonah spoke up. "We're sure. Just bring yourself."

"All right, then." Penny scrawled her number on a napkin and handed it to Rachael. "Text me your address, and I'll see you around five." Ducking away, she caught up with Belle. "I need to say good-bye to Mom and Dad."

Her sister groaned. "Fine. I'll be out at the car."

Mom and Dad sat across the room with Micah's parents. She headed toward the group.

"There's my Lucky Penny now." Dad engulfed her in his hug.

She breathed in his Old Spice as she slipped out of his arms. "Belle, Micah, and I are leaving. She mentioned you and Mom weren't coming tonight?"

"I think it's best if Dad and I head home." Mom rose from the table. "Besides, if we stayed, we'd get home late, and I need my beauty sleep." She smiled at Sharon. "I wouldn't want Micah to think we Thornton women don't age gracefully."

Dad placed a kiss on Mom's cheek. "That's something you'll never have to worry about, sweetheart."

Mom patted her white-blonde hair. "Yes, well, I've certainly been blessed, but it doesn't come without a lot of work. Right, Penny?"

Heat wound from her stomach up to her ears, and she tamped it down before the steam escaped. She'd never measure up to Mom's view of beauty.

She gave a simple nod and spun to Dad. "Drive safe."

He leaned in and whispered, "You're beautiful. Don't you forget it."

Her eyes moistened. Dad forever tried to fill the hole Mom dug, but that hole had grown into a chasm his words no longer touched.

"Thanks, Daddy." She brushed a stray tear. "I gotta go before Belle sends Micah to come find me."

She walked to the door, her eyes landing on Jonah as he spoke with one of the guests. With his hands in his pocket, suit coat open, and tie slightly loosened at the neck, he seemed ready to leave but unwilling to head out before the room emptied.

He truly was a nice guy. Was it sad that she looked forward to an evening with him and his sister more than one with her own family?

At least she did until he caught her staring. The corner of his mouth twitched, and he winked.

A hot blush worked its way up to her cheeks, and she scurried out the door.

He was not the man she was trying to make an impression on.

Tonight she was wearing sweats.

Chapter Eleven

Jonah let himself into Rachael's, and a large fur ball leapt up on him. "Down, Clooney!"

Four paws hit the ground, but Clooney still bounced around Jonah's feet, sniffing and barking. The dog needed a serious lesson in manners.

"Clooney. We need to work on your behavior." Jonah patted her on the head, attempting to calm her down.

The house was silent. Hopefully, that meant he beat everyone here—always better to be early than late.

Penelope's face came to mind and elicited a smile. Even in all black today, she'd been stunning. And the heels. She obviously was not comfortable in them, but they only showed off her amazing legs.

He swallowed.

Good thing Mom hadn't been there. She'd have swatted him for checking Penelope out at his grandmother's funeral. But he knew Gigi would have encouraged it.

A chuckle escaped and pushed back the tears. He missed them both so much.

"Hey, Uncle Jonah." Gavin leaned over the banister upstairs. "Thought I heard Clooney barking."

"Hey, bud. Where's your mom?"

"I'm here," Rachael called from the small pantry attached to the kitchen.

Jonah followed her voice. "Your dog needs obedience school."

"Tell that to the person who purchased her for me." Rachael walked out of the pantry. "Without asking first."

He inhaled sautéed veggies and baked chicken. "You two needed a dog."

"Yeah. One that came pre-programmed. I already have a child to train." Rachael started to shred the chicken.

Jonah peered over her shoulder. "Mom's chicken soup?"

"Sounded good tonight."

"It does." He leaned against the counter, facing her. "I'll find a place to train her, but I'd like Gavin to come too."

"I don't care who goes. I just want her to listen."

He snagged a piece of meat from the cutting board. Rach swatted him. "Stay back."

Thyme and rosemary settled on his tongue, and he reached for another slice.

Rachael pointed a fork at his hand. "I dare you." Her blue eyes possessed the same twinkles as Mom and Gigi's. She also shared their quick reflexes.

Jonah dropped his hand. "Fine. Let your big brother starve. The same big brother who tightened that leaky faucet for you and changed that light bulb you couldn't reach in the hall, and hung up your new blinds—"

"You mean the blinds Clooney broke?"

He glared at her. "You've offered me no proof it was that dog."

She laughed. "Right. Gavin and I chewed them."

"I give up." He scanned the room. "What can I do to help get dinner on the table faster?"

She wiped her hands on the towel thrown over her shoulder. "Leave my kitchen."

Her words were light, and he'd had her laughing, but dark circles rimmed her eyes. He tugged the towel from her shoulder. "You sure about having everyone over? We could still go out to dinner."

Rachael snapped the fabric of her yoga pants. "Are you kidding me? After the week we've had, I'm not going anywhere I can't wear these." She popped open a cupboard and ran her hand over the spices there.

He reached past, grabbed the basil, and held it out to her. "You sure I can't help?"

"I've already told you no about ten times today. You're really still asking me?" She took the spice, her eyes narrow as she watched him. "What's got you all fidgety anyhow?" Those narrow slits widened. "Oh wait. You're nervous because Penelope's coming over."

Jonah rubbed a hand over his bald head. As soon as Gavin's showed new growth, Jonah would grow his. "I'm not nervous, just don't think you need to be doing a whole bunch of work. You said yourself it's been a long week."

"Whatever. You're nervous, but I won't tell."

"Neither will I," Gavin added from his spot in front of the Xbox. "But it'll cost ya."

When had he come downstairs?

"Gavin—"

The doorbell cut him off, and Jonah headed for it, Clooney on his heels. He punched Gavin's shoulder as he walked by the couch. "Be nice. And take care of your dog."

Gavin grabbed Clooney's collar. "Got her."

Jonah opened the door, and a floral scent came in with the wind. Penelope stood behind Belle and Micah. He widened the opening, greeting Belle as she brushed past. "Glad to see you could make it, Belle."

"Micah didn't want to come alone."

Jonah tipped his head. "Penelope was coming."

"I know." Belle's light voice followed her retreating figure. She plopped down on the couch, and Micah joined her.

Penelope stepped inside, and Jonah leaned down to whisper in her ear. "Didn't know you were invisible."

"Unless she needs me for something." Her eyes stayed on her sister for a moment and then she peered around him. "Where's your sister?"

"In here," Rachael called from the kitchen.

Penelope headed in that direction, and Jonah studied her. The idea that anyone would think her invisible astonished him. Even in black sweatpants and an old orange Hope College T-shirt, she grabbed his attention.

The open main floor allowed him full access to her movements. She greeted Gavin and patted Clooney on the head as she passed by, bestowing her killer smile on them. Lucky boy.

Penelope continued into the kitchen area where she handed Rachael the dish she'd brought.

Jonah hurried to the counter. "Hey, sorry I didn't take that from you."

Her smile widened. "You're slipping. And in front of Gavin, no less."

"I told you not to bring anything." Rachael peeled back the tin foil on the dish. "But you're forgiven. These look fantastic."

Jonah peered over her shoulder. Brownies with melted caramel oozing out of them. "You had time to make those?"

"Actually, I already had them made. Figured I didn't need the whole pan to myself so I'd share."

"Generous."

"I try."

Rachael pulled dishes from her cupboards. "Here, Jonah. Make yourself useful."

"Where're your glasses?" Penelope asked.

Rachael pointed, and Penelope helped set the table while Micah and Belle chatted on the couch.

"Come on," Rachael called. "Soup's on. Literally."

They all filed to the dining room. Jonah waited until Penelope sat and then settled beside her. He blessed the food, and everyone dug in.

Jonah sipped his first taste. "Rach, this is exactly like Mom's."

Her face lit. "Thanks."

Micah grabbed the salt. "When are you planning on filing the will, Jonah?"

"Niles already has. He and I have a court date next Friday." Niles Davis was the family attorney for more years than Jonah could remember.

"Just let me know when you need my signature," Micah said. "Gigi was determined to see me in that company."

Rachael shook her head. "I think it was more Grandpa. Gigi was only carrying out his wishes."

"She'd made Jonah CEO; you'd think she'd have made him sole beneficiary, too," Micah said.

"Your grandmother didn't leave you the company?" Penny raised her brows at him.

"Nope." Jonah shrugged. "The shares will split fifty/fifty between Micah and me. Our grandpa wanted both us boys in the business, and Gigi thought she was honoring him by leaving things the way he'd planned." It still stung. But Jonah wasn't going to fault Gigi for the decision she'd made to stand by her husband's desires.

Micah pointed his spoon at Jonah. "Well, trust me, cuz, I have no interest in that company. You tell me when and where to sign, and she's all yours. Just make sure the trust keeps sending me checks and paying my med school bills, and I'm good. I'm going to need the extra money to make it through my residency." He patted Belle's leg. "With all the hours I'll be putting in, Belle's bound to get bored, and that means a lot of shopping."

Belle's lips twisted. "I'm sure I'll have plenty of distractions to pass my time with."

"Right. And shopping will be at the top of them." Micah laughed.

"Can I have another slice of bread, Mom?" Gavin asked.

Rachael passed the basket. "Do you know where your residency will be, Micah?"

"Not yet. I applied out East and also the West Coast. Both are places I've always wanted to live."

"And what's so wrong with living close to home?" Belle challenged.

Penelope stared at her sister, her brows drawn together. "You want to stay in Holland? I thought you were excited to move."

"I'm not allowed to change my mind?"

"Just surprises me, that's all."

"Your sister is full of surprises." Micah's low words pulled a glare from Belle. No one spoke for a long moment.

Belle cleared her throat, then focused her gaze on Jonah. "I can't believe that's you in the picture over the fireplace."

Everyone's gazes swung to the large family picture hanging above the mantle in the next room.

"Yeah. That was from a couple of years ago." Jonah stabbed at his lettuce. Out of the corner of his eye, he caught Penelope's squint.

"That's you?"

"One and the same."

She stared at the picture, glanced to him, and then back to the picture. "Your mother was beautiful."

That wasn't the statement he'd expected.

Jonah smiled. "She was."

While it was obvious who his parents were in the picture, there were still two others in the family who were missing from this table. He held his breath, unsure if he should say something or wait to see if anyone asked.

He needn't worry because Rachael spoke up. "The man standing beside Gavin is my husband, Chris. He was Jonah's best friend in college. The little girl is our daughter, Brianna." She swallowed. "They passed away shortly after that picture was taken."

All motion at the table ceased. "I'm so sorry, Rachael." Penelope glanced over at Gavin. "And you too, Gavin."

"Thank you." His voice was soft.

Silence dropped on them for a long moment.

Rachael cleared her throat. "Would anyone like more soup?" She stood. Everyone stared at her. "The living eat. And that's what we are—living, breathing, still here. So let's enjoy this meal. All right?"

Conversation pressed in around the awkward silence. Another round of soup filled their bowls, and laughter slowly reclaimed the evening. He hoped to see that trend continue. Pushing from the table, Jonah stood. "So. Who's up for a round of Dance Central?"

Gavin leapt to his feet. "I'll set it up." He dumped his dish in the kitchen and ran for the family room.

Rachael squeezed Jonah's shoulder as she stood. "Sounds fun, but I have dishes."

Penelope followed her with her own bowl. "I'll help."

"No. You're the guest, and you've already done enough. Go have fun."

"I'm not going to play in the living room and leave you with all these dishes."

Jonah stood. "I'll clear the table then help Rach with them tonight after you leave." Not arguing, Belle excused herself while Penny started stacking bowls. Jonah took them from her. "Go have Gavin show you the game. You'll want to practice before you take me on."

Penny reached for the butter dish. "I'm not dancing."

"It's easy," Gavin called from the living room.

Penny stood her ground.

"Afraid I'll beat you again?"

Her lips pursed. They were the perfect shape to kiss. "We've never played this game before."

"No. But I beat you at Scrabble, and I'm pretty sure that was a first for you." He focused on her. "I can see how you'd be worried to try and take me on in anything else."

She sucked in a breath and narrowed her eyes. "Pretty sure I can take you in a physical activity."

He ignored the dig. "And yet, you're still standing here."

Penelope peered around him to Gavin. "Set it up."

"Penny? Dancing? This I've got to see." Belle's laughter coated her words.

Gavin turned the TV on and brought the game to life. Techno pop music filled the air. "You have to stand here." He pointed to a spot on the floor. In front of the TV, a small, black rectangle moved up and down and colored figures appeared in the top corners of the screen. As Penelope moved, so did the pink one.

"That's me?" she asked.

"Pretty cool, huh?" Gavin smiled. "Now. You're player one so hold your right arm out and move it up and down to pick a song."

Penelope followed his instructions; her face pinched in concentration.

"Once you find the song you want, swipe your arm to the left," Gavin instructed.

Finished clearing the table, Jonah joined them. A piece of hair escaped Penelope's headband, and he itched to tuck it behind her ear. Wondered which would be softer, the dark strand or her skin?

"This one okay?" she asked.

"Huh?"

Her head tipped toward the TV.

Bananarama's 'Venus' played. He hid his grin. "That should work."

He selected his crew while Gavin walked Penelope through choosing hers and her level. Then the game began.

The dancers on screen started, and he mimicked the moves. Gavin fell on the couch, consumed with laughter. He pointed toward Penelope. Jonah turned. She stood stone still beside him, her brows arched. "What's that?" She pointed to the screen.

Jonah demonstrated the move, punctuated by more of Gavin's laughter. "It's called 'smush'. Just do what your dancer's doing."

"Penny's hips don't move that way," Belle said.

Red crawled up Penelope's neck. Jonah stopped. "Want to pick a different song?"

"Not on your life."

She threw out her hands with flair and swished her hips back and forth—not a bit of it on beat. He turned back to the screen, biting back laughter until the 'Aphrodite' move came on. Penelope's giggles exploded from her as she smoothed her hands across her body from her face to her hips. If she were going full-force, so would he. Beside her, his hands made the same track along his body, and he swished his lower half in exaggerated moves that kept time with the music.

Her eyes lit with laughter. "You're a guy. How on earth can you move like that?"

"Double-jointed."

Her shoulders shook. "Right."

"Don't look now, but you're losing."

She changed her moves with the dancers on screen. "I think I was set-up."

"You picked the song." True, he could have warned her he knew this one like the back of his hand. He'd danced it hundreds of times just to hear Gavin's laughter. All the hip swaying got his nephew every time, and he hammed it up almost daily to keep Gavin's mind on something other than being sick.

Penelope shimmied and shook, mostly from laughing so hard. The song came to an end, and she dropped to the floor, one arm flopped over her stomach, another over her forehead. Clooney stood over her and slobbered her with kisses, tail wagging furiously.

"Clooney, stop." Penelope giggled as Gavin tugged the dog away.

"I didn't just win. I crushed you." Jonah laughed.

"As if that was hard," Belle said from her perch.

He turned to her. "You want a turn?"

"Dance games are not my thing." Belle leaned into Micah.

Penelope sat up. "I'll play you again. That was a warm-up. Now it's for real."

Her cheeks were flushed and her eyes bright. He offered his hand. "Let me help you up." Hers fit his grasp as if made for it. Tugging her easily to her feet, he kept possession of it until she looked at him. "And I hate to break it to you, but that last one was for real, and you lost."

Her fingers wiggled against his. She had to feel the current moving between them.

"But if you want to lose again ..."

She pulled, and reluctantly, he released her. If they didn't have an audience, he would have held on, tugged her to him, and kissed those lips.

A light blush tinted her cheeks. "Not going to happen."

The corner of her mouth lifted, and he almost forgot they had one.

"Rematch!" Gavin's voice sliced through their connection. Their attention snapped to him.

"Same song," Penelope's voice cracked, and she cleared her throat.

"That hardly seems fair."

She tilted her head in a challenge. "Afraid you'll lose now that I know it?"

"Afraid it'll be no contest."

"It won't be." She pointed to Gavin. "How do I set it up?"

"You're sure you don't want a new song?" he asked.

"Same song."

"Glutton for punishment, are you?" Jonah tapped a finger against his lips. "All right. I'll play, but how about a bet? If I win, we go to dinner tomorrow, and you let me pay—no argument."

Belle's silky voice spoke. "Amazing. I never imagined my sister being asked out on two dates in the same week, let alone for the same day. Whatever will you do, *Penelope?*"

"You've already got a date for Saturday?"

A look passed between sisters. "Sorta." She shrugged.

"Sorta?" Belle stood behind them. "Her hottie of a personal trainer asked her out."

His stomach bottomed out to the basement. "East asked you out?"

"Yes. He did." Her shoulders straightened. "But let's not go there again." She nodded to the screen. "So pick a different bet, and let's do this."

Gladly. Because he didn't trust his foot to stay out of his mouth right now.

Belle reached for her purse. "I can't watch any more of this. I already don't feel well." She turned to Penelope. "I'm just glad I signed you both up for dance lessons."

Penelope turned to stone. "What?"

"There's no way you're dancing at my wedding like that." She held her arm across her stomach and turned to Micah. "I really don't feel well. Can you take me home?"

Concern cut deep lines in Penelope's face. "You're sick again?"

"I must have caught a bug."

"I'll grab my stuff." Penelope headed to the kitchen.

Micah wrapped his arm around Belle and ushered her to the door. "We'll meet you outside, Penny."

"Do you have another plate I can leave these brownies on?" Penny asked Rachael.

Rachael provided her with one, and Penelope quickly transferred the gooey treats over. Her own plate in hand, she headed to the door.

"Sorry your sister's not feeling well." Jonah walked with her.

"Me, too. I'm also sorry she signed us up for dance lessons. I'll talk to her about that."

Jonah held the door. "They might not be so bad."

She laughed. "Right. I'll see you later."

He watched her leave then turned to find Rachael behind him. "So ..." She pulled the word out. "Aren't you the one who put Micah and Belle in touch with Keegan and Melinda?"

Jonah brushed past her and snagged the last dish off the table.

"Maybe."

"No maybe about it." Rachael stayed on his heels. "You know Penelope's bound to find out."

Jonah set the dish down and filled the sink with bubbles. "Hey. I was only thinking of the bride. Thought she'd like to know I could arrange free dance lessons for her bridal party. What bride wouldn't want that?"

Beside him, Rachael shook her head. "Oh, the bride was thrilled, I'm sure. It's her sister you need to worry about."

He hadn't really thought about it when he'd fed the idea to Micah. All he'd been thinking about was taking the chance to twirl Penelope around the floor. A perfect excuse to hold her close.

Even after seeing her face at the suggestion, he still wasn't worried. He'd make sure she had fun. Besides, he had bigger issues to worry about.

Like her date with East Fisher.

Chapter Twelve

Penny glanced up as the front door of the Wilton house opened. Instead of Belle and Micah, her employee Ella Bronson walked in.

"How's it looking out there, Ella?"

The blonde stopped in front of her. With her hair in a ponytail, well-worn jeans snug over her hips, and yellow long-sleeve Loyola T-shirt on, Ella played the part of college co-ed to a tee. She held up the cards in her hand. "These Saturday-only sales draw a crowd. I've given most of the numbers out. There's nearly fifty people waiting with more coming up the street."

And she was two helpers short. Penny peered at her phone. She'd left three voicemails, and Belle still wasn't answering.

"Okay. I'd hoped to let them in fifteen at a time; instead, we'll do ten. Saige is already upstairs; you'll have to join her up there. I'll cover down here and the door, and we'll hope for the best."

"Maybe your sister will still show."

Doubtful. The grandfather clock in the hall dinged eight forty-five. If Belle wasn't here by now, she wasn't coming. Penny bit her lip and winced. She should have forced Belle to ride with her rather than naively holding to the belief that just this once, her little sister would come through for her.

"I'm going to take one last walk through." She handed a money belt to Ella. "If someone offers you full price, go ahead and take their money. Anyone bartering needs to see me. And no—"

"Personal checks. I know."

Ella disappeared up the stairway, and Penny surveyed the living room. Everything was set. She could do this. The lack of help would up the pressure, but it would also make the day move faster. And keep her thoughts away from her "date" tonight. They kept wanting to tease her it was real.

The front door opened, and Penny spun. "Sorry, but we're not letting people in yet."

"I come bearing gifts." Jonah stood in the doorway, a bag from Leitzia's bakery and four to-go coffee cups in a carrier. "And prepared to help."

His bald head was a site for sore eyes.

She shook her head.

"You don't want my help?" He turned.

"No! I mean, yes!" Penny rushed to his side and took the coffee from him. "Yes to it all."

He spun on his heel. "Good because I don't need to eat all these pastries by myself."

With a laugh, Penny nudged him toward the kitchen and set the treats on the dining room table. "Not that I'm not incredibly thankful, but what are you doing here?"

"Bringing you nourishment and help. Pretty sure I already said that." He sipped his coffee and handed her a cup. "This one's tea. I wasn't sure how you'd want it, so I brought cream and sugar."

He remembered she loved tea.

Her fingers brushed his as she claimed it. "Thanks. I actually like it plain." She sipped the spicy brew. "And licorice is my favorite."

"I thought that's what I smelled on the train."

Penny smiled. "Your mother did an amazing job with you."

"I like to think I'd have made her proud." He tapped the drink carrier. "Now, who do these go to?"

"Ella and Saige. They're upstairs." He started that way, but she stopped him. "And I'm sure you would—make your mother proud, that is."

He gave a small nod, the corners of his lips tipped upward. "Thanks."

"Oh, hey?" she asked.

"Yeah?"

"How'd you know not to bring two more?"

Jonah sighed, his hand on the banister. "Micah called this morning. He and Belle were on the road home."

Of course they were. "At least I know where she is now."

His brows lifted. "She hasn't called you?"

"Nope. And she's not answering my calls either." She let out a disgusted breath and shooed him upstairs. "Can't do anything about it right now. Go on and take those coffees to the girls and get back down here. If you're going to help me, I need to give you a quick walk-thru. Doors open in five minutes. You're crowd control for now."

Jonah saluted her and walked up the stairs.

Half a day later, Penny perched inside the door of the Wiltons' house, tired but satisfied. With Jonah's help, they'd been able to move customers in and out easily. Nearly everything had sold, and things were quieting down. Most buyers knew what they were doing and had shown up early with some extra muscle and a trailer or large van for loading their items—or small boxes to load all their collectibles into.

Now all that remained were normal garage sale items. A few pieces of small furniture, some non-collectible knick-knacks, kitchen utensils … she looked to the dining room—and the table.

Sunshine spilled across its dark wood. She'd been so sure the gorgeous piece would go first. It was beautiful, and she'd priced it more than fairly. What she hadn't stopped to think about was the sheer size of it. Nearly ten feet long. If her dining room were bigger, she'd take it home with her. One day Mr. Right would show up and help her fill it with kids. At least she hoped.

Penny walked throughout the first floor checking on what pieces were still available and then returned to the dining room table once again.

A throat cleared, and Jonah appeared beside her. "I've noticed you admiring that table off and on all day."

"It's an amazing piece."

"It is, and I've been looking for a new one." He joined her beside it.

She brushed her hand across the surface. "I was sure it would sell."

"Just needs the right buyer." Would that be him? He definitely seemed interested. He fiddled with the spindles on one of the chairs. "I enjoyed today, Penelope. You're very good at what you do."

Ah. Pre-discount-seeking charm. "Flattery will get you nowhere with me."

But there was no charm in the gaze he pinned her with. Only caution. "Remember that on your date tonight."

"You sound like my father."

Jonah inspected the intricate carving along the apron of the table. "Trust me; I'm not him."

The soft words barely reached her ears curling warmth through her. "What?"

But he remained focused on the wood pattern. "Did Allen Wilton carve this himself?"

Penny crossed her arms over her stomach and stared at him. She'd heard him. Just like on the train. But again, he wasn't owning his words. "Why do you do that?"

"Do what?" Mischief mixed with the steel in his eyes.

"Never mind." She'd already lost enough games to him. She pointed to the carving. "Yes. Allen built it out of solid mahogany to seat eight without a leaf. With the leaves, it seats twelve." Comfortably. "He made the chairs to match."

"It's amazing work."

"Rarely have I seen pieces like it. The only reason I have it priced the way I do is because Allen was not a known name in furniture making. Though he could have made a killing at it." Her fingers smoothed over the grain of the tabletop.

Jonah's hand followed hers. His fingers stopped as they grazed her skin. She looked up to find him watching her. But again, he didn't further his move. "Why aren't you buying it?" he asked.

"My house isn't big enough."

"But you love it."

No use denying. "I do."

Jonah studied her and then the table. His knuckles rapped across the top. "I hope you find the perfect home for it."

The man was going to give her whiplash. And not only over this table. "So you don't want it then?"

"No. It's beautiful, but I'm not sure it's right for me. Besides"—he turned to her, close enough for his cinnamon breath to tickle her face—"I didn't come for a table today. I came to help you. And now I'm wondering if you could help me."

People in her personal space typically bugged her—but not Jonah. It felt natural, which bugged her all the more. She stepped away and clasped her hands together. "I told you; I'm not training Clooney for you."

He laughed. "No. Though I'm going to wear you down on that one."

"So what then?" She had a good idea what was coming.

"I wondered if I could hire you for Gigi's estate?"

Had he asked before today, she'd have said no, convinced he'd been working an angle. But somehow an honest friendship had sprouted between them. Then he'd shown up on her doorstep unsolicited today to freely offer his help. How could she do anything less for him?

"No."

"No?"

She squelched her laughter at his surprise. "You can't hire me because I'll do it for free."

"I am hiring you." He crossed his arms. Must think he meant business, but she wasn't cowering.

A young couple strolled into the room. She'd nearly forgotten customers still shopped. That was a first. She smiled sweetly at Jonah. "I need to get back to work." Let him think she was giving in. This wasn't the time or place to fight him on it.

But she would. And she'd win.

The last customer left twenty minutes ago. Jonah leaned against the large column that separated the dining room from the living area and entryway. Perfect view. Sitting on her stool in the foyer, Penelope counted out the last dollar and typed something into her laptop. They were closing up for the day, but he wasn't ready to say good-bye.

He hadn't lied earlier. She was amazing at her job. Watching her mind for business and ability to work with even the most difficult customer brought out his respect. Especially when she'd kept her cool speaking with Allen and Frances' son who'd stopped by in the last hour.

But if he was honest, it was the bonus of spending time with her that had him asking her to tackle Gigi's estate. He chuckled at how she'd left him standing by that table earlier. Pitiful attempt at making him believe she'd conceded. That sugary smile had done nothing to dim the flames in her eyes. Stubborn as all get-out. Well, so was he.

His gaze tracked to the table. A beautiful piece made only more intriguing by Penelope's interest in it. He'd nearly purchased it and had it delivered to her until she said it wouldn't fit. And for a fleeting moment, he entertained buying it for his own home. Pictured the two of them sitting there surrounded by kids.

He needed to see it reflected in her eyes first. Or at least some interest. But he'd only seen glimpses and even those he wondered if he made up.

He'd never been one to give up easily, though.

"Can I walk you out?" He snagged her jacket off the back of one of the chairs and approached her.

Startled, she glanced up. "I thought you'd already left."

"I wasn't going to leave you here alone."

She closed the cash box and locked it. "I would have been fine."

"Probably, but now I'll know for sure." He held her coat open.

She shrugged her arms in and then picked up her laptop.

His hand found the small of her back as he ushered her through the door. She stopped next to her car. "Thanks again for helping today. I really couldn't have done this without you."

"My pleasure." Her light flowery scent trailed his way. "What perfume do you wear? I can't place the smell, and I've been meaning to ask."

"Smell?" She raised both brows. "You're slipping, Jonah Black."

"Is there a better word?"

"Yes. It's *scent*." She tightened the belt on her short yellow trench. "And I've no doubt your mother taught you not to ask a woman about her smell."

He chuckled. "True. She'd have swatted me." Sunlight created a soft hue around them. "Then told me that you're a good teacher, and I should listen to you."

Laughter spilled from her own lips, bringing his attention to them. "Wish I could turn those abilities on my sister." She leaned against her car. "She refuses to give in about the dance lessons."

"Or the dress?"

"Or the dress."

He joined her and crossed his arms. "It's not that bad."

"Right. Because you seemed so enthused to be wearing that lovely purple shade."

"It's one day." He shrugged. "You can make anything work for one day."

"Tell yourself what you have to so you can make it through."

"Is that what you do with your sister? Just try to make it through?"

Penelope stiffened. "It's complicated." She exhaled. "But no. With Belle, I'm trying to make a connection."

He waited for her to say more. When she didn't, he nodded—though he'd like to have pushed. "Then I hope you do." He straightened. "So how about dinner? To talk over Gigi's estate?"

Her car beeped as she unlocked it. "I have a date with East tonight, remember?"

He had—though he'd hoped she'd forgotten. Disappointment edged in, but he ignored it for now. "Good thing you need to eat dinner every night."

She smiled. "That I do."

"Maybe tomorrow then? We'll grab dinner before Gigi's house. Once you look it over, we can discuss fees."

She pulled out her phone and opened the calendar. "I'm donating my time."

He raised a brow. "Nope. I'm hiring you."

She dismissed him with a wave. "We're friends. And I don't charge my friends."

But he wasn't planning on staying in the friend zone or letting her think he was using her. "I happen to know you could use the money. Something about wanting to open your own shop?"

This pulled her attention to him. "How do you know I'm opening my own store?"

"You mentioned it at dinner with Gavin and me the other night."

"Huh." She breathed out the word as a group of skateboarders rolled past them. "You really are a good listener."

"Pretty easy to be when it comes to you."

Red tinged her cheeks, and she glanced at her phone, swiping it. "Tomorrow doesn't work. I try to take Sundays completely off—except for church."

Every time he pulled a brick off that wall she'd placed between them, she pushed it back in place. Fine. He'd scale it. Only at a slower pace. "One of the perks of being your own boss. Setting your own schedule."

"Exactly." She nodded, relaxing onto their common ground. "How long have you been running All Waste?"

"A few years now. I worked there all through high school and college. Once I had my business degree, Gigi let me in the office."

"So you had to get your hands dirty first."

"Literally."

He could listen to her laughter all day.

It tapered off, but her focus on him remained. "That was smart of her. Employees need to know you understand them and their job. Don't lose that aspect."

Interesting she'd say that. "I've actually been contemplating riding the trucks again. Just for a week each year."

"You should. And with a different driver each day." She tipped her head. "Maybe even make it a week in summer and a week in winter."

Even in the warm evening, he shivered. "Do you have any idea how cold those trucks are in winter?"

"No." The perfect mixture of mischief and sincerity sparkled in her eyes. "But your men do."

She had him.

He groaned. "Better mark down the date because you finally beat me at something."

"Ha!" She pushed off the car. "On that note, I really need to go, or I'll be late."

In this instance, late wouldn't be a bad thing.

He moved so she could open her door then grasped the corner to prevent her from shutting it once she'd slid inside. Couldn't prevent her from going on a date with East, but he could secure his own before she left. "What day works this week for dinner and Gigi's?"

She started her car. Her radio blasted Adele's latest song, and she turned it down. "Monday?"

"Gavin and I work out on Monday nights, so it would have to be late."

"Even better. I need to work out too. I've got that lovely purple dress to fit into, you know." She scrolled to the calendar on her phone and started typing. "I'll meet you at the gym instead of dinner. We can exercise, and then I'll follow you over to your grandmother's."

"It's a date."

"A *work* date." Her eyes twinkled up at him.

Yes, he caught the clarification. Didn't mean he had to agree with it.

He closed her door, and she pulled away, hand lifted in an absent wave. Hopefully, she'd try just as hard to keep East in his place tonight because he planned to scale her walls before that man was firmly encamped on the other side.

Chapter Thirteen

Penny grabbed a thermos from her kitchen cupboard, added hot water, and a tea bag. While that steeped, she carefully packed the picnic basket, trying to focus on anything other than the knot in her stomach. It was nearly time to meet East.

"You look great." Lacey leaned against the counter. "Though if you took the tank top off from underneath, I'm sure East would appreciate your outfit even more."

Not with the deep cut of this dress. A royal blue v-neck, she'd belted it around the waist and added the coral layer underneath. The skirt swirled just above her knees. She'd need to be careful when she sat, but the cut was flattering and hid the extra pounds she carried. Not that East didn't know she had them, but he didn't need to stare at them either.

She fingered the straps of her tank. "Without this, I give him more of a show than I'm comfortable with, especially if I lean over."

Lacey shook her head. "I've so much to teach you." She stood and dipped forward. "The key to securing date number two is no tank and making sure you lean over. Several times."

Licorice wafted to Penny's nose. She pulled the tea bag out of her thermos and threw it away. "I'm not crazy enough to think there'll be a date number two. East's a flirt who knows how to keep his clients coming back. He's not seriously interested in me. I only said yes to this one because Belle was there." Slowly, she tightened the lid. "You and I both know I'm not what guys are looking for in a girl." And she was done wishing for it. Done being embarrassed or hurt when reality set in.

"Stop selling yourself short. You're a great catch." Lacey plucked Penny's strap. "Now ditch the tank, and help East see that."

If there was an ounce of truth to Lacey's belief in her, it shouldn't matter if she wore the extra shirt. "Not a game I want to play, Lacey."

"I thought you said East was 'hot.'"

"He is."

"Then it's a game you need to play. Guys like him have expectations."

And her body met none of them. "If those are his expectations, and he actually aims them my way, then one date will be more than enough." She closed her basket and walked to the front door.

"Tell me that after he kisses you senseless."

Her cheeks warmed. Along with her blood. "Lace!"

"'Lace' me all you want; your face tells a different story." She spread the paper in front of her and started to read.

Penny lugged the picnic to the park. East was coming from work and meeting her. If she'd been thinking, she'd have invited him straight to her house rather than carrying everything. Her arms ached from the weight of the food and drinks. She'd packed way more than they'd be able to eat, but she wanted to make sure East left satisfied.

Wicker Park came into view. East sat on a bench and waved. His navy Abercrombie T-shirt and khaki cargo shorts showed off his toned muscles. As she neared, he smiled. His white teeth gleamed in the sun and pulled her attention from his chest. When she reached the bench, East took the basket from her. His hand brushed hers, and a tingle shot up her arm.

Not good. She needed to stow the attraction, and quickly before she embarrassed herself.

"You look great." He led her to a blanket in the grass, paused. "Would you rather sit at a picnic table?"

"No. This is fine." Penny knelt down and tucked her skirt under her.

East popped open the basket. "You burned some calories carrying this. What all did you bring?" He peeked inside.

Penny leaned in beside him and pulled the items out, setting them on the blanket. "I wasn't sure what you'd like, so I made a couple of different sandwiches." She placed a bowl between them. "I cut up some fruit and made a dip. Oh, and veggies too."

He pulled out another bowl. "What's this?"

"Pasta salad."

He dug in for more and found the pan of brownies. He raised his brow.

"Dessert," she offered. Maybe she shouldn't have brought that.

She waited for his reprimand, but he simply set them aside then held up a bag of gourmet chips. He smirked. "What? You couldn't roast your own chips too? Slacker."

His ease brought out hers, making it way too easy to pretend this was real. "I had to draw the line somewhere."

She unwrapped the sandwiches. "One's roast beef with horseradish and some caramelized onions. The other is turkey with cream cheese and cranberries.

Not sure which you'd like."

"How about we split them?"

"Sounds good."

Penny let East fill his plate first then made hers. Turkey and cranberry was one of her favorites, and after the long day, she was more than ready to eat it. She picked up that half and took a bite. Something cold plopped onto the front of her dress. Wonderful.

East handed her a napkin.

"Thanks." She scrubbed at the blob of cranberry on her chest, wishing she could disappear. Oh, she was making an impression all right.

Beside her, he held up his sandwich. "I bet it tastes a whole lot better if you're eating it, not wearing it."

And then he went and erased her awkwardness with laughter. "Probably does." She wadded up the napkin and tossed it in the trash bag she'd brought.

East took a bite. "So tell me about your family. You don't look anything like your little sister." He spoke around his mouth full.

She stilled. "So I've been told." And Mom planned it that way. "It might be due to the fact that she's adopted."

"Belle's adopted?"

"She is." Though it wasn't something they talked much about.

Birds chirped overhead, and children's laughter spilled over the green grass. East leaned in and brushed a strand of hair from her face. "Well, that explains it."

"Explains what?"

"Why you're so much prettier."

Prettier.

He smiled. Her cheeks warmed, and she blinked away. This was only about his job. Flattering her to keep her business. Except he didn't have to meet her here. Share dinner with her or ask about her family.

This line of thought was dangerous.

"Like I said before, you don't have to pour on the flattery or arrange this"— she waved her hand over the blanket—"to keep me coming into the gym. Having to fit in that dress is motivation enough." She strove for a lightness she didn't feel. Even maintaining perspective, being with East was messing with her. Teasing out hope.

"I know."

Two simple words, but his tone had her attention. It sounded like … no. He couldn't actually *be* interested. Her pulse picked up. "How about something to drink?" She fumbled with the picnic basket, and a sharp sting cut into her palm. "Ow!"

East straightened. Reached for her. "What happened?"

"A wasp." She pointed to the red welt already forming in the middle of her palm.

"Ouch." East dug into the basket. "Did you bring any ice?"

"Yeah. At the bottom."

He pulled it out and dumped a few pieces into his napkin before holding it to her.

The cool cloth immediately calmed the throbbing in her palm. His touch did the opposite.

Unsure, she pulled away. "Thanks."

"You're welcome—again." East dug into his sandwich.

She glanced around. Food spilled down the front of her, wasp sting on her hand ... she was a real prize.

He grabbed a strawberry from the basket and bit into it. "So tell me more about you. I know about your job, but what do you do for fun?"

Not flirting to keep her at the gym. Not trying to pick her brain about how to sell things. He wanted to know about her? A ball rolled across their blanket, and she tossed it back to the kids playing catch. "It may sound lame, but my job is fun to me." Okay, that did sound completely lame.

"That doesn't sound lame at all. I feel the same way about mine."

She did not expect them to have that in common. Or anything in common, really. "What got you into personal training?"

He waited a moment. "Honestly?"

She nodded.

"I haven't exactly been in this shape my whole life."

Her gaze traveled his body. "You've got to be kidding."

"Nope." He popped another strawberry into his mouth. "I struggled with my weight for years. In college, I decided to do something about it. Joined a gym, and my personal trainer changed my life. The rest is history."

"That inspires me to believe I can do it too."

He squeezed her leg. "All you've got to do is want it."

She stared at his hand on her bare shin. Her mouth went dry.

East looked from her to his hand, gave one more squeeze, and let it go.

An hour later, dinner was finished, the basket packed, and blanket folded. "Can I walk you home?" East asked.

Was he serious or being polite? No clue. But if he was offering ... "I'd like that."

They headed down Schiller at a leisurely pace. At one point, her fingers brushed his. East grabbed them and held on. Everything she'd been sure of flew out of her brain, replaced by everything she hadn't dared to hope. This was beyond an interest in keeping her as a client. This felt like interest in *her*.

He held her hand all the way to her house. The sun was setting in the sky as they reached her door. They climbed the steps together, and Penny reluctantly released his hand to reach for her keys. "Thanks for walking me back." Her heart pounded.

"My pleasure." He focused his blue eyes on her, a slow smile forming on his face. Dropping the basket, he dipped his head down to hers. "You're beautiful."

"And you're blind." Her insecurity escaped. But this couldn't be happening. East Fisher was not standing on her doorstep, calling her beautiful, looking like he was about to kiss her.

"No. You are."

She melted.

His lips brushed hers, slowly at first before pressing deeper. East leaned her against the door and closed in, one hand palmed against the wood behind her, one at her waist.

Penny's breath left her as she opened to him. He caressed her mouth, moving from the corner of her lips to the fullness of them, coaxing her on. His hand at her waist slowly moved up, cupping her neck before his fingers wrapped into her hair.

A horn honked, and boys' voices catcalled as a car drove down the street. Penny snapped her head up and pushed East off. Too hot. Too fast.

He leaned close. "Maybe we should take this inside."

The heat rolling through her ran cold. What was she doing?

"East. I'm not that girl." It was as much a reminder for herself as it was for him.

His eyes widened. "Sorry. Did I read that kiss wrong?"

She shook her head, unable to lie. "No. And I'm the one who's sorry. I shouldn't have kissed you like that. I barely know you." Didn't even believe he was interested until ten minutes ago.

He gave them some distance and ran his hands through his hair.

No way he'd ask her out again. He was way out of her league. She'd known it, but had chosen to ignore it and made a fool out of herself once again.

Penny picked up the basket. "I, uh, I guess I'll see you at the gym."

East grabbed her arm. "Penny, wait. You're a nice girl, and I'm not used to dating nice girls. I shouldn't have pushed that kiss so soon, but I've wanted to do that since the moment I first saw you."

Her heart dipped inside before it started to race. "Really?"

"Yeah. Really." His thumb rubbed the soft flesh on the inside of her wrist.

"And if I haven't already ruined my chances, I'd like take you out for a real date. Pick you up, take you to dinner." He paused. "Keep the kisses rated PG."

He wanted that? With her? She barely believed it. Mom and Belle definitely wouldn't. "I'd like that."

A gentle tug pulled her into his soft hug. "Next Friday then?"

"Sounds good."

"And I'll see you Monday at the gym?"

"Count on it."

He dropped a kiss on her forehead before trotting down the steps. At the bottom, he turned. "I think you'll be good for me, Penny Thornton."

She watched him walk down the sidewalk, her fingers brushing her lips that still tingled, her thoughts echoing East's, only he had it backward.

He was good for her.

Chapter Fourteen

With a huff, Penny tore off her gray T-shirt and tossed it on her bed. How could she not own one cute piece of work-out clothing? Probably because it hadn't mattered before. But now?

She eyed the clock. Four thirty-five. Her standing Monday appointment was for five. If she didn't get out the door in the next ten minutes, she was in trouble.

"You could always borrow something from my closet." Lacey leaned against Penny's bedroom door with a huge grin.

"Nothing of yours will fit me."

"It might."

"Maybe if I dropped six inches and twenty pounds." She rummaged through her drawer. "There's got to be something in here that will hide my middle."

"From what you told me about that kiss, East doesn't seem to have a problem with any part of you."

Warmth flooded her cheeks, and she fought the temptation to touch her lips. "I had no business kissing him like that."

Lacey walked in and sat on her bed. "But it was a great kiss, wasn't it?"

This time, her fingers gently slid over her lips. "Great doesn't begin to describe it."

"I knew it." Lacey jabbed a finger at her. "I knew there was a seductress in there. Told you if she came out, he'd ask you for a second date." She leaned back and propped herself up on one arm. "Need some pointers before Friday?"

Lacey's words threw cold water on the memory of that kiss. No seductress in here.

She dug to the bottom of her drawer and tugged out her old college T-shirt with holes then slid out of her running shorts and into an old pair of sweats. "No pointers necessary. East and I are going to take it slow."

"Uh-uh … and that's what that kiss told him, right?"

"That's what *I* told him."

Lacey snorted. "Yeah. I know. I'm sure it came out loud and clear with his tongue down your throat."

Penny lobbed a pair of socks at her.

Lacey shot up. "Hey!"

"Drop it." Penny slid her feet into her tennis shoes. "I never said I was perfect."

Lacey mumbled something.

"What?"

"I'm not repeating it." Lacey got up from the bed and followed her into the hall. "I don't want to be used for target practice again."

"Wise choice since I only have dirty socks left."

Lacey's laughter drowned out her own. "Love you, roomie."

"Love you, too."

And she did, even if Lacey drove her crazy.

"You want to catch dinner tonight when you get back?" Lacey asked.

Penny snatched her keys off her kitchen counter, then thought better of it. She may be running late, but East would not be happy if she drove.

"Can't." She headed for the door. "I told Jonah I'd check out his grandmother's house and give him pointers on how to sell it all."

Lacey's lips twitched.

"What?" Penny drew out the word.

"I always knew you were capable of hooking a man. Just didn't think it'd be two on the line at once."

"There's not!" Especially not Jonah. "I'm not even sure I have one on it."

"My view says differently."

"I've got to go." Penny slammed the door before Lacey could say more.

The silence of her hurried fifteen-minute walk did nothing to calm her nerves. Saturday night's kiss kept replaying in her mind, and confusion rang through her brain. What on earth did East see in her? And was it enough? Or would he look at her tonight and regret he'd kissed her?

She opened the glass door to the gym and immediately caught sight of him. He stood by the weight bench, spotting Jonah. East's eyes met hers.

"Penny. You're late."

No warmth in that greeting at all. Her smile froze in place. She checked her watch. "By a minute."

He raised a brow. "Late's late. Fifty extra push-ups and sit-ups tonight."

Her cheeks warmed. Oh yeah. He regretted it. And she was a complete idiot.

Jonah locked his bar back in place and sat up. "Quite an interesting way to inspire your clients, East."

"Either they're here because they're serious, or it's a waste of both our time."

The heat traveled from her cheeks to her blood.

"Didn't mean assigning extra reps." Jonah wiped his face with his towel. "I meant the disrespect."

Her heart shifted. Jonah was sticking up for her.

East's fist clenched at his side. Jonah put the towel down and stood.

"Jonah." Penny moved between them. "Let me know when you're finishing up, so I won't keep you waiting." She turned to East. "As for you, in the past minute, you've wasted as much of my time as I have yours. I think we're even. So can we get started?" But after tonight, she was finding a new gym.

She caught the corner of Jonah's smile as she stomped to the treadmill. Jumping on, she punched it to a six. Time to burn off her embarrassment and anger.

East walked over. "Penny—"

"Really don't feel like talking right now."

She'd been so stupid to think he could care for her.

Rolling his eyes, he stepped away. "I recommend you stretch first."

Her focus remained on the wall in front of her.

A moment later, Jonah appeared at her side and punched the treadmill down to near zero.

Penny reached out, but he grabbed her hand. "You may be angry, but that's no reason to get yourself hurt. You need to stretch first."

She caught his cool blue eyes. The color reminded her of a winter day, yet there was nothing cold about Jonah. No. Jonah was becoming more like a cup of her licorice tea—familiar and comfortable ... unexpected spice.

She shook her head.

He smiled and tugged at her arm. "Come on."

Jonah led her to a mat and worked through her warm-up with her. Mercifully, he stayed silent.

They finished the last stretch, and Penny sat there.

"Cooled down?" he asked.

"Thought the point was for me to warm up."

He laughed. "That too." He nudged her shoulder with his. "And I hate to add to your evening, but I have to cancel for tonight. Micah called a few minutes before you walked in here. He's asked for a meeting with Niles, our lawyer, and I need to be there. Would tomorrow night work to check out Gigi's?"

"Sure." She reclined on her palms. "Is everything okay?"

Jonah released a long breath. "I hope so."

This time it was his turn for quiet, and her turn to nudge him. "How was the rest of your weekend?"

"Good. Rachael, Gavin, and I took Clooney to Wicker Park. Thought maybe we'd run into you there." He stretched his legs out in front of him and leaned back on his elbows.

"Lacey and I grabbed brunch at Orange and then hung out along the lakeshore. It was a beautiful day." She'd thought Saturday had been too. Her gaze strayed to East, and her stomach knotted.

The edge of his lip pulled up. "We're friends, right, Penelope?"

Penelope. She smiled. "We are." And he was quickly becoming an important one.

"Then can I say something?"

"Sure."

He sat up. "You're better off without him."

Her eyes widened. "East?" She let out a nervous laugh. "Oh, there's nothing there. I let myself forget that one kiss doesn't mean as much to a guy as it does a girl."

If she hadn't been sitting so close, she'd have missed the tick in his jaw. Then he fixed his eyes on her, and it was like she was the only one in the room. "To the right guy, Penelope, one kiss means everything."

Mouth suddenly dry, she swallowed. They may be friends, but it might be better to keep the chats about her love life confined to Lacey's ears.

Unyielding in his focus, Jonah's lips parted. "Penelope, I—"

"Thanks for making sure she stretched, Jonah," East interrupted, standing over them. "She was too angry with me to listen, and I deserved it." He aimed puppy dog eyes her way. "Sorry for what I said. I've had a lousy day, and I took it out on you. Can we pick up where we left off Saturday?"

She looked at both men, side by side, and catalogued their differences. East stood a few inches shorter, had muscles on every square inch, and a full head of blond hair. They both had blue eyes, but even those weren't similar. Jonah's ice blue eyes gave her warmth, while East's sapphire blues brought fire.

She liked them both, but only wanted to date one.

The one Mom and Belle never would have set her up with. The one she'd never believed would even notice her. And the one who'd just apologized so sweetly.

Everyone was entitled to a bad day.

"Apology accepted."

His gaze flicked between her and Jonah. "So we're still on for Friday?"

"Of course."

Tension rolled off of Jonah. He'd made his feelings about East known, but this was her decision. As her friend, he should respect it.

Jonah picked up his towel. "I'm going to check on Gavin and then hit the shower. I need to get to the lawyers."

"What time tomorrow? For your Gigi's house?" Penny asked.

"Six?"

"Sure. Can you text me the address?"

What a difference a few minutes made. He'd gone from capturing her in his gaze to barely looking at her. "Sounds good."

As Jonah stalked off, East stepped closer. "You're not going on a date with him, are you?"

"What?" Jealousy? Or did he want to be exclusive? No, it had been one date. One kiss. She wasn't about to bring up that word, but she also didn't want him wondering about her interest. "No. I'm helping him with his grandmother's estate."

They walked over to the treadmill.

"I wondered what was up with you two." He strolled around to the front of the machine. "I don't really see the two of you together. Though I'm sure he'd like that."

Penny watched Jonah disappear into the locker room. "We're just friends."

East laughed. "When it comes to men and women, Penny, there's no such thing."

Jonah tapped his foot against the white marble floor of the glass elevator he rode. It had been a long work day that ended with his Chief Operating Officer resigning for no clear reason. And then he'd had to endure watching Penny with East ... hearing they'd kissed ... listening to them plan another date.

He checked his watch and groaned. Six twenty-seven. Not to mention he was nearly late for the meeting with Niles and Micah.

The elevator dinged open, and he hustled down the hall to the Law Offices of Niles Davis. Doris, Nile's secretary, met him at the door with a cookie and hug. "Go on. Niles is waiting with Micah, and they appear rather serious."

The boulder that had lodged in his stomach with the morning's first problem grew. He stepped down the hall and into Niles' deep blue office. A massive desk was flanked by a seating area on one side and overstuffed bookshelves on the other. Across the room, a picture window overlooked Michigan Avenue. Jonah didn't particularly care for the busyness of the Magnificent Mile, but Gigi had loved coming into the city. Somehow it seemed fitting that gray clouds created a backdrop for the buildings today. Nearly like the city was in mourning too.

Niles and Micah sat at the table as Jonah entered, inhaling the familiar scent of leather mixed with aged paper. Niles stood and offered Jonah a handshake.

Micah remained in his seat, not meeting his glance. The boulder doubled in size.

Niles motioned for Jonah to join them. "Need a glass of water?"

The Sahara had nothing on his mouth right now. "Sure."

Niles plucked a water bottle from the small fridge. Not quite six feet tall, his stocky frame still showed the muscles of a young man, though the silver around his temples spoke to his age.

After he handed Jonah his water, he settled across from them. "As you both know, Gigi made you the beneficiaries of her life insurance with the sole intent of fulfilling the buy/sell agreement in regards to All Waste."

Jonah nodded. Micah remained still.

"Upon receipt of the life insurance benefits, you both were to purchase fifty percent of the All Waste shares from Estelle's estate, effectively fulfilling the buy/sell agreement Estelle and William had put in place."

Another nod. Again, his cousin remained still.

"At that point, and after the estate was settled, you both had a verbal agreement to create a new buy/sell agreement allowing Jonah to purchase the shares from Micah, making you, Jonah, sole owner of All Waste."

Niles shifted to Micah. "Would you like to share with Jonah what you told me when you arrived today?"

Finally, Micah met his gaze. "I'm keeping my shares and going into business with you, cuz."

The boulder broke free and tumbled through his gut. "What?"

"I'm moving to Chicago after the wedding and running All Waste with you. Unless you need me here sooner."

Need him? Micah hadn't worked a day in the company. By his own admission didn't know the first thing about business—or care to.

"What about your residency?"

Micah shrugged. "Things change."

"Within the space of two weeks?"

"You can remain as CEO. I thought we could talk to the board about making me COO." His leg tapped a staccato beat on the rug. "I hear there's an opening."

Jonah gripped the arm of his chair. "You're why Thompson left?"

"Jeff's been talking retirement for years."

And just happened to finally take the plunge? Jonah wasn't buying it. "You know nothing about operating All Waste, Micah."

"I'm a quick study."

"No." It had taken *years* for Jonah to learn the ins and outs of this company. Years of experience coupled with school. Not once during that time did Micah show an ounce of interest or have anything positive to say about All Waste. Now he wanted to be COO?

Micah frowned. "I don't have to take the title right away. We can wait until everything is official with the shares."

Jonah shook his head. "No. Not just to the title, to all of it."

"You don't have a choice."

Niles caught Jonah's glance and shook his head. "You don't."

This could not be happening.

"I'm CEO. That gives me controlling power to make decisions regarding the company." He pointed to Micah. "Own your shares if you want, but you're not working there."

Micah gave a tight grin. "We can always have the board appoint a new CEO."

The board consisted of the two of them, Rachael, Aunt Sharon, and Walter Hamlin, an old family friend with several companies of his own. Walter was a skilled businessman, who also happened to have a soft spot for Micah. On this matter, he'd be the swing vote, and there was no telling which direction he'd swing.

Jonah nearly burst holding in his steam. "Fine. Come to work. But you'll start on the trucks and work each position up from there." Penny's words on gaining the employees respect returned. He'd never agreed more.

A sharp laugh poured from Micah. "If you think for one second I'm riding the trucks, you're wrong." He stood. "We've always gotten along, Jonah, and I'd like that to continue. You're in my wedding. We'll be working together. I don't want this to get ugly."

Neither did he.

But he wasn't willing to just let Micah come in and take everything he'd worked for.

He needed time to think.

Micah walked to the door. "I'm driving home tonight. I could have handled this on the phone but wanted to tell you in person. Plus I figured you'd have some questions for Niles." He left.

Jonah took a deep breath. "What are my options?"

Niles leaned back in his chair, clasping his hands over his chest. "Short of taking him to court, nothing. Unfortunately, your grandmother didn't do what I advised her, which was to make you sole beneficiary."

"She wanted to honor Grandpa. He always envisioned Micah and me working side by side, the two sons he never had."

"Well, he'd be happy right now, but he'd be the only one." Niles sat forward.

"You could push the board, but I'm not sure that would work out in your favor. You could try to contest the will, but there's no evidence of lack of capacity, fraud, or undue influence at the time Estelle signed this will. There are simply no grounds." He blew out a breath. "You're stuck with Micah until he grows tired of the company."

And it didn't sound like that would happen anytime soon. But why? What was pulling him away from his residency?

Jonah pushed back from the table.

"Find a way to fix this." He stormed from the office.

Chapter Fifteen

Tuesday evening, Jonah unlocked Gigi's door and held it open for Penelope. Her easy smile brought out his. He'd waited all day for tonight. "You find the place, okay?"

"I did." Her floral scent tickled his nose as she walked by.

She barely saw him as a friend, was falling for the wrong guy, and here he was; a goner.

Good thing he was a patient man.

Beside him, Penelope stared up through the two-story entry at the large wrought-iron chandelier overhead. "It's beautiful." She ran her hand up the staircase banister. "Craftsman style is my favorite."

Six inch wide, dark wood trim ran along both the floor and the ceiling. The windows were lined in the same fashion, and a full bank flagged the front room. Colorful light splayed across the entry, shining down from a stain glass window at the top of the stairs.

Penelope peered up at it. "Gorgeous."

He watched her. "Exactly what I was thinking."

She turned and caught him staring. A slight blush colored her cheeks. Jonah followed her up the stairs to the window where she caressed the glass. He stood close enough to again inhale her unique scent of flowers.

"Gigi had that window made for here. It's not exactly a traditional pattern for the style of the house." He touched the brown glass that formed the base of a large oak tree, brushing her shoulder in the process. "It represents her favorite verse."

He glided his fingers over the rippled surface.

Penelope stood still beside him, focusing on the window. "Which was?"

"Isaiah 61:3." Jonah dropped his hand but didn't step away. Her head tipped as she shifted her focus to him. This close, he could see the light green that rimmed the emerald pools of her irises. He'd never seen anything like it. He'd never seen anyone quite like her.

"That makes the window even more special."

Jonah followed her down the staircase, their footsteps echoing in the silent home. It was still hard to come here and not have this place full of life.

"This is a great space. You'll have no trouble selling it. Especially in this neighborhood."

"Wait until you see the kitchen." He nodded for Penelope to follow him.

Much like the Wilton house, the first floor was open from the entryway all the way back to a large cherry door that led into the kitchen. In the center of the massive room, two large square columns ran floor to ceiling, dividing the family room and dining room. Penny stopped, her eyes riveted to the dining table there.

"That's nearly as large as Allan Wilton's table."

Jonah smiled. "It is. This one is going to my aunt's house. I can't remember a time when it wasn't full. We weren't the largest family, but there was always room for one more at Gigi's house. She never met a stranger." He pushed open the swinging door and motioned her inside. "I've got to show you this."

Penelope brushed past him and froze. "These were all hers?"

Jonah walked over to the countertop full of teacups. "Every single one." He picked one up and held it out to her. "No matter how hard he tried, Gramps never got Gigi to drink a drop of coffee in her life. It was tea and tea only."

Penelope accepted the teacup. "This is Aynsley china." She scanned the counters. "Nearly every single piece, I'm betting."

Jonah shrugged. "I have no idea the importance of that. I did, however, know you'd be the one to tell me."

Over the next half-hour, Jonah reveled in watching Penelope in her element. She handled each saucer as if it was a newborn baby. Her eyes lit as she found a signature on a few of the cups, and she placed them in a different section. "Bailey." She'd whisper.

When she'd finished gently handling each one, her bright eyes focused on his. "I can't believe she has all of these." She picked up a deep-blue piece. "Some of them will sell on eBay for around thirty to forty dollars. But others"—she set the sapphire set down carefully and reached for a light-green set with white gardenias—"such as this one, could be worth quite a bit more."

Jonah slipped the cup from her fingers, their fingertips brushing together. "This was one of her favorites."

Penelope clasped the hand he'd touched and absently rubbed it. "Gardenias are my favorite too." She grabbed the matching saucer from the counter. "Maybe you'd rather keep this set? Good memories are priceless."

Her voice was a mere whisper and sadness suddenly clouded her eyes.

"Don't you have many good memories of your family?" He kept his voice soft.

"I do with my father," she finally answered.

"And your mother?" he pressed.

"Mom and I have never really gotten along."

"Why?"

Her finger touched her scar for a brief moment before she shook the emotions away. He was familiar with that action.

She handed him the saucer. "You and Rachael should go through these and pick out the ones you want. After that, I can help you catalogue them."

And it was back to all business.

"Before that, we need to settle on your fee."

Her back straightened. "I told you its free."

He set down the china and crossed his arms. "And I told you I'd pay."

"Guess we're at a standstill because I don't charge friends, and I'm not starting with you." She planted a hand on her hip. "So if you want to pay someone, you'll have to hire another company."

Their stare-down continued. Jonah stepped closer to her. "Your stubbornness isn't going to open the front doors of your shop. So stop thinking with your pride,"—he tapped the side of her head gently—"and start using this. I'm hiring someone either way, so why not let it be you?"

Her gaze flickered over him. *Come on, Penelope, let me help you here.* Her eyes narrowed slightly, and then she blinked. "How about a compromise?"

Intrigued, he tipped his head. "I'm listening."

"I give you a discount." She held up a hand to stop his argument. "I typically pay my workers a commission after a sale, but you worked one for free the other day. Consider the discount your pay."

Highly doubtful that pay would have amounted to anything near the discount she planned to give, but he'd work with it. With her ramrod spine and tight shoulders, if he pushed farther, she'd walk—and regret it later when her bottom line caught up with her steel backbone. "Okay."

She arched her brow. "That was easy."

"I don't always have to win, you know." Especially when his loss gained her more ground.

"Could have fooled me." She smirked as she passed him on her way to the living room. "What's your time frame?"

"We're in no hurry—especially since you're discounting your time. In that case, we come at the bottom of your to-do list."

She tapped her chin. "There's a lot of furniture, books, and knick-knacks in here." Then pointed to the ceiling. "What about upstairs?"

"Four bedrooms—one of them filled with trains—and above that is an attic." He cleared away any thought of working in the close bedroom quarters with her.

"Rach can help you out with the second floor while I'm at work during the day. I can tackle downstairs, and maybe together, we can go through the attic."

"That should work as long as Rachael is cleared to make decisions when you're not here."

"I'm only listed as executor so she won't have the legal headache. Whatever she wants is fine by me."

"You're a good big brother."

Wished he could have been even better. Still, her words soothed the edge of that ache. "Thanks."

"It's the truth, and you're welcome." She chased the words with a smile before focusing on her phone. "I have one more sale coming up two weekends from now that'll put me outside the city, but I could spare a few afternoons between now and then. Sorry I can't promise more, but after that, I'll be all yours."

"For you, I'd wait even longer. You're worth it."

And he wasn't simply referring to her work.

Penelope picked up her jacket from the couch, her back to him. "I appreciate your confidence." She struggled to get her arms in the sleeves.

Jonah grabbed the yellow fabric. "Here, let me."

Ever-so-slightly, she stilled before pushing her arms through. She buttoned up her jacket and flipped her hair out from under the collar. It brushed his nose, and once again, a sweet smell wafted to him. The desire to lean down, sweep the silky strands aside, and place a kiss on her nape nearly consumed him. Before he could, she turned. Her gaze centered on his collarbone, and slowly, she inched it up to meet his. His desire flamed into a deep need to kiss more than simply her neck.

Penelope cleared her throat and gave a quick shake of her head. Pink tinted her cheeks. "I should get going."

She was as unsettled as he was, and that was without the kiss.

He tipped his head. "I'll walk you out."

Even though he wanted her to stay.

Penny scurried down the sidewalk. What was going on with her? Whatever it was, she wasn't letting Jonah that close again. He was her friend, and only her friend. East had actually asked her on a second date. She couldn't mess that up.

"You don't have to follow me to my car," she tossed over her shoulder.

"I know." He easily kept pace with her. "But I'd like to."

Why had the only available parking spot been over a block away?

Jonah strolled along beside her, hands casually tucked in his pockets. "I appreciate you agreeing to help us out. Rach and I didn't even know where to start."

"It's really no problem."

Except she started to worry it might be. Working with Jonah. Seeing him more often—it might give him the wrong idea. She didn't want to lead him on like others had done to her. A groan lodged in her throat. How had this thing that wasn't even supposed to be a friendship turned into such a jumbled mess?

Silence settled around them, and neither seemed ready to break it. Her plan to keep it that way, however, was short-lived.

A sing-song princess theme trilled from her cell phone.

"Belle." Now the groan escaped. Penny dug out her phone, catching Jonah's lips twitching at the sugary tune. "I should change it." She answered the call. "Hey, Belle."

"I have the dates for dance lessons."

Penny started to sweat. "You're not going to let that drop, are you?"

"No." Belle heaved a sigh. "Do you have your calendar? I'm tired and have several more calls."

"That's easy. You can finish this one because I'm not taking dance lessons."

The open line buzzed with static. Then Belle's controlled voice. "Penny. Please take down the dates, and do this for me."

She sounded exhausted. And she had used *please*. "All right. Text them to me, and I'll do my best."

Jonah's phone rang.

"Where are you?" Suspicion laced Belle's voice.

"Walking to my car."

A muffled sound came over the phone, almost as if Belle was covering it with her hand. At the same time, Jonah answered his phone.

"Hey, Micah." He grinned at Penny. "As a matter of fact, she's right here. I'm walking her to her car."

Belle's shrill giggle nearly split Penny's eardrum. "You're with Jonah? Oh see, I knew that thing with East wouldn't last more than one date."

Penny clenched her phone so tightly she was surprised the screen didn't crack. "As a matter of fact, I have a date with him this Friday. A *second* date."

"Huh." Belle sounded truly stumped. Had to shake her world that East was interested in her big sister.

"We should double date the next time you're in town." Penny slapped a hand over her mouth. What craziness had just erupted from her lips?

"Or you could bring him here for the dance lessons." She was calling what she thought to be Penny's bluff. "I'll text those dates. FYI there's four, and they're all Saturday nights at Juliana's Dance Studio. You remember that place, right?"

How could she forget? Belle's picture was plastered all over its walls. Their hometown star.

"Saturdays? Coming home for that many weekends might not work." Penny noted Jonah was already off the phone. Men. Straight and to the point.

"Well, talk to Jonah. He's the one who suggested having the wedding party take lessons. I can't imagine he figured it would be on a weekday."

"Jonah—"

She turned to find him doing his best impression of innocence.

"I'll talk to you later, Belle." Penny hung up the phone and stared daggers into the man beside her.

He held up his hands. "In my defense, I gave her the names of local dance instructors. Apparently, that's too long of a drive for them to make each weekend."

"And you're surprised by that?" Her voice rose several notches. "Belle took lessons in Holland for years. She's scheduled them there."

"Oh." He had the good sense to look sheepish. "I'll pay the gas money."

"I'm not worried about the gas money," she bit out. "I just ..."

How did she even begin to explain she couldn't handle that much time around Mom and Belle? He adored his family—and she would too if she were him.

But she wasn't.

They came to a stop beside her car. "You don't want that much family time, right?"

How did he do that? Read her mind so completely.

She sighed. "You've met them. What do you think?"

"I think you're an amazing woman." He leaned his head down near hers. "And that I'm in this with you. I created the mess, and I'll fix it."

The space around them filled with his familiar scent, sandalwood and cinnamon. Like a hot fire on a frigid day, it comforted and enticed, but it was the promise in his icy eyes that beckoned her closer. Her breath hitched in her lungs. She hit the release button on her locks and jumped in her car.

"Penelope?"

"Sorry. It's been a long day. I've got to go." She shut her door and then rolled down the window. "I'll contact Rachael about meeting at your grandma's place." Then she sped off.

She needed to calm the beating of her erratic pulse. Try to understand why it leapt at his words, his nearness. Falling for Jonah made no sense. East was who she wanted. The man none of them thought she'd ever have, and now she did.

That had to be it! Worried it wouldn't work with East, she was sabotaging things before they fully began. And that needed to stop.

Which meant space and time away from Jonah Black.

Chapter Sixteen

The morning sun sparkled over Lake Michigan as Penny jogged the trail along Lake Shore Drive with Lacey. She was actually enjoying her new habit of exercise. Especially the mornings she and Lacey decided to run. The bright sunshine glinting off the lake, the fresh breeze, and the other joggers out so early energized her. Having lost nearly six pounds since starting with East three weeks ago didn't hurt either.

"Glad you could come this morning," Lacey huffed beside her. "I hardly saw you at all this weekend."

"Sorry." She dodged a lady pushing a stroller. "The sale was crazy, but I got rid of everything the Brown family was hoping would go. At a great profit too."

"Hopefully, that means you'll get a big commission. Put you closer to opening your own shop."

Penelope nodded. It had been a crazy two weeks and an even crazier weekend hosting a two-day estate sale on the outskirts of town. But the check she had in her purse to deposit today more than made up for it. "I think I can start seriously scouting places by summer's end."

"Good for you, Pen."

They jogged around a curve, and Lacey slowed. "Okay, gotta stop." One hand held her side. "Shouldn't have had breakfast before we started."

Penny walked beside her. "I was ready to walk anyway. I still can't go as far as you."

She was up to almost three miles, but even that took a bit of pushing. Lacey, however, annually ran the Chicago Marathon.

Lacey limped over to a patch of grass. "I'm gonna stretch this cramp out." She bent sideways at the waist, stretching her left arm over her head. "I forgot to tell you; Jonah stopped by to see you. He was walking that giant dog with his nephew."

Penny took a sip from her water. "When?"

"When you were out with East on Thursday night."

"And you're just now telling me?"

Lacey bent the other way. "Like I said, I didn't see you all weekend."

"You could have left me a note. Texted. Called."

"Would you have called him? Because you haven't returned any of his phone calls in the past two weeks—and those messages I *did* give you."

"I've been busy."

Straightening, Lacey looked directly at her. "Right. And yet you had time to go out with East."

The briny scent of the lake rolled toward them. "I don't want to give Jonah the wrong idea."

"Or maybe you're worried about giving yourself the wrong idea?"

"I'm with East."

"Three dates count as 'with'?"

"We had lunch too."

"Which he had you pay for." Lacey hopped up and down, jiggling her arms. "Has he kissed you again?"

The wind cooled down her warmed skin. East was a great kisser. In fact, she was discovering how much she loved that sport too. "Yes, but we're taking it slow."

Lacey stopped and raised one brow. "And you're sure this an exclusive relationship?"

"Where did that come from?"

"No place." She nodded down the trail, and they started walking. "Just be careful, okay?"

"I am." Penny went from a walk to a slow jog, needing to take the edge off her nerves. "And no, we haven't actually said we're exclusive, so he's free to date others if he wants."

The words left her mouth with ease yet filled her stomach with dread. Was that what East was doing? She'd allowed herself to think he was only going out with her, but she'd never asked because she didn't want to pressure him.

Lacey nudged her. "So you could date Jonah then if you wanted?"

"Jonah is just a friend."

"I typically don't work so hard to avoid my friends."

"Lace," Penny growled.

"Fine." Her hands shot up. "It's your love life; do what you want. But if I were you and had two guys chasing me, I'd take advantage of it. Just think what that would do to your mom and Belle."

"Oh, East is doing that all by himself."

Penny knocked on the massive oak door at Gigi's house, shaking out the sore muscles in her legs as she waited for Rachael to answer. They'd spent a few afternoons here in the past two weeks, but now that her schedule had cleared some, this would become her focus.

Familiar barking sounded above the tap of footsteps, and Penny braced herself just as the door opened. Clooney vaulted at her. Rachael lost her grip on the dog's collar, and Clooney planted her two big front paws on Penny's chest.

"Clooney." Rachael regained her hold and tugged. "Get down."

Clooney's paws remained where they were. Penny grabbed hold of them and pushed the dog off. "Clooney, you have awful manners. Now sit."

Clooney sat.

Rachael shook her head. "I think I'm going to send her home with you. You're the only one she listens to."

Penny bent down into Clooney's face. "That's because she knows I'd just as soon leave her on the curbside than put up with her." She looked up as Rachael shut the door. "Not that I would, of course."

"Yeah, well, I'm sorely tempted."

"Right. This dog has you and Gavin wrapped around her paws."

A half-sigh, half-laugh. "I know. Which is why she's always here with me rather than home alone."

Penny followed Rachael through the family room. "Sorry I'm a few minutes late. I went for a morning run with Lacey."

Rachael waved her off. "It's not me who has the hang-up about being on time. That's Jonah." She picked up a key from the dining room table. "I finally got a key made for you, so you can come and go as needed."

"Thanks." Penny slipped it into her purse.

"How did your sale go last weekend?"

"Great. And now I'm completely yours." She shed her jacket and placed it on a chair. "How's it going with the buttons?" Gigi had the most expansive button collection Penny had ever seen. Which would be a fantastic draw for the sale because button collecting was huge.

"I've sorted through the ones I want and taken them home. I know I can't keep them all"—Rachael touched a gold button lovingly—"but I'm still sad to see them go."

"Letting go makes things so final."

Rachael brushed a tear aside. "Yep. And it never gets any easier."

Penny stood caught between the moment of acknowledging or ignoring Rachael's comment. Hints of pain came through at different times, and though they'd spent several afternoons here together, Penny still wasn't sure if she could ask about it.

"Enough sadness," Rachael said before Penny could make up her mind, "let's get upstairs and started on those trains. Jonah's nearly finished with this level."

Looked like it. "He certainly has been busy."

On the stairs, Penny's eyes were drawn again to the beautiful oak tree that greeted them. An odd feeling curled around her heart as she remembered Jonah standing behind her, his outstretched hand warming her shoulder as he smoothed his palm across the stained glass.

"He's been here nearly every night. Comes straight over after working out with Gavin—which, by the way, I keep meaning to ask you. Are you still going to the gym? Gavin says he hasn't seen you in weeks."

"I am. Just had to change my scheduled time a little." To avoid running into them.

"I figured you were." Rachael opened the first door of the upstairs hallway. "You look great. Not that you didn't before."

"There was room for improvement. At least that's what my mom and sister told me." Penny entered the train room. A miniature city rose from the table with tracks running in every direction, and nearly a hundred trains lined the perimeter of the room. "I still cannot believe how many trains your grandfather collected."

Rachael laughed. "He didn't hunt, didn't enjoy sports. This was his thing."

"And Gavin took the ones he wants?"

"He did."

"All right, then. Let's get to work." Penny unzipped her iPad, and they spent the next three hours cataloguing and pricing. When they were down to only the pieces that made up the Norman Rockwell looking town, she stood. "Tea time?"

"Most definitely." Rachael scooted around a box. "Jonah restocked the licorice flavor you like. Oh, and the M&Ms."

Even when she was basically ignoring him, he still treated her kindly.

"I'll put the kettle on for you and coffee for me. You sit for a bit." Rachael left Penny standing in the living room.

Across from the couch, a set of built-in shelves held several frames full of family pictures. Rather than sit, Penny walked over to study them as she did nearly every time she came here. Clooney followed on her heels.

There was really only one that continued to capture her attention. One she hadn't been free to dissect the first time she saw it at Rachael's house, but the image had remained with her—along with the questions it produced. But here she'd had the chance to study it several times. Penny peeked at the kitchen door before picking up the frame. She ran her fingertip along the faces, stopping at

Jonah.

His blue plaid shirt was rolled up, giving a perfect view of tanned, muscular forearms. It stretched against him in a way that promised a solid chest underneath and tucked in at his waist that didn't have an extra ounce on it. His jaw was angular, he held the same killer smile, and had a full head of jet black hair textured along the sides and spiked in front.

The kitchen door swished open. "I cut you a slice of carrot cake too—"

Penny shoved the picture back onto the shelf.

After a pause, Rachael walked over. "I keep waiting for you to ask, but you haven't."

"Ask what?" She tried for innocence in her voice, but she wasn't fooling anyone.

"One of the many questions that picture brings up."

Warmth rose in her cheeks. "You don't have to share."

"I want to." Rachael reached out and picked up the picture. "Like I said that night at dinner, this was taken shortly before Chris and Brianna died." She ran her finger over their faces. "Brianna was a hoot, always laughing with the sweetest little giggle. I can still hear it. No one could make her laugh like Gavin. She was constantly on his heels, but still, she was a daddy's girl." With a deep breath, Rachael set the frame back down. "We lost them both in a car accident when she was almost three."

What did you say to someone who had lost so much?

"Gavin was nine." She crossed her arms over her stomach.

"I can't imagine."

Rachael's eyes leveled on hers. "I hope you never have to. But there's more to my story. A part I really want you to know."

Penny nodded her on. "I'd love to hear it."

She motioned to the couch where they both sat. "Two years after Chris and Brianna passed away, I took Gavin for his well-child check-up. He was turning eleven, and he'd kept complaining of headaches and how things were blurry. His father was severely nearsighted, so I figured Gavin might need glasses. We found out, instead, that he had a brain tumor."

Penny couldn't stop her gasp. "Oh, Rachael."

But Rachael smiled, yet again. "Every scripture you read is true, Penelope. I can't—" she faltered. "I can't say I don't still hurt at times, so badly it takes my breath away. But I can promise you that."

"You don't have to tell me all this." Uncertainty stole her earlier curiosity.

"No. I think I do." Rachael clasped her hands. "Gavin had to go through a lot. Chemo and radiation, two rounds of each. When his brain started to swell due to the position of the tumor, they needed to put him on steroids. So, not only did he lose all his hair, but he put on weight. I think that was the hardest for him."

Penny's gaze tracked back to the family picture as she contrasted the Jonah there to today's, accepting the conclusion her heart already discovered. Had suspected more each time she studied that photo. Even without knowing the motivation, she'd somehow known what he'd done. "Jonah went through it with him, didn't he?"

Rachael nodded. "Didn't even hesitate. They shaved their heads together, and Jonah went on a shake-fast with him when Gavin couldn't hold anything else down. Then when they had to put him on steroids, Jonah stopped working out and started putting on weight with him. He told him they'd put it on together and lose it together."

The man was crazy.

Crazy, kind, and incredibly sweet.

Penny shook her head.

"Gavin's still weak, but the tumor is gone. It's a miracle, really. And now that he's off the steroid medicine, he should start to lose the weight. The big thing we're waiting on is for his hair to start growing back. The doctor says that may take several months, though, due to the radiation."

"And Jonah's determined to stay bald as long as Gavin is?" He had a huge heart.

"Yes." Rachael stood. "I'm going to go check on our snack and bring it out here. Let you digest everything I just told you, and give me a moment to take a deep breath. I love talking about Chris and my little girl, even Gavin's healing, but it takes me a sec to pack all the emotions away again."

"Take all the time you need." Penny stayed on the couch until Rachael had disappeared into the kitchen, then rose and headed straight for the bookshelves. She honed in on the family picture, and her fingertips touched it just as her cell phone sounded a text received. She glanced at the screen.

East.

She smiled and slid a finger across the screen. Her smile dropped.

Have to cancel tonight. Keep Friday open. Will call later. Signed you up for a spin class.

Penny clutched her phone. East had canceled on her and asked for a date all in one text? Her gaze bounced between her phone and the picture.

If this was her dream life, maybe it was time to wake up.

Chapter Seventeen

Jonah pushed open the door to Emerge Fitness, the cool air a welcome change from the unseasonably hot night. Today had more than lived up to its reputation as a Monday. One of his trucks had a fender-bender with a little old lady; Micah was moving full speed ahead with his plans, and Jonah had to miss his workout with Gavin.

Truth be told, he'd have happily missed his own too—until he'd spoken with Rachael. Penelope was taking a spin class at the gym tonight, and as much as he wanted to tell himself it was sheer willpower that made him still show up, he knew it had more to do with the possibility of finally reconnecting with a certain brunette.

And the hope that maybe, just maybe, his day was about to turn around.

About twenty people filled the spin room, but his focus immediately landed on dark brown hair pulled back in a ponytail, orange T-shirt, and navy shorts. He walked over, thankful the bike to her left was still open.

"This seat taken?"

Penelope startled then quickly recovered. "I seem to recall answering that question on the train to no avail."

He dropped his water bottle into the holder. "Not that you answered it honestly."

"It was taken."

"By what? Your computer?"

She laughed. "Details." Rock music began to play at the front of the room, and people settled onto their bikes to warm-up. She patted the one beside her. "This time it's open, though."

He dropped his towel over the bars and sat.

Penny eyed him. "I'm surprised to see you here tonight. From what Rachael said, you weren't having the best of days."

"I wasn't." He adjusted the tension on his bike. "Gave me plenty of stress that needed to be worked out." Micah was at the top of that list. "Don't ever go into business with family."

"No problem there." The room continued to fill. "Though from the snippets

I've heard, it doesn't sound like you have an option."

"Not one that I've found yet."

"Wish I had more influence with my sister to try and help." It was sweet that she offered. "Have you tried offering him a larger buyout?"

"I don't have the extra capital right now." They'd just purchased all the new trucks for recycling and expanded their line to new suburbs. It would take time for that move to pay off.

"I'm sorry, Jonah. I can't imagine being forced to share my business, especially with someone who has no experience."

Neither could he. "I appreciate that." Appreciated her listening ear. There wasn't anything she could do, but she understood on levels others didn't.

The instructor walked to the front of the class and began stretching. Penelope bent over her bike, her handlebars too high and her seat too low. Strange position. Then he noticed her aqua and yellow running shoes. "Where are your bike shoes?"

"East didn't say I'd need any."

"This is your first class?"

"Yeah. He had to leave early tonight, so he signed me up for this class. Said it's even better than the treadmill."

"Seriously?" Another reason not to like the guy. "Didn't you see the sign on the door?"

"What sign?"

He pointed behind him to black letters on white paper that spelled out 'Advanced'. "The sign that says this isn't the beginner's class."

Her lips tightened into a thin line, and her shoulders squared. "I'm sure I'll be fine. I've been riding a bike since I was four."

He remembered his first class—and that had been at the beginner's level. "How about you and I go for a run instead?"

She began to pedal. "I can do this."

And if she stayed in that position, more than just her toes would be numb when this was over. He got off his bike. "Okay." He walked up beside her. "Then we need to get you correctly seated." The few adjustments were quick. "Hop on and lean forward on the bars."

She did. He walked around her, stopping when he reached the front. "Looks good."

She gave a half-smile. "Thanks."

Jonah pointed to her tension knob. "Start low on that knob. When we're approaching a hill, he'll call out a number of turns. You don't have to do them all, only what you're comfortable with. And don't worry about standing to pedal up the hills—even if he calls for it. Just because he says it, doesn't mean you have to follow it. Keep your own pace."

Their instructor took his bike. "Let's go."

Halfway through the class, it was evident they were never going to crest the hill. The guy was living up to his killer reputation. "Out of the saddle. Give it another quarter turn."

Jonah watched Penelope. Sweat ran rivers down her red face. She'd kept up with every command the instructor gave. Pride mixed with worry in him even as she stood, reached down, and twisted her knob. If she swayed once, he'd be off his bike.

Instead, Penelope knocked him out with her smile. "I love this!"

Most likely she'd feel differently tonight, but right now she beamed. That grin, her legs pumping away, and her cheeks full of color—as angry as he was at East for signing her up cold for this class, he owed the man a thank-you.

A half-hour later, Jonah dismounted, slightly sore and very sweaty.

Penelope swiped a towel over her face and guzzled her water. "That was amazing."

"Come on." He tugged gently on her arm. "You need to get off that bike and walk."

She swung a leg over her seat and attempted to stand but swayed instead. He steadied her. "Whoa there."

"Sorry. I didn't realize how wobbly my legs would be."

"You just spent an hour climbing Mount Everest. That was one of the toughest classes I've done."

She finished off her water. "It was a lot harder than I expected." Her eyes shone. "But I did it."

"And you should be proud. No one starts with Adam as an instructor. I'm surprised East signed you up with him."

She shrugged. "He likes me to push my boundaries."

His mind went places he didn't like. "I hope that's only with your exercise routine."

If possible, her red cheeks deepened in color. "Sounding like my father again."

"More like a concerned friend."

They headed for the showers, Penelope's gait slow and with a slight limp. "There's nothing to be concerned about."

Unfortunately, he didn't agree.

"Did you walk here tonight?"

She stopped at the entrance to the ladies' locker room. "I did, and as much as I loved that class, it's going to make for a long walk home."

"Let me drive you."

Her head tipped. "Want to grab a coffee too?"

Surprise lit through him and nearly stole his tongue. "Sounds great."

And his day finally turned around.

Showered and ready, Penny exited the locker room still wondering how that offer had escaped her lips. Maybe it was because East had canceled their date. Or maybe because of everything she'd learned today about Jonah. Whatever the reason, she wasn't digging further. It was enough to finally accept the realization that she enjoyed his company. Even sweating next to him in spin class. And not one drop seemed to make a difference to Jonah.

She stepped into the warm evening, locking eyes with him as he leaned against the brick out front. He'd changed into a black polo, khaki cargos, and leather flip-flops. A shadow of black stubble traveled from his chin along his strong jaw and up to where his sideburns would be—if he let his hair grow back.

She squinted against the sun and sudden warmth in her chest.

Jonah straightened. "You look great."

"Um … thanks." Her hand instinctively touched her scar. In a rush, she hadn't covered it after her shower—something she rarely forgot. That very mark was the reason she hadn't remained Mom's belle. Without it covered, how could anyone pay her an honest compliment?

She followed him to his car where he unlocked her door and held it open, his gaze snagging hers again. "Our scars are a part of us, Penelope. Being vulnerable enough to show them only makes you more beautiful." He tucked her inside, then he walked around and slid into the driver's seat. "Leitzia's?" Asked like he hadn't just attempted to shred years of personal beliefs with two small sentences.

Swallowing, she nodded. "Sure."

Silence settled for a few minutes before he peered her way. "How are your legs feeling?"

"A little sore."

"You should take some ibuprofen. You'll be even more sore tomorrow." He turned left. "I've got to say, though, you kept up better than any other first-timer I've seen."

"Once I commit to something, I'm all in."

He cast her a look. "Good to know."

She watched him as he drove. He'd lost weight too. And spent time in the early summer sun. The dark polo shirt showed off the muscles in his arms. The only definable muscles on his current body. She squinted her eyes and tried to reconcile him with the man in the photograph she'd studied today.

He turned. Caught her staring and smiled. Suddenly, she didn't need to squint anymore because the man from the picture came alive before her. Her heart tripped.

"A spot right out front, like it was meant to be."

He parked, and Penny jumped out, ready for a little space to reset whatever he was doing to her emotions. Jonah beat her to the door, opening it, then following her to the counter. They ordered and found a seat just as her cell phone rang. The screen showed East's name. She tapped the option to send it to voicemail and placed it on the table.

Settling across from her, Jonah pushed her scone toward her. "I don't mind if you answer."

"It was East." She broke off a corner of the yummy treat. "I can wait to speak with him." It felt too awkward to do otherwise in front of Jonah. Especially tonight.

He waited for her to swallow before lobbing a question. "Do you really like him?"

"I think so."

He sipped his coffee and grimaced.

"Too hot?"

"Yeah." Jonah took off the lid. "So, you think you do, or you do?"

"No. I do." She hesitated. "But he canceled on me tonight."

Jonah took another sip. "Good."

The words came out on a low breath, and Penny leaned forward. "What?"

He pointed to his cup. "My coffee. It's cooler."

"Glad to hear it." Though she highly suspected that wasn't what he referenced. She sipped her own tea, then, "I'm glad I ran into you tonight, Jonah, because I wanted to apologize for not returning your phone calls. Although I only found out today that you'd stopped by last week, too. I'm sorry."

He studied her for one long moment. "Apology accepted." He plunked down his cup. "So you worked on the train room today?"

She held up her hand. "Wait. You're not upset that I've pretty much ignored you for the past two weeks?"

"Did you mean that apology?"

"Yes."

"Then no, I'm not upset." He leaned back in his chair. "So you got them all priced?"

She tugged her hands through her hair. "Just like that?"

"Are we talking trains or forgiveness now?"

Penny eyeballed him.

He chuckled. "Yes, Penelope, I forgive you just like that. Now tell me about the trains."

She'd never met anyone who forgave so easily. Such a foreign concept, but she liked it. She sipped her tea. "I think you'll have a lot of collectors interested in them. Your gramps kept them in impeccable condition—he even still has some of the boxes. We got all of them priced, then worked a little more on buttons." Penny paused. "You know, what you're doing for your nephew is amazing."

"Rach told me she'd said something." Jonah shrugged. "But she makes it sound a lot more selfless than it is. What I did was as much for me as it was for him."

Penny doubted that. "How so?"

"I'm not a doctor, and I couldn't take the treatments for him. I felt helpless and this"—he ran a hand from his bald head down to his thick middle—"was something tangible I could do."

"Not everyone would do what you've done. Shave their head, maybe. But put on the weight too? So I disagree. That's an incredibly selfless thing."

"That's love." His forearms rested on the table, and he leaned on them, his steel blue eyes holding her in their strong grip. He didn't move. Didn't blink.

What it must be like to be loved by him.

She shook her head.

A slow smile slid across his face. "What thought are you trying to get rid of now?"

Her cell phone rang, saving her from an answer. Thankfully. Because with that look on his face, the lie on her tongue would never have passed for the truth.

For once, she was happy to take her sister's call.

"Hey, Belle."

"Could you come home on Friday instead of Saturday? We're going shoe shopping for the bridesmaids' dresses because I want you girls in your heels for dance lessons."

"Sorry. I have plans that night." At least she hoped that's why East called.

"What sort of plans?"

"A date." She savored the words.

Jonah sat back in his chair.

"Don't tell me it's with East."

"Actually, it is." And those words tasted even sweeter.

Silence. "Then bring him like we talked about," Belle challenged.

"No, my offer was to double date next time you're here. It's way too soon for me to invite him home." Wasn't it?

Across from her, Jonah's eyebrows lifted.

"It's probably better that you don't, anyway. You want my advice?" She didn't wait for an answer. "Cancel on him, and stop saying yes all the time. If you're always available, he'll lose interest."

Belle's comment cut deep—especially since they echoed her fears. It would only be a matter of time before East woke up and realized he was dating an overweight, mousy-haired, scar-faced woman. Maybe that was why he'd canceled tonight.

"I'll think about it." Probably too much.

"As long as your decision involves you here Friday night. We're going to dinner first so be home by six."

Belle hung up. Penny dropped her phone onto the table and pushed her scone away.

"Not hungry anymore?" Jonah's arms crossed over his chest, and he watched her closely.

"Talking to my sister is the best diet around. I always lose my appetite."

"She expects you to bring East home with you for the weekend?"

"No. What she expects is for the world to be at her beck and call." It was how Mom had trained her.

"If you have plans, don't go. Speaking from personal experience, the word "no" is in your vocabulary." His lips twitched.

Yes, well, she could be funny too. "I'll try that with Belle if you try it with Micah."

"I don't currently have that option." He leaned back and pointed at her. "You do."

"True. But with Belle, it's much easier to say yes."

Concerned eyes snared her. "That's a dangerous place to be, Penelope. Saying yes to a person when you should say no."

His focus didn't relent. He didn't even blink.

So she did. "You sound like Belle." Only while their words held similarity, she had no doubt Jonah's intent was the direct opposite of Belle's. "Can I ask you a question, as a guy?"

"You're a girl, but go ahead."

"Ha ha." She added an eye roll, but his ability to layer in the light with the serious made talking with him so easy instead of awkward. "Does that hold true for a relationship? If a woman says yes all the time, is always available, would you lose interest?"

His smile dropped. "What kind of availability are we talking about here?"

Warmth infused her cheeks. "Dates. Being available for dates."

"Belle advising you to play hard-to-get?"

Penny nodded.

Jonah sat for a moment. "I'm not East, but from where I sit, relationships aren't about playing games. So if you like him, say what you mean, and be yourself. That's more than enough." He stood up and offered her his hand. "And if East doesn't think so, then he's the one missing out."

"Thanks for the advice." She placed her hand in his and allowed him to tug her to her feet. Peering up at his bald head, she again took in the rough new whiskers on his face. Her free hand came up and rubbed his cheek. "I like the new look. You should definitely keep it."

The blue in his eyes darkened, and she caught her breath. Inhaled sandalwood and cinnamon.

His hand covered hers, his fingers brushing over the back of it, his skin rough, his touch soft. And for a moment, she froze. Touching him had seemed as natural as their easy banter, a simple extension of it, but now … she tugged herself free. Now *she'd* made things awkward. "I can walk home from here." Alone. Because she agreed with his advice. She refused to play games. Especially when it felt like they'd both lose.

With a fast wave, she hustled out the door as her phone rang a second time. East.

This time she slid her finger across the screen. "Hey, there."

"I was hoping you'd answer if I kept calling." His voice was low. "Sorry about canceling, but my dad was rushed to the hospital."

Relief at his reason flooded through her, quickly followed by worry for his father. "Oh, East. How is he?" She stopped walking.

"He'll be okay. I think he'll even be released tonight. So, can I make it up to you Friday night?"

Jonah's intense gaze from earlier swirled together with the disbelief in Belle's voice, the strange image taking hold of her brain. "Actually, I have to go home this weekend for dance lessons." She hesitated. "You wouldn't, by any chance, want to come with me, would you?"

"Spend the weekend with you?"

Putting it that way made it sound … "I'd get you a hotel room."

"Of course you would." Light laughter coated his words. "I'd love to come home with you, Penny."

She smiled. "Great. I can pick you up Friday afternoon. As long as that works with your schedule."

"It does. I'll see you then."

Her phone went silent, and she slipped it into her purse. East was coming home with her. Along with his six-pack abs, firm muscles, and perfect smile. She spun.

And came to an abrupt halt.

Jonah stood behind her with her gym bag. "You left this in my car."

Maybe he hadn't overheard her phone conversation. She accepted her bag. "Thanks."

He pushed his hands into his pockets. "So you took my advice?"

"Your advice?"

"Decided not to play hard to get."

So much for hoping he hadn't overheard her.

Penny hitched her bag over her shoulder. "I didn't really follow anyone's advice. I was talking to East, and somehow we leapt from him asking me out on a date Friday night to my inviting him home for the weekend."

"Quite the leap."

The words were low and to the side.

"What?" Penny stepped forward.

"I said that's quite a Jeep." He nodded to one parked along the curb.

"You did not." She took another step. "You do that all the time. How 'bout you take your own advice? If you've got something to say, say it."

He met her step and stayed silent. She held his stare. Jonah rubbed a hand over his shadowed head. "Fine. I said it's quite a leap, going from a Friday night date to a weekend together."

"It's not a weekend together." She bracketed her words with finger quotes. "Penelope."

"It's not. He's staying at a hotel."

"It doesn't matter where he's staying. All East heard was you invited him away for the weekend. That implies things."

Penny crossed her arms. "Really? Would it have *implied* things to you if I'd invited you instead?"

"I'm not East."

"No. You're not."

Jonah flinched, and her stomach tightened.

"Well,"—he turned on his heel—"as long as we have that settled, I'll head home."

Penny stood staring at his retreating back. He hadn't taken five steps before she stopped him. "Jonah. Wait."

He paused and turned slowly. "What?"

She came near and saw the hurt on his face he tried to cover. "My words came out wrong."

"No. They were correct. I'm not East." He leaned closer. "I look nothing like him, and I act nothing like him, but I'm still a man, and I can think like him."

Penny's breath stilled.

Jonah's gaze stole over her face. "Do you have any idea what your invitation says to him?"

"East isn't like that. He knows where I stand."

"He does as long as you don't move that line." Jonah shook his head. "Which is exactly what you just did."

Said yes when you should have said no. The words were there even though neither said them.

"I think you're wrong."

Jonah studied her for a moment. "Let's hope I am."

He turned and stalked to his car, once again trying to tear apart her beliefs with his truth. Except this time it wasn't as palatable to swallow.

Chapter Eighteen

Penny dropped a pack of Dentyne onto the counter of Walgreens. Last night's conversation with Jonah had replayed in her mind all night long. Lacey easily pulled it from her over breakfast this morning, and rather than standing on her side, she'd taken Jonah's.

Maybe she was naïve to think East wouldn't misinterpret her invitation. And to believe she and Jonah could maintain a friendship. This whole men and women as friends thing was harder than she thought. Good thing she was determined. She'd need every ounce to ensure both relationships worked.

After paying for the gum, she headed over to Gigi's house, letting herself in with the key Rachael had given her. Today she'd take some pictures of the Aynsley china and keep working on the button collection. She'd spent yesterday researching a few of the buttons to know what they were worth and hoped Jonah and Rachael would be pleasantly surprised.

In the kitchen, beside the huge bowl of peanut M & M's Jonah had left earlier in the week, she set out her tiny peace-offering for when he'd arrive later. Finding a sticky note, she scrawled his name with a smiley face and left it beside the gum.

See. This friendship thing would totally work.

Snagging a handful of M & M's, Penny started arranging the teacups. Within an hour, the front door opened, and a fur-ball appeared in the kitchen. "Hey, Clooney." Penny patted the dog's head. "Good morning," she greeted Rachael who joined them.

Rachael held a cardboard carrier with two cups. "I brought you a tea."

Penny reached for it. "I was just going to brew a cup, so thank you." She nodded toward the counters. "China's nearly priced."

Rachael ran her hands over several pieces. "And these are the ones you think will sell better online?"

"Yes. They're worth more money, and we'll hit a wider base of collectors who are willing to pay for them."

"Sounds good." She called Clooney. "We're going to head to the attic and keep going through boxes."

Something inside twisted. "I thought Jonah was going to help us with the attic."

"He's pretty slammed at work right now, especially since he's got to be in Holland this weekend." Rachael sipped her own drink. "You're heading there too, I hear."

If Jonah had spoken with her, how much had she really heard? "I am." Penny trailed a finger along the plastic lid of her cup. "I invited East."

"I heard that too."

So Jonah had told her. She wasn't sure how that made her feel.

Rachael started up the steps. "I'm going to get started. You want to have lunch later?"

"Sure." Penny shuffled into the dining room, the words between her and Jonah last night suddenly alive in the air. She shoved open a window and went to work organizing buttons by color and size, the monotonous task calming her.

Several hours later, Rachael clomped down the steps. "Getting hungry?"

"Just about. I'd like to finish this section before I break for lunch."

"How about I go grab us a couple of salads?"

Penny rubbed a milk-green button between her fingers. "Sounds good."

By the time she was sliding the last group of buttons into a tote, Rachael returned and set a white plastic bag on the table. Penny grabbed them water then returned to the table where Rachael had their salads set out. They said a quick prayer and dug in.

"The place is shaping up." Rachael speared a tomato. "Think we'll be ready in time?"

"Definitely." They were actually ahead of schedule. "All the work you, Gavin, and Jonah are doing has helped."

"You're practically donating your time. We figured the least we could do was pitch in." She sipped her water. "I wish you'd let us pay your full fee, though. I know it would put you closer to your goal."

"It's okay. There's nothing out there that's a fit right now anyway." She'd been scouring online sites. "So even if I had every penny, I'd be waiting. I want to make sure it's right and not rush things."

Rachael's upper lip tipped slightly. Oh, did she resemble her brother.

"What?" Penny asked.

"You know what you said could be used to draw a strong parallel to another area of life, right?"

Penny recounted her words, the parallel suddenly in neon. "Oh. Right." She tucked one foot under her and reclined in her chair.

"Why do you like East?"

The question seemed harder than it should be.

"Well, he's funny, kind, a little adventurous." A lot handsome.

And he looked at her. Called her beautiful.

Rachael seemed to hear those answers even though they remained locked in Penny's mind. "Does he share your beliefs?"

"He respects them."

The chair squeaked as Rachael leaned in. "Can I share something?"

Penny nodded. "Of course."

"Chris wasn't Gavin's dad."

Not at all what she'd expected. Penny stilled but said nothing.

"I was sixteen when I had him."

Penny quickly did the math. Rachael was only twenty-nine. That was a lot of life in not quite thirty years. "I had no idea."

Rachael smiled. "It's not a fact I advertise. I don't hide it, though, either." She folded her hands on the table. "As far as Gavin is concerned, Chris was his father. His biological dad left the minute the extra line showed up on my pregnancy test. Gavin never knew him."

"Does Gavin know ..."

"That Chris wasn't his biological dad? Yes. But it's never mattered to him."

"So why tell me this?"

"Because I see myself in you." Rachael's focus strayed past Penny for a moment, taking a deep breath before connecting their gazes again. "Not many guys paid attention to me in high school. I didn't exactly blossom early if you catch my drift. Girls were quick to tell me how I didn't measure up, and all I wanted was one person to notice me ... tell me I was beautiful." She shoved a lock of hair behind her ear. "I wanted to prove to those girls that I was as good as them. Prove to myself that I was good enough."

"Teens can be mean."

"People can be mean." Rachael sat forward.

She didn't say Belle or Mom, but Penny heard the words anyway.

Rachael continued, "But you know what people say has no bearing on who we actually are, right?"

"I do."

Across from her, Rachael lifted her brow. "Well, that's good because I didn't, and all it took was one boy saying the right thing, and I wound up pregnant." She tapped her empty ring finger. "Didn't matter that I wore a pretty little silver 'love waits' ring, because it didn't speak louder than that boy's voice. Not when I'd made his truth my truth."

Conviction rang in her words, but it was placed there by Penny's own heart.

She backed away from it. "I appreciate what you're saying, Rachael, but I'm not a sixteen-year-old girl. I know what I'm doing."

"I hope so because I've been there. Trying so hard to find yourself in a man that you end up losing yourself in the process."

"That's not what I'm doing." Penny pushed the rest of her salad away, no longer hungry. Rachael's words were filling enough.

The next night, Penny pinned her last curl in place just as her doorbell rang. Her stomach flip-flopped. East had called earlier today. He had an evening cancelation so he'd asked to squeeze in a late night date. The past two days had shoved hesitation into what should have been an easy yes response. But she owed it to herself to pursue this relationship. To prove that a man like East would pursue *her*. So she'd donned her black wrap dress, tamed her hair, and perfected her makeup.

The doorbell rang again as she hustled down the hall, snagging on her turquoise flats. She managed to open the door before the third ring.

"I was starting to worry you weren't home." East stood on her front step, every blond hair in place. His dark green shirt pulled against his chest, and a pair of perfectly worn jeans hung off his hips while the full wattage of his smile aimed directly at her.

She returned it. "Spin class got out late. It put me behind. Sorry."

"Don't apologize. You look great." His eyes traveled along the scooped neckline of her dress, past her waist, to her bare legs and back up again.

Penny turned to grab her purse off the small table by her door before he caught the blush on her cheeks. She'd known this dress showed off her new curves.

"You hungry?" East moved back as she stepped out and turned to lock the door.

"Starved."

His lips brushed the back of her neck. "So am I."

Penny swiveled, and he winked. "For dinner, of course."

He grabbed her hand on the way to his car, his thumb stroking her wrist. They reached his silver Mazda Miata, and he let go, rounded the car, and slipped into the driver's side. Penny slid into the passenger's seat.

East glanced at her as he pulled into traffic. "You did spin again today?"

"Yeah. I really like it."

"How are your legs?"

"Fine. Definitely better than after yesterday's class."

He flipped on the stereo. Hard rock beat the air. "Yeah. Sorry about that. I didn't realize the class was advanced." He tapped his steering wheel. "Adam said you handled it well. He also said Jonah was there helping you."

Was he jealous? "I wouldn't have been able to make it through the class without him."

"Glad he was there then." He merged onto 90 East, giving her leg a little squeeze. "I don't have anything to be worried about, do I?"

"We're just friends. Like I've said before."

"I don't get that vibe from Jonah."

"Well, we are, so no worries." But did this mean he wanted to be exclusive? She was so not good at this.

East checked his blind spot before merging into the left lane. "Glad to hear it. I was worried I might have some competition." Then he laughed.

She must have missed the joke. And she didn't want to be the butt of one, so she'd shelve her relationship questions until later. "So where are we going?"

"You like heights?"

"Roof at Wit?"

"You got it."

She glanced at her watch. Seven. Even on a Wednesday, it would be hard getting in at this time. Reservations had to be made a few days in advance, and he'd only called her this morning.

"Relax, Pen. I've got a friend there. She'll take care of me." He got off at Washington and turned on Dearborn to park. "It's a great night for walking."

It was early May, but the night resembled a mid-summer evening. East placed his hand on her back and guided her the block to The Wit. They stepped inside, its chrome and black along with open stairway greeting them as they strolled the few short steps through the lobby to the elevators. As the doors rolled open on the twenty-seventh floor, a tall, platinum blonde woman with a shirt that should have a few more buttons done, straightened from studying something at the hostess booth. Her eyes lit.

"East Fisher." She strolled over and hugged him.

"Kelly Hanning." He squeezed her back. "I hoped you might have the table open on Hangover for me."

"I might, but you'll owe me." Her perfect red lips slipped into a smile. "And I'll have fun collecting."

Penny cleared her throat.

East slipped his arm around Penny. "Kelly, this is Penny."

Kelly's smile twitched. "Your friend?"

"My date."

Her smiled thinned into a line. "Right." She grabbed a couple of menus. "Follow me."

East motioned for Penny to walk in front of him. She followed the blonde through the crowded room. If the woman swayed her hips any harder, she'd knock over one of the tables they passed.

Kelly stepped outside onto Hangover and led them to the table along the glass wall overlooking the Chicago skyline. She held out the chair that faced the glass and motioned for Penny to sit. East slid into the seat with a view of the patio.

Kelly handed them both their menu. Her hand lingered on East's. "If you need anything tonight, let me know."

"I think we're all set."

"Just want to make sure you're taken care of." Kelly nearly purred.

She stepped away, and East put his menu down, a sheepish grin on his face. "Sorry about that. Kelly's always been a bit of a flirt."

Penny leaned back in her seat, dropping her menu onto the table. "A bit?"

He laced his fingers through hers. "Okay. A lot. But don't let it bug you. She's not my type."

"What is your type?"

"You have to ask?" He raised a brow.

Her cheeks warmed, and she pulled her hand away to pick up her menu again. Maybe she could hide behind it. "So what's good here?"

"I like the sushi and the oysters if you're up for sharing."

An order of raw fish and slime did not appeal to her. "I think I'll order salad, thanks."

"Oh, come on. Where's that adventurous side?"

She waffled. "I'll try some of yours, but I'm ordering a salad."

"Suit yourself." He picked up the drink menu. "What do you want to drink?"

"Water's fine."

He closed the menu. "You don't sleep around, you don't drink, and I'm going to guess you're at church every Sunday. Penny Thornton, you intrigue me."

Their waitress appeared and saved her from answering him. They placed their orders, and then East excused himself to the restroom. By the time he returned, his oysters were at the table.

"Sorry," he said as he slid into his seat, "I think the line for the men's was actually longer than the women's for once."

She pointed to the oyster platter. "Care to show me how to eat one of those? I've never tried one before."

He picked up a shell and nodded for her to do the same. Then he touched it to hers as if in a toast. "To the first of many things I'd like to help you experience." Then he tipped his head back, slurped his first oyster, and reached for another.

Penny still held hers. She eyed the slimy creature.

East stopped his second helping at his lips. "You'll love it. Trust me."

With a deep breath, she tipped one of the shells to her own lips and tossed her head back, sliding the oyster into her mouth. The cool slime hit her tongue, and she gagged. Sweet mercy, she was going to hurl all over East.

Penny grabbed her napkin and spit, East's laughter drawing stares. She peeked at him. "I think I'll let you eat those. I'll stick to my salad."

He held another one up. "If you're sure."

"I'm sure."

"At least you tried it."

A few minutes later, their waitress brought East's sushi and Penny's salad. East didn't offer her a sample of his dinner, and after the oyster fiasco, she was fine with that. She dug into her Mediterranean salad, the crunchy greens a welcome contrast to the oysters.

As they finished their meal, East hauled out his phone.

"Looks just like mine." Penny held up her iPhone in the same blue case.

East smiled. "Nice taste in cases." He nodded out the window. "It's such a beautiful night, how about we walk to Millennium, maybe stop at Grant Park, check out the Bean? Play the tourists?"

"Sounds good."

Kelly slid up to their table. "Bringing your check." She laid it next to East before sashaying away. Her phone number filled the top of the slip of paper.

East pulled out a few bills and placed it on the tray, shaking his head. "Sorry again." He nodded to her scrawled number. "That crosses the line. I'll say something to her."

"No. Let's just go."

Crossing out her number, he folded, then pocketed the receipt. "Most women would want to claw her eyes out."

"I'm not most women."

"No, you're most definitely not." He stood. "Shall we, then?"

Kelly wiggled her fingers in a wave as they passed her. East grabbed Penny's hand, not sparing the woman a glance. They rode the elevators down to ground level and strolled through the lobby into the now dark night. Outside, they headed toward Millennium. "So, Penny, what other goals besides fitting into that purple dress do you have in life?"

"A lot."

He laughed. "Share."

"Well, there's opening my own store someday."

They dodged a group walking toward them. "Really? What type of store?"

They'd talked about this before, but apparently, he'd forgotten. "A place to sell all the items I repurpose or to take things on consignment that don't sell at the estate sales I put on."

"Oh, that's right. You've mentioned that." He squeezed her hand. "When did you want to open again?"

"If my finances remain strong, and I can find the right place, I'd like to open no later than a year from now."

He popped out his bottom lip and nodded. "Well if you keep at it like you have your weight loss goal, you'll definitely make it." His gaze trailed over her. "You're doing an amazing job."

"I was. But I can't seem to break that eight-pound plateau."

"That's normal. We'll need to shake up your routine some. And remember, you're changing fat to muscle and losing inches. You'll fit into that dress." He grinned at her. "I never fail at a goal."

As they approached Grant Park, music filtered from whatever group was playing in the amphitheater. They strolled the perimeter and made their way over to the Bean.

"What do you think about a movie after this?"

Penny walked under the Bean, her hand trailing against the cool surface as the shadows darkened around her. "I could be up for that. What did you want to see?"

His breath tickled against the back of her neck. "I can think of a few things."

She shivered. Turned. East dropped a kiss on her lips and tugged her to him, deepening it. He released her lips, his forehead leaning against hers. "You sure about that hotel room this weekend?"

Her mind whirled from his kiss. His nearness. Somehow she found her voice. "I'm sure."

He tugged her closer. "I figured you'd say that, but a man has to try." He let her go and took her hand, turning her to face the Bean. "I mean, look at you. You're beautiful. Can you blame me?"

She laughed. Her distorted reflection stared back at her.

"Come on." East tugged her into the night. "If I can't convince you to change sleeping arrangements, can I at least convince you to sit in the back row at the movie?"

It was an addicting feeling, his desire for her. She smiled and flamed it. "Oh, I don't know, you might be able to convince me." She kissed his cheek.

His return kiss curled her toes.
Good thing he had his own hotel room for the weekend.

Chapter Nineteen

With the speed which this weekend at home had arrived, Penny held high hopes it would pass as quickly. But no. Just like her slow-motion shoe shopping with the Royal Court last night, today was moving at a snail's pace. And she still had Sunday left.

If only East hadn't canceled.

But his dad wasn't doing well again, so she couldn't be upset with him—just the situation. Turning the key off in her ignition, she leaned her head against the steering wheel, peeking up at the dance studio in front of her. She was late, and still she had no desire to make herself leave this car. She so did not want to take dance lessons tonight.

Or see anyone inside that building.

But there wasn't a legitimate reason to stay in this car. With a groan, she slowly opened her door and then strolled across the parking lot toward the building marked *Juliana's Dance Studio*. Her heart rate tripled with the sight of Jonah's Ford Focus in the parking lot. They hadn't spoken since their harsh words over East coming home with her for the weekend. He'd spent opposite hours at Gigi's house. Though the Dentyne she'd left for him had disappeared with a smiley face left in its place. Did that mean they were on good footing?

She pulled open the door and walked inside, inhaling the familiar musty scent of the old building. Penny had spent hours here as a child while Belle took ballet, hip-hop, and tap—all to make her the best beauty pageant contestant in all of West Michigan.

It had worked too. Belle made it all the way to Miss Teen USA—and won.

Voices spilled from the dance room, and Penny sought them out rather than following her desire to run in the opposite direction. At least she wouldn't have to see Mom until later tonight. Dad had arranged dinner to celebrate Penny and Belle's birthdays after dance lessons. Born five years and four days apart, it had been years since they celebrated their birthdays together.

"Penny, you're finally here." Belle spun away from her friends to find Juliana. "Do you want to show us the dance now?"

"Sure. Let's get started."

She plugged in Micah's phone while Penny found a seat in the back and by the door. Juliana and Dylan took center stage as music filled the room. They twirled effortlessly across the floor—more like floated seamlessly as one.

How on earth was she ever going to learn to do that?

"This seat taken?"

A nervous tingle grabbed her stomach, but it was powerless to stop the smile Jonah's deep voice always tugged out of her. She looked up into his familiar blue eyes. "Depends on who's asking."

"An old friend." It sounded almost like a question.

"For him, it's open."

He filled the chair beside her, his shoulder brushing hers, and nodded toward the floor. "They're good."

"Incredibly. I hope Belle doesn't expect us to dance like that."

"Hey. Have a little faith."

"Oh, I have plenty of faith, but even buckets of it won't have me moving like that. The woman is floating."

"It's because she trusts him."

Penny watched them for another moment. "So it's all about trust?"

"Well, he's got to be strong and confident in where he's going. But yeah, it won't work unless she trusts him."

She let silence fill in between them, both their focus on the dance floor. Oh, to look that graceful. Even to simply not trip. But she was pretty good at doing that—and not only with dance.

The music slowed, and she sucked in a deep breath then turned to Jonah. "East didn't end up coming."

He faced her. "Really?"

"Really."

"How come?"

"His father is sick again, so he went home to help his mother."

"Really."

"Is that the only word in your vocab tonight?"

He laughed. "Only one that seems appropriate. I'm not looking to start another fight."

"Is that what we had?"

"Didn't we?"

"I suppose." She tipped her head. "And I'm sorry for how I acted."

"Me too."

The music stopped, and applause filled in behind it. Juliana and Dylan bowed. "Okay, we need everyone to pair up with their partner and take the floor."

Jonah stood before Penny and offered his hand. "Ready?"

She put her hand in his. "It's that easy?"

"One foot in front of the other." He pulled her up.

"Come on." She stiffened. "I mean us, our friendship. The air's cleared? Just like that?"

"You really have a thing about guilt trips, don't you?" He leaned down toward her. "Penny. We're friends. Friends have disagreements at times, but they move past them and don't hand out guilt along the way."

"A novel idea."

"One I hope you'll eventually get used to."

Get used to him?

"I think I already am."

Jonah offered her his arm. "Then shall we?"

"We shall." She took it, and he swept her onto the dance floor.

Jonah waited patiently through Juliana and Dylan's instructions. It was Ballroom 101. After demonstrating, Dylan began working with the women to help them learn the frame and how to follow a male's lead.

Juliana took the men. When it was his turn, Jonah spun her around the floor, his eyes on Penelope who was with Dylan—fighting him every step of the way. Kind of like how she could be with their friendship. The time away had done him good, though. Made him certain he wanted to fight right back for it. For her.

"You've danced before." Juliana tapped his arm.

"Maybe just a few times."

Her focus followed his. "You'll have your work cut out with your partner. But judging by your smile, I'm going to guess you won't mind the extra work."

Jonah stumbled. The song ended, and Juliana grinned at him before strutting to the middle of the floor. "Okay, everyone, find your partner, and we'll start the music again. Dylan and I will watch and jump in to help as needed."

Penelope stood before him. "If you value your toes, you may want to reconsider this."

"I'll take my chances." He put her left hand on his shoulder. "Now grip here, tightly." He then took her right hand in his left, clasped it, and stretched their hands out together. His right hand came around and grasped just below her shoulder blade. "Keep your elbows tight, your muscles engaged, and lean into me."

She leaned forward.

He chuckled. "I mean, lean into my hold."

"Oh, sorry." She pressed back.

Never had anyone felt so perfect in his hands. He inhaled flowers, still curious over what scent she wore. The music started. "Follow my lead."

"You sure you know what you're doing?"

He grinned. "Trust me."

She hesitated a moment. Then relaxed into his grip.

"Keep your head up," he noted. "And close your eyes."

"Excuse me?"

"Close your eyes. Let me lead you."

She narrowed them instead. "I still don't know the dance."

"Close your eyes, Penelope. Picture what Juliana showed you. And then keep leaning into me."

"I'll step on your feet."

"You may." He tightened his hold. "Just trust me."

Skepticism crossed her face before she finally obeyed. She nibbled her lip, but her eyes remained closed—she trusted him.

The thought twisted around his heart, tightening her grip on it. He could stand here all night.

She cleared her throat and peeked at him. "Are we going to dance?"

"Right." Everyone else moved around them. "Here we go."

Jonah whirled her around the room, thanking Gigi and Mom every second for the dance lessons they forced him to attend.

She was beautiful.

And not simply because of how stunning she looked.

Penelope was beautiful through and through. Her quick wit. The way she lit up when she held a precious piece of history. Her determination. Even those things she saw as flaws attracted him. She wasn't perfect, neither was he, but those imperfections were what made her stunning. Allowing people to see them, growing from them, that was incredibly attractive.

Penelope's fingers tightened around his as he spun them, wishing the music would go on all night. He spun in another circle, pulling her closer and taking advantage of her nearness to study her. The way her hair fell in waves, the light scar he still wanted to ask about but didn't know how to, the floral scent he couldn't seem to place.

The music stopped, and slowly she relaxed into him. He held still, barely breathing, wanting this to last.

Penelope slowly opened her eyes. "You can dance."

"So can you."

"Only because I have a great partner." She stepped back, the moment slipping away with her.

But it was quickly recaptured as another song began, and Penelope slipped into his arms again. With each twirl around the floor, she relaxed into his hold even more. A few times, he'd caught her staring. He'd smile. She'd blush.

She kept it up; he just might kiss her.

He spun them toward a corner of the floor, ready to catch her stare again. It took a moment, but those big green eyes of hers found his.

This time, she held his gaze, studying him as if seeing him for the first time. Her hand inched up, trailing a path from his shoulder to his neck where she brushed against the stubble along his jaw. "It really does look good on you." She continued up along his cheek, her breath calm, her gaze steady. Did she have a clue how her touch sent his pulse racing? Featherlight, her fingertips traced over his ear. He wanted to capture them. Climb in her mind and discover her thoughts. Know if she'd let him kiss her.

Or if with one move from him, she'd run again.

He didn't get the chance. Belle's hand grasped his arm, tugging them to a stop. "Penny, you're doing great. I didn't know you could dance like that."

Penelope's gaze stayed on him. "Neither did I."

"I think I have you to thank." Belle squeezed his arm. "Pen, we've got to get going. Dad and Mom made reservations for six so Micah and I could cut out early."

Her attention swayed, pushing her into motion. "I didn't even realize the time. Let me grab my stuff."

Belle caught his eye. "Since East was a no-show, do you want to join us? We're celebrating Penny's birthday too."

"It's your birthday?" he called to her.

"Belle's is tomorrow; mine is not until Thursday."

"And dinner is to celebrate?"

"I guess." She stopped. Shrugged. "It's no big deal, Jonah. If you've already got plans—"

"I don't."

Her lips slid into a smile before she nibbled at the lower one. "Well, I guess if you want to come."

"I do."

"You know where CityVū is?"

"Inside CityFlats hotel. I'll follow you there."

Because he wanted more than just dinner. He wanted a future with her.

The thought settled in and took root.

"If you're sure." Penelope started for the door.

"Never been more sure of anything."

He followed her to the lot on Seventh, noticing how she took the speed limit signs as suggestions. She was already leaning against her car as he exited his. It beeped as he locked the doors. "You drive fast."

"I drive the speed limit ... ish."

He chuckled. "It's the 'ish' that will get you."

The heels of her flats clicked along the cement as they strode out of the parking garage and into the night. They turned toward CityFlats.

"How come you drove instead of taking the train?" she asked.

"Micah and I had different schedules this weekend. No easy way to and from the station or all the places he needed me to be." He pushed his hands into his pockets. "Speaking of which, how did shoe shopping go last night?"

"Depends on who you ask." She dug out her phone and pushed a button. "Take a look."

His lips twitched. "Those are nice."

"Really?"

His shoulders shook under restrained laughter. "Yes. Really."

"Go ahead, laugh. Just remember, she's dressing you too."

"Not in three-inch sparkly heels." He grabbed her hand and held her phone in front of him. "That purple bow on the heel is a nice touch."

His hand warmed hers, and he noticed her breath hitch. Talk about nice touches.

But she pulled away and tucked her phone into her purse. "If you like them so much, I'll let you borrow them when I'm done."

"Not exactly my style, but thanks."

He held open the glass door that led into CityFlats. Laughter erupted from the bar as they passed it. Penelope snuck a glance. The entire wedding party plus some were there. She kept walking. They reached the elevators, and Jonah punched the button. The door opened, and Penelope stepped inside, holding it with her hand. "This is your last chance. You don't have to subject yourself to my family torture."

No way he was leaving her. He took her hand. "Dinner with you is far from torture, no matter who's there." The elevator doors slid closed, and he inched closer. She backed away, the wall stopping her in the small space.

She was flustered.

"Don't say I didn't warn you." Laughter tinged her words. Her attempt to lighten the moment. Except her eyes held his, and there was anything but humor in them. They flickered over his with questions ... interest. Both he was willing to meet.

"Duly noted. But I think I'll take my chances." He leaned closer. "You're worth it."

She looked to his hand covering hers, and he tightened his grip. Kept his focus steady on hers. She blinked up. Her breath small puffs against his cheeks.

Then she shook her head.

He gently took her chin. "Some thoughts you don't need to shake away, Penelope." The elevator opened, but his gaze remained directly on hers. "You go first."

Did she hear the deeper meaning?

With the way she dodged past him, she did. And had no clue what to do with his offer.

He waited a beat before following her. He needed to step back, give her time to catch up with him.

Because she would.

He'd seen it in the way she'd looked at him tonight. Eyes wide and inviting— until he got too close. Like just now. He needed to simply enjoy dinner with her. It was night and day difference from how he'd imagined this weekend. For the past two days, all he'd thought of was Penelope making the three-hour drive with East, introducing him to her family, dropping him off at his hotel.

Jonah wasn't stupid. He knew where things could lead if East got his wish.

East canceling was the best news Jonah had received all week. The guy was too smooth. Had too many excuses. His gut said East was playing Penelope, but he didn't know why or have any proof. And sharing his thoughts? He'd done that once before—with Rachael—and it had only pushed her farther into her boyfriend's arms. No. Unless Penelope caught East in his own lies it wouldn't matter what Jonah said.

At the hostess stand, Penelope supplied her name, and they were ushered to her family.

"Penny." George Thornton placed a kiss on his daughter's cheek. He then reached out a hand to Jonah. "Great to see you again, Jonah."

"You too, sir." He shook George's hand then held out a chair for Penelope. She slid into it with a slight nod to her mother. Jonah settled into his seat. "Adelaide, you look beautiful tonight."

She fingered the pearls around her neck. "Thank you, Jonah."

Micah groaned. "Getting a little deep in here, cuz."

His cousin's voice grated sore nerves. Penelope had been right when she'd said dinner tonight could amount to torture.

Belle swiped her fiancé. "Be nice." She smiled at Jonah. "So glad you could come with Penny. I was worried she'd be alone tonight."

"I'm sure she'd have been fine with that." Jonah reached for his water glass. "But I'm glad I came too."

Even with Micah here acting like he hadn't a care in the world.

Probably because he didn't. Niles had yet to find a reason to contest the will, which meant Micah was getting exactly what he wanted.

Fifty percent ownership in All Waste without having to lift a finger.

Jonah swallowed his anger. This was not the place for their family problems.

The waitress appeared. "What can I get everyone for drinks?"

Micah tapped his empty tumbler. "I'll take another of these. And this gorgeous lady will take a glass of—"

"We'll both have water." She moved her arm under the table, and Micah grunted. He narrowed his eyes on her before donning a tight smile.

Maybe Micah's world wasn't as carefree as he portrayed.

"Water sounds great."

Penelope's gaze bounced between Micah and Belle. "Same here."

"Sounds good," Jonah added.

The waitress left, and everyone opened their menus.

"The salads here are amazing, Penny." Adelaide ran a manicured nail down the page of her menu.

Beside him, Penelope stiffened. "I had a salad for lunch."

"Well, it's not like you can eat too much salad."

"I can." Penelope opened her menu. "I'm thinking a steak sounds nice."

"Honestly, Penny." Adelaide stared at her daughter. "Must you get so defensive? If that's how you act when East tries to help you, then it's no wonder he didn't come home with you this weekend."

White-knuckled, Penelope clenched her teeth.

"Adelaide." George tapped his wife's hand. "Pick out a salad for me. You always seem to know what I like."

"I'll take one too." Belle smiled at her mother.

Jonah leaned over. "I'm ordering the Strip. You?"

"New York Strip?"

"With mashed potatoes, asparagus, and red onion marmalade."

She closed her menu, relief and playfulness in the glance she snuck him. "Guess that'll cover my veggies then, too."

Their waitress took their orders. An hour later, they were all stuffed. Well, at least he and Penelope were. Belle had barely touched her food; Micah had somehow refilled his tumbler and mainly drank his dinner, and Adelaide wound up only ordering a small appetizer. And poor George had stared longingly at their steaks all through the meal.

Jonah tossed his napkin on the table. "That was fantastic." The food had been. The conversation, however, had been stilted. Jonah possessed an entirely new insight into who Penelope was after dining with her family, and no doubt this only scratched her surface.

George pulled out two gifts. He handed the first one to Belle. "Belle. It's your last birthday as just my girl."

Tears sprang up in her eyes. She took the gift. Gingerly opened the package and gasped. "Thanks, Daddy." She hauled out a sapphire bracelet.

"Your mother and I thought you needed something blue for your wedding day."

Adelaide touched her youngest's cheek. "He's talked about doing that ever since you and Penny were little. I was starting to wonder if he'd ever have the chance."

Next to him, Penelope wiped a finger under her eye. Her lips trembled. He reached over and squeezed her hand. She squeezed back.

George took the other package. "And for my Lucky Penny."

Penelope gingerly accepted the package. She slowly removed the layers of gold wrap and stilled when she opened the box that lay underneath. Jonah fought the urge to lean over and sneak a peek.

"What is it, Pen?" Belle asked.

Penelope pulled out an empty glass bottle with bumble bees etched across it. "Where'd you find it?" Her hushed voice dropped across the table.

Whatever that bottle was, it meant the world to her.

George's grin matched Penelope's. "At an antique sale I went to with Grandpa and Gran. I'd wanted to buy the full bottle from the Wilton sale, but with the wedd—" he stopped. "Money's a little tight right now."

Penelope shook her head. "No. This. It's perfect." She kissed her father's cheek. "I wouldn't have worn it anyway. It costs too much."

Jonah touched the glass. "What is this?"

Micah sucked back the last of his drink. "I wondered the same thing."

"It's an old, empty perfume bottle," Adelaide supplied.

The waitress delivered their check, and Jonah reached for his wallet. "George, let me get my dinner."

George waved him off. "No."

"But I crashed this party. I didn't expect for you to pay."

George grinned at him. "You want to pay for something? Stay and have dessert with my little girl."

"I thought we agreed no dessert tonight, George." Adelaide touched his arm.

"We did." He threw a few fifties onto the bill. "They didn't."

Belle stood too. "I'll come home with you."

"But all our friends are downstairs, honey," Micah said. "They're waiting for us."

"I'm tired, Micah. I'm ready to go home."

"It's your birthday celebration. Can't have a birthday party without the birthday girl."

Belle hesitated, and they stared each other down.

Penelope broke their silence. "Belle. I'm only ordering tea. Go on down with your friends, and if Micah's not ready to leave when I am, you can ride with me."

Belle's shoulders slumped. "Fine."

Micah left the table. "Works for me."

Belle and her parents followed Micah to the elevators. Penelope watched them closely.

"Something's up with her."

"She's just stressed with the wedding getting closer."

"It's more than that."

Knowing his cousin, it could be more. "Maybe. But until she's ready to talk, all we can do is pray for them."

Penelope crushed her linen napkin. "Belle will never be ready to talk. At least to me."

"Well, it was nice of you to offer her a ride home. Maybe that will open a door."

"No matter what I try, there's never been an open door between her and me. More like one bolted shut—with multiple locks."

"Why is that?" He leaned in.

"Uh-uh. We've talked far more about my family woes. Time to work on yours." She crossed her arm. "You barely said two words to Micah tonight."

"Because I didn't have any polite ones to say."

She uncrossed her arms, her features softening. "My turn to share some advice."

He preferred to be on the giving end. But it didn't look like she would take no for an answer. "Go ahead."

"Find common ground before the space between you grows too large."

"I'm worried it already has."

"Jonah." His name spoken with compassion and understanding. If anyone knew strained family dynamics, it was her. Her advice was hard-earned. That she'd be vulnerable enough with him to share it had him listening. "It hasn't had time to. You still have far more good memories than bad ones. Don't let hurt feelings and misunderstandings begin to flip that precious balance because trust me, it's nearly impossible to regain." She paused while a large group passed. "I often wonder if I'd talked to Belle more about ... our differences, been open about how I felt instead of shoving it down, maybe we wouldn't be where we are today."

"I know keeping silent isn't helping." He clasped his hands, rubbing them together. "But it's not going to be an easy conversation. Not what I need to say to him or swallowing my frustration long enough to say it."

"Since when have you walked away from anything hard?" Her focus shifted to his bald head.

The appreciation in her eyes ... how'd he keep it there? "Never."

"Then don't now."

He had no intention to—from her or this mess with Micah. If anything, her encouragement and belief in him tonight only strengthened his resolve for both to work.

"I don't plan to." He picked up his menu. "So what are we getting to celebrate this birthday of yours?"

"Not sure about you, but I'm just getting tea."

"Not acceptable. It's your birthday."

"Again, not till Thursday."

Jonah twisted his mouth and nodded. "Then how about cake on Thursday and tea tonight? Well, tea for you, I'll stick with coffee."

The waitress appeared, and Penny ordered. "I'll take licorice tea, please."

"And I'll have a decaf, cream and sugar."

Their waitress cleared their plates and left. He felt Penny's stare. "What?"

"You assume I'll be spending my birthday with you."

He nodded. "You're right. I should have asked." The ding of silverware and hushed conversations kept their table from being silent. "Can I take you out for cake on your birthday?"

Her lips twitched. "Now you're assuming I like cake."

He added playful to the long list of what he found attractive in her. "Pie then?"

She slowly shook her head.

He clasped his hands, forefingers outstretched, and tapped them against his lips. "Enlighten me."

"Homemade cream puffs with my gran's chocolate sauce smothering them."

He'd need to get a hold of her gran. "Sounds amazing."

"They are."

The waitress arrived with their drinks, and they sipped their desserts for a few moments, a comfortable quiet around them. Then Jonah pointed to the box beside her. "Tell me about your gift."

Penelope set down her tea and picked up the glass bottle. "It's an antique perfume bottle."

"You said that earlier." He held out his hand. She paused, then cautiously placed it there.

"Careful," she nearly whispered. "It's extremely expensive."

"And important to you." Their heads were nearly touching. He struggled to keep his eyes off of her lips, inhaled her flowery perfume, and nearly lost the battle.

Penelope blushed. Leaned back. "It is."

"So, um …" He touched one of the bees etched onto the bottle. "What's with the bumblebees?"

"It's a Guerlain trademark. This was a bottle of their Apres L'ondee, my favorite perfume."

"Is this what you wear then?"

"Oh no. The empty bottle alone for a vintage … well, if it were filled, it would be much too expensive."

Jonah could hear the "for me" she didn't say. "But if you had it, you'd wear it?"

Her eyes widened. "In my dreams." She tucked the bottle back into the box. "But like I said, it's beyond expensive. And incredibly hard to find—only available in France, and even that is reformulated."

"Come again?"

"Basically it means if I want the real thing, I'll only be able to find it from collectors. That's where Dad found this."

"Have you ever run into the real thing?"

"There was a vintage bottle at the Wilton sale. It was slightly different, though. Smoother sides with a honeycomb top."

"And you didn't buy it?"

She laughed. "I sold it for them on eBay. Guess how much it went for?"

"Couple hundred?"

"Try a couple thousand."

His brows arched. "Special perfume."

"It is." She sipped her tea. "I have a small decant of the reformulated at home. I only wear it for special occasions. Even that doesn't come close to the original, though."

"So what do you normally wear then?"

"Monyette, Jo Malone, or if I'm really splurging, Chanel or Illuminum."

That's why he couldn't place her perfume. She constantly changed it.

"You like scents as much as you like teacups."

"I do." She relaxed into her chair. "Smells evoke memories. Help tell stories. Make the everyday a little more special."

"Yet you've never had a day special enough to wear your vintage Apres L'ondee?"

"You forget, I don't even own it."

"And why is that again?"

Penelope shrugged and met his gaze head-on. "I haven't found the memory special enough to make with it yet."

He planned to help her rectify that.

Chapter Twenty

How had she let that slip out?

Jonah had his hopeful eyes trained on her.

His steel-blue, kind, incredibly gorgeous eyes.

Gorgeous? Penny shook her head.

"And what type of memory are you searching for, Penelope?" he asked.

Apres L'ondee was the one scent she'd saved for her wedding day. The day when she'd finally be special enough to wear something so extravagant.

And connect that one scent with the one man who loved her that much.

It was a dream she wasn't ready to let slip past her tongue out into reality. Not when the man across from her was far from who she dreamed of fulfilling that role. And yet still, somehow, kept pulling her farther into him.

"I'll let you know when I've got it figured out," she lied.

Like earlier in the elevator, that gaze of his delved into her again, made her feel seen. The connection was unlike anything she'd felt before. It held an intensity she wasn't ready for.

He was only a friend. Not what she expected. Not what she needed.

Or maybe everything she needed.

Crud. She was beyond confused.

Jonah released her. He leaned back in his seat. "Deal."

Penny cleared her throat. "Deal?"

"Letting me in on that memory once you've got it figured out?"

"Oh. Right."

She finished her tea while Jonah paid, needing the distance from him. By the time he'd signed the slip, she had her bearings back.

"Thanks for my tea."

"You're welcome." He motioned for her to step in front of him. "I was serious about taking you out on Thursday."

"I know, but honestly, I don't celebrate my birthday."

"Seriously?"

She glanced over her shoulder. "Yeah. Birthdays lost their fun years ago."

"We'll just have to bring the fun back, then."

Celebrating another birthday while facing down her little sister's nuptials did not conjure up fun thoughts.

"Pretty sure that's an impossible task." She hit the button for the elevators. "No, my plans are to hang out in my yoga pants and have a Cary Grant movie marathon."

They stepped into the elevator and hit the button for the ground floor. "Now that's a way to celebrate a birthday."

"I sense sarcasm in your voice."

He laughed. "You sense correctly."

The doors slid open, and rowdy voices spilled inside.

"Sounds like quite the gathering." Jonah followed her toward the wedding party that crowded the small bar area.

"I liked my quiet tea better."

Belle sat surrounded by friends—a few of their faces new to Penny—and waved her over. "Hey, everyone, here's my big sister, Penny." Her loud voice boomed across the room.

Penny held in her cringe and waved. "Hey, everyone." She turned to Belle. "Ready to go?"

"Not yet."

A waitress appeared beside her. "What can I get you?"

The front door?

Belle sucked down her drink. "Sit and order something, Pen. You need to get to know the girls a little better."

Because shopping with them last night hadn't been enough.

Jonah's hand touched Penny's lower back. He leaned in. "I'll stay too."

Relief soaked through her. "Water's fine," she informed the waitress.

"Same here."

Jonah held out the chair beside Belle for Penny to sit.

Moments later, the waitress delivered their drinks. Cotton-candy wafted through the air as Belle leaned over. "If all my friends were like you, Pen, I could afford to do an open bar at the wedding."

"Thanks. I think."

Belle giggled again. She gestured around the group, pointing at everyone as she filled in names to the people Penny didn't know.

Taylor smiled across the table. "You look great, Penny. Of course, with what I've heard about your personal trainer, I'd be at the gym all the time too."

Penny tensed.

Ava jumped in. "We were hoping to meet him. Belle said he could be on the cover of GQ ... preferably without his shirt."

Jonah clunked his glass on the table.

"Hey." Ava's boyfriend nudged her.

"What? I don't have a ring on this finger." She smiled sweetly at him. "If you don't want me looking, do something about it. Preferably before Penny shows up with this personal trainer because if he's as good looking as Belle says, I'll definitely be checking him out."

Micah held up Belle's hand. "This ring didn't stop her from checking him out."

Belle jerked her hand back. "And it hasn't stopped you from checking other women out."

He laughed and put both his hands in the air. "No ring on my hand."

"Yet." Belle glowered at him.

"Two more months, babe."

"Thought the commitment started when you proposed," Jonah's deep voice challenged.

"Oh, I'm committed to her all right." Micah grinned. "But that doesn't mean I can't appreciate a good-looking woman. Right guys?"

Disgust colored Jonah's face as the men laughed. "Yes, it does."

"Hey. Looking doesn't hurt anything. Not if we promise not to touch."

"Much."

Laughter exploded over the table again. All of it coming from the groomsmen.

Penny shook inside. She didn't belong at this table. Neither did Belle. So why were they both here?

Belle crossed her arms and narrowed in on Micah. "Maybe it's time to switch to water."

"You know I'm only kidding, Belle. It's all in good fun." He sobered. "Remember what that is?"

"Unfortunately."

Micah clenched his jaw.

"Dance lessons went really well tonight, Belle." Penny cut through the tension.

It took her a second, but she pulled her thin gaze from Micah. "They did, didn't they?" Her voice grew louder. "I'm so happy you all made it for the lesson. It truly shows how much you care. So I know you'll all be at the remaining ones."

"One down, three to go," Chad called out then winced as Kinley elbowed him.

She held her glass in the air. "To Belle and Micah and learning how to dance."

Everyone toasted, and then pockets of conversation resumed, the noisy chatter floating over the table. Jonah's quiet words tickled her ear, "And now I understand your hang-up with guilt trips."

She turned. He was close. So close. Her breath hitched. What was happening between them? She studied him, searching for answers. Only the more she received, the more ground he captured in her heart.

"I appreciate you guys staying." Belle's voice startled Penny.

She blinked. Tried to focus. "You're welcome."

"Not a problem." Jonah gulped his water as if he hadn't just completely unsettled her. Yet his face announced he knew exactly what he'd done. It wasn't a cocky confidence, though. No, this was ... attractive?

Belle kept talking. "I'd have told you to leave, but Micah's in no shape to drive me home."

That had her attention. Penny peered around her sister. Micah's bloodshot eyes focused on whatever story Chad was telling. She focused back on Belle. "Am I driving him too?"

"No. He's staying here at the hotel with the guys."

"Okay. Then I'm ready whenever you are."

"I'm ready now, but Micah planned this with our friends for my birthday. I told him I'd stay until eleven."

It was nine fifteen.

Micah draped an arm over Belle's shoulder and leaned around her. "Look at us, almost all family. Except I bet you wish you were losing one instead of gaining, huh, Jone?"

Jonah's hand tightened in his lap.

"It's the alcohol talking. Don't let him get to you." Penny placed her hand over his clenched one.

"Sorry I'm messing up your plans." Micah took a swig of his drink. "I know that sucks, but plans change, and if you love the person, it's no big deal." He dropped a sloppy kiss on Belle's neck. "Right, babe?"

She pushed him away. "Stop it, Micah."

He brought his hands up in surrender. "Can we say touchy?"

"Can we say drunk?" Belle glared at him.

Penny stood. "Micah, how about we find some coffee?"

He swiveled his gaze to Penny. "You don't even like coffee." He chuckled low. "Or are you just trying to get me alone?"

Jonah jumped to his feet and snagged his cousin's arm. "Enough, Micah. Let's take a walk."

Micah shrugged him off. "I don't need a walk. I need people who know how to have a good time." He stood and leaned down in Belle's face. "Used to be you. Guess you're more like your sister than you thought." He charged from the room, Jonah on his heels.

Belle's face crumpled. She pushed away from the table with tears in her eyes as she ran for the bathroom.

"Nice." Penny stood. A hush had fallen over the table.

Kelsey sipped her drink. "Wondered if we'd make it through the night without another fight."

"Another?" That was news. "Have they been fighting a lot?"

"The closer it gets to the wedding, the more tense they are." She shrugged. "They always make up, though. I wouldn't worry about it." Her attention strayed to her drink and Chad.

Penny stared at the woman. She was supposed to be Belle's Maid of Honor. Some friend. Instead, it was Penny who tracked Belle to the restroom and knocked on the stall. "Belle?" Sniffles answered. "You okay?"

"My fiancé just hit on my sister and called me a drag. So no."

"He's drunk. You said so yourself."

Another sniff. "Lousy excuse."

Silence filled the room.

"You want me to go deck him for you?"

A sad giggle. The door unlocked, and her little sister's big blue eyes peeked out. "You'd do that for me?"

"I would."

Belle swiped toilet paper across her cheeks. "I don't doubt it." She propped herself against the brown wooden door. "He's not always such a jerk, you know. He's just stressed right now, and his friends ordered him one too many."

"Didn't mean he had to drink them."

"I know. He never used to, but lately ... things have just been so crazy." With her thumb, she twisted her diamond ring. "It helps that he's not doing his residency. We'll settle down. Things will go back to normal. It'll be good. It has to." Her tears sped up, and she buried her face in her hands. Penny reached out tentatively. When Belle didn't shrug her off, Penny wrapped her arms around her. "Hey, Bella Rose." She smoothed down her hair. "It's okay." After a few moments, the crying calmed. "You want to talk?"

Belle shook her head, then straightened and dried her cheeks. "Nothing to talk about."

"Belle. You were sobbing. All over the man you're supposed to be marrying. I'd say there's lots to talk about."

"I told you; he's just stressed."

"Stressed or not, he shouldn't treat you like that. You deserve better."

"So you're saying I should break up with him?" Her voice pitched high.

"I'm saying the man you marry should respect and cherish you."

She stilled. "That's right. You think because Micah slept with me, it means he doesn't respect me, and couldn't possibly cherish me."

"What?" Penny stepped back from the ice shooting from Belle's eyes. "I never said that."

"You didn't have to." Belle pushed past her. "Because it always comes back to the same thing for you, Penny. But it's not because you care about me, it's because you can't get over the fact your younger sister found love and is getting married while you sit in Chicago all alone. You can't handle that no man wants you."

"Belle!"

"What? The truth hurts?"

"It's not the truth. I'm dating East."

A cruel sound snaked past Belle's lips. "You couldn't hold onto a man like him even if you tried. If you could, he'd be here." She stormed out, her words ringing truth into Penny's world.

Jonah hit the door, shoving through it with the same strength he was using to tamp down his anger. He checked the street to his right. Then to the left. Micah's tall frame stalked down the sidewalk a few feet away.

"Micah!"

Micah slowed but kept walking.

Jonah easily caught up to him. His legs were longer, and he wasn't drunk. He grabbed Micah's arm and swung him around. "What is wrong with you?"

Micah yanked away. "I could ask you the same thing."

"You owe your fiancée an apology." Penny's face flitted through his mind. "And her sister."

A hard laugh escaped Micah. "Belle will be fine. As for Penny, she oughta take my joke as a compliment."

Jonah's fingers curled into a fist. He'd never hit his cousin before, but if ever he deserved it, now was the time. Micah laughed again, and his breath nearly knocked Jonah back. Penny's calm voice replayed in his ear. It was the alcohol talking, not his cousin. His hand relaxed.

"What's going on with you, Micah? I've never seen you touch a drink."

"Then it's been longer than I thought since we've hung out."

A group of college kids walked past, most of them in the same state as Micah.

"Has this become a regular thing?"

"Only on the weekends."

Jonah crossed his arms and stared him down.

"Okay. Mainly the weekends." Micah perched against the half-wall lining the sidewalk in front of CityFlats hotel. "Why does it matter to you anyway?"

"Because if you're coming to work with me, I can't have you drunk."

"Well, too bad. You have no say over my personal life, and you definitely have no say over my part in the business." He crossed his own arms. "Fifty/fifty, cuz."

"You come in drunk, and you'll hand me the reason to have a say."

They stared each other down. After a minute, Micah released a long breath, his sneer loosening. "Relax, Jonah. I won't be showing up drunk." He ran a hand through his blond, spiky hair. "Once the wedding is done, and we're moved, things will settle down, and so will my drinking. It was a habit I got into at school. No more school, no more drinking."

Jonah didn't think it would be that easy, but he could only tackle one issue at a time. Something told him Micah's drinking was not the place to start. He walked over and leaned against the wall with him, staring out across the street. "Why aren't you taking your residency, Micah? All you've ever wanted was to be a doctor."

Micah remained quiet. Cars sped down Seventh Street, and Jonah counted them, patiently waiting his cousin out.

"For my family."

Surprised, he swung his gaze to Micah. "Your parents are pushing this?"

"I meant Belle."

That was even more surprising. "She wants you to give up med school?"

Micah nodded. "I received my residency placement. It's in California." He shrugged. "She didn't want to move."

"But she knew that was a possibility when she said yes. And it doesn't have to be permanent, right? You can come back to the area once you finish your residency."

"Depends on who's hiring. Even then, she could barely handle my school hours. The thought of living that far away, starting a family, the hours I'd put in as an ER doc ... it all became too much for her."

"You don't have to start a family right away."

A deep, guttural laugh pulled out of Micah. "Tell that to her. I've tried."

Another long beat of silence fell between them.

"So your solution was to come work at All Waste?"

"Sort of."

Jonah tensed. "Sort of?"

"I think we should expand. Open a division in Holland."

It took a moment for words to find their way back to Jonah's tongue. At least words he could voice. "We just expanded throughout the Chicago area. We're not opening another division too, Micah."

"Not right away. I'll work in Chicago for a year, learn the ropes, then Belle and I will move back to Holland."

He really thought it was that easy? "It's taken me nearly fifteen years of working in this company to 'learn the ropes.' You can't come in, play owner for a year, and think you have what it takes to open another office." Jonah paced away then stalked back. "Even if we were going to open another office—which we're not."

"We can talk about it once I start."

"The discussion is closed. It was never even opened."

Micah pushed off the wall. "Look. I get it. You've run the company by yourself since Gramps died. It'll take you a while to get used to the fact that you've got a partner who's not as silent as Gigi was, but you need to because it isn't changing."

"Don't make me fight you on this, Micah." He towered over his cousin.

"How are you going to fight me? Call a board meeting? We all know how that will go."

Maybe it was time to call Walter. Take the risk. Sure, it could wind up backfiring, but Walter was a businessman. No way he'd go for Micah's crazy idea.

The pounding music of a passing car caught their attention. After it turned, Micah stared back at him. "Why fight me on this? Think about it. You'll work with me for a year, and then I'll be out of your hair." He stalked back to the restaurant.

As tempting as Micah's words sounded, Jonah wasn't about to make a costly business decision based on his personal desires. He followed Micah, shoving the conversation aside for now. As they entered the lobby, Belle stormed out of the restroom and to the bar. After a moment, Penelope followed, her jaw clenched as if it was the dam holding back her tears.

Jonah halted Micah. "You owe her an apology."

"Sure. I'll get right on that." He shrugged him off. "Soon as I've had another drink."

"You can't drive home," he called to Micah's retreating back.

"I know. I'm bunking here for the night, so my place is all yours." He turned and smirked. "If Penny's anything like her sister, you can put it to good use."

Disgust filled him. "You're an ugly drunk."

"Why? Because I have the courage to say what you're hoping for? That doesn't make me ugly, just honest." With a cocky salute, he disappeared into the bar.

Jonah counted to ten and unfurled his fist. Penelope stood in a corner, her back to him. He approached her. "Penelope?" He reached out.

She turned, her eyes red-rimmed. "What?"

That one word held a million more filled with emotion.

Laughter erupted behind her, Belle's carrying on top of everyone else's. Penelope's gaze flicked over her shoulder. Jonah followed her stare and caught Belle locking gazes with Penelope, her smile tight, her eyes narrowed. Then Belle turned away.

It never ceased to amaze him how women could speak so much with one look.

Penelope sniffed. "I need to leave." Her voice broke.

Anger lit a fire inside of Jonah. He'd about had enough of Belle's cruel behavior.

He squeezed her arm. "Stay here. I want to walk you to your car, but I need to take care of something first."

She shrugged.

Assured she was staying put, Jonah crossed to the bar and leaned down into Belle's face. "She stayed for you. She was the only one to come and check on you. So why not try treating her as well as you do these so-called friends of yours. She's the only sister you have, and she's been there for you no matter how horribly you've treated her."

Belle barely broke her attention from those friends.

He wasn't letting her out of it so easily. "You have no idea how much she loves you, Belle."

This brought her blue eyes to his. "And you have no idea what you're talking about, Jonah. No one loves their replacement."

"Replacement?"

She opened her mouth then clamped it shut and waved him away. "Good night, Jonah."

Jonah waited, but Belle didn't expound. Instead, she jumped into the conversation between her friends. He pulled away and turned to the door.

Penelope was gone.

Penny stormed up Seventh Street, completely lost in the words Belle had thrown at her. If someone could shut off the repeat button on her brain, she'd be beyond thankful.

"Penny. Wait up." Jonah's voice snagged her. She slowed but didn't stop. Within a minute, he'd caught up. "I thought you were waiting for me."

"I never said that."

"True. You only shrugged." He tugged her gently to a stop. "Hey. You okay?"

"I will be." She offered a wobbly smile. "I just made the mistake of trying to play big sister and learned my lesson—again. Don't know why I even bother."

A soft breeze picked up. "Because you love her."

Penny swiped at a lone tear. "Crazy, right?"

Because it *was* completely crazy. Belle was nothing but awful to her, and yet she loved her … wanted to protect her. To be important to her again.

"No. Not crazy at all." Jonah's warm voice calmed her aching heart. In the distance, a train whistled. "Why don't you two get along?"

"Long story."

"Long? Or just one you don't want to share."

"A little of both, I guess."

Jonah jingled the change in his pocket. "Back inside, Belle referred to herself as your replacement."

His words startled her. "She did?"

"That surprises you?"

It took her a moment to formulate an answer. "It's an accurate description, but yes, I'm surprised she used it."

"Why?"

"Belle's adopted. If anyone should say she's a replacement, it's me, and I've never said that." Though she had more than enough reason too. "As far as I knew, Belle's only seen herself as the perfect gift to our family."

Jonah's brow rose. "Belle's adopted?"

She nodded. "She came home on my fifth birthday. It's the gift that keeps on giving."

He didn't call her out on her harsh words. Didn't offer advice. Didn't spout off about reconciliation or forgiving her sister. Simply gave silent understanding.

Penny took it and regrouped, hauling in a deep breath then blowing it out.

Jonah watched her and then nodded toward the hotel. "You still need to wait for her?"

"No." Belle had made it clear she wasn't needed. "She changed her mind and wants to stay at the hotel with her friends."

"Then can I walk you to your car?" He offered his arm. After a moment, she wrapped hers around it. They walked a few steps, and she shivered. "Cold?"

"I'm fine."

Jonah stopped them. "That's not what I asked." He shrugged out of his coat and draped it over her shoulders.

"Thanks." She didn't talk. He didn't push. She didn't need to hit the play button on Belle's catty words again.

They arrived at the parking garage, and Penny returned his jacket, missing the cinnamon scent and light warmth that had enwrapped her.

"Did you ever catch up with Micah?" she asked as she released the locks on her car.

"I did."

"How did that conversation go?"

"Hard doesn't begin to touch it. He shared his drunken ideas for All Waste."

She peered up at him. "Drunken ideas are never good ones."

"Even sober, they wouldn't be sound. He wants to open a new division in Holland."

"But you recently expanded your service line. Added new trucks. You can't open a new division right now."

"Nearly the exact same words I used." He paced. "And they weren't ones Micah wanted to hear. He's never been someone who likes being told what to do, but he'll sink All Waste if he doesn't listen."

She let him pace off steam. Except he only grew more agitated. "Rather than wearing a hole in this concrete, let's gain some perspective." He stilled. Good. She had his attention. "Micah was drunk, so take anything he said with a grain of salt. Wait until he's sober, and then reopen the conversation."

He scrubbed a hand down his face. "I know, but he's so stubborn, I don't think it'll change anything."

"He's marrying Belle. Stubbornness is a prerequisite."

That elicited his laughter. He relaxed against her car. "True."

She joined him. "Is there a board in place to help with decisions?"

"There is, though there's a good chance they'll side with him."

"Even if it's not fiscally responsible to do so?"

"The head of the board has a soft spot for Micah. Always has. And he's the tie-breaker in this one."

She could relate. "And if things go Micah's way?"

He closed his eyes. "I don't know."

She squeezed his shoulder, the comforting touch coming from pure instinct. How many times had he comforted her? "Start with what you do know. You are still CEO of All Waste. Go to the board with your concerns before Micah brings his ideas. Your years of experience are far more valuable than any emotional ties someone has to him."

Beneath her touch, Jonah's muscles relaxed. He brought his hand up to rest on hers. "Thank you."

"I didn't say anything you didn't already know."

"No." A car started at the other end of the garage. "But it's nice to have someone else on my side."

"You didn't leave mine all night. So where else would I be?" As she spoke, his hand trailed up her bare arm, heating every square inch. She panicked. "I mean, that's what friends are for, right?"

Her words worked exactly as she'd planned. Jonah's movement stopped, and he cleared his throat. "Right." He pushed off her door and opened it for her. "It's late. You should get home."

She slid into the cool interior. "Good night, Jonah."

"Good night." He hesitated. "And Penelope?"

"Yes?"

"I will always stand by your side."

Chapter Twenty-One

Penny smoothed down her skirt. She'd spent so long picking out her outfit that she'd practically had to jog back to the gym to meet East. He'd extended his weekend with his parents, staying through Tuesday, so she'd worked out alone the past two nights. East more than made up for his absence, though, putting her through a killer workout tonight. While she wanted to break through the plateau she seemed stuck on, she'd also like to be alive to enjoy the results. Like East asking her to dinner as they'd finished out their last reps. She'd agreed to meet him here after his final client.

The sun glared against the front window, and Penny checked her reflection. She'd tucked a loose white scooped-neck T-shirt into her vertically striped navy and white skirt that landed just above her knees. It had been years since she'd tucked anything in. Her long hair was secured into a loose, wavy bun laying against the nape of her neck. A few tendrils had escaped as she'd scurried here, but she liked the look. She was starting to like everything about her reflection.

East was still busy inside, so Penny leaned against the building and took out her cell phone. She'd spent the afternoon working with Rachael but had to leave before Jonah arrived. Yesterday had been the same. They'd missed each other at the gym too. Texts, however, had been flowing between them. And she'd discovered he loved corny puns. She shot off the latest meme she'd unearthed along with a short text saying she'd be off-grid for the night and then pulled up Facebook, her hand hovering over the keyboard. The weekend still hung in her memory. Temptation to broadcast her evening events across her status made her fingers twitch. Belle would see it, most likely Mom too.

The glass doors opened, and East walked out. He wore another pair of his faded jeans that hung off his hips perfectly with a very fitted gray T-shirt showing off his incredible physique. No. A picture would serve much better than a status update.

Only she never got the chance. He sauntered over and tugged on one of her loose locks of hair. "You look beautiful."

Her pulse shot into overdrive. Confidence soared as he leaned over and dropped a kiss on her lips. Short and sweet. Then he turned and started walking.

"You coming?"

Oh yes, she was coming. She caught up to him. "Where are we headed?"

Her phone dinged a text before he could answer. She peeked and laughed. Jonah had sent one final meme with a good night.

"What's got that grin on your face?" East peeked over, his lips thinning. "Huh. I never pegged that guy with a sense of humor."

Funny. It was one of the first things she'd noticed about him. She slid her phone into her purse. "Guess he's taking his workouts seriously then." Then she leaned into the arm he wrapped around her. They strolled another block but were headed away from restaurants. "So where's dinner?"

"My place."

She stiffened.

East's fingers brushed her shoulder lightly. "Relax. I know your boundaries."

"I know you do, but—"

"There's no hidden agenda here, Penny." He pressed a kiss to her head. "But I've missed you, and I don't want to share you with anyone tonight."

Hesitation crawled up her spine. "No agenda?"

"Well, there was one small one." He leaned close. Paused. Then, "I wanted to blow that picnic you made for me on our first date right out of the water."

She laughed.

"So you'll come?" he asked.

All her life she'd heard how relationships took compromise. And really, he was only inviting her for dinner—no hidden agenda. How big of a compromise was that to make their relationship work?

And she wanted ... needed for this to work.

"Yes. I'll come."

East lived on the second floor of a dark gray brownstone halfway down North Wolcott. He unlocked the door and walked in. Penny followed him, skirting around his bike in the hallway. He dropped his keys on the small table there and led her into the kitchen and living area.

The room was painted the color of cement with black leather furniture in front of one of the largest wall-mounted televisions she'd ever seen. A set of weights filled one corner of the room, a large sound system in the other corner. A small black table sat in the nook next to the kitchen.

He pointed down the hall that extended from the kitchen into the back of the apartment. "Feel free to check out my bathroom and bedroom while I get dinner started." He reached into the cupboard. "Want a glass of red wine?"

Penny settled on a chair at the table. "Water's fine."

He shut the cupboard and opened the fridge instead. "Here you go." He tossed her a bottled water. "Make yourself at home."

"I'll just watch you cook if that's all right?"

"Definitely is."

East dug through the fridge and came out with a handful of vegetables, thyme, rosemary, and a couple of chicken breasts. He opened the pantry next. "You like pasta?"

"I eat pretty much anything."

He peeked over the pantry door. "You better not be eating just anything anymore."

Heat pricked her skin.

His laughter cooled it. "Sorry. Hard to shut-off work sometimes."

Within minutes, the kitchen was filled with wonderful aromas. East wiped his hand on the dishtowel over his shoulder, then took another swig of his water. "This is one of my father's favorite dishes."

"So he's doing better?"

"He is, but I'll need to be home more often. Mom can't help him out on her own."

"Was it a heart attack then?"

"Yeah. Then he had to undergo a bypass."

"I'm so sorry, East."

He shrugged. "He'll be fine as long as he takes it easy." His cell phone rang, and he glanced at it, surprise across his face. "This is them, actually. Mind watching the onions and mushrooms while I take this in my room?"

"Of course." She stepped over to the stove.

East disappeared down the hall. The veggies on the stove were nearly cooked. Penny stirred them as the water on the next burner bubbled. She turned it down some, grabbed the box of whole wheat pasta from the counter, and added half of it to the boiling water. The chicken cooked on the small grill he'd plugged in beside the stove.

"You look good in my kitchen." East stood at the end of the counter.

His compliment brought out her smile. "Just hope I didn't ruin your dish."

He walked over and peeked in the pan. "Doesn't look like it." He took the wooden spatula from her, his fingers brushing hers along with his lips at the back of her neck. "Go sit down, and I'll serve it up."

Wobbly legs carried her to the table. She sat, pulling in long, deep breaths as East filled two plates. He set them down and joined her, placing a napkin and silverware in front of her. Penny folded the napkin over her lap. Across from her, East dug into his pasta.

She quickly bowed her head. When she finished, she found East watching her. "Sorry," he said, "I was so hungry, I forgot."

"It's okay." She forked a bite of pasta. "This smells delicious."

"Typically, the simple dishes are."

Rosemary and thyme melded on her tongue. "You're right. So simple, yet so good."

"So tell me, really, how did things go last weekend for you?"

Penny finished another bite before answering. "They went fine."

"That's not how you sounded when we texted."

She shrugged, not wanting to ruin the good evening with her bad memories of the weekend.

East reached over and squeezed her hand. "The wedding will be different. I'll be there."

The warmth of his hand, and the picture he'd created filled her. Hopefully, he wouldn't cancel again. Not when he knew how important it was to her. She set down her fork.

"Full already?" he asked. "You barely even touched your dinner."

"Guess I wasn't all that hungry."

He released her hand. "Want to watch a movie?"

"Sounds good."

He picked up her dish and pointed toward his TV. "Check and see if I've got something that interests you. If not, we can find something on Hulu or Netflix."

Penny opened his TV cabinet. Her hand slid over several movies. "East Fisher, you like chick flicks."

His laughter flowed from the kitchen. "My sister, Charlotte, stocked those when she bunked with me for a few months. She keeps them here for when she visits." Dishes clinked as he loaded them into the sink. "And since your weekend was so awful, I'll even suffer through one."

She scanned the titles, her hand stilling on *27 Dresses*.

"Now that would be a perfect pick, don't you think?" East reached around her and grabbed it.

She jumped. "I didn't even hear you come over."

He popped the movie into the Blu-ray player. "Mind grabbing a blanket from my room while I set this up? There's one on the end of my bed."

"Sure."

"I'll stay out here, I promise." He winked.

With a good-natured eye roll, she shuffled down the hall. The bathroom door stood open, and the only other door in the hall was on the left. She opened it to find a gray-blue room with black furniture and another TV mounted across from the bed. A gray throw lay at the foot of his bed, and as Penny grabbed it, her eyes landed on a cream-colored cardigan thrown over a chair on the other side of the bed. A cardigan that appeared to be much too small for East, not to mention nearly identical to one she owned.

Penny picked it up.

"I know I said I'd stay in the living room, but I wondered if popcorn sounded good?"

Her heartbeat nearly drowned out his words. She held out the sweater.

His eyes widened. "Oh man. Penny."

She swallowed, blinked back tears. He walked over to her, and she stepped back, anger pulsing through her. She'd been so stupid to ever think—

East grinned. "It's not what you're thinking." He took the sweater from her. "It's Charlotte's, my sister. I had it out to bring home to my parents' this weekend but forgot it."

Her stomach unclenched. "Your sister's?"

"Give me a little credit, will you?" He placed it back on the chair, reached up, and brushed her bangs back, his hand lingering on her face.

"Sorry, I thought—"

He stopped her with his finger on her lips. "You just can't believe that I may like you, can you?"

She shook her head.

"Well, I do." He stared at her. "If only you'd let me show you." His hand slipped from her lips to the back of her neck, and he brought her close.

Her stomach tightened, and she met him as he leaned into her. His kiss started slow, then deepened as he coaxed her lips open with a kiss that literally stole her breath. Coming up for air, he trailed from behind her ear down along her neck and to her collarbone.

Her hands moved between them to break the contact, but he tightened his grip. "Not yet." It was barely a whisper, so quiet she didn't know if it was his words or her own crazy thought.

He continued making a path along the delicate skin of her neck, his hands untucking then sliding up under her shirt to rest against the small of her back. A fire started low in her belly then traveled up to where his breath whispered across her skin. She leaned her head back, all other thought suddenly lost in his exploration and the revelation that East wanted her.

She delved deeper into his kisses, pressing into him, seeking what he was giving. East twisted her around and walked her backward. The bed bumped into the back of her legs, and she stilled, caught in his desire for her.

"Stay with me." His words came out urgent. He tipped her toward the bed. If she fell, she'd be lost.

Or would she be found?

"I want you, Penny." East gave a slight push, and she nearly toppled.

But did *she* want *him*? Want this?

His mouth swept across her jaw, and he pushed again.

She twisted from him, trying hard to slow her pulse. "East, I ... I can't."

He reached for her. "Don't you want me too?"

Cold and hot flowed over her in equal measure. "Agh." She swiped hands through her hair and took another step away. "I don't know what I want."

East stilled. "Seriously, Penny? Because based on the way you were kissing me, it was pretty clear."

Embarrassment flooded her. How had she ended up here? In his bedroom. Nearly—oh ... this wasn't as easy as she'd always thought. Always said. Especially since her blood still coursed so hot through her that with one touch, she'd be his.

She moved to the door. "I know, East, and I'm sorry. I'll grab my things."

"Penny, wait. You don't have to leave." She stilled and looked at him, her gaze avoiding the bed beside him. "It was just a kiss, totally PG rated. Let's not blow things out of proportion."

If that was PG ...

He stood where he was, but his eyes seared into her. "Can I help it if you drive me a little crazy? Make me forget you're a slow mover." While he spoke, he stepped across the room until he was completely in her space again. He trailed a finger over her scar. "I mean, you're just getting more and more beautiful."

She leaned back into his hand, letting his warmth and words soothe that spot in her soul that would never feel pretty enough.

His hand cupped her cheek. If he kissed her, there'd be no stopping.

She waited.

He dropped his hand. "Let's go watch that movie. I'll even sit in the chair and let you have the couch."

She released her breath. Let him walk past her into the hall. Disappointment mixed with relief, and she followed.

East grabbed the remotes, and she settled onto the couch. He started the movie then stepped toward the hall. "All that water." He laughed and headed for the bathroom. "Don't pause it for me. I've watched this with Charlotte too many times to count."

Penny nodded, her mind still caught on what happened in East's bedroom. She brushed bangs from her forehead and snuggled into the blanket he'd snagged as they left his room. The blanket she'd been sent to get before things got out of hand.

As the kiss played through her mind, Penny dissected it. Her fingers touched her lips gently, and she smiled. When East had kissed her tonight, for one long moment, her beauty felt like truth.

East rejoined her. "Did you still want popcorn?"

"No. I'm good."

He settled into his chair, and she watched him. His short blond hair, perfect smile, tan skin, toned body, muscles … what did a man like him see in a girl like her?

Maybe a little more kissing would help her find out. He'd promised to keep them PG-rated, and she suddenly liked his idea of PG.

She tugged the blanket back, softening the warning bells in her brain. "East?"

His cell phone rang, and he dropped his gaze to his phone. "Sorry. It's my mom. I've got to take this."

"Oh. Of course."

He picked it up. "Hey there." His mom spoke, and he nodded. "I'll come right now." He hung up and stood. "Sorry, Penny, but my mom needs me."

"But you just got home."

"I know, but I told her to call for any little thing. Apparently, she took that very seriously."

"No, don't apologize." She was being selfish. "Go on, and I'll walk home."

He grabbed his keys and followed her out of his apartment. "The rest of my week is crazy, what with fitting in all the appointments I missed. How about I call you this weekend?"

He'd miss her birthday. Not that he even knew it was tomorrow.

"I'd like that." She waited while he locked his door, then they walked downstairs and out into the warm night. They stopped by his car, and Penny leaned in and gave him a hug. "I'll say a prayer for your parents."

"Thanks." He dropped into his car and rolled down his window. "Sorry to cut the night short. I'll make it up to you this weekend."

He pulled away from the curb, his taillights getting lost in the dark night. She stepped back from the curb and started down the walk, one thought pricking her; what else would have been lost tonight if his mother hadn't called?

Chapter Twenty-Two

Penny bolted upright in bed as her door slammed against the wall. "Happy birthday, roomie!"

"Seriously, Lace, you're going to give me a heart attack." She flopped back in bed and burrowed under her covers. She'd tossed and turned all night, guilt and desire playing tug-o-war in her brain.

Lacey placed a tray on her bedside table and yanked on the covers. "I hope not. You'd miss out on all this amazing food I just made you."

Chocolate croissants, thick bacon, and fluffy eggs accompanied a steaming cup of tea sitting beside a bouquet of gardenias. "You made all that?" She sat up.

"Sure did. Well, at least the bacon, eggs, and tea. I got the croissants from Leitzia's."

"And the flowers?"

"Oooh, I was hoping you'd ask." Lacey picked up the small, rose-colored glass vase and dragged one of the flowers under Penny's nose. "These I had nothing to do with."

Penny inhaled. "East?"

Lacey laughed. "Right, because he'd know what your favorite flower is."

"Who then?"

"Seriously? Are you that clueless?" Lacey snagged a piece of bacon.

Penny slapped her hand. "Hey!"

"What? I made extra for me too." She held out a second slice. "You really don't know who'd buy you gardenias?"

Penny munched on the bacon, more than its taste bringing a smile to her face. "Jonah?"

Lacey nodded, mischief in her eyes.

Penny stopped mid-munch. "He's not here, is he?" Their friendship wasn't at crazed hair and morning breath level yet.

"Relax, birthday girl; I wouldn't let him come inside. Not that he asked." Lacey reached into her robe pocket. "He did, however, ask me to give you this."

Penny reached for the white envelope. Opening it, she slid out a black and white card with Fred Astaire and Ginger Rogers dancing on the front. Her smile grew, and she flipped to the inside.

Trust me?

She nearly grabbed Lacey. "Did he say anything?"

"What's that card say?" Lacey grabbed it from her. "You two are so weird."

"What'd he say, Lace?"

Lacey snuck another slice of bacon. "To enjoy your breakfast and then meet him out front."

Penny stood and scooted down the hall where thick curtains still covered the window overlooking their steps and front sidewalk. She peeked out from behind them. Jonah relaxed on a bench, sipping coffee.

She dropped the curtain and spun around to Lacey. "I planned on spending the day on the couch watching old movies and eating ice cream."

"You hate ice cream."

Penny peeked outside again, her heart beating wildly to a completely different tempo than last night. She'd missed her friend these past few days. Texts were nice. In person was better. She glanced to Lacey. "Did he say what his plan is?"

Lacey shook her head. "Probably where the 'trust me' comment comes in."

Penny raced for her phone and dialed Jonah's number.

"Happy birthday, Penelope." His deep voice rumbled in her ear.

"Thanks for the gardenias. They're beautiful."

"I hoped you'd like them."

"And the card."

He chuckled. "How long until you're ready?"

"What's the plan?"

"Did you even read the card?"

Her turn to laugh. "I did. Did you remember my big birthday plans?"

"Did you remember I asked to celebrate your birthday with you?" His voice was so warm. "Besides, we're watching Cary Grant tonight with Rachael and Gavin."

Peeling back a corner of the curtain, she snuck another peek. Jonah's eyes met hers from where he now stood on the street. With a yelp, she hid.

"Shy in the morning, Penelope?" he teased.

"Bed head does that to a person."

"You looked good to me."

"Me and the one eyeball you saw."

"Go get ready. It's a cool morning out here, and my coffee is almost gone."

She shuffled toward her room. "I still have my eggs and tea—oh, and the most delicious chocolate croissant to finish."

He groaned. "You're cruel."

"If you give me a sec, you can come in."

He hesitated a moment. "No. It's your birthday, and you deserve that breakfast in bed. I'll head over to Leitzia's. Text me when you're nearly ready."

"Give me twenty minutes."

"Take what you need. I've told you before; you're worth waiting for."

Her heart caught on his words, and she hung up.

"I don't think you've ever smiled that way over me." Lacey watched her from her bedroom doorway.

Penny rolled her eyes. "What are you talking about?"

"Only that you could light the room with the wattage you're putting out."

"He's a friend."

"My point exactly. So am I, but you never look like that when we're talking."

Penny perched on her bed. "I'm finishing my bacon. Want to join me?"

"It's bacon. You don't have to ask twice."

She hopped on the bed. They both sat cross-legged as Penny slid the tray between them. "Dig in."

Lacey broke the croissant in half. "Sorry I got in so late last night. I wanted to hear about your date with East."

Penny rubbed the edge of her sheet, remembering the kiss.

"Oh boy." Lacey dropped the croissant back on the plate. "Tell me that red is from what you want to do and not something you already did."

Penny's mouth dropped. "Lace! You should know me better than that."

"I do know you, but I also know guys like East."

"What's that supposed to mean?"

"Is East sitting out front, waiting for you? Does he bring you flowers or open your doors for you? You know, all those things you always tell me are so important?"

"Since when do you notice things like that?"

"Since you started pointing them out for me." Lacey squeezed her hand. "Just because I let my standards slide sometimes, doesn't mean you should."

"I'm not dropping my standards."

"Where was your date last night?"

Penny glanced out the window.

"Let me guess, his place?"

"Nothing happened."

Lacey snorted. "If that's true, it's not because he prevented it, am I right?"

"He likes me."

Lacey snorted again.

Penny shot up from the bed. "Why doesn't anyone believe that East could like me?"

"Whoa, hold up a sec, Penny." Lacey stood next to her. "A guy would be crazy not to find you amazingly beautiful inside and out. You're the whole package."

"And then some." Penny patted her waist.

Lacey took her shoulders and twisted her around to face the mirror hanging on her wall. "Pen, you're dropping pounds left and right. You've got this crazy, gorgeous hair, amazing style, and stunning eyes." She spun her back around to face her. "And a huge heart. But honey, I don't think East appreciates any of it. I think ..."

"You think what?"

Lacey shifted her weight, puffing her bangs up off her forehead with a hard breath. "Never mind what I think. Just be careful with him, please?" She hugged Penny and then thrust her toward the hallway. "And go take a shower. Your friend, Jonah, will appreciate it. Trust me."

Penny stood there for a moment, but Lacey was through talking. A twinge of hurt twisted inside that even Lacey didn't think East truly wanted her. She shoved it back. They'd see. East wasn't going anywhere. She'd make sure of it.

On her bedside table, her phone chirped, and she picked it up to read the new text.

Meant to tell you, dress comfy, we'll be walking.

"There's that smile again." Lacey picked up the tray. "Tell Jonah I'm jealous."

"Whatever." Penny grabbed her towel and headed for the shower.

Jonah found a spot, dropped his car into park, and looked over at Penelope. Her black hair was tied in a loose braid with a few waves escaping. The fitted jeans she wore showed off all the hours she'd put in at the gym, and the green cardigan she'd thrown over a white tee shirt made those eyes of hers stand out. Eyes that sparkled as she took in the area around them.

"Seriously?" she asked.

"I was going for 'fun.'" Now he wasn't so sure of his impulsive choice. "If you don't like rides, there's always bumper cars and funnel cakes."

She jumped from the car. As he climbed out, her sparkling eyes found his over the rooftop. "It's perfect." She nearly bounced off the pavement.

He grinned. "You like coasters?"

"Love them! I've done King's Island and Cedar Point numerous times growing up. But it's been years since I've been on one." Her head tilted up as she took in a large steel coaster. "Hope I can still keep up."

"We can start small."

"Oh no. If we're going for fun, we're heading straight to X-Flight." She grabbed her wallet, stuck a few bills in her pocket, and slammed the door. "I've heard it'll take your breath away."

His was already gone.

He locked the car. "Let's go."

They wove their way through the parking lot and up to the line at the entrance. Excitement rolled off Penelope in waves. Jonah breathed out and began to relax. It had been a long shot, taking her to a theme park for her birthday, but that shot seemed to have hit its mark.

"Two, please." He shooed Penelope away as she shoved bills at him. "It's your birthday."

"This is too much of a gift."

"You're worth it." He turned toward her. "And far more."

She shook her head. "You keep saying that."

If only he could climb in that pretty head of hers and shove out all the other voices. "So when are you going to believe it, Penelope?"

She didn't answer him, just panned her attention around all the rides.

He paid for their tickets and handed hers over. "X-Flight is at the back."

Fried goodness and sweet cotton candy mixed in with the smell of chicken grilling as they navigated to the rear of the park.

"No line." She nearly ran through the gate.

"Helps when you come this early in the season. Kids are still in school."

"Guess I picked a good birth date then." She laughed.

They walked straight up to the ride.

"You a front or back rider?"

Her grin grew. "Let's start in the front."

"Start?"

"With these lines, we can ride it a couple of times."

He swept his hand out. "I'll follow you."

The attendant helped them lock in. "Ever ride X-Flight before?"

"First time."

"Best ride in the park." The guy tugged on the bar over their shoulders. "Have fun."

He gave a thumbs up to another attendant who completed his safety spiel, and then the ride began. Pushed back in his seat through barrel rolls, twists, and turns, Jonah could only add his laughter to Penelope's. Her screams covered his, and as the ride rolled into home, she twisted up and around the shoulder bar.

"Now *that* was fun!"

"Again?"

"Definitely."

Five hours disappeared under the warm late spring sunshine, fourteen coasters, bumper cars, and a trip through the arcade. He discovered Penelope's aversion to water rides and the ones that spun in continuous circles; otherwise, she was up for anything in the park. Along with all the food. Even, he found, giant turkey legs.

That picture was nearly enough to make him create an Instagram account.

They walked off the Batman coaster, and Jonah pushed his hands into his pockets. "Rachael and Gavin were planning on dinner at their house, but I'd like to squeeze in one more ride."

"I'm game."

Once she saw it, he wondered if her answer would change. "Come on then." He led her toward X-Factor.

"Finishing where we started?" she asked.

Keeping silent, he continued walking until they stood in front of Dare Devil Dive.

"Oh, no." Penelope stepped backward. "Are you crazy?"

"Nope." He offered her his hand. "Trust me?"

She hid hers behind her back. "You, I trust. Those harnesses, not so much."

He wiggled his fingers at her. "Come on. It'll be *fun*."

"That word only works until we splat on the pavement."

"Trust me."

She hesitated, her eyes searching his. Her hand reached out and touched his. "If I die, I'm so going to kill you."

He towed her along behind him, her hand warm in his. He kept her tucked to his side as they explained how this attraction worked. They'd each be put into an individual harness, then harnessed together in a larger one with a cable attached to the back of it. Then they'd end up lying on their stomachs, facing the ground as they were hauled one hundred and twenty-five feet into the air where they'd have to pull a cord, releasing them into a free fall.

Penelope shook beside him, and he wrapped an arm around her shoulder. This was the ride he'd waited all day for. A small bit of remorse pulled on him as trembles ran through her.

He leaned down to whisper in her ear. "We don't have to do this."

"No way. I'm committed now and when I commit—"

"To something, you don't back down."

She smiled at him. "Ahh, you really do listen."

"To everything you say."

Her cheeks pinkened. "Then listen to this: you so owe me chocolate tonight."

"Oh, there'll be plenty of chocolate."

The girl suiting them up tugged on their harness. "You guys are a cute couple."

Penelope's cheeks went from pink to red. "We're just friends."

Jonah bit back the "for now" he wanted to add.

The girl shrugged. "Could have fooled me." She gave a thumbs up to the man running the ride. "They're ready."

And he was. He just hoped Penny would be soon too.

So far, this was the best birthday she'd had in years, and it wasn't even over yet. Jonah had dropped her off at her home while he went to shower and change. Dinner was in forty-five minutes at Rachael's house, and she'd meet him there.

Crossing her room, she ran a hand over her perfume bottles then grabbed the Illuminum and sprayed it lightly along each wrist. Gardenias filled her senses. This birthday started with them, and now it ended on the same note, sealing the two together in her memory.

She quickly slid into yellow flats before snagging her phone and a wristlet then exited into the early evening, locking the door behind her.

"Wondered how much longer you'd be."

She jumped and twirled around. Jonah stood at the bottom of her stairs.

"What are you doing here?"

"I came to escort you to dinner."

"I could have walked by myself." She dropped her key into her tiny purse. "It's even still light out."

He offered her his arm as she hopped off her last step. "Rach kicked me out. Apparently, I'm not allowed to sample your birthday dinner before you show up."

"I like your sister."

He laughed. "I think the feeling's mutual."

They walked in silence for another block, the breeze slipping gently between them.

"What's your scent tonight? I don't think I'm familiar with what you chose."

"Illuminum's White Gardenia."

He slowed their pace. "I noticed gardenia is a common theme to most of your perfumes."

"Most. But not all." Pink laced the sky in front of her. "Apres L'ondee has no gardenia in it if you can believe that."

"And yet it's your favorite."

"It is."

They strolled the blocks between her house and Rachael's. The streets were strangely quiet tonight. Birds filled in the evening sounds around the calls of children as they played. Penny relaxed beside Jonah, breathing in the light cinnamon smell he carried. She couldn't remember a better birthday in years.

She slipped her arm around his, leaning her head against his shoulder. Comfortable. That was how she felt with him.

"I keep meaning to tell you, I visited your church on Sunday while we were in Holland, but I didn't see you." Jonah's deep voice rumbled through her.

"You went to Beachside?"

"Yep. Saw your parents and Belle." He looked down with a raised brow.

"East texted. I hadn't spoken to him all weekend, so we started chatting, and I lost track of time."

Jonah slowed their speed. "How's it going with him?"

The kiss from last night lit through her.

She shook her head, removing the image before the heat of it played across her cheeks.

"What are you trying to dislodge now?" Jonah asked, his hand gently grasping hers as it rested on his arm.

She startled and tried to pull away. "Nothing."

He held tight, searching her gaze. "Nothing?"

Penny stilled, maintaining his stare for a second before it became too intense, before he read her too clearly. With Jonah, she always felt like an open book. Right now, too open.

She averted her eyes. "Looks like we're here."

"Lucky you." A light challenge filled his voice.

Instead of answering, she pulled them up the stairs. If he refused to let go of her arm, then he could just come along for the ride.

And he did.

With his free hand, he knocked and then opened Rachael's front door. "We're here."

Clooney clattered down the stairway, Gavin behind her. "Happy birthday," he called.

Penny wiggled once again against Jonah's hold, and this time he released. Gavin engulfed her in a hug, and Clooney danced, barking at her feet.

"Jonah, control your dog." Rachael hustled from the kitchen.

"She's all yours, sis."

A grunt escaped Rachael as she greeted them. "Happy birthday, Penny."

"Thanks." Penny stood from where she'd bent to pet Clooney and gave Rachael a hug. Clooney scooted in between them, her wet nose burrowing into Penny's palm. She scratched her snout.

Rachael led her to the kitchen. "Can I get you something to drink?"

"I'm good." She inhaled. "Something smells great, though."

"Grilled steaks, stuffed mushrooms, asparagus, garlic bread, and dessert—something chocolaty."

"You made all that for me?"

"I promised you chocolate, didn't I?" Jonah leaned against the counter, grinning at her.

Rachael tossed a pot holder at him. "As if you had anything to do with it."

"I got you the recipe, didn't I?"

"Fine. I'll give you that." Rachael pointed at a serving platter. "Now help put the food on the table."

Fun. The word encompassed this entire day. Even as they joined around the table, laughter filled their conversation. And the way they sang her Happy Birthday? Her stomach still hurt from giggling at their awful singing.

But the best was dessert. Jonah had called Gran for her crème puff recipe, and Rachael recreated it to perfection. She'd nearly licked her plate clean; it was so good. After clearing the dishes, they'd settled into the family room. Gavin disappeared only to return with a couple of wrapped gifts in his hand.

Penny straightened. "What's this?"

"Looks like birthday presents to me." Jonah reclined in the large chair across from her.

"You guys didn't need to buy me anything."

"We know, but we wanted to."

"Technically, I didn't buy you anything." Rachael handed Penny the larger of the two packages. "I made you something."

Jonah shared a smile with his sister.

Curiosity grabbed Penny, and she tore open the paper. Her mouth dropped open. "You made this?"

Jonah answered before Rachael could. "She's good, isn't she?"

The watercolor in her hand was a gardenia, the detail exquisite. She panned around the room at the paintings on the wall. All were landscapes or flowers. Penny had noticed them the last time she was here but missed their significance. "You painted all those too?"

Rachael nodded. "It's a hobby."

"Don't let her lie. She used to have showings. She's known at several art studios. It's not just a hobby."

Penny set her gift down. "Do you have any showings coming up?"

"I don't do them anymore."

Silence filled the room. Whatever was going on, Penny didn't pursue it. "Well, thank you for this. I know right where I'll hang it."

Gavin handed her a small gift. "I got you something too."

Penny opened it and chuckled. A copy of *White Christmas*.

"If you already own it, you can exchange it."

"I don't, and it's perfect. Thanks, Gavin."

Jonah handed her another envelope. "Now mine."

Their generosity nearly had her in tears. "Seriously, you guys are spoiling me."

"Everyone deserves a little spoiling, especially on their birthday." Jonah nudged the envelope into her fingers.

She slid a finger under the flap and opened it. Another black and white picture greeted her, this time of Millennium Park, and as she turned the card, tickets slid out from inside it. Her hand stilled as she read the name on them.

Adele.

She found Jonah's eyes on her. "I can't take these."

"Of course you can."

"Jonah, it's too much. This was a sold out concert."

"Good thing I have connections."

She narrowed her eyes at him. "Did they give them to you for free?"

"Didn't your mother ever tell you it's rude to ask someone how much they paid for your present?"

She snorted. "No. Just the opposite."

His brows raised.

Penny released her frustration. "Never mind." Her thumb brushed the tickets. It was a dream to see Adele. But it was too much. "I can't take them, really."

"Listen. You have gone above and beyond in helping us with Gigi's house for a fraction of your cost. This isn't just a birthday present, but a way for us to say thank-you."

She hesitated. "Then it's from you and Rachael?"

"If that'll make you keep them, then yes."

Adele. In the park. Sold out concert. She touched the tickets, finding only two. "How come you didn't buy three then?"

Rachael cleared her throat. "Because I don't care for Adele."

"Come again?"

Jonah laughed. "She's a rocker."

"Seriously?"

"Very serious." Rachael nodded.

"Yeah. I have to ask her to turn down her music when she's painting," Gavin added.

Penny pointed to her painting. "You listened to hard rock while painting that."

"TFK, Decyfer Down, 12 Stones. The louder—"

"The better," Jonah and Gavin finished for her.

Straight-laced, prim, and proper Rachael, a punk rocker. Penny laughed.

"So you see," Jonah said, "I need someone to attend Adele with me."

Tempting. The day spent with Jonah was such a drastic contrast to last night with East. Both made her feel wanted in such different ways.

She closed the card around the tickets, sealing in her decision. "Then I guess I'm your lady."

His smile nearly knocked her over. "That you are."

Chapter Twenty-Three

Jonah turned onto North Huron and parked, the memory of Penelope's birthday dinner last night warm enough to calm the nerves jumping around his stomach. Walter Hamlin's four-story white townhouse stood in front of him. It was a familiar place. Gramps, Gigi, Walter, and Walter's wife, Celeste, had been close friends, and as a result, so had their entire families. His gaze went up to the roof—over the years he'd consumed at least a hundred hotdogs on that rooftop patio.

He jogged up the front steps and rang the bell, familiar enough to just enter, but wise enough to wait for Tony to answer. For all intents and purposes, Tony was a butler. You just never called him one.

After a moment, the door opened. Tony's wrinkled hand stretched out in a handshake. "Jonah. Early as usual."

"Good to see you too, Tony."

He should introduce Penelope to Tony. The old man was a Cary Grant look alike. And he played it up, too.

"Nice glasses." Jonah pointed to the dark black frames.

"Figured if I had to start wearing them, I might as well put them to good use." He shut the door behind Jonah. "The ladies love them."

"Find one you want to settle down with yet?"

Tony's rough laugh popped out. "Goodness, Jonah, why'd I want to do that?"

The old man would never change.

He was also all talk. His heart had never gotten over the death of his Maggie.

Tony walked with him to the stairs. "He's up in his office, waiting for you." He waited until Jonah was two steps up. "You ask me, it's a shame what Gigi did, allowing Micah to step in the way she did."

Jonah bit his tongue. To agree would betray his Gigi, and no matter how much he might feel the same, he couldn't do that to her. "Gigi did what she thought best."

And now it was time for him to do the same.

Jonah climbed to the third floor, then strolled down a long hall to the dark cherry door. He rapped his knuckles across it.

"Come on in, Jonah."

Walter Hamlin sat behind his massive desk, the navy walls of his study brightened by the morning sunshine that filtered through the floor to ceiling windows. While Tony had allowed his hair to turn silver, Walter kept his such a dark black that in the right light it had a blue tint to it.

He nodded to the sitting area on the other end of the room. "I had Tony bring coffee. Thought we might need it."

Jonah followed Walter across the wool rug that had been made for this room. Most likely it cost more than all his own furniture combined. He settled into one of the dark leather chairs across from Walter and poured himself a steaming mug of coffee.

"So let's get to this." Walter stirred creamer into his coffee. "Tell me why you've been calling my house all week."

And that was Walter. Straight and to the point, life moved at his schedule, not a minute earlier, not a second later. Which is why when Walter had called this morning, Jonah dropped his plans and headed straight over—even though it would mean being late to Gigi's. He twisted the watch on his arm until he couldn't see the face.

"Micah and All Waste." Jonah gripped his mug. "He's going to ask the board to make him COO, and I'm not in agreement with that."

Walter nodded. "No. I don't suppose you are. You've had All Waste to yourself all these years. It's going to be hard to share."

"I'll be happy to share—once Micah learns the business." Jonah kept his voice even. Emotion and business did not mix well for Walter. "But he can't step into All Waste at that level. He's never worked a day there, or anywhere else for that matter. He's not qualified to make the decisions he'd be making. Nor would he have his employees' respect."

"Or yours."

"I won't lie." Jonah left it at that.

Walter drew in a deep breath and set his mug down. He watched Jonah. "So you want to maintain control."

"I want to do what's best for the company."

"And you don't think that's Micah?"

He didn't. But he was willing for that thought to change over time.

"I'm asking you to keep me as CEO. Allow me to continue making decisions for All Waste, including—if need be—the positions Micah is allowed to work. As he learns the business, I'm open to him advancing. But he needs to do it the right way."

Walter nailed him with a look. "Like you did."

"Like Gramps and Gigi wanted me to." He didn't shy away. "And the experience was invaluable. It gave me the knowledge and confidence to run the company today."

Across from him, Walter nodded, then returned to drinking his coffee. Jonah allowed him the silence. After a moment, Walter spoke. "I think Micah could be a great asset to the company."

"So do I ... someday." Jonah shook his head. "Walter, he plans to open an All Waste division in Holland, Michigan. Not because he's studied the market, but because it's convenient for him and his fiancée. Does that sound like an asset to you?"

Again, Walter was silent. This time Jonah couldn't wait him out. "Would you take someone on in one of your companies, place them in a COO position, no experience, no background, and let them make decisions of that magnitude?"

Walter's stare remained out the window. After agonizing minutes, he turned. "I'm sorry if you thought you'd have an easy answer today, Jonah, but I also spoke with Micah this week, and I'm simply not on board with relegating him to the garbage trucks because you're unwilling to share nicely."

His answer knocked the breath from him. "That's not what—"

Walter held up his hand. "Don't get me wrong. You've made some excellent points, but I'm not prepared to give you what you're asking for today. So, for the time being, you'll need to accept the fact that Micah is coming on board with you."

"It's not what's best for the company."

"Worry about what's best for you. And right now, pushing me is not on that list." Walter stood and walked from the room.

Penny twisted her hair into a bun and rammed a pencil through it to hold it in place, her gaze straying to the clock. How long was Jonah's meeting with Walter going to take? He'd texted on his way there, and with every tick of the second hand, she wondered how things were unfolding.

The front door burst open, and Jonah stormed through. She'd never seen his eyes so cloudy or his face so twisted in anger. Apparently, there'd been wrinkles.

She stood slowly and met him halfway across the floor. "Bad meeting?"

"How could you tell?"

"Your nostrils."

He gave her a blank stare.

"They're flaring. I didn't even know you possessed that ability."

His blank stare gave away to laughter. He ran a hand over his bald head and groaned. "Thanks. I think."

He may have laughed, but frustration still rolled off him. "Want to talk?"

Instead, he scanned the room. Penny had started setting up collections throughout the first floor, creating small areas that flowed well together. In the dining room, she'd set the table with one set of Gigi's china and placed another on the butler. "You've been busy here."

So "no" to the talking then.

"Your sale is in a week. I better be busy here."

He shed his suit jacket and tugged off his tie. "Okay then, I'll take the kitchen."

"It's already done. What I need is your brawn, so go home and change first, or you'll ruin your suit."

He rolled up his sleeves. "Not going to fit me much longer anyway."

As if he couldn't have it altered. She'd seen the tag as he'd draped it over his arm. Gucci. And by the cut, new.

"Jonah."

He laid a hand on hers. "It's fine." But was *he*? He didn't give her a chance to ask. "Let me grab a drink of water, then I'll get started." He disappeared into the kitchen. It was too easy to forget that he had the money to ruin that suit and buy another one—Jonah didn't flash his wealth. And that's not what he was doing now. No. He was willing to trash the suit because he'd given her his word that he'd help here, and he'd already been running late.

Due to a crummy morning, apparently.

"Did I hear Jonah?" Rachael clomped downstairs.

"You did. And by the looks of it, his meeting didn't go well."

Rachael plopped onto the sofa. "Unfortunately, I'm not surprised."

Could she convince him to leave? He needed to focus on his business, not helping with hers. She typically hired students to help with moving furniture, but because she'd given him a discount, Jonah insisted on doing it. And even with the morning he'd had, he was stubborn enough to stay.

As if to prove it, he stepped from the kitchen. "Where do you need me?" His blue dress shirt tugged across his chest, but in a good way. How had she missed that? Penny followed to where it tucked into his pants. His waist was thinner, too.

He cleared his throat, and Penny's gaze slammed into his. His gray-blue eyes crinkled around the edges. "Like what you see?"

"Pardon me?" she choked out.

His hand swiped across the empty room. "Wondering if you like how the room looks, or if you need me to move anything in here for you."

"You drive me crazy when you do that."

"Do what?"

Penny shook her head.

He grinned. "Not sure I want to know what thought you're dislodging right now."

"Trust me; you don't," she said.

"What do you need me to do next?" Rachael stood.

"Get your brother to head to his job."

"That's not happening." Like flipping a switch, frustration edged his voice.

Looked like after his meeting with Walter, he wasn't backing away from another argument. She could give him the fight he was primed for, or help him work it off. Choosing the latter, she pointed to the ceiling. "Let's start with taking furniture down from the attic."

She gave them credit. Neither groaned.

By the time they were finished, it was late afternoon, and by Penny's count, they'd run up and down the three flights of stairs a million and one times. Her thighs burned, but the house was nearly set for next weekend's sale. She had a few more small things to attend to, but she should be able to handle them in the next few days.

You two hungry?" Rachael reached for her purse. "I've got to pick Gavin up, and we can stop for food."

Jonah collapsed on the couch. "I'm not picky."

"Me either." Penny joined him.

"Remember you said that." Rachael slipped out the door.

"Great. We're going to end up with kale smoothies."

Penny rested her head against the armrest then stretched herself across the couch. "Should have been more specific."

"You like kale smoothies?" He picked her feet up and placed them on his lap.

"They are delicious."

"Liar."

She nudged him with her foot. "Like you, earlier today?"

"When did I lie?"

"When you pretended everything was fine."

He squeezed her ankle. "Everything was fine once I got here with you."

"And before that?" she pressed. He'd had enough time to cool off, but distraction had dogged him all day. "What happened with Walter?"

Outside, a car blasted its horn. Jonah's attention shifted to the window. "I brought up my concerns about Micah."

"And?"

"He doesn't want to make a decision yet, and I have a feeling if he was forced to right now, he'd side with him."

"You told him about Holland too?"

He massaged the back of his neck. She ached to do it for him. Hated to see him so tense. "I did, but Micah had already been by with the idea. I'm not sure how he sold it, but Walter didn't seem to think it's an awful one."

"Did he say it was a great idea?"

"No." He dropped his head back against the couch and stared at the ceiling. "Which is what I can't figure out. Walter isn't known for his emotion, but talking to him today, I got the feeling like that was what was swinging his decision."

"Think he likes Micah better than you?" Because she knew how that felt. Playing second fiddle to someone—except with her, she knew the why. Jonah was left with questions.

He hesitated. "I don't know. There was something there I couldn't put my finger on, but whatever it is, it's keeping Walter from making a clear business decision."

"Then we pray." Penny hauled herself off the couch and reached for her phone. "And text Rachael to bring grease instead of green leaves." Before she could do that, her phone rang. She checked the screen. Awful timing, but she had to answer. "Sorry, I need to take this."

"East?" Jonah's smile disappeared.

"Um, yes, actually. We've been playing phone tag, and his dad's not doing well again." Penny hurried to the kitchen and answered. "Hey."

"Hey yourself." His voice was light.

"How's your dad?"

"Doing okay. It's Mom I'm worried about. She's really struggling with all this."

She leaned against the counter. "I'm sorry, East. I'll keep praying for them."

"You are as amazing as you are beautiful, you know that?"

Her insides warmed. "And you're sweet."

"I'll be home tomorrow night. Are you free? I know it's a Saturday, and you've probably got plans, but my sister is coming in the morning to cover the rest of the weekend with Dad and Mom, and I'd like to make it up to you for bailing on you the other night. Thought we could grab takeout and finish that movie you picked out."

"Sounds perfect." Actually, it sounded better than perfect. "When do you want me to come over?"

"Six work?"

"It does. I'll pick up dinner."

"And I'll make the popcorn."

"See you then."

She turned to leave the kitchen and saw Jonah standing there. "You're really going over to his house?"

"For dinner? Yes."

She waited for him to move from where he blocked the door. He didn't.

"Anyone else going to be there?"

"No."

He watched her for a moment. "Think that's wise?"

"It's dinner, Jonah."

"And you think he's going to keep it to that?"

The kiss from Wednesday night roared to mind, warming more than her cheeks.

"Exactly," Jonah stated.

"What about 'trust me' like you're always asking?"

A low laugh escaped. "Oh, I trust you, it's East I don't trust. I've known guys like him."

"You really think I'll just fall for a line? I haven't yet."

Came close. But she could handle it.

Jonah opened his mouth, then snapped it shut. He rubbed his jaw, his gaze never leaving hers.

"What, Jonah? You want to say something, so say it." How could they go from the ease of their conversation on the couch to this?

"I don't want to fight with you, Penelope."

"That's the last thing I want, too."

He held her gaze another moment then sucked in a deep breath. "Just be careful, okay?"

She stepped into his space, touched over his concern she'd be hurt. "Like I said, trust me."

Warmth radiated off of him. "And like I said, I do trust you, but no way I'm trusting him."

The tone in his voice warned her she shouldn't either.

Chapter Twenty-Four

Penny stepped onto the scale and peeked. Then groaned.

Who'd decided to make Friday weigh-in day? That right should be reserved for a Monday.

The number glowed, and she wanted to scream.

Another long week of busting her bum to get off this stinking plateau. She'd changed her diet, and even with her crazy-busy week, she'd gone through every new exercise East threw her way, taken more spin classes with Jonah, and ran twice with Lacey. And *this* was the result?

"Everything okay in there?" Lacey called from the hallway.

"Fine." Penny placed her toes on the cold tile and shivered. "As long as I can have the alterations lady work a miracle on my dress."

A gentle knock sounded on the door. "I'm coming in."

"Whatever."

Tightening her robe, Penny sank to the edge of the tub. Lacey plopped down on the floor. "Still on that plateau?"

"No." The tears she fought spilled over. "I gained." Everything was going in the opposite direction lately.

"Seriously?" Lacey thumped the scale. "This thing has got to be wrong. You look great."

"It's not wrong. I hoped the one at the gym was, but they match."

Lacey stood, picked up the scale, and walked out of the room. The front door opened and metal crashed. Lacey returned, swiping her hands together. "Fixed that problem."

A laugh strangled out. "I wish it was that easy."

"It is that easy. You're more than that number, friend, so start acting like it. Ever since this wedding came along, you've gone a little crazy."

"My mom and Belle tend to do that to me."

"You don't have to let them."

No, she didn't. But somewhere along the line, this became about more than them. She wanted to lose the weight, wanted to be pretty—she'd always wanted that, but it wasn't until East that she felt she could have it. If her number started to creep back up, he'd be long gone.

She needed to get on top of things.

"You want to take a run this morning?" she asked.

"Sorry, Pen, but I've got work." Lacey picked up her toothbrush. "I thought Gigi's sale started today."

"It does, but I can squeeze one in. The sale doesn't start till eight."

Toothbrush in her mouth, Lacey smiled at her. "Hey, how was your date with East last night? I wondered if you'd be home this morning or if you'd stay there again."

Her insides twisted. Lacey wasn't letting her forget she'd fallen asleep at East's after dinner and finishing their movie. "It was one time, and I slept on the couch. Nothing happened." Nothing major anyway.

Lacey raised her brows and finished brushing her teeth. She finally spoke as she capped the toothpaste. "I think your idea of nothing keeps changing."

"My idea is the same it's always been." A few lines had blurred, but she hadn't crossed the line of having sex with him. And she wasn't sleeping there again.

"Sweetie, staying over at a guy's house doesn't exactly scream you want to remain a virgin."

Penny bristled. "Seriously! Why does everyone think I can't control myself alone with a guy? Obviously, I've proved I can."

"Whoa, reel it in there a little." Lacey twisted to see her. "I was just teasing you." She ran a brush through her hair. "So Jonah didn't like you going over to East's either, huh?"

"Who said anything about Jonah?"

"You and your touchiness, that's who."

Lacey had her nailed, and it bothered her. It bothered her even more that Jonah had caught her working at Gigi's last Sunday and realized she'd missed church. Again. But at least he didn't know why. He was worried enough that she'd dare have dinner alone in East's apartment. If he knew she'd spent the night there …

Penny glowered at her.

Lacey giggled. "You sure have it rough, two guys chasing you and all." She darted around the corner before Penny had a chance to lob anything at her.

"Chicken!"

After changing into her workout gear, Penny stopped in the kitchen where Lacey sat at the counter. "And for your information, I didn't go out with East last night. He texted me that he wouldn't be home until late because his dad's doctor's appointment ran over. Had you been home, you'd have known that. Where were you, anyway?"

"I was with Shawn. East canceled again?"

"Shawn, the guy who I met in the hallway last month?"

"Yes. So what's up with East?"

"His dad is really sick." She eyed Lacey. "What's up with Shawn? You two getting serious?"

"Maybe." She waved away that subject. "You should stop at East's apartment on your run. Say hi."

"You think?" The thought did pull at her. She stretched her arms over her head.

Lacey stood with her dishes. "I do."

"I'll think about it." With a wave, Penny headed out the door. Her sneakers hit the sidewalk, and she checked her watch, hesitated. Nearly seven. East would be up right now. Probably eating breakfast. And he *was* always the one to call her for a date. Maybe it was her turn to take the initiative. Drop by for breakfast. See how his dad was doing.

They were dating, after all.

Decision made, she pooled her energy into a run. Her feet pounded the pavement, her heart rate picking up the closer she came to East's house. She rounded the corner, and his brownstone came into view. Penny stopped, nearly second-guessing herself. How would East react to her just showing up? Would he be bothered, or would he smile and welcome her?

She pulled in a breath and jogged up the steps two at a time, pressing his buzzer before her nerves got the best of her. Seconds ticked away, but no one answered. She peered at it to make sure she'd pressed the right one. She had. Maybe he was still asleep. Or in the shower.

She eyed the button, wondering if she should press again, and just then the speaker came alive.

"Yes?"

It was a woman's voice.

Had she pressed the wrong button?

Slowly and deliberately, she pressed the button next to East Fisher's name.

"I already buzzed back. Who is this?" The same woman responded.

Penny turned and ran.

Jonah sat on the front step of Gigi's house and waited for Penelope to arrive. Already, a crowd was lining up in the morning heat. Spring had somehow skipped right into summer this year. Fine by him, he loved being outdoors.

He leaned into the sun, letting the warmth seep out the frustrations from yesterday. He'd spoken with Niles, who still hadn't found a reason for him to contest the will. Then he'd debated calling Walter—who'd yet to reach a decision after a week—but Walter's warning had been clear. There was nothing Jonah could do at this point. The future of All Waste rested in others' hands. Sad when the thought of that gave him less stress than the thought of Penelope's having dinner at East's house again last night. He'd overheard them making plans at the gym.

She was changing for him.

All week, he'd encouraged her to think twice about her relationship with East. What he needed to do was back off. Unfortunately, what he needed to do wasn't winning over what he wanted to do. Not when he kept picturing her with East.

Footsteps clacked against the sidewalk, and he looked up to see Penelope. "Hey," he greeted even as he caught sight of her puffy eyes. "Hey," he softened. Jumping up, he reached out to grab her.

She shrugged him off with a glance at the crowd. "We need to set up."

He followed her inside, shutting the door with one hand and clasping her arm with the other. "Slow down. What's wrong?" Again, she tried to shake him off, but this time he held on. "You've been crying." The sight ate at him.

She blew her bangs out of her eyes. "I'm fine."

"You don't look it. Tell me what happened." He stepped closer. "Talk to me, Penelope."

"It's nothing, really. Let's just get ready for the sale."

He gave her arm a squeeze. "It's not nothing if it's got you this upset, but if you don't want to talk right now, I get it. Just know I'm here if you need me."

She gave a half-smile. "Thanks."

Within minutes, the doors were opened, and the first twenty people came in. Jonah stationed himself in the living room, a watchful eye on Penelope. She dealt with each customer in the same graceful yet direct way she always did, and anyone else would never know how upset she was under her calm façade. The focus of work was good for her, but whenever she had a slow moment, he caught the tears welling in her eyes again. The clock could not move any slower.

Midway through the morning, Ella snuck inside. "Hey, Penny? There's some guy out here who doesn't want to shop, just wants to see you."

Penelope's head snapped up. "What's his name?"

"Didn't say, but he sure is hot. Tall, blond, lots of muscles."

Penelope's face turned to stone. "Tell him I'm working."

East.

Jonah tensed. Penelope had been at his house last night. Her tears this morning. He stormed past Ella. "I'll tell him."

"Jonah," Penelope called.

But he kept moving, straight out to the sidewalk and into East's space. "Penelope wants you to leave."

East pulled a cocky grin. "Then why's she coming out to see me?"

Jonah turned. "I've got this, Penelope."

She stopped beside him and leaned her lips next to his ear. "This isn't good for your sale. People are getting uncomfortable. Go inside; I can handle this."

Jonah turned so only she could hear him. "He's the reason you were crying this morning, isn't he?"

She didn't deny it.

Anger coiled in him, building. "What'd he do last night?"

Penelope's eyes widened. "This has nothing to do with last night."

East stepped up next to them. "No, it has to do with this morning. Right, Pen?"

Jonah swung around, but Penelope held his arm. "Stop." She addressed East. "I'm busy. If you want to talk, it'll have to be after hours."

She tugged on Jonah's arm, but he could barely see past the rage of her with East. Why else would she still be there this morning?

"You ... stayed with him?" His throat loosened enough to choke the words out.

She dropped his arm and backed away, her head shaking. There was no emotion in her words. "Just go, both of you. This isn't the place for this."

Hurt ran over every one of her features, the question he'd voiced hanging in the air around them. "Penelope?"

She raced to the door.

Jonah turned on East. "What'd you do to her?"

Smugness rolled off of him. "It's eating you, isn't it? Not knowing. Her not talking."

No way he was giving him the benefit of seeing that truth. "I don't see her talking to you either."

"She will." Hands in his pockets, he sauntered off.

If it was up to him ... Jonah linked his hands behind his neck and growled. That was the problem. It wasn't up to him. East held some strange power over her. She'd talk to the creep again.

But would she talk to him?

Jonah stomped inside. Rather than Penelope on the bottom floor, Rachael was there. "I don't know what you did, big brother, but I suggest you stay down here for right now."

"I screwed up."

"Yeah. I got that much."

The rest of the day trudged by. He didn't even bargain with customers, just agreed to what they offered. At one point, time moved so slowly he checked to make sure the clock in the kitchen still worked. It did.

Five finally struck, and Jonah locked the front door. The three college girls who worked the sale dropped off their money belts to Rachael. She tallied what they'd sold. Penelope descended the steps and joined her. She scanned the tally sheet and then removed cash from the metal box in front of her. She handed each girl their pay, barely breaking a smile as she thanked each of them. When they left, the house settled into silence.

Rachael moved to the stairs. "I'm going to tidy upstairs and shut off all the lights. You two play nice."

Penelope stared across the room at Jonah. The betrayal in her eyes cut him. "You think I slept with East."

He pushed his hands into his pockets. Thought about her reaction outside earlier. Weighed what he knew about Penelope against the situation and went with his gut. "I did. But I don't now." He stepped over to her. "I was wrong. And I'm truly sorry."

Her face softened with his apology. "Accepted." Jonah started to relax, but she didn't let him off that easily. "What I don't understand is how after our last conversation you still jumped to that conclusion."

Jonah hesitated, then sat on the couch and waited until she joined him. "Because like I said, I don't trust East. I've seen this before. Men like him say what a woman wants to hear, and suddenly they're doing things they always said they wouldn't."

"Wait." She held up her hand. "You're talking about your sister, right? Rachael's told me her story, but I'm not a sixteen-year-old girl, Jonah."

She most definitely was not.

"I know, but you asked why I jumped to the conclusion I did, and my reaction partially has to do with what I saw happen to her."

Penelope took a deep breath. "So you think East is simply telling me what I want to hear?"

He thought through his words before using them. "I don't know. What I do know is I'm watching you make decisions that just last month you were upset Belle was making. Skipping church, being alone with East, staying over at his house last night. You may not have slept with him yet, but where do you think it's going to lead?" He shoved that encroaching mental image away. "And you might be mad at the picture I colored earlier, but what outline did you give me to work with?"

Penelope nibbled her lip. "I didn't spend the night at his house … last night."

The way she carefully chose her words, and the tentative twist of her face mangled his gut. His mind rewound to last Saturday and the date she'd had at East's—the one he'd warned her about. He wanted to push but worried if she had spent the night there, she'd only find excuses to justify her actions not only to him but herself. So he stuck with the issue at hand.

"So why did East—"

"Because I stopped by there this morning."

"Why were you crying when you came here then?"

Penelope shook her head.

He wished she'd shake it hard enough to dislodge East's hold.

She twirled a piece of her hair around a finger. "East canceled last night because his dad is sick. I went to check on him this morning, and when I buzzed his apartment, a girl answered."

Anger flared, but he held it in check. He stilled her hand, pulling it away from her hair, and wrapped his fingers around hers. "I'm sorry." He may not like East, but he didn't want Penelope hurt.

"It's okay. He texted a little bit ago and told me it was his sister, Charlotte." She blew out a short breath. "I should have known. She's been visiting a lot lately. I guess I just can't wrap my head around the fact that East really likes me."

"He'd be a fool not to."

Her green eyes met his. She searched his face. He couldn't stop himself. He brought his free hand up and traced along her scar. Stopping his fingertips at her chin, he gently nudged her closer. "Why do only his words count?"

She didn't answer, barely even breathed. His other hand still clasped hers, and he rubbed his thumb against the inside of her wrist, her pulse racing beneath his gentle touch. He leaned an inch closer, and she didn't back away.

"Upstairs is closed up." Rachael thumped down the steps.

Penelope bolted from the couch. She pushed her hair back with both hands. "Good. Um, thanks, Rachael." She grabbed her purse. "I've got to go. Dinner with Lacey."

"Penelope?" Jonah called, pushing down his laughter at her actions. He affected her. She may not be ready to pursue it, but he could wait.

"Yeah?" She headed for the door, barely turning.

"Don't forget our date tomorrow after we finish this sale."

She turned, palm against her throat. "What?"

"The Adele concert. It's tomorrow. Or did you forget?"

"Adele?" Her voice squeaked. "No. No, I didn't forget. I, um, I'll see you tomorrow."

She slammed the door behind her, and Rachael's giggles followed. "Did I interrupt something?"

"Nothing to interrupt. Yet." He peeked out the window at Penelope hurrying to her car. "Check with me after tomorrow."

Chapter Twenty-Five

Penny slipped a thin black headband into her hair, positioning its red flower slightly over her left ear. She dabbed on red lip gloss, smoothed down a few fly-aways, and then headed to her room. Three pairs of flats lined up in front of her floor length mirror, and she stepped in front of each one, contemplating.

"And who exactly are you trying to impress?" she muttered to her reflection, still unsettled over how she'd reacted to Jonah yesterday. At least today her heart rate had maintained its normal pulse around him as they finished Gigi's sale.

"The good guy." Lacey leaned against the doorframe.

Penny met Lacey's gaze in the mirror. "Ha ha."

"Wear the teal ones."

"You think?"

"I do. Not many people can pull off red and teal, but you are one of them."

Putting them on, she nodded. "I like it."

"Of course you do. So will Jonah."

"*The Princess is calling, pick up the phone ...*"

Saved by a ringing phone, even if it was Belle calling.

Lacey chuckled. "Thought you were going to change that ringtone."

"Yeah, well, my last trip home changed my mind." She answered. "Hey, Belle."

"You have a second? Or did I call at a bad time?"

Politeness? Penny checked the screen. Yep. It was Belle calling. "Um, I'm just getting ready to go out, but I have a couple of minutes. What's up?"

"First, let me get business out of the way. I have a few dates to run by you to see if they'll work."

"More dance lessons?"

"Actually, you and Jonah did so well I'm fine if you can't make it back for more. I'd like you to come to my showers, though, if you're able."

She widened her eyes at Lacey. "Okay, what are the dates?"

Belle rattled them off. "But those ones aren't as important as the party two weekends before the wedding. We're hanging out with the whole wedding party. Friday is the bachelor and bachelorette parties. Then Saturday, there's a big shower for both Micah and me. Mom and Dad and Micah's parents will come for that, and we're renting rooms at a bed and breakfast in South Haven. I'd love for you to come. You can bring East—if you two are still together."

And there was the Belle she knew.

"I'm sure we will be."

"Things are going well then?"

"Very well."

"So I should book one room for you guys?"

"No, Belle, book two."

"And he's still dating you." It was as if she was trying to discover the solution to a quantum physics problem.

"As implausible as it sounds, yes, Belle, he is."

Complete silence and then, "I'm sorry, Penny. I called to apologize, and then I end up nearly picking another fight."

Wait. "You called to apologize?"

Lacey coughed on the water she stood drinking.

"I was a little harsh when you were here for lessons, and I'm sorry. Jonah kind of laid into me that night, and a lot of what he said was true. Just took me a bit to think about it."

"Jonah what?" Her mind reeled to catch up. She'd left him in the lobby when he said he had something to take care of. Belle was that something? "He put you up to this?"

"No, but he did make me take a harder look at how you've been there for me." She stopped a moment before continuing, "I know we're not exactly close, but you are my sister. I shouldn't have said what I did, at least not in the way I said it. I mean, I don't see you and East together in the long run, but if you're having fun with him now, then go for it. He's really helping you lose the weight, and that's important. You look great."

Penny nearly dropped her phone. This was Belle's idea of an apology?

"Thanks, I think."

"So I'll see you in South Haven?"

If Belle was willing to meet her halfway ... "I'll be there." The clock caught her attention. "Hey, I've got to go. Jonah's picking me up in ten minutes."

"Jonah?" More curiosity flooded her voice.

"Yes. He's taking me to a concert to say thanks for helping out at his grandmother's."

"The fact you have two men chasing you absolutely amazes me."

"Good-bye, Belle." She hung up before Belle could ruin her apology any further.

"From this end, that sounded like a real interesting conversation," Lacey said.

"Oh, you don't know the half of it." Problem was, the satisfaction Belle's amazement should have brought was mysteriously absent. This moment had been years in the making, but nothing like she'd dreamt it would be.

Thoughts churning, Penny moved to their front window to watch for Jonah. Knowing him, he'd be early. When they'd left the sale at three, he'd told her to be ready by six. Sure enough, five minutes before her wall clock rang, he arrived. She stepped outside and hurried to his car.

"Hey." He jumped out and opened her door for her. "Don't you know a guy's supposed to come to your front door for you?"

"Sure, for a date, but not when it's a friend."

"The best dates are between friends."

He shut the door on her open mouth.

Jonah schooled his tongue before returning to the driver's seat. He needed to play things low key tonight, let things happen naturally. Penelope almost let him kiss her on the couch at Gigi's yesterday, and if he wanted to get back to that place, he needed to move slowly. He knew she cared about him. She just wasn't ready to admit it.

It didn't help his game that she looked beyond gorgeous tonight. Or that her fragrance permeated every inch between them, enticing him.

"What're you wearing tonight?"

"Illuminum."

It was the same one she'd worn on her birthday. "I wondered. I'm starting to place each one."

"I'll keep you guessing."

"You do that."

He started the car and pulled away. Forty-five minutes later, they were near Millennium Park, swallowed by the traffic trying to attend the sold-out venue.

"Mind walking a bit?"

"Not at all."

He found a spot a few blocks away, parked, and grabbed a small backpack from the rear seat. They stepped out, and Penelope strolled along beside him. His fingers itched to take her hand, but he pushed them into his pockets instead. They'd walked a few feet when Penny spoke up. "Belle called while I was getting ready."

"Oh yeah?"

She slowed her pace. "Get this; she actually apologized to me. Pretty amazing, right?"

"Really? What for?"

She stopped, her brows nearly in her hairline as she regarded him. "Give it up, Black. I know you laid into her."

Was she angry? "Penelope, I—"

"Completely deserve my thanks."

His worried pulse relaxed. "You're welcome. I'm glad she decided to listen to what I had to say."

"Which was?" They started walking again.

"That you have common ground."

The streets were packed, and he only had eyes for her. Especially when she peeked at him through a sidelong glance filled with appreciation. "Like what?"

"Like you're her only sister. You want her wedding to be perfect for her. And you care about her. I reminded her that you were the only one to check on her. The least she could do was be grateful."

"I bet she took all that well."

"Not so much." Jonah jingled the change in his pocket. "That's when she made the comment about being your replacement."

He wondered if he could pull the story from her tonight.

"Oh." Penelope tipped her head. "So, how's it going with Micah and All Waste?"

All right. That story was still off the table.

Jonah moved forward with her. "Things are about the same. I'm going for no news is good news."

"Very optimistic of you." She laughed.

They chatted effortlessly for the next few blocks until they came to the entrance, and Jonah handed over the tickets. The place crawled with people. Great excuse to do what he'd been waiting to. He grabbed her hand and laced their fingers together. "Don't want to lose you."

She tightened her grip. "Lead the way."

He strolled toward the back, weaving in and out of people and taking his sweet time to find them a spot. Eventually, he settled about halfway back and along the edge. The main crowd was in front of them, but they still had a good view of the stage.

"This okay?" he asked.

"Perfect. I'm not one for big crowds, and I'm sure I'll be able to hear just fine from here."

Jonah unfurled a blanket from his bag and helped her to sit. Joining her, he tugged out two waters and an economy size bag of Peanut M&M's. She laughed as he opened them and held the bag in front of her. "Happy birthday again."

She pulled out a handful and tossed a few in her mouth, a wide grin on her face as she bit into them.

Jonah clenched his hands against the desire to pull her near and kiss her right then and there. "Good?" he asked.

"It's Peanut M&M's. Need you even ask?"

The red flower in her hair drew his attention to her red lips as it had several times tonight. But right now, it was the carefree joy spilling across her face, sparkling in her eyes, and turning those lips up that stopped him cold. Oh man, she had no idea how beautiful she was.

And he nearly told her, but the stage erupted in lights. Music pounded, and the crowd roared as Adele took the stage. Midway into her set, Penelope edged closer to Jonah. He leaned back on his palms, and she mimicked his stance, her shoulder bumping his.

"Happy?" he asked in a lull between songs.

"Incredibly." Her pinkie finger hooked his. "Thanks for this."

"You're worth it."

With a smile, her gaze swung back to the stage. Another song began, and like a wave, people stood, swaying with the music. Penelope jumped to her feet and peered down at him. "Gonna join me?"

He dusted off his hands and rose. Beside him, Penny belted out the lyrics with Adele. He couldn't take his eyes off her. She was much more entertaining than the woman he'd paid to see.

Bouncing during the fast songs, swaying during the slow, she even pulled her cell phone out at one point and held it up like a lighter during a ballad. He chuckled and tugged his out too. There weren't many Adele songs he knew, but there was one he was waiting for. And after another fast song, the first strands of it hummed through the air.

Penny reached for her cell phone again, but he grabbed her hand instead. "Dance with me?" Around the lawn, other couples moved in close to one another. "For practice?"

She rolled her eyes. "Like you need any."

"I didn't say it was for me."

Her soft punch connected with his shoulder, but she stepped into his arms. At first, he kept to what they'd learned on the dance floor two weeks ago. As the familiar music gave way to its lyrics, he shifted subtly, pulling her closer until their clasped hands rested on his chest. He wrapped his other arm around her waist and called himself the liar he was—this was completely for him.

"This isn't the hold we were practicing." A light tease colored her voice.

"Humor me."

She sighed and laid her cheek against his chest.

He swayed with the music, stepping her slowly around their small patch of grass.

Was she listening to the words? His chin rested on top of her head. She fit perfectly. Could he convince her to stay with him? Because he had known from the moment they met that this was right where she belonged.

Adele sang, her words creating a bubble around them. Penny's fingers clung to his, tucked in tight to his chest. She didn't move her cheek from his chest, and while the melody rode the air around them, no other sound penetrated. He inhaled sweet flowers, the Illuminum she'd worn tonight bringing him back to her birthday. Another day he'd have liked to last longer.

He spun them around. How much would it cost to have Adele keep singing?

The song wound toward its end, and he slowed them to a stop. Penelope remained still in his arms, her hair tickling his chin, her body warm against him. He barely breathed. If she tilted her face up, with her lips that close, he'd kiss her.

The final note clung to the air, and the crowd erupted around them. Penelope startled and stepped away. "Thanks for the dance." She stared at the ground.

He pushed his hands into his pocket. "It was nice."

Nice.

Understatement of the century.

Holding her that close … he couldn't walk away from tonight without giving it his all.

"Penelope?"

She peered up, her lip caught between her teeth.

Jonah bent and retrieved the gift he'd brought with him. On stage, Adele announced intermission, and the crowd began to disperse. He'd picked their seats along the edge of the lawn for this reason. They weren't in the way of anyone.

She eyed the wrapped box in his hand. "What's that?"

"A gift. For you."

"This concert was my gift."

"Doesn't mean I can't get you another one." He held it out.

She sighed but took it, slowly unwrapping the white paper to uncover a simple white box without any markings. She slid her finger around the opening and lifted the top. Then stopped. Her eyes widened, then her gaze slammed into his. "I can't accept this."

Penny pulled out the carved glass bottle with the honeycomb top filled with original Apres L'ondee.

How he found it … why he bought it … none of that mattered because she couldn't accept it. What that would say to him was far more than the dance they'd just shared. The dance she enjoyed more than she was willing to admit.

She shook her head.

"Don't," he said.

"Don't what?"

"Listen to that voice in your head that says you're not worth it."

For once, he was wrong in reading her thoughts.

"I wasn't." She handed him back the bottle, but he refused to take it.

"Then what were you thinking?"

No way she was telling him. She'd confused their friendship enough with that dance. Accepting the bottle would only add to the cloudy state of whatever they'd become.

"That I can't accept this. I know how much you paid for it, and it's too much."

"There you go again, talking about the price of your gift."

"That worked getting me to accept the Adele tickets, but not this. I won't even spend it on myself."

"Which is why it's a gift. You don't think you're worth it." But she was. In fact, "I think you're worth far more."

She shook her head. "You're wrong."

"I'm not." The steel in his eyes darkened. "I know how much you're worth to me, and it's more than a million of those bottles." His finger followed her scar from her cheek to her lips. "You are the most amazing, beautiful woman I've ever met. You make me laugh. You challenge me, you—"

Her pounding heart nearly drowned out his words. She had to stop him. She grabbed his hand and pulled it from her cheek. "I'm dating East."

He stilled. Tightened his fingers around hers. "East is the wrong guy for you."

"And you're the right one?"

"Yeah. I am."

His soft words settled inside her, sinking into that hole she could never quite fill. They rang with a truth she wanted to ignore.

"I'm not attracted to you in that way, Jonah."

"You may have a shot of convincing me of that if you looked me in the eye when you said it."

She brought her gaze to his but didn't repeat her words. Couldn't. Not when she no longer knew what she wanted. But it had to be East. He was the man she'd always wanted if just given the chance. The man no one ever thought she could have. The one who could make her finally feel enough—make Mom and Belle realize she was enough.

"Attraction is far more than physical, Penelope. It's emotional too." Jonah stood inches from her, his right hand still in hers. With his left hand, he tucked her hair behind her ear then trailed his fingers down to her chin. He tipped her face toward his. "And you might not want to admit it, but we're having no problem with either one."

She couldn't move. Everything about him pulled her to him. Sandalwood and cinnamon cocooned her, and she sighed. One kiss. One kiss to prove how wrong he was.

But what if he was right?

She twisted away. "No, Jonah." Coolness slipped across her face where his hand had been. "The feeling doesn't go both ways." Defiantly, her eyes found and held his. "I'm sorry, but it just doesn't. You're a good friend. That's all."

The crowd buzzed. Laughter among friends. Couples walking hand in hand. Light music drifted from the stage. But silence held their corner of the lawn.

A low breath escaped him. "If I looked like East, would your answer be different?"

"What did you say?"

"I think you heard me."

"You seriously think that about me?" His words stung with a truth she fought against facing.

"I think"—he leaned in closer—"that you're with East to feed something in your self-esteem. To prove a point to your mom, your sister ... yourself. And I think you're using the same yardstick they measure you by to measure me."

She stared at him a moment, unable to combat his words. Scary how well he read her. How well he seemed to know her—and right now, that was better than she knew herself.

Penny pushed past him. "I need to leave."

He grabbed her arm. "You're not running because I'm wrong. You're running because I'm right."

A tingling slid up from where his hand held her. She shook him off. "I'm running because if I stay here much longer, I'll say something I regret." Like admitting how right he was, on oh so many levels. She laid the perfume box on the blanket. "I'll get myself home."

She disappeared into the crowd, half expecting Jonah to chase her. But he didn't.

Chapter Twenty-Six

J onah grabbed his coffee and cheesecake from the counter at Leitzia's and slid into the seat across from Rachael. "How did Gavin do on his science test?"

"He passed. If he passes the exam and hits summer school hard, he should be able to catch up with his class."

"I'll help him."

She sipped her coffee. "I know."

Jonah slid a key across the table.

"What's this?" she asked.

"Studio space, for you." He held his hand up to stop her. "It's only a block from where you live. Great natural light, exposed beams, well-insulated walls for you to blast your music. Much better than that little room you've been using at your house."

She didn't touch the key.

"Come on, Rach. It's time, don't you think?"

Another sip of her coffee. She plunked her cup down. "How's Penny?"

"Oh no, you're not changing the subject."

Her brow rose. "So I'm the only one who has to talk about things I don't want to?"

That would be ideal.

"I have no idea how she is. I haven't talked to her since the concert."

"Not one phone call in two weeks?"

"Nope."

"You're giving up, just like that?"

"What am I supposed to do, Rachael? She wants to be with East."

"Because she's messed up right now."

He crossed his arms. "Exactly. And all I keep doing is pushing her farther toward him. Been there, done that, and don't want to go back."

Rachael's face dimmed. "You're not responsible for my getting pregnant."

"If I'd have kept my mouth shut—"

"I'd have slept with Kurt anyway. I was young, and I thought I was in love."

"Penelope thinks she loves East."

The door opened as a family walked in. Rachael waited until they walked past their table. "Has she told you that?"

He thought back. "No."

"Just for the record, she hasn't told me that, either."

He sat up. "You've talked to her?"

"We had coffee last week."

"And you're just telling me this now?"

"Seems that way." Her nonchalant attitude wasn't funny. "When's your next wedding duty?"

"We don't have anything until the joint shower in South Haven."

"When's that?"

"Next weekend."

"And you aren't planning on seeing her until then?"

He sighed. "I was going with the thought that absence makes the heart grow fonder."

Rachael laughed and finally picked up the key. "A block away from my house?"

"Give or take, but it's within walking distance."

She twirled it in her fingers.

"Want to go check it out?" Jonah coaxed.

She stood and pocketed it. "I do, but by myself, if that's okay with you. Will you text me the address?"

"Sure. Call me if you need me?"

"I always do." She kissed his cheek. "Go see Penny. You've had enough absence. Time to check on that fondness." She strolled out the door.

He peered out the window. Outside, the bright sky opened up behind puffy white clouds. He needed to get to the office but wasn't ready to deal with Micah who'd come for a visit. If Walter sided with Micah, Jonah wasn't sure he'd stay in Chicago. If Penny stayed with East, he was sure he wouldn't.

He pushed back from the table and walked outside, heading for his car parked across the street. He'd just reached it when his phone rang. Stifling a groan, he answered. "Hey, Micah."

"Are you always this late to the office?"

He was never late. "It's not even eight."

"Our trucks start out before dawn."

"I know." He slammed his door. "I've ridden them before."

Silence.

Then Micah started again. "I want to know if anyone's using the space at the end of the hall, or if I can move some things in there."

212

"I thought today was just a visit. Didn't think you were moving here until after the wedding."

"I figured since I already signed a lease in town, I might as well move in. I can stay in Holland on the weekends."

A couple walking toward Leitzia's stopped. The man leaned down and kissed his girlfriend, the kiss quickly becoming more than what should be witnessed on a public sidewalk. Jonah glanced away but then suddenly jerked his gaze back.

He nearly dropped his phone.

"Micah, I'll be there in a few."

He hung up on his cousin mid-sentence.

East Fisher. Kissing some blonde.

They disappeared inside, and Jonah's fist curled into a tight ball. Deck East. Call Penelope.

He didn't know what to do first.

He reached for his door handle then stopped. Memories of this situation years before pressing him into his seat. Penny's voice defending her choice to be with East only cemented his decision.

No. East would have a convenient explanation, and if Jonah stepped in, it would only push Penny closer to the guy. She'd already made it clear where her allegiance stood. All he could do was pray she'd see East for who he really was before it was too late.

He'd happily help show her if it would make a difference.

Penny closed the heavy wooden door and leaned against it.

"Another great sale, Penny." Ella stood two feet in front of her.

"It was, wasn't it?" She was ready for a nice, long soak in her tub. "I couldn't have done it without you."

"Need any help shutting this place up?"

"No. I've got it covered." She went over Ella's sales with her and the commission amount she'd be receiving. "You ever want to come on full-time, I'll take you."

The girl groaned. "Don't tempt me. I'm so over school."

"Good thing it's summer break." They walked to the door. "What are you doing with the rest of your day?"

"Meeting a bunch of friends at the beach. You?"

Penny leaned on the doorframe. "Going home to soak in my tub." In her very quiet apartment, by herself. Lacey was spending more and more time at

Shawn's.

"No date with East tonight?"

"No. He's with his parents for the weekend."

"You've been seeing a lot of him lately. Things getting serious?"

"Maybe." He'd definitely been pushing harder for exactly that. But ever since the Adele concert, the passion she'd felt for East had started to cool considerably. "We'll see."

Ella tipped her head. "Whatever happened to Jonah?"

A band clenched around her heart. "Jonah was just a friend." And she missed her friend, dearly.

"Really? I read that totally wrong." She shrugged. "So I'll see you Monday for inventory?"

"Plan on coming around nine."

Ella left, and Penny finished closing up and settling with the homeowner. Within the hour, she walked through her front door. Time for tea and a tub. Maybe she'd pull out an old movie after her soak. She padded to her bathroom, ran a hot tub, added bath salts, and returned to the kitchen to make her tea. A ringing door stopped her mid-pour. Setting down her kettle, she crossed to the family room and peeked out her front window. Her pulse leapt.

Jonah Black.

She nibbled her lip. They hadn't spoken in weeks—ever since she left him standing in the middle of Millennium Park.

The doorbell rang again, and she snuck another glance. He ran a hand over his stubbled jaw. Still as bald as could be on top, but the black fitted shirt and well-worn jeans he had on played well with the look.

He turned, his eyes catching her, mischief there. "You going to open the door or make me ring the bell again?"

"I haven't decided yet."

He leaned into the bell and held. "I could just do this." The buzzing continued.

She couldn't help it. Laughter escaped. "Stop. I'll open up."

He didn't let go until she threw the door open. His own laughter faded, and his lips fell into a straight line. "I'm sorry."

Warmth spilled into her house from her doorstep. She held the doorknob, found his eyes, hinted at a smile. "Me too."

And she was. She didn't simply miss him; she wanted him in her life. The harder she'd tried to forget him these past weeks, the more he rooted in her mind and her heart. Somewhere along the line, Jonah Black had become a part of her.

And she didn't quite know what to do about it.

She leaned on the doorframe. "We're getting good with apologies."

"Yeah, we are, aren't we? That's what happens when you put two imperfect people together." Together. She liked that word. "If we stop giving them, then we'll worry. Deal?"

"Deal."

He held out a small white box that looked incredibly familiar. "Good. Now that we've got that out of the way ... you left this with me the other night, and I believe it's yours."

"Jonah—"

"From one friend to another. No strings attached."

"Just that easy?"

"Just that easy."

And there was his grin, the one that reached all the way to his eyes. She took the box from him and stood back from the door, waving him in. "You want to come in?"

He hesitated for a fraction of a second then nodded. "Sure."

Penny shut the door behind them. Jonah stood in the entry, and she motioned him toward the couch. "Come sit down." She sat, cradling the box of Apres L'ondee in her lap, still unsure if she'd keep it.

Jonah stood over her for a moment, then settled onto the couch beside her. "How's work?"

"It's been busy, but good. I hired Ella to help over the summer so I can organize my basement."

"That's where you keep all your extra inventory?"

"Yeah. That basement is a lifesaver. It's why I pay extra for this place. There's twelve-foot ceilings down there. Can you even believe it?"

"In this city, no way."

"Yes way. And it's all stocked with pieces from sales that I've run on eBay. Only it's gotten away from me, so Ella's going to take that part over for me this summer. Hopefully, by next summer, I'll have my storefront because quite honestly, I'm running out of room here."

His smile was full of confidence. "I have no doubt you'll have a place by then."

A group of kids skateboarded past her open window. Their laughter drifted in and coated the comfortable silence that had descended between them.

He nodded at her fireplace. "I like where you put the picture Rachael painted for you."

"It fit there perfectly." The gunmetal frame played well against her blue walls while the white of the gardenia matched the color of her fireplace mantle. Penny moved her gaze from the picture to Jonah. "Are you planning to attend the party in South Haven next weekend?"

He shrugged. "I'm not sure. Depends on if I'm still a part of the wedding party by then."

"Business not good between you and Micah?"

"As far as he's concerned, things are great."

"But ..."

"But that might change soon." He leaned back. "When are you heading over?"

She debated pushing him. Wanted to. But didn't know if she still had that right. So she answered his question, even though that was a landmine all of its own. "Friday morning." She hesitated.

"I already know he's coming." His focus remained straightforward. "Belle told Micah, and it eventually made its way to me."

"I'm sorry."

He folded his hands together. "Penelope, if we're going to be friends, then I'm going to have to get used to that fact that you're dating East. I don't like it, but I've liked the alternative a whole lot less."

"Which is?"

"Us not speaking. It's why I came by today, to clear the air."

She nudged him. "Is it clear now?"

"It was the moment we said 'I'm sorry'." He turned toward her. "So things are going well with you two?"

That was still a question she was trying to answer, but she wasn't ready to share that struggle. "They are. He's at his parents right now."

"Oh? Again?"

"His father being sick has been really hard on his mother."

Jonah frowned. "Where do his parents live?"

Penny sat forward. East had never really told her. "You know, I'm not sure, but it's a little over an hour from here."

"Have you spoken with him lately?"

"No. I had a sale today, and he's pretty busy when he's at his parents'."

"Did he know about your sale?"

"Yes." She narrowed a glance at him. "What's with all the questions?"

He gave her a long hard look, his mouth opened, and then he clamped it shut. "Nothing. Just making conversation."

Right. Something was up.

"Jonah. Whatever it is, spill."

He shook his head. "It's nothing."

Penny tapped his chest. "Right. I don't believe you for a second."

She jabbed playfully again, and Jonah grabbed her hand. "Stop poking me."

"Why? You ticklish?" She wiggled her fingers in his.

"No, I'm not ticklish."

"Then you won't mind if I do this." She lunged, her free hand assaulting his ribs.

"Hey!" Jonah fell back, their clasped hands pulling her along with him. Penny kept attacking his side until he had both her hands in his grip. A wicked grin slid over his face. "What're you going to do now?"

She matched his grin and dug her chin into the middle of his chest, wiggling it back and forth. Oh, she'd missed laughing with him.

"That's it." He rolled and twisted until she was under him. With one hand he held her wrists, with the other he aimed for her side. "You asked for it."

She writhed underneath him, giggles escaping in gasped breaths. "Okay! Stop," she cried. "Uncle."

"Too late to beg for mercy."

Penny twisted, and her shirt rode up. Jonah's hand connected with bare skin, and he stilled. The warmth of his rough palm on her waist deepened her breaths. His eyes held a question she wasn't sure she had the answer to, but as he leaned down, she suddenly wanted to discover it.

His breath touched her lips.

Beside them, her cell phone rang, the sound like a pin against the bubble surrounding them.

Jonah slammed to his feet. "You should get that." He wiped his hands on his pants. "And I should go."

Penny stood with him, silencing her phone. "You don't have to." She tugged her shirt back into place.

His eyes trailed her movements, and he swallowed. "Yeah. I do." He backed to the door. "I just came to clear things up between us before the wedding activities are fully underway. Didn't want things to be awkward."

Right. Because they weren't awkward now for a whole bunch of other reasons.

"I'll see you in South Haven." He slid outside with more speed than she knew he possessed.

She watched him through her front window. What had just happened?

Her gaze caught on the bottle of Apres L'ondee. She grabbed it and ran for the door. Maybe in his mixed-up state she'd actually be able to convince him to take it back. "Jonah!"

He stopped on the bottom step and turned.

She lifted the box. "I can't keep this. It's too much."

With a long sigh, he climbed the steps until he was eye level with her then held her stare for a minute before speaking. "What if I told you I only paid ten dollars for it?"

"Right." She held it out to him. "I know better. This bottle cost a hundred times that."

He tipped his head. "Why is it," he asked softly, "that you can so easily recognize the worth of that bottle of perfume, but fail to see your own?" His fingers touched her chin. "Stop selling yourself short, Penelope. You're worth far more than you realize."

Her skin warmed beneath his touch. But it was his words that pricked heat into places cold for far too long.

Then his touch was gone. "I need to head out."

She used her words to reach for him. "You really don't have to go. We could have that Scrabble rematch you owe me."

Jonah hesitated.

"I promise to keep my hands to myself. No more tickling."

His eyes went to her untucked shirt at her waist, and the tiniest of smiles raised his cheeks. "Another time, maybe?"

"Oh, okay." She clutched the box of perfume. "Well, it was good to see you."

"You too, Penelope." He watched her for one more long moment and then jogged down her front steps.

Penny stood there until his car disappeared around the corner, the box in her hand a tangible reminder of Jonah's words. With a sigh, she headed inside and back to her lukewarm bath. She placed the white box on the table in the living room and went to drain her tub and reheat her tea.

A few minutes later, she took her drink and snuggled up on the couch. Almost against her will, her hand reached out and grabbed the box with the Apres L'ondee. She opened it and pulled the bottle back out. A small slip of paper fell to her feet. Penny picked it up.

Beauty doesn't come from the outside, but the inside. Make sure you're looking in the right places, Penelope. 1 Peter 3:3-4, Jonah

She thought she had been.

Only now, she wasn't so sure.

Chapter Twenty-Seven

She'd never seen so many Victorian Mansions in her life. Penny turned down a quaint tree-lined street watching for The Windsor Inn. Lake Michigan peeked out from behind the homes, sparkling in the June sunshine, and midway down the road, she spotted the pale blue sign welcoming her. It was the largest house on the block. Caught somewhere between white and cream, it towered three stories with a balcony at the tippy top ringed in by a wrought iron fence. Black rocking chairs filled the porch that wrapped around the entire first floor where bright red flowers dipped low from hanging baskets.

"Finally here," East said as he pulled out his earbuds. It was the first time he'd spoken since they'd set out on the nearly three-hour drive. "And right on the beach, too. Nice."

"It's beautiful, isn't it?"

He nodded. "Beautiful place. Beautiful woman." Then squeezed just above her knee. "Hopefully, some beautiful memories."

Did he think … her cheeks heated. Of course he did because his charm had worked before. Now it was growing old. She parked in one of two spots left in the private lot then snagged her bag from the backseat. East grabbed his and waited for her.

"Looks like a full house." Except Jonah's vehicle wasn't there, but maybe he'd taken the train.

"Is it just the wedding party?"

"I'm not sure. There are ten of us in the wedding, and I think my parents and Micah's are coming tomorrow, so I suppose we could easily book this whole place up."

The front door was dark wood and at least nine feet tall with small leaded-glass rectangular windows lining the top. East reached for the oval iron knob and strolled through.

"Good afternoon," a young woman greeted them. "You must be Penny and East."

"We are." Penny dropped her bag by the front desk.

"Welcome to Windsor Inn. I'm Delaney, and my husband and I own this place. Your sister, her handsome groom, and their wedding party are already down by the beach." She tapped a few buttons on her computer and then held up two antique-looking skeleton keys. "Do you have more bags?"

"No, this is it." East shrugged his higher onto his shoulder.

"All right." Delaney handed the keys to Penny. "You're in the Queen Elizabeth room. Top of the stairs to the right. I'm supposed to inform you that you're to change into suits and meet your sister on the beach."

The beach. Great.

Penny turned. "And my friend is in what room?"

Delaney consulted the computer screen. "I have him in your room."

"No." A sinking feeling settled in her gut. "We're in separate rooms."

A small frown pinched Delaney's face. "You might need to speak with your party. Belle supplied all the room assignments, and everything is booked. I can shuffle things around once you let me know where you'd like them."

"Let's drop our stuff in your room, Penny," East spoke up. "We'll change and find your sister to sort things out."

Yes. They would. "Fine."

"I'm so sorry, Miss Thornton."

"It's not your fault." It was Belle's. Penny snagged her bag. "Top of the stairs and to the right?"

"First door."

East followed her to their door where Penny hesitated.

"If you let me stay, I promise I won't bite." He laughed. "It's not like we haven't shared a room before."

She was tired of him pushing, reminding her that she'd crossed that line before and trying to tug her back over it even farther. Jonah's words pulsed through her mind. *You're worth far more ... stop selling yourself short ...*

"It wasn't on purpose, East. I fell asleep on your couch, and it's not happening again." She shoved the key in the lock. "We're staying in separate rooms."

He kissed the back of her neck. "You sure?"

She turned on him.

He stepped back. "Can't blame a guy for trying, right?"

"You can come in and change, but you're not staying."

Inside, gray washed wooden floors flowed to a set of French doors on the opposite wall. A king-size canopy bed filled the right side, a fireplace the other, and a tiled-in large Jacuzzi tub occupied the corner of the room.

"Nice." East dropped his bag on the bed.

Penny set hers on the small chaise at its foot. She dug out her bathing suit. "I'll change first."

The all-white bathroom was narrow and long with a glassed-in rain shower, pedestal sink, and toilet. Penny nearly slammed the door. How could Belle do this to her? Frustration welled. She needed to get a handle on her temper, or she'd make a scene on the beach. Bad enough that she had to don a swimming suit to meet with everyone, but then Belle stuck her in the same room with East.

After she'd told her not to.

She was about to lose it on her little sister.

Knuckles wrapped across the door. "You going to be a while? Because I'll just change out here."

Penny took a deep breath. It wasn't just Belle she was fed up with.

"Go right ahead." She removed the elastic band from her wrist and shoved her hair into a knot, thankful for the extra moment to breath. Laughter poured through the small window in the bathroom, and Penny peeked out. The Royal Court, decked out in their bikinis, was playing a game of touch football with the groomsmen. Belle stood on the sidelines, her white strapless cover up with the word 'BRIDE' ensuring everyone knew her role.

Quickly changing into her emerald green tankini, Penny faced the mirror. Turned sideways. Sucked in her gut. She'd finally broken through her plateau, but even with the ten-pound weight loss, she still wasn't a match for any one of those women. Thank goodness for cover-ups.

Another knock. "All set."

With a deep breath, she exited the bathroom and tossed her towel into a bag along with some sunscreen.

"Want me to spread some of that on before we leave?" East snagged a hold of her waist.

Penny wiggled free. "I'm good." She brushed past him.

It took less than five minutes to make it from the room to the sand.

"Penny, you're finally here." Belle made a 'T' with her hand. "Time out guys. We've got a few new players."

The group stopped mid-play. The girls' gazes landed on East, appreciation and a hint of surprise filling them. Micah tossed the football in the air, caught it, and tossed it again. "We needed some more muscle. These girls are killing us."

Taylor laughed. "Because you guys are too easily distracted."

Hoots and hollers erupted from the groomsmen. Belle introduced East, and he jogged over to the men's team. Penny joined Belle on the sidelines. "You're not playing?"

"No. Someone has to be the ref, and since I'm the bride, I nominated me."

The game restarted, and Penny waited for a few plays before she made her own tackle of a tough subject. "Belle, why did you book East and I in the same room?"

"I didn't figure you'd want him rooming with Jonah."

Jonah? So he was definitely coming. The thought warmed her heart. The memory of their near-kiss on her couch heated it another degree.

She shook her head.

"Are there any other rooms East could stay in?"

"Nope. Everyone else is paired up already." Belle looked her over. "And honestly, I didn't think by now it would still be an issue. You've been dating for nearly two months. Nobody holds out that long and stays a couple."

She refused to rehash this with Belle. Especially since she'd come dangerously close to proving her right. "I'm not sharing a room with East. You need to fix it."

Belle gave an exaggerated eye roll. "Fine. I'll take care of it later tonight. All right?"

"Thank you."

They watched the game for a few more minutes. East seemed to have no problem tackling any of the ladies. He did throw a few winks in Penny's direction. She humored him with a grin.

Belle pushed down her sunglasses, surprise in her eyes. "You honestly haven't slept with him yet?"

"Really?" Sometimes one heated word did better than several.

Belle's hands lifted. "Fine. I won't say another word." Doubtful. "The guys are going out tonight after dinner. Think he'll want to join them?"

"You'll have to ask him yourself. Where is dinner, anyway?"

"I have a chef coming here." Belle plopped to the sand. "Sorry. Tired of standing, and I don't think they're quitting anytime soon."

Penny settled beside her. Dark circles lined Belle's eyes. "What about you and Micah? Are you getting along any better?"

"I'm marrying him, aren't I?"

Not exactly an answer, but with her jaw set and arms crossed, there was no way she was pushing Belle on her answer.

Belle leaned on her palms, wiggling her toes into the sand. "Oh, hey, Mom found this great makeup to help cover your scar for the big day. If it still shows in wedding pictures, she'll have them Photoshop it out."

Because she'd never be perfect on her own.

Jonah opened the door to the Windsor Inn and landed in complete chaos.

Penelope towered over her little sister near the front desk. Sun-kissed skin said they'd spent the afternoon on the beach; only while it was sunny outdoors, their faces were anything but.

Carrying his suitcase, he skirted around the bridesmaids who'd congregated by the stairway.

"… he's welcome in my room," Taylor declared to the other girls who crowded around her, laughing.

His gaze skipped from them to the groomsmen walking in from the beach. East broke away from the guys and headed toward Penelope. Jonah doubled his stride to beat him there.

"You told me you'd take care of it." Penelope's harsh whisper found him.

"I told you I'd try, but there's nothing I can do." Belle huffed. "So deal with it. You're making a scene."

"I wouldn't have to be if you would have listened. I'm not sharing a room with East."

Jonah's stomach clenched tighter than Penelope's jaw. He joined the sisters at the same moment East did.

"Pen, don't stress your sister. It's a huge bed. I'll stay on my side, and we can take turns in the bathroom. No big deal." East slid his arm around Penelope's shoulder.

Jonah struggled to not knock it off—along with the smug smile on the guy's face.

"It is a big deal." She shrugged away and turned to Jonah. Her lips lifted. "Jonah. You made it."

He returned her smile. "Room problems?"

"Nothing we can't figure out." East pulled Penelope a few feet away. "Come on, I've proven by now you can trust me, right?"

She sighed. "East."

He cupped both her arms in his hands. "If it really bothers you that much, I'll bunk on a lounger outside or a couch down here. I just want you to feel comfortable."

She shifted from one foot to another and nibbled her lip, then peered around him to the couch in the main room. "You'd never fit on that."

"I'll be fine."

"I guess if you promise—"

No way was Jonah letting her finish that sentence.

"Room with me," he spoke over her.

They both looked his way.

"Sorry. Wasn't trying to eavesdrop."

Penelope's eyes widened. "It's okay. You wouldn't mind?"

"Not at all."

Not entirely true, but he'd mind it a whole lot less than East in Penelope's room, sharing her bed.

"That okay with you?" she asked East.

He scanned from Jonah to Penelope before dropping a kiss on her lips. "Sure. Anything for you."

Jonah's fist clenched. "I'll check in and get a couple of keys."

Behind him, Penelope whispered something to East. He wasn't turning around. Unfortunately, a nice, big mirror hung behind the desk. Acid buzzed through his gut as East nuzzled her neck. But then she shoved him off. Ha. Thatta girl. Maybe this weekend wouldn't be so bad after all.

A woman named Delaney punched a few keys on her computer then handed him the keys. "Head up the stairs, take a left, end of the hall on your right."

Jonah rejoined Penelope and East who couldn't seem to keep his hands off of her. He handed him a key. "Here you go, roomie." Hopefully, the floor was carpeted because he was sleeping in front of the door.

A few hours later, dinner wound to an end. The food was some of the best he'd ever tasted, but it was Penelope who stole his full attention. Her silky coral dress played up her lightly tanned skin, stopping at just the right length to show off the toned legs she earned from running and spin classes. She'd been beautiful before all her exercising; now she was stunning. Or maybe it was simply because how well he'd gotten to know her these past two months.

That's where tonight's highlights had ended, however.

Micah and the groomsmen were annoyingly loud. All the girls were busy giggling, and Taylor kept flirting with East who had one hand on Penelope the entire night. He'd kissed her cheek twice and neck once ... one long, lingering kiss, which only made Taylor flirt more. It was like some sick game. And Penelope didn't notice any of it. Her gaze had strayed out the window for most of the night, and she seemed a million miles away. Though once he'd caught her staring at him. When she realized she'd been caught, she'd flushed and hadn't looked his way again.

East leaned in for another kiss, and Penelope presented him with her cheek.

His conscience ate at him. He should tell her East was cheating on her.

Belle whispered something to Penelope. Her brows drew together, then she turned and leaned into East. This time when he kissed her, she didn't turn away.

No. Revealing it would only push her farther into his arms to prove she belonged there—just like with Rachael.

Dessert came, and Jonah waved his away.

"You love chocolate." Penelope's focus shifted to him.

"Not hungry for it tonight." He'd stomached enough sickeningly sweet things already. "Think I'll change and go for a run instead." Tossing down his napkin, he stood and started toward the door.

"The guys are going into town," Micah called after him. "Want to join us?"

"Sorry, cuz, not tonight." He needed out of this room before he said or did something he'd regret. Like reach across the table and throttle East … or pull Penelope into his arms.

When would she see East for what he was?

He bypassed the stairs and went straight out to the beach, no longer looking for a run but just a quick escape. The fresh air, star-filled night, and silence called to him.

By the time he'd walked to the lighthouse and back, a little over an hour had passed, and he was in a slightly better mood. The bed and breakfast was another fifty feet down the sandy beach. A figure moved along the water's edge toward him.

Penelope.

He would have recognized her even without her perfume floating on the wind. He stilled. Waited for her to notice him. As she came closer, he could see her eyes were trained on him.

"I was looking for you." She stopped a foot away.

"Where's East?"

"He went into town."

And she'd come looking for him.

"Where are all the ladies?"

"The Royal Court has taken over the bottom floor of the bed and breakfast."

"Royal Court, huh?"

She shrugged. "Belle already opened my gift. She won't notice I'm gone." A light breeze brushed her hair away from her face. "Why'd you let East room with you?"

"You really need to ask that?"

Intensity built in her eyes. She blinked it away. "I'm glad you came." She reached for his hand. "But I hate that our friendship is still so awkward even after we talked."

"It's not awkward."

"Tell that to your face during dinner."

He chuckled. "Fine. It's awkward when I'm around you and East." He broke their contact before he did something foolish. "Found a memory for your perfume yet?"

She hesitated, her eyes locked on his, studying him. They crinkled slightly in concentration as if she was weighing some important decision. "No. But I do smell it every morning."

"And tonight you chose Illuminum."

"It reminded me of you." Said so simply as if she hadn't needed to weigh that thought at all.

He stilled. Unsure what to make of it. Of her, out here with him instead of with East.

"Jonah ... I—" She reached to touch him, then drew back. No. He wasn't letting her doubts creep back in. His hand caught hers, and he tugged, engulfing her in his arms. If she'd come looking for him, he would make darn sure she found him.

The edge of a wave ran over their toes, but neither moved. Time slipped between them. He didn't let go. Couldn't. Her hands pressed against his chest, her head tucked under his chin, and Jonah held them in one spot, barely moving. Penelope stilled with him.

If she gave him access to her lips, this time he wouldn't be able to stop himself.

Her breath heated the skin beneath his shirt. Slowly, she inched her face up, and her eyes found his.

He shook his head.

"What thought are you trying to dislodge?" she whispered.

"Penelope." He drew her name out slowly, and in that moment, he offered her the chance to walk away. She raised her mouth instead.

A low groan escaped him, and he met her raised lips. His hand tightened its hold against her waist, pulling her in deeper, her fisted hands at his chest a gentle barrier between them.

He explored her, tasting licorice, and delved for more. His fingers tunneled into her hair, finding it as silky as he'd been imagining for weeks. A tiny sigh escaped her, and she flattened her palms against his chest, pressing there for a moment before tentatively sliding up along his collar then linking at his nape. She stood on tiptoes, her body curved into his, fitting to him as if she were made to be by his side.

He wasn't letting her go.

Nestling in, he pressed a kiss to her temple. "Penelope," he whispered, his breath tickling her by the way she shivered in his arms. He held her closer.

"Mhmm?"

"Penelope, I'm falling—"

Belle's laughter spilled across the sand from the open bed and breakfast window.

Penelope tensed.

No. He lifted her, twisting her around, away from the voices, willing Belle out of her mind. He claimed her lips again.

She pushed against him.

He pulled all his strength and released her. She wouldn't look at him.

"Penelope."

When her eyes met his, they were wet. "I ..." She tugged her hands through her hair. Confusion clouded her face. "I shouldn't have come looking—"

"Don't, Penelope."

She shook her head. "I've just missed you so much, your friendship. Then here, you holding me ... I got lost."

He let out a hard breath. "Did you? Because it certainly didn't feel like it."

"Jonah. You know I'm with East. I haven't given you reason to think otherwise."

This time he laughed and stepped closer to her. She wasn't getting out of it that easily. He ran a finger over her lips. "Right."

She backed away. "I am with him. One kiss doesn't change that."

"You're trying to tell me you feel nothing for me?"

He held her stare until she dropped it. Then he waited out her silence. No way he was making this easy for her. He loved her too much to just let her walk away.

The surf crashed along the beach. A few crickets called from the long grass lining the path to the bed and breakfast. Light laughter trickled from inside the house.

"No."

His head snapped up, his eyes holding hers. "What?"

"I care for you, Jonah, I do." The wetness in her eyes spilled over, and he heard her unspoken 'but.'

"Don't say it." He tried to reach for her.

She took another step. Shook her head.

Belle's voice carried on the wind.

And Penny straightened her shoulders. "But I'm not breaking things off with East."

He took her sucker punch, softened by her tears. She was caught and couldn't even see it. "You're too good for him, Penelope, not the other way around."

A debate warred in her eyes. One he desperately wanted to win ... but only she could do that.

A low breath escaped him. "I wish you could see what I see."

"What, Jonah. What do you see when you look at me?" Her words were whispered as if she were seeking the answer to a question she'd never solved and couldn't believe he'd supply it.

The wind picked up her curls, and he grabbed one long lock. Tucking it behind her ear, his hand remained there. "I see you." Her eyes searched his, their deep green depths delving into his. A tear spilled over those dark lashes, and he wiped it away with his thumb. "Thoughtful, loving, sarcastic ..."—her doubtful laughter broke his words—"stunningly beautiful, you."

She pressed her cheek into his palm, her eyes not leaving his. Oh, he was a hundred types of stupid. He leaned in and kissed her again. Pure sweetness. "Break things off with East." He pulled away. "Be with me."

Her teeth caught her bottom lip, nibbling slowly then releasing it. "I ... I'm so confused. I just need time." Conflict and angst swirled around her. "After the wedding. Let me have until then." She shoved her hair away from her face. "Let me figure things out."

Yeah. Make that a million times stupid.

"It's not something to 'figure out,' Penelope. Either you want to be with me, or you don't." Against every desire screaming otherwise, he let her go. "And you just gave me your answer."

Pretending he hadn't heard it would only ruin them both.

Chapter Twenty-Eight

Penny stood on the beach, chilled by the wind. She wrapped her arms around herself, watching Jonah's retreating back until he disappeared into the night. What was wrong with her? This amazing man was walking away ... and she wasn't stopping him.

Her heart screamed to run after him.

Her mind cemented her feet to the ground.

She touched her fingertips to her mouth. That kiss. No one had ever kissed her like that. Like she was seen. Known. Cherished.

And she was letting him go?

Penny took a tentative step forward. Why did her past hold her in such a tight grip? Could what one man saw in her be enough to fill those places left empty for years? But wasn't that what she was doing with East? How was it any better to shift her emotions to Jonah?

Things were so jumbled. And until she could figure herself out, she wasn't worth anything to anyone.

Light from the bed and breakfast spilled onto the beach, and she followed a narrow path to the house. Avoiding Belle and the Royal Court, she scooted around the side to the front entrance so she could sneak upstairs to her room

"... but do you really think she'll fit that dress by the wedding? I mean, she's lost some, but not two sizes worth." Kelsey's voice drifted through the open window.

Belle spoke. "The bridal shop wouldn't let me order it smaller than what they measured. I only told Penny that to motivate her because I knew she could lose the weight if she tried."

"She definitely looks better," Ava's voice answered.

"Good enough to catch East's attention?" Back to Kelsey.

Taylor laughed. "But not to keep it."

"Yeah. What was going on between you two?" Ava asked.

"Just a little light flirting. For now."

"Enough you guys ..." Belle's voice cut in, but Penny had heard all she could stomach.

Embarrassment flooded through her, and she dashed to her room. She sat on her bed and hugged her pillow, seeking solace and answers. What did she want?

The cloudiness in her mind didn't lift. If anything, as she dissected the past couple months of her life, comparing East and Jonah, her confusion grew until the only way to avoid the storm was to roll on her side and let sleep claim her.

She woke to something wet pressed behind her ear. A heavy weight pushed against her back and over her shoulder. Still half asleep, she shoved at it, but whatever it was only pressed in harder. The wetness trailed across her skin toward her lips.

Warm fingers slid from her waist up under her shirt.

Fingers?

Penny sat up and pushed them back. The hands moved. The lips didn't.

"Hey." East's breath touched her cheek.

And the full stench of a brewery hit her.

His hands now lay on either side of her, and he dipped his mouth to hers. She shoved him away. "You're drunk."

He laughed. "Nah. Just feeling good." He slid a hand onto her waist again. "Wanted to share the feeling."

She stopped his hand. "How'd you get in here?"

"My key." His hot breath came in too close. "You didn't take it, so I just assumed—"

Penny shoved against the headboard. "You assumed wrong." She avoided his hands and lips, pointing toward the door. "Leave. Now."

He didn't move. "Don't worry. No one saw me come in, and I'll leave as soon as we're done playing." He slid closer. "Trust me; you'll enjoy this game."

He was quick for as drunk as he was. His lips found hers again, pressing her into the headboard, while his hands roamed over her body. She shoved against them, turning her head at the same time so he connected with her cheek instead.

"You just need some persuasion." He kept kissing. "Give in, Penelope. You know you want this. You've wanted to for a while. I've felt it."

"No, East." She kept her face turned.

"Oh wait, I forgot." He pulled his lips from her cheek and leaned in close to her ear. "You're beautiful. That's what you need to hear, isn't it?"

Her skin chilled.

"I make you feel beautiful, don't I?" His wet mouth brushed her jaw and along her neck. "You have no idea how beautiful I could make you feel if you just let me."

His slurred words, his hands, his lips … she felt nowhere near beautiful.

Pulling her knees in, she kicked at him.

Wind sailed from his lips.

"Hey." He straightened, swerved. "What was that for?"

"Get off." Red hot anger seared through her veins.

He laughed. "I'm trying to."

That anger boiled over. He came at her again. She kicked again, nailed him in the gut. If he didn't get the message this time, she'd aim lower.

"You're serious?" His eyes widened.

"Do I look like I'm not?" Her jaw clenched so tightly that the words came between her teeth.

She struggled not to flinch at the name he called her. Not that he'd noticed if she had, could barely stand.

"This is how you thank me for all the work I've done on your body?" He lunged again, this time more clumsy than before. His words slurred closer together. "You owe me."

She slapped his hand away. His eyes turned to ice. "You think you're the only choice I have tonight?" he scoffed. "Being with you only makes them throw themselves at me even more." He crawled toward her, grabbing her foot. She nailed him again.

"You little—" His slurred words dropped off as he collapsed on the bed. He'd passed out. Scrunched up against the headboard, she eyed him. His short blond hair, tan skin, toned body, and muscles no longer spelled perfection for her. Her stomach threatened to revolt.

What had she ever seen in him?

Her reflection in the mirror across from the bed captured her. Shirt pulled to the side, hair in a tangled knot, and empty, sorrow-filled eyes.

She'd tried to see herself.

Oh, Lord, I'm so messed up.

Tears fell hot across her cheeks. She held her head in her hands and sobbed, East's snores coming from the end of the bed. He wasn't the reflection she should have been using to see who she was. The verses Jonah had written inside her gift bubbled to mind like a cool spring in a desert. They spoke of where her worth truly was rooted.

Worth.

East always used the word beautiful, manipulating her with it.

But Jonah spoke of her worth.

How many times had he whispered that word to her? Tried to get her to see her own value, while all she'd done was cling to East, attempting to prove her beauty through him.

She'd been so wrong. Giving in to things she never should have in hopes that East would satisfy the hole in her heart. Rachael's warning had been spot on—she'd nearly lost herself in East.

The erosion had been so subtle, she hardly noticed it happening. And now the ground beneath her shifted as she grasped the truth Jonah had tried to share all along. She was worth so much more than she'd been willing to accept in trying to prove what was already true: she was beautiful.

For the first time in her life, she began to feel it.

And it didn't matter what Belle or Mom saw. It didn't matter who she was with—

Who she was with.

Jonah's words from the beach fell over her. *"I see you."*

Her heart broke.

All along, he'd seen and accepted her—imperfections and all. Known her worth. Her mind might have missed it, but her heart knew it.

She picked up her cell phone and tried to call him. His voicemail picked up. "Um ... Jonah? I know I'm probably the last person you want to talk to, but ... if you get this ... call me. Please."

Penny dropped her cell phone onto the covers and stood. East still snored, not having moved a muscle. She nudged him, but he didn't respond. At least if he was passed out in here he wasn't bugging any other woman. She may not like the Royal Court, but she wouldn't wish this jerk on anyone.

His snores grew louder. Penny rolled her eyes and reached for the blanket under him. She tugged, not caring if East ended up on the floor or not. The blanket gave way, and her cell phone clattered across the floor. She picked it up, snagged a pillow and the Bible from the bedside table, and headed to the bathroom—where she could lock the door. And wait for Jonah to call.

Hours later, sunlight streamed through the bathroom window, waking Penny from a fitful night's sleep. Her phone still rested on the bathroom counter where it had remained silent all night.

She'd really made a mess of things.

Tossing off her blanket, she stood and stretched. Hard, cold, tile floors did not make the best of beds. She'd be feeling this one all day.

Her reflection caught her attention in the mirror, and she smiled. Last night, she'd shed the lies she'd listened to for so many years. The freshness of this morning fell on her new heart and mind. And of all the revelations a long evening stuck in this bathroom with her new thoughts brought, only one had her pulse racing over a bundle of raw nerves.

It wasn't only her own beauty she'd missed, but Jonah's. He was incredibly beautiful on the inside ... and suddenly the most handsome man she'd ever seen on the outside. And right now, all she wanted to do was see him. Tell him how wrong she'd been and let him know how much she loved him. Because she did. The full strength of her feelings hit her in the middle of the night, and it wasn't something she wanted to say for the first time over the phone.

Penny tiptoed to the door. No sounds came from the other side, so either East was still passed out, or he'd left. Her hand touched the knob, and she slowly opened the door to peek out. He was sprawled face down on her bed. The sheets were in a tangled heap on the floor, and the stench of him reached her all the way across the room. Wow, had she been blind? A wave of thankfulness washed over her. Last night could have ended so differently.

With a shudder, she silently closed the door and relocked it. Her suitcase was in the bedroom, but at least her bathroom supplies were in here. She turned on the shower. Hopefully, he'd wake up and head to his own room while she was getting ready. No way she wanted to see him.

After a quick, scalding hot shower, she tossed on the hotel's fluffy white robe and peeked into the room a second time. East was stirring on the bed. She shut the door and locked it again. She'd stay in here until he left.

A ring filled the room. Jonah. Her heart stopped, then started beating twice its normal speed. She lunged for her phone. A familiar blonde's face smiled back at her. Along with the name 'Kelly Hanning'. The hostess from Roof?

It took one long moment for understanding to dawn. Her eyes narrowed.

She'd taken East's phone last night instead of hers.

Her finger slid across the screen, but the call had disconnected already. A text appeared.

Pretty sure your mom needs you home again(:

Pieces of a puzzle began to shift into place. She didn't like the picture.

The bathroom door shook beneath a knock.

"Last night everything you hoped for?" East's smooth voice penetrated the room. "Come on out, and the morning can be just as great."

Seriously? Did he think—

Fury wrapped around her, and her hand touched the knob just as a knock at her bedroom door sounded.

"Oh. Did you order room service?" East's footsteps traveled across the room.

Penny's hand hesitated over the doorknob. She couldn't kill him in front of an audience, but she could humiliate him.

She flung open the door and nearly lost her breath.

East leaned against the doorframe, shirtless, smirking at Jonah. "Jonah, hey, Penny's a little uh, indisposed, at the moment."

Jonah's gaze caught hers, dropped to her bare feet, and then traveled up past the robe she wore to her wet hair. He spun on his heel.

"Jonah! Wait."

He didn't stop. Penny made it to the door before a tug on her robe stopped her.

"You might want to put some clothes on first." East slipped an arm around her waist and nuzzled her neck as he pulled her into the room and shut the door. "Or not."

Her hand clenched in a fist, and she decked him.

East grabbed his mouth. "What was that for you crazy—"

"Get out." She shoved him.

He shoved her back. "Fine by me. Just need my phone."

Penny stormed to the bathroom, grabbed his phone, and threw it at him. "You might want to call Kelly. Something about your mom needing you at home."

East didn't even blink an eye. "Right. Thanks for that. You may not have let me into your bed, but you certainly got me into hers."

She recoiled. "What?"

Cold laughter raked over her. "Why do you think I took you to Roof? That heated Kelly right up." He grinned. "Needed to prove she could turn my head over someone like you."

"You used me?" To get in bed with another woman?

"That was just a side-benefit." A sick smile taunted her. "At first, you were just a challenge. No one's said no to me before. Then Jonah came into the picture, and I wasn't about to let him take what I couldn't." He rubbed his jaw. "Guess Kelly and I are more matched than I realized."

Hurt and anger warred inside her. "Was your father ever really sick?"

"Only when I was sick of you, sweetheart." He grinned and walked out the door.

Penny slammed it and slid to the ground in tears.

East had never been her dream. She'd been blinded to think so. But that hurt didn't even touch the searing burn coming from the pained expression on Jonah's face. In that awful moment, East had smashed a possible future that had eclipsed her dreams.

Jonah didn't stop until he was in his car. Even then he kept going. He drove for an hour, not even sure where he was headed until he ended up at some beach near Saint Joseph. Abandoning his car, he walked hard and fast.

No matter which way he turned, he couldn't get the image of Penelope in that robe out of his mind. Or of East's smirk as he leaned against her doorframe.

He wanted to hit something.

Preferably East's face.

He reached for his cell to call Rachael. It had died last night, and he'd forgotten his cord. Unable to sleep, he'd left early this morning to buy one and charge it. He'd noticed voicemails from Penelope, but instead of listening to them, he'd gone straight to her room. What he'd intended to tell her he needed to say in person. East had remained MIA all night, and Jonah had honestly thought—after watching him flirt with Taylor all afternoon—he'd been creating the proof Jonah needed to inform Penelope he was cheating on her.

Man had he been wrong.

The phone rang, and Rachael answered. "Hey, Jonah. How's it going over there?"

He ran a hand over his eyes. "Not good."

"Oh boy. Hang on a sec." A door closed on the other end of the line. "What's wrong?"

Except he couldn't get the words out. "Just talk, Rach. Tell me something good."

A moment's hesitation before, "Walter called this morning. Said he couldn't reach you."

That Walter's call was her something good momentarily lifted a portion of the weight he carried. "What'd he say?"

"That he's thought things through, and he'll vote with you as long as you don't make Micah ride the trucks. Start him at the bottom, that's fine, and the COO title will be revisited within a year's time, but no Holland division. He's sending an email to Micah."

At least one small victory today. But the timing of that victory may cost him. "Micah hasn't seen it yet."

"Meaning he hasn't kicked you out of the wedding yet?"

"Exactly." Or he'd have been at his door this morning. Of course, maybe then Jonah wouldn't have discovered East in Penelope's room.

He swallowed acid. Pretending it wasn't true didn't make it a lie.

"You're positive this is the route to go?" Rachael's question beckoned him back to their conversation.

"I don't see any way around it. He needs to learn the ropes if he wants to understand the decisions we make, or even if he wants the guys' respect. I won't make his training status permanent or any longer than it needs to be. If he applies himself, he can advance quickly."

"You don't have to convince me." She paused. "Why'd you call, Jonah?"

He stayed silent. Voicing it meant facing it.

"Jonah?"

It took another long moment before the words choked out. "Penelope slept with East."

"What?" Shock. "You're sure?"

He shoved against the image of her in that robe. East shirtless in her room. This time there was no miscommunication. "He answered her hotel room door this morning."

"Jonah. That doesn't mean—"

It did. Things had been heading that way for a while, and he couldn't pretend otherwise anymore. If she hadn't made it clear on the beach, her actions afterward left no room for wondering. Or hoping. "She doesn't want me, Rach." Those words hurt. The reality hurt more. "She made it clear last night. Her choice is East."

"I don't believe that, Jonah. I've seen how she looks at you." No doubt she was now pacing. It was how she worked her problems. "Did you tell her East was cheating?"

"No." He scrubbed a hand against his bald head, second-guessing that decision. "I was going to this morning, but I wound up the one surprised. I read this whole thing wrong." Would she have chosen differently if he'd admitted what he knew? Or would it only have pushed her there sooner?

"I don't think you did."

"You didn't see what I saw." He stared at the sun hoping to burn the images away. "Thanks for letting me know about Walter."

"Don't hang up."

But he had nothing left to say. "Tell Gavin we're finding a new gym on Monday."

She didn't respond immediately. Then her soft voice drifted across the line. "Love you, big brother. I'm sorry you're hurting."

"Love you too." He wasn't only hurting. Anger was slipping in as well. "Thanks for listening."

"Always."

They hung up, and Jonah checked the time. The shower was in two hours. With all the people there, he could sneak in for his things and then leave. Avoid seeing Penelope with East.

He slammed his fist into his palm.

What was she thinking?

What had *he* been thinking? If he'd told her about East ...

No. He wasn't playing 'what ifs'. Penelope had made her choice. Would have made that choice anyway. He'd been a fool not to see it. The only thing she cared about was how East's perfect smile and words aimed her way. And after what he'd witnessed this morning, that choice was a permanent one. Nothing she could say would erase the imprint it left on his mind.

Defeated, he dropped his head in his hands. He was angry at her, but he was livid with himself. Because the ultimate truth stared him in the face: nothing she could say or do would erase his love for her either.

Chapter Twenty-Nine

"Are you going to stand there all afternoon?" Belle held a glass of ginger ale. Penny glanced at her little sister. "Do you need me for anything?"

"You are a bridesmaid. You should be mingling."

"I have mingled."

Belle laughed. "You talked to Dad, Gran, and Gramps. That's not mingling." She peered around Penny. "Who are you waiting for, anyway? And where's East?"

He'd called a cab to take him to the train station an hour ago. Didn't Belle notice anyone other than herself?

Stupid question.

"Wait. You're waiting for Jonah, aren't you?" Belle nearly danced around her. "I knew something was up between you two. He is such a better fit for you than East."

For once Belle had it right, only for all the wrong reasons. Penny looked her up and down. Her light blonde hair perfectly styled, nails a shiny pink, diamonds in her ears that rivaled the ring on her finger, and an outfit that could have walked off the pages of Vogue ... yet her smile never reached her eyes. Belle wasn't as happy as she portrayed.

"Do you even know what makes a perfect fit, Belle?" Penny crossed her arms.

"I must have some idea. I am the one getting married." She wagged her ring in Penny's face and walked away.

Penny leaned against the wall of the large foyer and waited. She'd stood there an hour already, and she'd stand another twenty if necessary. After tossing East from her room, and getting control of her tears, she'd thrown on her clothes and searched for Jonah. She'd scoured the property for him before realizing his car was missing. So she'd come in here to wait for him. Belle and Micah's shower was in full swing behind her, and the bed and breakfast's entrance stood in front of her.

"You all right, honey?" Dad approached.

His soft question coaxed tears from her again. She swiped at them with the back of her hand. "I will be once I talk to someone. If he'll listen."

Dad's green eyes crinkled. "He will."

"I'm not so sure."

"I am." Dad's voice held a quiet assurance.

Micah made another pass through the entry. He'd been stalking the door, same as her, but she couldn't figure out why. "What makes you so sure?"

"Because Jonah loves you."

And she'd hurt him. Terribly.

Behind her, Mom announced it was time for the bride and groom to open their gifts. With a glare at the door, Micah rejoined his guests. Dad kissed her cheek. "I should go back in."

So should she. But she couldn't make herself.

She stood alone, staring at the door, willing it to open. The crinkle of gift wrap mingled with oh's and ah's. At one point, teasing sounded from an elderly great-aunt over a bow Belle had broken on one of her gifts.

"Every broken bow equals a baby."

The women giggled; the men groaned. Penny cast a glance over her shoulder. Belle sat on a padded folding chair, her face chalky white. Beside her, Micah's face appeared etched in stone. If having babies together elicited that reaction, why were they getting married?

Penny refocused on the door. She had her own problems to fix. She couldn't fix Belle's.

More laughter caught her attention, but the front door creaked open. Jonah walked through, eyes fixed on the stairs. Heart pounding, Penny launched across the foyer. "Jonah?" Her voice faltered, nerves getting the best of her.

He turned her way, and the steel in his eyes flashed. He cut them back to the steps, not breaking his stride. If anything, his pace increased.

"Jonah, wait." She caught up to him and reached for his hand.

When her fingers touched his bare arm, he snatched back as if she'd burned him. "Leave it alone, Penny."

She stilled. His voice was so cold.

"Jonah, please, we have to talk."

"No. We don't."

She jumped in front of him, barring his way to the stairs. "We do."

His muscles tightened. She braced herself, sure he was about to push past her and unwilling to let him through. After a moment, he narrowed his gaze on her. "Fine. You want to talk. Let's talk." He grabbed her arm and led her into the room across the hall from the shower. The second the door closed, he released her. "Let's start with how I poured my heart out to you on the beach last night. How you made me think for one split second that maybe, just maybe, you might actually care for me—"

"I do ca—"

His snarl stopped her. "Right. That's why you slept with a guy who's cheating on you."

She stilled. He knew?

"What?" Her voice whispered past her lips.

"Not that it likely matters. All you care about is that he's looking at you too." He pushed her aside, moving toward the door. "Feel beautiful now?"

The breath left her lungs. She wrapped her arms around her middle. "You knew that East was cheating and didn't tell me?"

"Like I said, wouldn't have mattered."

Hurt lanced her. "How can you say that to me?"

"Because that's what it's all about, right?" His hands raked over his head. "I was such an idiot for sticking around, hoping ..." He stopped and spun, looking at her. "Forget it. You're so focused on proving to your sister and mom, to yourself even, that you can have someone like him." He let out a short, unhappy breath. "Not the bald, fat guy."

"You're not—"

"Never mind how incredibly hypocritical that is."

"Hypocritical?"

"I'm sure you know the word." His face twisted. "Saying one thing, doing the other. Kind of like how you claim your sister and mom can't see past your outside ... yet when it came to seeing me, you did the same thing."

The truth sliced her. "I know, and I'm sorry, Jonah. I was so wrong, and last night I realized it. I told East to leave. I was waiting for you. I choose you."

"What? You bagged the hot guy so now you can lower yourself to my level?"

"Jonah, stop. This isn't you."

A hard, cold laugh slipped from his mouth, and he got in her face. "Thought it wasn't manners you cared about, Penny, just the looks."

His words forced her to take a step back.

"Or did East disappoint last night?"

She slapped him.

Jonah rubbed his cheek then turned toward the door. He pulled it open, slammed it against the wall, and started up the stairs.

Penny followed just as Micah barreled out of the room across the hall. "Jonah."

A groan escaped Jonah, and he turned. "Not now, Micah."

Micah hauled him off the stairs. "Yes, now. I've been waiting all morning for you." He tugged his phone from his pocket, lit up the screen, and shoved it in Jonah's face. "Explain this email."

Jonah didn't touch it. "We can talk about it later."

"Now."

"You've got guests, and your bride waiting for you."

"I don't care about them." A gasp came from behind Micah as Belle walked up to them, but he kept going. "I want answers."

Jonah towered over Micah by a couple of inches. He narrowed in on where he'd gripped his arm. "You've already got them; you just don't like them." He tugged free. "Call me on Monday, and we can discuss this."

Bright red splotched Micah's neck and face. "We'll discuss it now."

Belle stood at his side. "Micah, please. Our guests—"

"Can wait, and so can you. You're the one who's pushed this, so if you don't like the timing of it all, tough." Micah brushed her aside.

Belle's eyes widened. She turned and ran through the crowd.

What was going on? "Hope you two are proud of yourselves."

Jonah's gaze swept her way then dismissed her. Without a word, he stalked up the stairs.

"You're out of the wedding, Jonah. Pack up your stuff and get out of here," Micah called after him.

"With pleasure." Jonah's voice drifted to them as he disappeared down the hallway.

Fighting tears, Penny turned to discover the shower guests' open mouths and wide eyes. She rushed past them, searching for her parents and little sister. Belle found her first.

"You," Belle's voice strangled out. She stood beside a large display of cupcakes. Chocolate. They looked amazing. Perfect for what was intended to be another perfect day for her little sister.

Belle advanced. "You ruined my shower."

Mom corralled the guests toward the French doors. "Everyone, lunch is about to start on the veranda. Follow me, please. There's nothing more to see ..." She wrung her hands together nervously. Her concern was for her reputation, not her daughters. Penny was sure of that.

Micah's parents stepped forward and opened the doors. "Come on, everyone." They shooed people outside then followed, closing the doors behind them.

Mom exited with the guests, but Dad remained in the room. "Girls. You're sisters. You love each other," his voice soothed.

Belle's lower lip trembled, and fat tears rolled down her cheeks. "She ruined my shower."

"I?" Penny switched her gaze from Dad to Belle. Sure, she'd fought with Jonah, but she'd done that well away from the guests. Micah was the one who had made a scene in front of everyone. Her *perfect* groom. The one who had implied she wasn't important to him.

"Yes, you." Belle pushed a finger into her chest. "Are you happy now?"

"What?" Penny stepped back. "No."

Laughter popped from her sister's mouth. "Right. You've hated me since the day they brought me home. Why would I ever think you'd want to celebrate my happiness?"

Hated her? "I don't hate you, Belle." Disliked her at times, sure. Crazy jealous of her, yes. But she didn't hate her.

"It's not my fault that Mom picked me. Or that she changed your name."

Penny drew back. Belle knew?

Belle's lips lifted, her eyes piercing Penny. "Yeah. I know. And I know it's why you hate me. But it wasn't my fault."

"I … I know it wasn't. You weren't even here yet." Penny stepped back, still trying to catch up with her sister's words. They'd come out of nowhere. All these years she'd thought Belle hadn't known. Penny had carried her hurt deep, believing she was the only one in the family who'd been affected by Mom's decision.

But all this time, Belle knew? Words deserted her.

Dad cleared his throat and stepped forward. "It wasn't either of your fault. It was your mother and me, and what we did was wrong."

That was the first time Penny had ever heard him say that. It was actually the first time any of them had ever really talked about it.

The twisted ball of hurt inside her pushed toward the surface, but she kept quiet.

Dad placed a hand on both of them. "If I had known how a simple name change would have played out, I never would have allowed it."

A simple name change?

"It wasn't that simple, Dad." The words barely made it past Penny's clenched throat.

Belle stepped forward too. "There was nothing simple about it."

He shook his head. "No, maybe there wasn't." He sank to a folding chair. "I owe both you girls an apology."

After over thirty years, they were going to talk about this now? Here?

The French doors behind them opened, and Mom walked in. "Honestly, do none of you realize there are over fifty guests out there waiting for your attention?"

Dad stood back up. "Our daughters need our attention more, Adelaide."

"What's their problem now?"

"The problem we created when we took one daughter's name from her and eventually gave it to another."

Mom's eyes widened. "Oh, honestly." She stalked over to Penny. "You were a baby. How could you even know?"

"I saw my original birth certificate."

"So did I," Belle added. "It was tucked in with the paperwork from my adoption."

Mom huffed. "So I changed Penny's name from Bella Rose to Penelope Rose." She pointed to Dad. "You were constantly calling her your "Lucky Penny" after your darling mother anyway."

No way. Penny had waited too long to hash this out. Now that it was out in the open, she wasn't letting Mom off that easily. "That's not why you did it, Mom. I saw the date. It was right after my surgery." Penny touched her scar. "I wasn't your Bella anymore, your 'beauty.'"

Mom clutched her chest, silent for a moment. Then her voice whispered, "You have no idea how hard it was to see my dreams die when that doctor messed up your face."

"You pushed for that surgery, Adelaide. They said the birthmark would likely clear up on its own, and that having the surgery caused a greater chance of defect."

"I didn't think it would." She touched Penny's face. "I just wanted you to be perfect."

Belle watched the two of them. "And since she failed at your idea of perfection, you found me to take her place."

"Found you?" Mom turned to Belle. "No, Bella Rose, I picked you."

Dry laughter poured from Belle. "Yes, you did, didn't you? I saw the papers. You were very specific in what you were looking for. Lucky me. I fit the bill and could wear the name, right?" She rounded on them all. "Do you know what it feels like to be a replacement? Needing to stay perfect all the time. Knowing if you fail, you'll be replaced too?"

"About what it feels like to be the one already replaced." Penny traced her scar. "Knowing you'd already failed ... that you weren't ever enough."

Mom clucked her tongue. "Oh, please stop, both of you. You're reading too much into this." She pointed to Penny. "It's not my fault the doctor messed up the surgery to remove that birthmark." Then she pointed to Belle. "Nor is it my fault that you were blessed with beauty. I did what I felt best."

Dad stepped forward. "And I let her. For that, I'm sorry." His eyes implored them. "Don't hate each other for a situation your mother and I created."

"Situation?" Mom shook her head. "The only situation here is that crowd outside." She hooked Belle's arm. "Come on and take care of your guests. Not to mention your groom looks like he could use you by his side."

Out on the deck, Micah sulked at a table, red solo cup in his hand.

Belle ripped from Mom's grasp. "That's all you care about, isn't it? Image." She stepped away. "And it's all you've taught me to care about, but I've had enough." Her little sister's gaze found hers. "I never wanted to replace you, Penelope. I wanted a sister. I wanted to be accepted. Loved." Her eyes filled with tears. "But you hated me. I mean, how could you not?"

Belle knew. All this time she knew that the name Bella Rose was Penny's first. And somehow that changed things. It cracked open a door that had been shut.

"I don't hate you." Penny grasped her hand. "Bella Rose."

Her sister's big blue eyes widened. "You don't?"

"No. I don't."

"Then why did you leave me?"

"Leave you?" She was right here. Had been there for her in each step of this wedding.

Before Belle could respond, Mom spoke. "This is all well and lovely, but you're really needed outside, Belle. People are beginning to stare at us through the windows."

"Enough, Adelaide!" It was the first time Penny had ever heard Dad raise his voice. "There are far more important things than what those people will think." He faced his girls. "I'll handle the crowd. You come out when—or if—you're ready."

"George—"

Dad grabbed Mom's arm and forced her out the French doors.

Silence filled the room. Penny finally broke it. "When did I leave you, Belle?"

"You moved to Chicago."

Oh. "That was more of me running away."

"Yeah. From me." She sniffed.

"From never being good enough." Penelope approached her little sister and took her hand. "We sure have made a mess of things, haven't we?"

A hiccup-sob came from Belle. "Think we can ever fix them?"

Fresh light shone on her little sister. Belle had lived under the constant pressure of perfection for fear she'd be brushed aside if she fell short. She was raised believing her beauty was the only reason she was loved.

Her cruel words had come from her own deep hurts and insecurities.

Maybe she and her little sister were more alike than Penny had ever realized. "I do, Bella. In time, I do."

Belle sucked in a deep breath and nodded. "I should go check on Micah." She swiped at her tears.

Penny reached out and squeezed her little sister's hand. "Want me to come with you?"

"You'd do that?"

"I'll be right by your side."

Belle shared her smile, and they walked through the door, hand in hand.

Jonah slipped farther down the hall, away from the room Penelope and her sister had just deserted. He stopped in the empty foyer; his eyes settled on the deep blue paint of the walls, his mind on what he'd just overheard. He curled his fingers into fists. The conversation he'd listened to between Penelope and her family explained so much.

From day one, she'd been told she wasn't beautiful.

Stripped of her name, Bella ... *beauty* ... as a baby ... and then to know it had been given to someone else her mother thought was more deserving? No wonder her idea of beauty was so messed up.

No wonder she fell for East's lines.

East.

Jonah squeezed his eyes closed. As much as he'd just gained understanding of Penny, it had come too late. He may have the whole picture now, but it would never erase the one in his mind of her with East.

Or the decision she'd made. And it was so obviously not him—no matter what she'd said.

She'd made her choice last night.

Pain pricked at his heart. If he didn't create some kind of distance from her, that pain would only grow stronger. And all of Chicago wasn't distance enough.

He dialed his father's number, picked up his bag, and walked out the door.

Chapter Thirty

J onah knocked on Rachael's door a second time. He'd been in California for
the past two weeks, visiting with Dad and mulling over his future. Now he
needed to share his decisions with his sister.

He knocked again, and she still didn't answer. Jonah didn't have his key on
him. He pulled out his phone and dialed her cell.

"Hey, Jonah. What's up?" Skillet played in the background, and he could
barely hear her.

"I'm at your house. Where are you?"

"You're back?" The music quieted.

"I just got in."

"Well, I'm at the studio you rented for me."

He started up the sidewalk. "Mind if I swing by?"

"You're always welcome; you know that."

"Be right there."

They disconnected, and he pocketed his phone. Up ahead, Rachael's studio
space came into view. She'd already painted the door a teal blue and added a
silver knocker to it. It brightened up the corner and made it easy enough to spot,
even from the street. As he approached, music thrummed from the building.
She'd turned it back up.

Before he could knock, Rachael opened it. With her light brown hair pulled
back into a loose knot, paint-splattered jeans, and a streak of white across one of
her forearms, she was a sight for sore eyes. But her smile was the best. When he'd
purchased the studio space, he prayed she'd use it.

He'd also hoped Penelope would move her antique shop into the space
beside it. Though he'd never told anyone as much.

And he had no business thinking it now.

He smiled at Rachael. "Looking good."

"Wish I could say the same."

"Hey!" He flicked her shoulder.

She dodged him and closed the door, then walked over to her wireless
speaker. With one press of her finger, the room quieted.

Jonah crossed to where she'd been working. "This is beautiful, Rach."

Her forehead leaned on his shoulder. "You think so?"

"I do." He turned to study another piece she'd recently finished. Bright blues raced across a field and met with a striking orange sunset. It erred on her more abstract side, and the colors she'd picked were breathtakingly bold. "Have you shown this to any galleries yet?"

"No." She started capping her paints. "Not sure I want to do that."

"You could easily sell it." He scanned the room. She'd brought in some of her older pieces and hung them on the walls. "You could even have another showing."

"I don't know, Jonah." She brought her brushes over to the sink. "Can it be enough that I'm just painting again?"

He joined her in the small kitchen and sat at a barstool. "Bet it feels good."

"It does." Her lips barely lifted. "When I can get past the guilt."

When her first tear fell, Jonah stood and wrapped his arms around her. "Ah, Rach, I shouldn't have pushed—"

She shook her head against his chest. "You didn't. And it was time ... I missed this." After a long moment, she pushed from him and wiped her eyes. "So what's got you coming over here in the middle of the afternoon?"

He'd rather talk about her problems than his own, but she'd find out soon enough. "I wanted to tell you I'm going to California."

"Isn't that where you just came back from?"

He stood silent.

Rachael grabbed a root beer from the small fridge, handed it to him, and grabbed another for herself. "Come on." She led them to the small patio off the back of her studio. Once they were seated, she cracked open her drink and tipped it at him. "Okay, spill."

He set his bottle on the cement. "I'm moving."

Rachael pulled her drink from her lips. "You're what?"

"I'm letting Micah have All Waste, and I'm moving." Jonah held up his hand as she opened her mouth. "There's conditions, and it won't happen right away. Walter is going to step in as CEO and work with Micah while I still hold my shares. Once Micah's at a place I feel confident he'll be able to run All Waste, I'll sell them to him."

Silence dropped over the patio. Jonah grabbed his root beer and cracked it open, giving Rachael time to digest what he just said.

"So, California."

He nodded. "I'm going to join Dad, learn the ropes out there."

"Helping Dad's a noble thing, Jonah, but running away is pretty cowardly."

"I'm not running."

She huffed. "Oh no?" Rachael picked up her phone. "I've been meaning to have Penny over here to check out my studio. I think now's a great time."

He snatched her phone. "Leave it be, Rach."

"I have for nearly two weeks. I've listened to you sulk on the phone, and frankly, I'm tired of it. You love her, so go after her."

"She slept with East."

"So?"

He opened his eyes so wide it hurt. "So?"

"Yeah, Jonah. So what?" Rachael scooted forward on her seat. "You set me up with your best friend when I had a toddler. Wasn't exactly Virgin Mary, now was I?"

He bit his cheek.

"What if Chris had the same reaction to me sleeping with someone before I met him? Gavin wouldn't have had a daddy. I'd never have had Brianna." She touched Jonah's arm. "I'd have missed out on the love of my life."

He tensed beneath her touch, her words. "You didn't know Chris when you were with Kurt. It happened years before."

"You're making excuses." She squeezed harder. "We all make mistakes, Jonah. Don't let Penny's keep you from her. Forgive her, or it will become your biggest mistake ever."

Jonah flew to his feet. "I need to go. I've got a lot to pack up before the move."

"And you called her the hypocrite," Rachael scoffed.

Anger flooded his veins. She had no right.

He turned and walked out the door.

Penny perched on the edge of her childhood bed. She'd hoped to sneak up here unnoticed, but Belle had been waiting for her car to pull in the drive. Hard to believe her baby sister's wedding was this weekend. Even harder to maintain her smile. Oh, she was happy for Belle, but her heart stung from missing Jonah. He hadn't returned a single one of her calls.

It had taken nearly a week to get past the last words he'd thrown at her before the desire to call him started to eclipse her anger. It took another three days for that desire to surpass the hurt over his keeping quiet about East.

But love truly did conquer all—or at least it conquered most things, because if it conquered all, Jonah would pick up his phone.

Maybe he didn't love her, after all.

Belle knocked and entered, the infamous purple dress in her hand. "Ready to try it on?"

"I suppose." Anything to take her mind off its current trajectory.

She quickly donned the dress, and Belle zipped it up. "Oh, Pen, you're beautiful." She twirled Penny around to face the mirror.

How many years had she waited for Belle to say those words? Now, she didn't need them. Dressed in the same purple dress with the same glittery brooch, a very different woman stared back. Her waist and hips had shrunk. She hadn't lost all the weight and would never be as thin as Belle, but she wasn't meant to be. Finally she liked the woman in the mirror. But the reflection didn't bring the satisfaction she'd once imagined it would.

"You still hate it. Don't you?" Belle asked.

"No." She spun. "I mean, it's not my style, but I don't hate it."

"It's okay. They weren't my first choice either. Pink is more my style."

"Mom?" Penny shared a conspiratorial look with her sister.

"Mom." Laughter flowed between them. "I have to say; Gran did an amazing job with the alterations." Belle walked around her, then stopped as she faced her. "I really am sorry I lied about the size I ordered. I truly did only want your happiness, and I thought losing weight would bring that. I was wrong." She nibbled her lip then plunged forward. "I was also wrong to let Mom talk me out of your being my maid of honor."

Pain she didn't realize she still carried cracked away. "It's okay. We've both been wrong about a lot of things."

"But I haven't only been wrong. I was awful to you. Would you please forgive me?"

Belle shifted her weight from her right to left foot. It reminded her of when they were little, and Belle couldn't sit still. She'd bounce along beside her, begging to play. They'd been inseparable once until hurt and misperceptions wedged a wall between them. Slowly they were removing that wall. "Of course I forgive you, Belle."

"Just like that?"

Good memories of the man who'd demonstrated true forgiveness danced in her heart. "Just like that." She missed him. Wished she had the chance to ask for his forgiveness again. But this was the relationship she could work on right now. "And I'm sorry I put distance between us. I should have tried harder to keep us close."

"Make it up to me by standing right beside me at my wedding. Be my maid of honor?"

She hugged her little sister. "I'd love to." There'd been a lot of tears these past few days. Penny swiped hers and chuckled. "Honestly, I owe you a thank you. If you hadn't pretended about that dress size, I'd never have discovered my love for running."

She'd been aiming for lightness; instead, Belle's eyes widened. "You're not still going to that gym, are you?"

"No." The mere thought turned her stomach. "I have no desire to see East Fisher ever again."

"I don't blame you." Belle wrinkled her face and shivered her disgust. "He's a creep. That's why I was surprised you were with him. It had nothing to do with his looks or yours."

"Really?" Every time they spoke, another misperception ended.

She nodded. "I've met guys like him before. I know what their type is, and for so many reasons, you weren't it. But Jonah ... the minute I met him, I could tell he was different. He was funny, kind, and a business owner like you. I really thought you two could be a match."

Jonah. How could his name carry hurt and joy all at the same time?

Penny swallowed tears. "The only match around here is you and Micah, and you're getting married tomorrow." She stood. "Now get me out of this dress so it doesn't wrinkle before your big day."

The zipper gave way easily, and Penny let the dress slide off her. Belle picked it up and walked it to the hanger on the closet door. "Pen?"

"Yeah?" Penny slipped on her pants.

"I know you're trying to change the subject, but I thought you should know that Jonah called Micah."

Penny stopped, her blouse halfway over her head. "Oh?"

"Yeah. Last night."

She pulled the shirt down. "What about?" Her heart pounded in her ears. Was he coming to the wedding? Had he asked about her?

"Apparently, he's heading to California."

Disappointment flooded her. Those hopes snatched away in one sentence.

"California?" Worry joined the disappointment. "Why?" she asked, but she didn't really want to know. His father lived out there ...

Belle's tentative expression answered before her words.

Penny's stomach bottomed out.

"He's moving there, Pen." Belle stepped toward her. "He's letting Micah take All Waste, though with some conditions I'm still not sure of. He's moving to California to help at his dad's company."

He wasn't just ignoring her calls; he was leaving her behind. Permanently.

Tears threatened. Belle hurried to her side. "But he's coming to the wedding tomorrow."

And just like that, hope inched in.

"He is?"

Belle nodded. "He's driving in tonight. He and Micah patched things up on the phone, and Jonah said he'd come."

"Did Micah put him back in the wedding?"

Please, oh please, say yes.

"He offered, but Jonah declined."

Her heart tore a little more, but she chose to focus on the fact that he was coming.

Even if he didn't want to see her, she had every intention of making sure he did.

Chapter Thirty-One

Penny stood outside the bridal room door. She'd gone in search of a water for Belle, and from the sounds of it, a major catastrophe had occurred in her absence. The Royal Court's voices reached fever pitch inside as Penny thrust open the door.

"What's the matter?"

Belle twirled from the mirror, jumbo size tears sliding down her cheeks and marring her professionally applied makeup.

Penny grabbed tissues while Belle's friends whispered to each other. "Belle, you've got to stop crying." Penny dabbed at her cheeks. "Save the tears for the altar."

Belle brought a trembling hand to Penny's. "My dress ..." She sobbed again.

Penny inspected the front of Belle's princess-style wedding dress. No stains. No rips. Not even a thread out of place. She raised a brow to the Royal Court.

Kelsey shrugged. "We can't get it zipped all the way up."

"Zippers get stuck all the time." Penny soothed Belle. "Let me see."

Taylor's snide voice cut in. "It's not stuck. She gained weight."

Penny stilled, then ever-so-slowly turned to Taylor. "Why don't you go check your makeup or something?"

Taylor turned on her heel. "Whatever." She stalked from the room while Belle sobbed in the corner.

Penny touched Belle's arm. "Ignore her. I'm sure it's just the zipper."

Ava looked at her over Belle's head and gave a little shake of her own.

"Serves me right," Belle moaned. "What's that they say about karma?"

Penny leaned into her little sister's face. "You don't believe in karma, and neither do I. Now turn around."

Slowly, Belle turned. The last inch of the zipper was still undone. Penny bent and examined it. It most definitely wasn't stuck.

Belle's shoulders shook. "I can't walk down the aisle like this."

"You're not going to. We're going to fix it." Penny focused on Ava. "Can you go find my gran and tell her we need her and her sewing kit in here—but don't let my mom overhear."

"Got it."

Penny next turned to Kelsey. "Go find Taylor and run interference, will you? Don't want her spreading any nasty rumors to anyone who'll listen."

Kelsey headed out the door.

Belle swiveled around. "After how awful I was to you about fitting into your dress, I deserve this."

"That's in our past, remember? So leave it there. Gran can fix this easily. You're going to be a beautiful bride."

Belle's bottom lip trembled. She opened her mouth just as Gran entered the room.

"What's this I hear about a bride not fitting her dress?" She bustled into the room, stopped at Belle, and spun her around. "Oh, well this is an easy fix." She pulled out a needle and thread. "You just hold still. I'm going to sew you into this dress, and no one will see a thing."

Penny grabbed the water she'd fetched earlier and handed it to her sister. "Drink this, and then I'll fix your makeup."

Belle sniffed. "Family pictures were supposed to start already. The photographer was going to do our family and then Micah's."

"Want me to tell him to start with Micah's family instead?"

"Could you?" Belle's big blue eyes fixed on hers.

She sucked in a deep breath. "Sure."

Penny snuck from the room and crossed the hall to the opposite side of the sanctuary. She'd alert the groomsmen, then find the photographer. She rapped her knuckles across their door. "Micah?"

Butterflies danced across her stomach. Would Jonah answer?

Nope. Tim did. "Micah's not here."

She peered inside. Neither was Jonah. "Do you know where he is?"

Tim shook his head. "We haven't seen him yet. Told us to be here and ready by eleven, but he's MIA."

The butterflies quickened their wings. Only this time for her sister. "I'll try calling him."

Penny rushed back to the bridal room. Her hand touched the doorknob, and she schooled her features, letting out a slow breath before she slipped a huge smile across her face and opened the door.

"How's it going in here?" She hurried past Gran and grabbed her phone, then dashed back to the door.

"We'll have her ready in no time." Gran smiled.

"Okay, well maybe we can still do the bridesmaids' pictures first." Penny stepped into the hall. "After all, we'll want to have time to freshen up before the ceremony. Think about it." The door closed behind her.

Penny dialed Micah's number, but it went straight to voicemail. Her finger hovered over Jonah's number next. Would he have stayed at Micah's last night? Even if he had, would Jonah answer her call?

She hesitated one more moment, then pressed send.

"Micah, you can't mean that." Jonah ran a hand over his bald head. His cell rang again in his pocket, and he ignored it again. He'd spent the last hour trying to talk Micah into going to the church. The ceremony was supposed to start—he looked at his watch—now.

And Micah's tuxedo still lay on his bed.

"I do." Micah zipped his duffel bag then walked into his adjoining bathroom. He started throwing toiletries into another bag. "I can't do it, Jonah. I tried putting that thing on"—he pointed to the tux—"and I froze."

Jonah blocked his exit from the bathroom. "Lots of men get a bad case of nerves before walking down the aisle. I mean, let's face it, Belle and her mom have made this wedding quite a production. But I bet if you call Belle, tell her how nervous you are, she'll run off to the Justice of the Peace with you."

A dry laugh ripped from Micah. "Even if that were remotely close to the truth, it wouldn't change things. I can't marry her."

"What's going on, Micah?"

His cousin's shoulders stiffened. "She's pregnant."

He might have well have thrown a bucket of cold water at Jonah.

Micah let out another laugh and shoved past. "Exactly how I took it." He tossed the small bag beside his duffel and flopped down on his bed. "I tried, man, I really tried to picture myself as a dad, but I'm just not ready."

"It doesn't matter if you're ready or not because you're going to be one."

"Not if I don't stick around."

Seething anger worked its way up from Jonah's gut. "That baby is yours whether you're here or not."

Micah's shoulders drooped. "I have no idea what to do with a kid. Not to mention I'm nowhere near ready to provide for one."

"I'm giving you the way."

"I don't want All Waste."

Jonah struggled to keep up with his cousin's ever-changing news. "You don't—"

"I tried it for Belle. She didn't want me to accept the residency. Not when it meant moving her so far from home with a baby on the way and me working eighty hours a week. She wanted family around and me in a nine to five job. All Waste was the only way I could make that happen." Micah stood. "But when I tried putting that tux on today, I realized what Belle and I want are two different things. She's better off without me."

Jonah thought of Rachael as a single mother ... and of Gavin who missed his dad so much.

He stared Micah down. "And your child?"

"Will be better off without me." He picked up his bags. "I watched my dad work a job that he hated for years, Jonah—a job my mom forced him in to. It didn't make him a very happy guy. I'm not about to repeat history. I thought I could, but when it comes down to it, I can't." He grabbed his keys from his bedside table. "I can't do that to her ... to my kid." Micah stopped in the doorway. "I'm going to take my residency, establish myself, and then I'll come back. Maybe we'll work out, or maybe she'll be with someone better by then. It's a chance I have to take."

Jonah grabbed his cousin's arm. "You tell her this face to face, give *her* a chance to make a choice. Don't just walk away like a coward."

"Mean like you're doing with Penny?"

The words hit their mark. Jonah flinched but didn't let go. "I wasn't engaged to her, and she's not carrying my child."

"No. She only has that possibility with East, right?"

Jonah's fingers curled into a fist. Micah was looking for a fight, and if he kept pushing, he'd get one. "This isn't about Penelope or me. This is about you and Belle. You can either go to the church on your own, or I'll take you there, but you are going to talk to her."

Micah shook out of his grasp. "I've got a plane to catch. Tell Belle ... tell her I'm sorry."

Jonah grabbed for him again, but Micah twisted out of his grasp. Jonah stayed on his heels all the way to the car. He lunged for him again. "You're going to the church to tell her yourself."

Micah reared back and slugged him, laying him flat on the ground. "Sorry, cuz." He stood over him, shaking his hand. "If it's any consolation, that hurt me as much as it hurt you."

Cheek and eye throbbing, he sincerely doubted it.

Micah climbed into his car and rolled down his window. His hands clenched the steering wheel.

Jonah sat up but stayed put on the ground, waiting out the indecision warring its way across Micah's face. Then it was gone, and with a squeal of tires, so was Micah.

Jonah dropped his aching head into his hands.

Belle would be devastated.

He slowly stood up. How could Micah do this to her when he claimed to love her? Leave without so much as a goodbye. Not giving her the chance to work things out.

Like you're doing with Penny?

Micah's words haunted him—because they were true.

So were Rachael's. He'd been a hypocrite, just like he'd accused Penny of being.

Jonah glanced at his watch. It was too late for Belle and Micah, but hopefully, it wasn't too late for him and Penelope.

He climbed into his car and headed for the church.

Belle sat in a crumpled mess on the floor. Her big floofy skirt billowing out around her. Penny locked the door and slipped down beside her.

"It's going to be okay, Belle."

Penny had spent the past hour trying to locate Micah and keeping the fact that he was missing as far from Belle as she could. In fact, they'd be lined up at the back of the church right now if Jonah hadn't called Dad to tell him Micah had left.

Jonah. She'd called him five times during that hour, and even in this situation, he refused to speak with her. He'd called her father instead.

She shoved her own heartbreak aside to focus on her sister's. Locking them in this room until Dad had emptied the church seemed like the best idea.

Penny slid her arm around Belle. "Hey, it's okay."

Belle shuddered in Penny's grasp. "It's not."

The words came out broken through the sobs. Penny held her tighter. "It's going to be, Belle, you'll see."

"I'm pregnant, Pen."

Penny leaned closer, sure she'd heard wrong. "What?"

"We were going to tell everyone after the honeymoon." Her eyes dipped down, pain and uncertainty in their blue depths. Penny hugged her close. "Oh, Belle." And she cried with her sister.

Cried because she understood her like never before. Had she kept on the same path, it could have been her someday.

They sat on the floor for what felt like hours, but when Penny looked up, it was closer to fifteen minutes. Belle stirred in her arms and then stood. "Will you help me out of this?"

Penny stood too and hunted for Gran's sewing kit. "Just need to find a scissors to cut out the stitches Gran put in."

Fabric ripped behind her. Startled, Penny swung around. Belle slid out of her dress. "Guess you don't need those scissors anymore."

Standing there in her wedding corset, Penny noticed her little sister's rounded belly. The princess style gown had hid it well, although now she understood why it wouldn't zip up past her chest. Penny thought Belle simply had pads sewn into the dress. She hadn't.

"Apparently, I've popped," Belle bracketed the term with her fingers.

Penny didn't know whether to laugh or cry. Instead, she reached down for Belle's bag and handed it to her sister. "Want to talk, or just have silence?"

"Silence for now." Another tear slid down her cheek. Penny waited for her to change, picking up the room around them. After a moment, she realized Belle still stood in her underwear.

"Belle?"

Belle held up the white Juicy Couture sweatsuit she'd worn into the church that morning. The word "Bride" glittered in pink sequins across the back. "I can't—"

Penny grabbed it from her and threw it in the corner. She passed over her own bag with her navy sundress in it. "Here. I'm sure my dress will be big on you, but I've got a cardigan you can cover it up with in there too."

"But what are you going to wear? That grape dress?"

Penny smiled. "You got it."

Belle slipped the navy fabric over her head. Then she tugged on the cardigan, kicking her wedding gown away from her. "Can you get that thing out of here?"

She scooped it up and tossed it into the corner with the sweatsuit then handed Belle another bottle of water. "How far along are you?"

"Just over fifteen weeks." Her lips turned up. "I found out when we were staying at your house."

Penny recalled her sitting in tears on the edge of her tub. She'd thought it was because of their fight. "Do Mom and Dad know?"

"No. And don't tell them. Especially right now—they've got enough to deal with." She slumped onto a chair. "How am I ever going to repay them for this wedding?"

"That's the least of their concerns." Penny grew hot. "If anything, it's Micah's. Does he know?"

Her little sister nodded, more tears erupting.

The jerk left her at the altar, pregnant. Penny could easily wring his neck. Instead, she wrapped an arm around her sister.

Belle trembled. "What is wrong with me that makes everyone leave?"

Such deep pain in those words. Penny hoped one day to show her what she'd learned—there was nothing wrong with her. And she was loved dearly. For now, she'd start with a promise. "I'm here, Bella Rose, and I'm not leaving ever again. Promise." Someone knocked on the door, and Belle tensed. Penny stood. "I've got it; don't worry."

"It's me, sweetheart." Dad's voice called softly through the door.

Penny waited for Belle's nod before opening the door. "Hey, Dad."

He slipped inside the room. "I sent your mother home. Gran and Gramps are taking care of the reception hall." He knelt in front of Belle. "Ah, honey, I'm so sorry."

She laid her head on Dad's shoulder and sobbed what appeared to be endless tears. Penny passed him the box of Kleenex. She worried what this stress would do to the baby.

"Are you taking your sister home?" Dad asked.

"Yes." Just needed her keys. A question burned her lips. Hand on her purse, she sucked in courage. "Dad?"

"What is it, sweetheart?"

"Did Jonah ... did he ask about me?"

His hesitation was all the answer she needed.

She'd cry later. Blinking tears away, Penny picked up her things. "I'm ready whenever you are."

Dad stood up, watching them. "My girls."

Penny stepped into his embrace. "What a pair we are, huh?"

Belle coughed a laugh and stood. She found her bag and dug through it, producing a thin sheet of paper. She scanned it, all the while pinching her bottom lip between two fingers. Then she stuffed it into her purse. "I'm ready. But can Dad drive me? I have something I want to talk to him about."

Understanding dawned.

Dad watched them. "Am I missing something?"

"I'll tell you on the way to the airport." Belle opened the door.

"Airport?" Penny's voice covered her dad's.

"I'm not ready to face people yet. I'm going to take the honeymoon. It's already paid for."

"You're sure?"

Determination filled Belle's face. "Positive."

Penny hugged her. "If you need me, call."

Dad and Belle left while Penny gathered her own things. A small bit of gold protruded from the top of her bag. She lifted out the bottle of Apres L'ondee she'd brought today. The seal around its honeycomb stopper finally broken. The scent finally on her skin because it wasn't her wedding day she needed, it was Jonah. He was the memory she'd waited for, and she desperately wanted him to know it.

She'd been so sure he would come.

Been so sure when he caught the new scent, realized what she wore, he'd know how much she loved him.

Penny eyed the wedding dress crumpled in the corner. Belle's dreams weren't the only ones crushed today. She returned the bottle to her bag then collected Belle's dress from the floor. Grabbing them both, she headed for the car.

The only people who remained were church staff who'd stayed to clean up. Penny descended the stairs, toddling on the three-inch sparkly heels she still wore. The heat of the early summer day wound around her. The sky held no clouds, just a perfect cerulean blue. A light breeze brushed a few tendrils against her cheek, ones that had been expertly pulled from her loose up-do and curled to frame her face. She laughed. All this perfection had not brought one ounce of happiness.

Oh, how she'd learned that painful lesson these past months.

Juggling her bags, she pressed the button to unlock her car and release the back hatch. She dropped the wedding dress into her trunk and then slipped off her heels and chucked those in too. The pavement warmed her toes, nearly to the point of being too hot, but it was better than still wearing those shoes. Next came the bobby pins, and she shook her hair free.

Penny shut the hatch to her trunk and leaned against it. The thought of going home curdled what little food she'd eaten that morning. Mom would be unbearable, and Penny wasn't in the mood to handle her. A small courtyard sat off to the side of the church, its flower-lined gravel paths and wooden bench inviting her to sit. She crossed the parking lot, tiny stones pressing into her feet until she reached the grass. A few steps farther, and she collapsed onto the bench.

She stretched her legs out in front of her, crossed them at the ankle, and tipped her head back against the wood. Closing her eyes, she tried to focus on the sound of the water in the nearby fountain and not thoughts of Jonah.

But that proved impossible.

Tears pricked the back of her eyes, and she squeezed them tighter. Gravel crunched beneath someone's feet. She kept her eyes closed, not wanting to invite their company. The crunching stopped directly in front of her.

"This seat taken?"

Chapter Thirty-Two

Penelope shot straight up, her wide eyes focused on his, alarmed.

Not quite the response he'd hoped for when he'd finally found her. He'd searched the entire church and had been about to exit the lot when he'd spotted her sitting out here alone ... in that awful purple dress.

He grinned and settled beside her, leaving some space between them.

"What happened to you?" She reached up gently to touch his bruised eye.

Apparently, the car mirror hadn't done justice to how bad it looked. "I had a run in with Micah's fist." He stilled her exploration of his face, taking her hand in his. "But I don't really want to talk about him right now."

Her hand warmed his. This time, he wasn't letting go.

Not that she was pulling away.

"You came. Belle said you were coming and then when you didn't ...." Her lips turned down as worry entered her eyes, and then words started to tumble from her. "Jonah, I stayed at East's apartment once, but we didn't ... and that night at Windsor Inn we never ... I never ..."

He stopped her. "It's okay, Penelope, even if you did—"

"But I didn't. He came in drunk that night—"

Again, he stopped her, pressing his finger gently to her lips. "You don't owe me any explanations."

She brushed his hand away. "I do." Water trickled through the fountain beside them. "I need you to know the truth. I stayed with him one night, weeks ago, and it was wrong even though nothing ... major happened." Her gaze dropped to the ground then slowly eased up to his, nearly hidden beneath her long dark lashes.

If he pressed, she'd likely tell him everything from that night. But he didn't need to know. Didn't want to know because it wouldn't matter. He'd listen if she needed to tell him, but he loved her regardless. The thought brought out a smile, which he quickly held in when her serious face found his.

With a quick breath, she continued, "When we were at the Windsor Inn, East came in drunk and passed out in my bed. I slept in the bathroom." She shifted beside him. "I called you that night, and I waited for you to call me back.

I've been waiting, and I keep calling, but you haven't answered any of my calls."

Because he'd been an idiot.

"I know. And I'm sorry." He scrubbed his free hand over the top of his head. "What I said to you that day was so wrong, Penelope. I was a jealous idi—"

"Okay."

"Okay?"

She grinned. "Yes. Okay. You're forgiven."

"Just like that?" He smirked.

"Isn't that the way it works between friends?"

A new floral scent floated past him. "I was hoping maybe we could be a little more than friends."

Penny stilled her fidgeting, her dark green eyes honing in on his. How he ever thought he could walk away from her ... yeah, he was an idiot.

The breeze swirled between them carrying that new scent with it again. Penny stood absolutely still, watching him, her eyes telling him something ...

The new floral scent.

She knew he was coming today.

Jonah picked up her wrist, bringing it under his nose. He inhaled. Her lips slowly lifted. He tugged her closer, and she slid across the bench until her knee pressed against his. He leaned down, his cheek brushing hers as he inhaled near that soft spot behind her ear. Her chest rose as she pulled in a sharp breath.

He kept his face close, slowly moving until his eyes were locked with hers. "Apres L'ondee?"

Ever so slowly, she nodded.

No more waiting. He lowered his lips to hers.

The taste of cinnamon teased her mouth as his lips touched hers. Gently, he pressed her closer to him. No kiss—no man—had ever possessed more of her. Her hands skimmed up past his chest, locking together behind his neck.

He released her lips and kissed along her jaw. Heat touched her skin as he trailed softly to her ear. "I love you, Penelope Rose."

His words wound around her heart. She'd never grow tired of hearing them ... or saying them.

"And I love you, Jonah Black." She eased away. "I'm sorry I was a little late to the game in realizing it."

He pressed another kiss to her lips. "For once, I didn't mind the wait. Like I keep saying, you're worth it."

She so didn't deserve him, but she wasn't about to give him up. Wait! She dropped her forehead against his chest. "Except if I'd been on time, you wouldn't be moving to California." She'd never be late for anything again. Ever. "What are we going to do?"

His chest rumbled under her with chuckles, and this time he kissed the top of her head. "I'm not moving, Penelope."

She straightened. Found him staring at her with that smile she loved. "You're not?"

"No. I wasn't moving to begin with; I was running." His fingers trailed up and down her bare arms. "I don't want to run anymore."

"But your dad?"

"Doesn't need me. He was kind enough to offer me a job, but he has things covered out there. Here, though …" His jaw ticked. "Micah's leaving the company just like he left your sister." Disgust was evident in his voice. "I'm so sorry he hurt her."

She squeezed his arm. "Not your fault."

"No. But I'm still sorry."

A breeze brought out goosebumps. Or maybe it was his nearness. Yeah. It was definitely him. She placed her palm on his chest. "Your huge heart is one of the many reasons I love you so much." And kissed the corner of his mouth.

He shifted to fully claim her kiss. Heat flared between them again, and he broke away. "You know, there's a church behind us and a pastor who planned on a wedding today." Jonah's eyes crinkled at the edges. "Though I'm not so sure this is the wedding dress you envisioned—even for a proposal. So we'll hold that thought." He grinned. "Just not for long."

She placed both of her hands on the side of his face covered in light stubble, then ran them up along his bald head. Bald head, black eye, rumpled shirt … and never more handsome. "I'd say yes any day you asked, Mr. Jonah Black."

He dropped another kiss behind her ear, inhaling deeply. "Would that be the memory you've been waiting for?"

"I already have it." She turned his face to hers and kissed him long and slow. "And you're better than any memory I've ever dreamed of making."

THE END.

Made in the USA
Lexington, KY
04 November 2018